*"You feel it too, don't you?"*
*Celeste asked her cats quietly.*

On the street, the new woman's pickup went by, gleaming white as a ghost. Three heads appeared in the cab. The woman drove, the companion dog she was never without sat in the middle, and Nick Alessandro filled the rest of the space.

Celeste lifted her hand to wave. At fifty, she wasn't too old to appreciate a good-looking man with soulful eyes and a body that—well, a very nice body.

Just then, the mysterious woman and her dog turned at exactly the same time to look at her, and everything within Celeste froze.

This woman had taken a terrible journey and her struggle would end here in Blanchefleur.

Shaken, Celeste hurried into her house to lay her tarot cards, her hands trembling. She laid them again and ̲ ̲ ̲ ̲, changing the pattern, fearing to b̲ ̲ ̲ ̲ ̲ ̲ ̲ ̲ ̲

̲ ̲ ̲ ̲ ̲ ̲ ̲ ̲ ̲ ̲ ̲ ̲ure, *she brought*
d̲ ̲ ̲

# CAIT LONDON

## With Her Last Breath

AVON BOOKS

*An Imprint of* HarperCollins*Publishers*

This is a work of fiction. Names, characters, places, and incidents are products of the author's imagination or are used fictitiously and are not to be construed as real. Any resemblance to actual events, locales, organizations, or persons, living or dead, is entirely coincidental.

AVON BOOKS
*An Imprint of* HarperCollins*Publishers*
10 East 53rd Street
New York, New York 10022-5299

Copyright © 2003 by Lois E. Kleinsasser
ISBN: 0-06-000181-X
www.avonromance.com

First Avon Books paperback printing: July 2003

Avon Trademark Reg. U.S. Pat. Off. and in Other Countries, Marca Registrada, Hecho en U.S.A.
HarperCollins® is a registered trademark of HarperCollins Publishers Inc.

Printed in the U.S.A.

10  9  8  7  6  5  4  3  2  1

*Always for Lucia, my editor, who envisions my story before I actually write it. To the kind residents of Michigan, who helped me to research near their famed lighthouses. To the notable master wine makers in Michigan and Missouri, who were so kind to let me interview them.*

# PROLOGUE

Maggie Chantel crouched just beyond the reach of the dog's chain. Tethered to a stake, the young female Labrador braced her paws in the mud and snarled.

"He's not going to destroy you the way he did my sister," Maggie said quietly as she placed a plastic bowl in front of the dog. Black as the night, the dog showed white teeth, a warning growl low in her throat.

At eleven o'clock at night, the exclusive San Francisco suburb was quiet, draped in sheets of April rain. Maggie continued to talk quietly and poured dry dog food into the bowl—not too much, just a tentative offering. She eased it toward the young dog, who began to eat.

"My sister's name was Glenda. She was beautiful, just like you. Her life was beautiful, too, and the same man who owns you killed her, in very slow ways. That's why I'm taking you with me. I couldn't help her, but just maybe—if you'll let me—we can save you."

Uncertain how the dog would react to her, Maggie waited until the plate was empty. Then she placed food in her hand,

and slowly extended it to the dog. "Friends, okay?"

*Oh, Glenda, why?* she sighed to herself. Pale and sweet once more, her sister's face flashed in front of Maggie. Overdose was listed as Glenda's official cause of death, but Maggie knew that there was so much more—the enticement and the betrayal and the loss of her self-respect.

Ignoring the tears on her cheeks, Maggie held her hand steady as the dog nibbled on the food. As children, the sisters had always been close. Later, they had both married, and Glenda's boys, Seth and Cody, had made her life almost perfect.

Then one man had insidiously poisoned Glenda's life, luring her into an affair, which had destroyed her marriage and her self-respect.

And Maggie's husband wouldn't help; he didn't want to offend his top business associate and investor and entrepreneur—the man who had ruined Glenda. As a final blow, her husband hadn't believed that Maggie had been attacked in their home; he'd chosen a divorce from Maggie, rather than support her battle to avenge Glenda . . .

"I loved him, but that wasn't enough," she said aloud. "Ryan wanted me to apologize to the man who ruined her and who tried to rape me. I couldn't do that." Driven by hunger, the dog accepted more food, greedily now, and Maggie cautiously reached out a hand to pet him and the dog instantly stepped back, teeth bared and hackles raised.

She lowered her hand and thought about the many times she'd tried to reach out to her sister.

"I don't blame you. I wish my sister would have fought more."

While sheets of rain slid by her, Maggie settled in to make friends with the dog. As a personal physical trainer, Maggie heard many stories. One of them was that this high-priced hunting dog would not obey her master's commands. She was terrified of guns, and when she had refused to retrieve in water, the man had been shamed in front of his elite hunting club. He'd vowed to break her.

Nothing could bring Glenda back, or paste the pieces of Maggie's life together, and now she'd planned carefully.

The cold rain pounded at her, but she crouched, patiently feeding the dog, little by little, until she accepted the touch of Maggie's hand. "Good girl. You're coming with me, okay?"

Hours later, Maggie drove through the dawn. Everything she owned was packed in the back of the small white pickup truck. The dog was curled up, asleep on the passenger seat, covered by an old blanket. Maggie laid her hand on the dog's head, absorbed her quick jolt of terror, and waited for the bite. Instead, with a tired sigh, the dog settled back into an exhausted sleep.

Maggie touched the small gold locket at her throat, a tiny reminder of the sister she couldn't save or avenge. Instead, Maggie had lost everything—her job, her marriage, and her life. Her tears were dry now, just the sheer need to survive remained.

"So here we are. Be my friend, will you?" To still her fears, Maggie stroked the dog's matted, dirty head. "So we're off to scout our futures, together. And what's a good name for you? Something brand-new, just for us?"

With another sigh, the dog moved closer on the pickup's bench seat. She tentatively placed her muzzle on Maggie's jeans-clad thigh. "We'll be fine," Maggie said quietly and prayed they would be.

# ONE

He ran from the past, from his guilt and his dead dreams. Yet they tangled in the late April air and caught him. Locked in his own private hell, Nick Alessandro ignored the brush bordering the jogging path and the highway running beside it. He didn't see the happy patches of daffodils, bright yellow in the afternoon sun, or the signs meant to attract tourists. On the five-mile run from his home and vineyard to Lake Michigan's small town of Blanchefleur, his lungs ached for air as he pushed himself to the limit, the gravel crunching beneath his running shoes.

Nick fought the nightmare of twelve years ago, the vision of his young bride sprawled on the pavement after a motorcycle accident. Alyssa, his lifetime sweetheart, his wife, his dreams. Alyssa was dead, and he could have prevented her death.

Guilt spiked, almost choking him.

The motorcycle was a toy he'd had to have.

Alyssa was a sweet necessity to his life, his heart, his soul.

The baby she had just told him about was gone, and so were his dreams.

How many times had he damned himself for that motorcycle? For not insisting that she wear a helmet?

The scar along his side and down his thigh reminded him every minute of how he had painfully crawled to her. He hadn't felt the burn of his own torn flesh; terror had moved him across the pavement.

As her husband, he'd been the one to sign the legal papers to take Alyssa off life support. Nothing, not even the land he'd sold to pay for her medical expenses, could bring her back.

"Nice muscle formation." As a personal trainer, Maggie appreciated the smooth flow of the muscles in the jogger's butt, and from the back, the rest of him wasn't bad either. His sweaty tank top clung, and with each stride, power surged beneath the skin from his powerful back, tapering to his waist—no love handles there, just man in smooth motion—a symphony of cords, muscle, and bone. He ran easily, sweat glistening on his dark skin, running shoes eating up the gravel path leading to Lake Michigan's small tourist town.

She gauged the man to be about mid-thirties, and he was one sweet piece of male animal, moving easily despite his size. Those defined muscles said he weighed more than he looked, but Maggie's expert trainer's eye estimated him to be about two-twenty.

Seated beside her in the passenger seat, Scout watched the man, and the quiver of muscle beneath the Labrador's thick black coat said she wanted the same freedom of late April's crisp air and sun.

Maggie slowed her pickup truck just a bit to better appreciate the man's bare shoulders and back, the tight butt in the worn loose shorts, and the defined muscles in his thighs and legs. She noted clinically that the brand-name shoes were expensive and worn and should be replaced.

Her appraisal was that of a dispassionate, assessing professional, not a woman. Maggie's fingers tightened on her steering wheel. In trying to survive, she'd lost something—the ability to feel like a woman.

It had been almost two years since her divorce, even longer since she'd made love. Her interest in the man wasn't sexual, she told herself. She was just a physical fitness professional appreciating a fine-looking male body. That was as far as it went—it would be a long time before she trusted anyone up close and personal.

When trusted friends, fearing for their own fortunes and welfare, turned from her, hadn't listened or helped, the scars ran deep. Maggie's husband's defection had been the worst—he wouldn't endanger his business by standing with her against the powerful man who had caused her sister's ruin and death.

Maggie had recognized something of herself in how this man fought his body's limits, pushing himself, focusing within where the shadows weren't warmed by sunlight's kiss.

More heavily built than a sleek competitive runner, the man was evidently prowling over the darkness in him, seeking and frustrated, and fighting the realities he'd found.

Maggie's fingers tightened on her steering wheel. Once her engagement ring and wedding band would have caught the light, and now they were gone. But she'd also lost more than jewelry. She'd lost confidence in trusting the right people and in making the right choices. She'd lost a deep, intimate softness and a lifetime of dreaming about a husband, home, and family. After moving from town to town, trying to reclaim herself, she was bone-tired.

"I'm going to make it work right here, Scout. I'm going to build a clientele, then a business. I'm going to take my parents' things out of storage and make a real home with a real kitchen, my own bathroom, and a nice big backyard for you. I've been running from reality for a year, taking part-time jobs, but it's really time to settle in for whatever peace I can find. But I'm never forgetting Glenda. She'll be with me always."

Maggie had chosen the battlefield on which to fight her past—and her fear of water, putting all behind her, attempting to manufacture some happiness in her life.

Maggie intended to meet her fear of water—and conquer it—in the small Lake Michigan tourist community. She would attempt an everyday familiarity, a gradual sampling, to still her overwhelming fear of water—in short, she would face the beast in a very private battle.

After waging another furious, futile battle to avenge Glenda, Maggie had learned to hide her emotions, to share little.

But running beside her small truck, the man's emotions slid stark and savage across his face. Whatever darkness stalking him nipped at her through the patches of sunlight and shadow.

A storm of shaggy black hair whipped around his darkly tanned face. In profile, the man's face was hard—as if he'd known the depths of hell and it still gripped him. His skin ran taut over jutting bones and shadowy planes, slashing cheekbones and a jaw dark with stubble. His damp hair gleamed, curling at the ends, and sweat plastered against his cheek.

In motion, all gleaming sweaty skin over cords and powerful muscle, he could have been a broad-shouldered gladiator battling in an arena. Fighting his demons, he pushed himself to the limit, locked in a battle that only he could understand.

Side by side, Maggie's pickup truck and the man glided through the patches of sunlight shafting through the trees. She recognized and understood his dark mood; they traveled together for that short space of time and distance, companions in darkness and light, seeking answers they could not find.

For just that few heartbeats, it was good to have someone to share her life, to understand the depth of her pain.

But life moved on, and she had to make a life and income for herself. This guy wouldn't need her services to coach him into a land of target heart rates and no flab.

She passed the man, noted his six-foot plus height absently, and frowned slightly when his face, all planes and harsh edges beneath that sweaty dark skin, appeared in the rectangle of her rearview mirror.

He looked like a man you wouldn't want to push, because he'd push back and hard.

Was he addicted to jogging? Possibly, but he was too focused, and that came from looking within, digging at yourself for answers. Maggie knew too well how a person could punish his body when he was fighting his emotions . . .

Maggie's professional, detatched survey took in the man: neck and shoulders strongly developed, pecs taut and leading to a washboard stomach, good thighs and calf development. His body was defined, rougher, edgier, than that of a man who spent hours in a gym, using exercise equipment. Add that to his primitive, warlike expression, and you had the look of a fighter.

Raw, tough power summed up his total appearance. Or maybe she felt just that tug of sexual attraction, because in her mind, for just another heartbeat, she fantasized about stopping the pickup and hauling him off into the brush for a fast stress, slick sweat and skin reliever. Just a mindless, momentary release before they cruised their separate ways . . . something, someone physical to pit herself against instead of nightmares and daylight regrets.

In reality, she knew that she wasn't made that way, not good girl Maggie Chantel, the virgin bride, now divorced ex-wife with thin finances.

Now, running with Scout and extreme exercise helped relieve Maggie's daytime physical tension, but the nights still brought a kaleidoscope of frustrating, painful scenes from the past. Early on, she had decided not to take her sister's path—drugs to dull her mind.

Instead, Maggie trusted her collection of good luck charms—and herself.

She pulled onto the small main street of the picturesque town, and her pickup did the cobblestone-bump routine.

For an instant she almost felt the need to say goodbye to her troubled companion of the shadows and sunshine and wish him luck. Then she forgot him as she focused on taking the next step of her long town-to-town journey. It had to end in this town, and she prayed that she would be able to get what she needed . . .

In the sunlight, Blanchefleur nestled in the shallow valley, Lake Michigan spreading a blue line beyond the homes that seemed stacked on the hills. The town was bright and clean, and birds flitted among the trees, not yet full with leaves, lining the streets.

A boy on a motorcycle soared from behind Maggie and passed her, cutting in a bit too close, a reminder that she was the visitor, not him.

Blanchefleur's streets were lined with two-story 1900-era buildings, labeled by an arty collection of shop signs meant to attract tourists. Restaurants and shops gave way to side streets fingering off into residences. As she drove closer, Lake Michigan was pure blue silk blending into the clear sky, expensive homes studding the hills. Past the beach grass and the thin fencing to hold the sand, a concrete pier shot like a spear into the blue water. It ended with a red lighthouse, one of many along the Michigan coast. The small red building propped against the lighthouse added to the picture.

Guided by concrete sea walls on either side of the entrance, a large channel fingered inward from the lake; it ended with a harbor clustered with boats and ships and docks. A tiny drawbridge raised to allow the tall sailboat masts poking at the sky, and a charter fishing boat motored smoothly into the harbor, trolling lines already sloping into the water like silver threads. A small aluminum boat followed in the gentle wake. The two men in it were bundled against the cold, trolling lines in place.

Maggie had chosen this lakeshore town, not only to face her fear of water, but because many of the year-round residents were retired wealthy, and in summer, the streets would be filled with tourists. She hoped to snare more than a few of them as clients. Now, a young woman fast-walked behind her baby's stroller and an elderly couple, arm-in-arm, paused to look at a window display of pottery.

Maggie pushed up her sunglasses, found the mirrored reflection of the contoured silvery surfaces, shielding her eyes. Who was she really?

She'd had a high school sweetheart, gone to college with him, and married him. They'd begun *Ryan's* dream of a physical fitness gym, and she'd designed her life around his.

Now, at thirty-one and divorced, the physical fitness business was what Maggie knew.

Scout's black nose did that twitching I-smell-people-food thing; her pink tongue dangled from her mouth and her black eyes pinned Maggie.

"You are absolutely ruthless. You know I'm running on a few dollars and change. If I can eat peanut butter and jelly sandwiches for a month, you can eat dry dog food. Me, a health professional, whose body is a magnet to fat. It's supposed to be the off-season here and rooms are cheaper, but you're a real problem. Not all hotels will allow pets, but hey, we've slept in the pickup before, right? We do seem to share the same eau de dog."

Scout spotted Lake Michigan and went into her soft whine, eye-pinning, panting, I'm-so-hot water-dog mode.

"Okay, okay. It's forty-five degrees, you know. Not exactly tropical. You can play along the shoreline and that's all." Tired from the long drive from lower Missouri and needing time to walk and stretch her muscles, Maggie followed the street likely to lead to the lake. The street swung downhill, running parallel to the channel, and she drove slowly down it, leaving the town. With Lake Michigan ahead of her and the channel running alongside the road, Maggie eased onto paved parking lot.

An elderly man sat on a park bench, considering the boats that passed in the channel. Evidently a tourist site, a manicured park and concrete walk led from the town down to the sandy beach and too much water.

The blue expanse of glittering waves, the white seagulls bobbing on the surface, took away Maggie's breath, and terror chilled her body. In the bright cold sunlight, she remembered her sister bobbing like a cork in her life jacket. Glenda had been terrified, but no more than twelve-year-old Maggie. Somehow, their mother had saved them both from that sudden summer squall, dragging them to the upended family sailboat.

From that moment on, it was only the three of them . . .

Maggie shivered beneath her sweatsuit. She'd never forget Glenda's terror and the sight of their father drowning—his hand, still reaching out to Maggie, then sliding beneath the waves.

Her mind pulled her back to another time. Her family had gone sailing, laughing and enjoying the day. Then a sudden squall had changed everything, capsizing the boat . . .

She forced herself to step onto the sand, to ignore the sink of it beneath her shoes, and made her way to the sprawling beach.

She released Scout to run on the beach and slowly walked across the sand, struggling against her fear of water. It seemed to always be there, ominously waiting for her . . .

Scout leaped into the water and began swimming happily away from shore. Locked in fear, Maggie screamed the dog's name. "Scout!" She looked at the waves caressing the brown sand and panicked, her scream freezing in her throat; she couldn't move and she couldn't save Scout.

At the top of the street leaving Blanchefleur's Main Street and leading to the lake, Nick Alessandro dragged air into his lungs. A short distance behind him was his family's restaurant, and his brother's pickup was parked along the sidewalk, in front of a small engine repair shop. The owner of a small boatyard, Dante was evidently inside on an errand.

Nick braced his hands on his knees as he scanned the sandy beach in the distance. In the off-season around Lake Michigan, newcomers were easily noted. He was curious about the woman who had been framed in the shadowy pickup cab, her ponytail pulled through the back of a ballcap, her sunglasses silvery wraparounds.

Now that white pickup stood alone in the beach's parking lot, and he wanted to strike back at her.

Nick resented her intrusion into his private hell, the aching of his lungs, the loneliness and grief of his heart. Somehow she'd peered inside and tangled with his darkness; somehow she knew that he fought what he could not change.

He should have died that day, not his beloved and his child. But he couldn't change Alyssa's death, or their baby's, one in the same, one in the same, his child within her, just a tiny particle of himself . . . dreams as shattered as Alyssa after the motorcycle accident.

Nick's punishment was to go on living with the knowledge that he could have saved her life, that he should have made her wear that motorcycle helmet that day . . .

And somehow the woman had cruised beside him, almost companionably, understanding somehow what he did not.

At first, the big dog had sat beside her, looking almost human. Then the dog had placed its muzzle on the door's open window, giving a better view of the woman. Nick had felt just that snap of recognition in the woman before she'd pulled away, as if she, too, had had a disaster in her life.

He'd heard her call frantically to the dog, "Scout!" Now she was obviously scolding the Labrador retriever as it swam back and came to hunker down on the sand in front of her.

Focused on the woman, Nick answered his brother's wave from inside the repair shop with a nod. The breeze from the lake was too cool on Nick's sweaty body, and he reached into Dante's pickup to grab a sweatshirt, tugging it on.

The dog's breed was water loving. Why would the woman chastise the dog for swimming?

Nick walked slowly down the concrete walk along the channel toward the beach and the woman. He and his two older brothers had grown up on this same beach, familiar with the sand and grass and tourists, the fishing of Coho salmon, trout, and whitefish.

He paused in the paved parking lot beside her pickup. From a short distance away, he saw that her sunglasses had been discarded carelessly to the sand. She was crying now, the wind whipping her ponytail, sending a burst of reddish color into the sunlight. She dashed away tears as she fell to her knees, hugging the dog.

Framed by the wide expanse of sky, water, and brown sand on the empty beach, she looked small and alone.

Nick glanced down at her pickup's license plate, noted the Missouri tags, and wondered if she had plans to meet someone at Blanchefleur. Couples often met here; the town's off-season rates ensured a good room at a cheap price for lovers' rendezvous.

At just past three o'clock in the afternoon, the school's Frisbee crowd hadn't made it down to the beach with their overloud boom boxes.

Nick turned, intending to return back up the hill to the town and his family's restaurant on Main Street. He took a few steps and stopped. The woman wasn't his concern—nor were her tears. He wouldn't get involved; he just had time for a shower before starting work at his parents' restaurant.

He stopped and swept a hand across the tall beach grass—but then, she had reached into his life for that moment, hadn't she? Only a stranger passing by, she'd seen his dark storms, the furious life battle he could never win. In just that moment, she'd pushed some wrong button, nettling him as she drove coolly by, leaving him adrift in that endless river of doubts and shadows.

Nick tilted his head and turned. Tit for tat, he decided darkly, and began walking toward her.

With one fist, the woman clasped something at her throat, and her other arm tucked the dog tight against her.

Hugging the dog and murmuring to "Scout," the woman didn't see Nick until he stood beside her. Instantly, the dog neatly maneuvered her one-hundred-and-seventy-five-pound body between the humans and sat, watching Nick, a protective barrier for her mistress.

The woman stood abruptly, her hand roughly swiping the tears on her face. Just reaching his shoulder, she had hazel eyes, more meadow green than brown now, and too bright. The sun caught the sheen of tears spiking her dark brown lashes, and Nick resisted reaching out a fingertip to dry them. He wondered if he touched that shimmering dampness, would he feel what ran so deep and aching inside her?

But beneath the brim of her ballcap her frown forbade him.

Nick noted the Nordic influence in her face, slanting cheekbones and that rounded jaw. Her long sleek ponytail held the sun in red highlights, the wind flicking at the strands. With winter white buttermilk skin, she'd probably wear more freckles in summer, just across that pert nose. Soft as a baby's and twice as enchanting, tendrils of chestnut-colored silk framed her face, stirring in the wind.

The curve of her cheek, damp and gleaming, caught him and tossed aside his nasty mood as lightly as a dandelion fluff on the wind.

The set of her lips and jaw said he wasn't welcome; the tense lock of her compact body and her fists at her thighs said she was ready to defend herself. Nick adjusted her ethnic mix, adding a drop of fighting Irish. Judging by the dark circles beneath her eyes, she'd lost some sleep. What had happened to make her react defensively, suspiciously?

But then, Nick decided, the extensive Alessandro family had always been friendly and not too adept at taking hints from loners. He crouched to look at Scout. Nick extended his hand, letting the dog become familiar with his scent. "Nice dog."

"Leave her alone."

Fear sailed through that sharp, low command. Had someone tried to hurt her dog?

A gold locket gleamed on the woman's chest, and Nick realized that was what she had been holding. Small and oval, the locket didn't require the heavier chain that held it. The contrast was unusual and curious, when women usually matched such things. "Okay, but she seems friendly enough."

But then, when a dog extended a paw, it was only polite to shake it. Nick obliged and added a rough ear rub for the favor; the dog leaned into his hand. At least *one* female on the beach could stand him.

"New in town?" he asked the woman as he smoothed the dog's wet coat. However shabby and worn the woman's green sweatsuit was, the dog's thick coat reflected good care.

As he studied her, her body tensed. A curious thing, Nick thought, how the brown and the dark green of her eyes changed with her mood, the gold flecks picking up, stirring in impatient anger.

But then he was a patient man, set on his course, and someone else's impatience was his best game. Nick settled in to enjoy who would win the toss—the woman with the gold-green eyes, or him.

With the ease of a man who admitted his arrogance and a certain amount of charm that he could use when needed, Nick bet on himself.

"If you're finished, we're leaving. Come on, Scout."

She stared coolly down at Nick, and with that slight remaining thread of fear, her voice was low and husky. He wondered what it would sound like without the drench of tears. Would the tone be sultry as the air before a summer squall, or light and gentle as a spring breeze?

There was just that edginess about her, the way she glanced down the empty beach and latched her hand onto the dog's collar. Nick could almost smell her fear—and apparently, so could the dog, who edged just that protective bit in front of her. "Hello, Scout," Nick said softly.

Impatience against patience was one game, fear another. If he could help her in this moment, he would.

Two small boys, laughing as they played tag, ran along the beach, their mother calling out to them, and, through the inches separating them, Nick could feel the impact of the woman's rigid body. The hiss of her indrawn breath slid along the wind. In profile and as still as a doe caught in headlights, she followed the flight of the boys, and the gentle longing in her expression, that wistful curve of her lips, couldn't be missed.

So his mystery woman had a family, then—somewhere—and she missed them.

Nick scanned the lake, waves caressing the shoreline where the boys dipped and splashed water at each other. The lake seemed to melt into the clear blue sky as Nick's thoughts tumbled on. Did she think of her own children? And what kind of a woman would leave them? And why?

"Let's go." The woman abruptly patted her thigh as though tearing herself from another time, and the dog sat, looking up at her and at Nick. "Now, Scout," she added impatiently.

When she said, "Treat, Scout?" the dog stood, wagging her tail.

Because Nick came from an Italian background where "Eat, you'll feel better," was a standard cure-all, his instincts told him that she needed a good meal. While Nick was a winegrower, his family served the best food in town. He dug into his pocket, extracted his wallet, and held out a "Good for One Free Meal at Alessandros Italian Restaurant" coupon. Because he sensed her pride wouldn't allow her to take charity, he said, "It's a promotion. Trying to get new customers in off-season. No obligation. Just say that Nick sent you. I get points for how many new customers I send in. It's good food. There's some health rule about pets being off-limits in the restaurant, but if you say I sent you, they'll ask you to come back to the private family room, next to the kitchen. Just turn up before they get busy at six."

Her indecision said she didn't like relying on anyone else and questioned gifts or kindness. He followed the swallow down her pale throat, the telltale sign of a hungry stomach. When she reached for the coupon, her hand was squarish and strong, a working hand, nails neatly trimmed. "Sure. Thanks."

"Staying around awhile?" he asked, reaching to scratch the dog's ears. The woman didn't look like a tourist, set to relax and enjoy the beach. She looked restless and edgy. In contrast, Scout pushed her substantial weight against him, and the sturdy thump of her tail said she was happy.

Her mistress wasn't. She frowned at him, eyes shadowed warily. "Maybe. Why?"

"Just wondering. I get a free meal at the restaurant if I can send someone to take the upstairs room. They take pets." So he hedged the truth a bit—he'd been raised on his parents' food, and they loved animals.

"Expensive?"

The question was too quick for casual interest. Mystery Woman was down on her luck, needing food and money, and she was fighting pride and tears. "It's cheap enough. Usually the extra summer help stays there. Mom and Pop Alessandro live upstairs. Their family is grown, and she likes someone in that room. They had a dog like this once. His name was Benny."

Nick and his brothers had loved Benny, who had lived to a ripe old age. He'd spent many nights at the foot of Nick's bed.

The woman's hand clutched the coupon as if it were a lifeline, knuckles showing white. "Thanks."

A guarded loner, Nick thought, as she said, "Treat, Scout" again and began running down the beach. With a huff, the big female Lab followed. Woman and dog ran, side by side, almost one with each other. Nick placed his hands on his hips, admiring the picture, taking note of the woman's easy stride. Not lithe or willowy, she ran more to the healthy five-foot-six "armful," as Nick's father was fond of saying. If she had any body fat at all, it was all in the right places beneath that sweatsuit.

And that brief glance back at him over her shoulder said she didn't trust him.

Because he was still nettled that she'd passed him by so coolly earlier and knew he was fighting his life, Nick smiled—just a little payback for the intrusion. He waved as if they were friends—and she clearly didn't want to be friendly.

When he started back up the hill toward town and the restaurant, Nick wondered about the shade of her eyes just then. Were the gold sparks stirring, or were they as green as grass?

And he wondered why, when the wind feathered through those soft reddish-brown tendrils, something stirred in him . . .

Maggie placed the foil-covered pie plate of Italian food on the neat second-story apartment's small table. There were too many carbs in the pasta, but then she wasn't complaining about free food. Beneath her apartment, Alessandros Restaurant was in full swing, soft dining music filtering up through the well-varnished board flooring. The sixtyish Alessandros had been bustling and friendly; both had hugged their new renter soundly, surprising Maggie.

"You're alone then," Rosa Alessandro had said, as she'd filled the ravioli dough with a spinach mixture. "No husband coming later, a boyfriend perhaps?"

"I'm divorced," Maggie had answered a little too sharply. Ryan's betrayal, his desertion when she needed him most, still stung. She hadn't meant for that pain to leap out unexpectedly—*he hadn't believed she'd been attacked; Ryan, her husband, didn't want to endanger his business to support her . . .*

After a long, torturous road of pain and decision, she blamed herself, not Ryan. Her choices were as she made them—but she would never regret fighting for Glenda, risking everything.

"You'll be comfortable here," Rosa had said, one woman sensing another's pain. She wiped her hands on her apron. "Are you needing protection?" she had asked cautiously.

"I'm trying to start a new life by myself," Maggie had said quietly.

At that, Rosa had hugged her again, adding a kiss on her cheek that surprised Maggie. The soft gush of motherly Italian words stunned her. It had been years since she'd been comforted, and she truly appreciated the gift. "Thank you. Whatever you said, you have no idea how much it means to me."

Rosa smiled warmly. "Poor little bird, you have come to the right place. This will be your new home."

The building had a comfortable, worn feeling, as though lives had passed happily there, and without even looking at the apartment, Maggie had taken it at the affordable price. Mr. and Mrs. Alessandro had merely given her directions upstairs from the restaurant's kitchen. They'd told her to bring the plate, fork, and spaghetti spoon down to the kitchen later, and that meals—whatever was the daily special—came with the room. If she got hungry between times, she was to use the family's private, roomy kitchen, dishing up the leftovers from the refrigerator; cleaning up the kitchen's range was a must. Rosa spoke like a woman who had run a family, giving Maggie no more, no less firm instructions than she would give her sons.

While the large family kitchen behind the commercial one looked comfortable, with the muted sounds of the restaurant on the other side, Maggie preferred to eat alone.

The Alessandros' upstairs apartment was across from hers, and that gave Maggie an odd sense of safety and homecoming.

Safety fled when Maggie noted the ancient door lock and the skeleton key. Experience told her that a chair backed into the knob and a rubber wedge beneath the door would offer some comfort, but a child could open the lock.

*Her sister's seducer had come straight into Maggie's bathroom at home and had found Maggie soaking in mounds of scented bubbles. Furious that she'd gone to his powerful social friends, exposing the dark side of his life, using her sister, he'd wanted to prove his power over her by rape—*

And after eight more months of Maggie struggling to save her marriage, Glenda was dead of an overdose. Maggie had tried everything to pull her back from the edge, and nothing had helped.

With experience, Maggie pushed back the memories that could still slither into life. She hefted the backpack filled with Scout's dry dog food and bowls onto a chair. "How do you like our new home?"

The small, neat, one-room apartment overlooked the picturesque Main Street. An air conditioner filled one tall window, and an aged radiator had been painted several times. The sturdy bed didn't match the big dresser, but when Maggie tested the mattress, it was firm and good. She flipped back the worn chenille bedspread and cotton sheets and found the scent of sunshine.

Scout padded after her into the compact bathroom. "Good. A shower and no bath," Maggie noted.

*She would never take a bath again, never let herself be so defenseless . . .*

Maggie firmly closed the bathroom door and shut out thoughts of her past. She was going to look to the future. She was going to change her life here in Blanchefleur, meet her fear of water, and get the home that she desperately needed.

In San Francisco, Brent Templeton watched the prostitute walk toward him, her generous hips swaying, that knowing, hard look on her face. In his pocket were the ropes with which he would tie her. She would serve his purposes tonight, because no one would believe a prostitute, just as no one had believed Glenda that she had once been righteous.

Except Maggie Chantel, fighting for her sister, fighting to avenge the pitiful excuse for a woman. Maggie had raised enough doubt with her constant harassment to make his heiress wife listen and eventually leave him.

Evelyn took her time arranging their divorce, her strategy perfect as she lined up the reasons for a quiet breakup, carefully extracting his name from her accounts. His ex-wife deleted his name from her insurance and made him wear the limp—the reminder that he'd failed to rape Maggie and that she'd badly injured his knee.

Oh, Maggie had described his attack perfectly to Evelyn, and his ex-wife had made him pay every day by her coldness.

Two weeks after his dog was stolen, Evelyn had delivered her final coup—papers for a quick, quiet settlement.

He'd had quite the scramble at first, trying to maintain lifestyle appearances, trying to get his old friends' support while searching for Maggie. But without Evelyn, the doors were closed to him. Then he'd started his search in earnest for the woman who destroyed his life. Evelyn's get-lost money didn't last long, and when he couldn't pay the bills for his lifestyle, he'd borrowed, and the collectors hadn't been sweet.

He'd furnished drugs and prostitutes for his powerful friends, including attorneys and a judge, Sam Jones. Brent was an expert at moving in to use the soft underbelly of private vices and sins. He'd gotten information for blackmail, enough to push through big-money deals that weren't supposed to happen. Once, he'd been a member of an elite club for hunters, a tightly woven group of powerful men with enough dark secrets to keep a blackmailer happy. They shied from him now, fearing for their reputations even though once he'd helped them. Blackmailing them had worked only a few times, and then they'd sent experienced muscle men after him.

Surgery could correct his broken nose, the long scar down his cheek, if only he had money. The slight paunch on his thin frame would take hours in the gym, which he could no longer afford. Gone was his Jamaican tan, replaced by a sallow, mottled complexion.

He'd wanted Maggie from the first moment he saw her five years ago. When she'd rebuffed his advances, he'd taken her sister instead, using her to prod Maggie. But the she-devil fought him and everyone else and had taken everything from him.

He would find her, and when he did, Maggie Chantel's death would be very, very slow and painful. He'd have her first, of course, in many painful ways. She'd ruined his life, taken his pride, his home and prestige, and now the country club set laughed at him, avoided him.

All because of Maggie Chantel.

Now he had nothing left but the hatred that drove him, the need to find Maggie and see the fear in her hazel eyes, making her pay, feeling the pain. Whatever hole she'd found to hide in, he'd find her.

The hunted had become the hunter . . .

Later, when the woman tied to the bed cried out in pain, he was powerful again and in command. He viciously ordered her to tell him that she loved him.

Just as Glenda had.

Just as Maggie would.

# TWO

Down on the street, a car honked and Maggie snapped back to the present. With a steadying breath and shaking hands, she began unpacking.

With more to retrieve from her pickup, Maggie opened the upstairs apartment door and stepped out onto the landing.

The stairway was narrow, the varnished wooden steps firm, but worn with use. The man standing on the bottom of the stairs startled her. It was the same man—the jogger beside the road, the man on the beach from the restaurant, dressed as a cook, with a long apron over his short-sleeve black T-shirt and worn jeans. Apparently he not only promoted the restaurant, but worked in it, too.

The single bald bulb overhead hit Nick's face, all jutting angles and planes. Head tilted down, the arrogance was there, and just that bit of anger. He held a large glass of milk. His black brows had drawn together in a scowl, his mouth hard as he faced a tall graceful blond, dressed expensively in a flowing cobalt blue silk suit. Obviously locked in a disagreement, the blond pressed, "You'll call me, won't you, Nick? It was so good between us."

His deep voice cut through the shadows at the bottom of the stairs. "It's over, Lorna. We dated a few times and that was it."

Then the woman's furious blue stare rose up the stairs to pin Maggie. She inhaled and stepped back into her apartment, softly closing the door. Maggie didn't want to be involved in someone else's business ever again and went to the window overlooking Main Street.

Families strolled about in the sunshine. A father protectively carried a small child across the cobblestone street while his heavily pregnant wife latched her hand to the back of his jeans. An elderly man and woman strolled along the sidewalk and stopped to admire something in an antique shop window.

Maggie turned from the peaceful scene, and her mind flipped back to the upsetting one on the beach, where she'd sensed that Nick was angry at her. At first, he was determined to push her; she'd offended him somehow.

She'd seen arrogance in the tilt of his head, and a rough intimacy in his deep tones, man to a woman, the sound of a man whose arms could frame a woman against the wall, trapping her until she didn't want to leave. She was certain he could be charming, and by the look of the woman pressing him, he was paying for playing.

Maggie shrugged, because now another woman was calling him to task, and that was fine with her.

Caught by movement down on the street, Maggie moved aside the lace curtain. A woman in a long dress covered by a full-length black cape with a hood was just locking the door of a small shop opposite the restaurant. The wind licked at her hem, and she gathered her cape around her. The word "Journeys" in silver scrolled artistically across the shop's window, and the woman stopped, almost as if she were frozen. She seemed wary and scanned the street, her face

narrow and pale within that shadowy hood, and then she disappeared into a side street.

Maggie wondered what had caught the woman in that moment, what had made the fear leap to her face. But it wasn't
Maggie's purpose to understand. She'd been drained by
knowing too much, trying to help . . .

Like books of different colors propped up side by side, the
two-story buildings were narrow and had bench seats and
flower boxes in front of them. Sunlight flashed in the windows of the tavern directly opposite the restaurant. While the
other shops seemed well kept, the dark windows of Ed's
Place held a timeless, seedy look, probably highly sought by
tourists wanting local flavor.

Blanchefleur seemed peaceful, exactly what she needed.
Maggie removed her baseball cap and the band that confined
her ponytail, placing them on the big sturdy dresser. She win-
nowed her fingers through her hair as she looked into the
mirror. She looked like she felt, road miles dragging on her.
If she could just stay long enough to set up a clientele, to get
a little money saved for her own business . . .

Scout looked up from lapping water and Maggie lifted the
plate's foil, inhaling the aroma of spaghetti and garlic bread.
"If there's one thing I don't need, it's to be involved in someone else's life," Maggie said as she settled in to enjoy the
meal.

She looked at the ceiling when the woman's voice dropped
the soft pleading and raised sharply. "She's not coming back.
I can make you forget Alyssa. Don't forget that I've got business connections you could work years to make. Let me help,
Nick."

The answering low male rumble was indistinguishable,
and then only the sound of the busy restaurant carried up the
stairway.

So he'd lost his woman, had he? Maybe he deserved this
woman, pushing him. But then, Nick wasn't Maggie's business.

She ate quietly, determined not to enter any more scenarios that didn't concern her. The food was delicious, the sauce just spicy enough and the pasta-carbs settling in to make Maggie sleepy. She sat, propping her jogging shoes on the other chair, and decided to wait a little longer before unloading her pickup, giving time for Lorna to work on the reluctant Nick.

"Mine is really good. How was yours?" Maggie asked as Scout padded around the apartment, sniffing the unfamiliar scents. Maggie had planned to eat only a bit, saving the rest to parcel out the next day, but suddenly her plate was clean.

Scout stilled, turned, and went to sit at the door, announcing a human on the other side.

Maggie froze; she hadn't locked the door. She forced herself to wait in silence and then the brisk knock sounded. "Yes?"

"I'm supposed to bring you this glass of milk to go with your dinner, and to check the refrigerator to see that it's working."

She recognized Nick's voice and glanced at the small refrigerator doing its humming-happy thing. "It's fine. I've eaten. I don't need the milk now."

On the other side of the door, Nick issued a tired sigh and uttered a smothered "Women."

Scout's look begged Maggie, who stood reluctantly, stretched, and said, "Okay. So he's having a bad day, fending off his blond friend who wants to get married. He's only a handyman or a cook or something doing his job and taking orders. He did steer me here and to good food. I'll be good."

Maggie slowly opened the door six inches and met the scent of garlic and onions. Nick's black waves were damp, and just a drop of milk clung to his earlobe. A few more white drops beaded on his tanned throat. The damp spot on his white apron looked suspiciously like he was wearing the rest of the milk over the red spaghetti sauce stains. He held a glass of milk in one hand and a bottle of wine tucked beneath one arm.

There was too much of him, and his eyes were so black she could see herself reflected in them. The light in the landing did not soften the jut of his cheekbones, those fierce, drawn eyebrows. A muscle moved along his jaw as he studied her face, and he lifted the glass of milk, grimly prompting her. "I got detained. The first glass of milk got spilled on my head."

Maggie had learned never to ask the whys. They were outside her life now. "The refrigerator works fine. You don't have to come in."

He sighed again and explained firmly, slowly. "Mom told me to."

Since apparently everyone called the Alessandros "Mom" and "Pop" or "Dad" and they had invited her to also, Maggie dismissed any relationship. Scout was muscling her head by Maggie's thigh, sniffing at Nick, who reached a hand down to pet her. The dog's bulk prevented Maggie from closing the door, so she opened it wider. "Just do what you have to do— and I don't drink."

"The wine is a welcome gift. It's from the Alessandro Winery, an estate red, grown on the company's vineyard."

Maggie didn't like gifts; they usually came with a high price tag. When she'd set her course to avenge her sister, the gifts to make her stop were expensive and the price she needed to pay very high—her honor and her pride.

When Nick moved into the apartment, Maggie was disgusted by Scout's flirtation with the man, bumping against him, her tail wagging happily. Maggie would have staggered with Scout's playful leap upon her chest, but Nick didn't. He placed the glass and wine on the table, then petted the dog. "Hi, Scout. How's it going?"

"Sorry about that. I've been working with her, but she gets excited. Get down, Scout," Maggie ordered, but the dog continued to enjoy the man waggling her head playfully as she stood, paws on his chest.

In the small apartment, Nick seemed taller, his shoulders broader. At six-foot-four and in excellent shape, he could easily overpower her. Maggie's sense of danger leaped; no one would hear her scream; she'd fought desperately in her own bathroom against a big, powerful man—

"You look scared, as if you're going to jump out of that window. What's wrong?" Nick asked quietly.

Maggie grabbed Scout's collar and hauled her back from him. The dog plunged, dragging Maggie slightly, as she made her way back to her new playmate.

"Sit." Nick's voice held firm command, and Scout instantly plopped her bottom, her tail thumping on the floor. He bent to waggle her head and Scout looked at him as if he were her doggie chew treat, a perfect delectable dried pig's ear. "Good dog."

Great. After all those futile hours of trying to get Scout to respond to "sit," she now obeyed a stranger. Maggie's dog was in love. Irritated that Scout would obey Nick and not her, Maggie crossed her arms. She was road-tired, full of good food, and after she walked Scout, she'd be ready for a shower and bed. She needed privacy and quiet and not the man invading her space, challenging her, or taking control of Scout. "Do what you have to do and get out."

Nick's slow smile mocked Maggie's irritation, and the set of his body said he'd move when he wanted. "Friendly type, aren't you?"

She let that pass and stood, disgusted by the way her dog was obviously trying to make friends. With her tail wagging, Scout followed Nick to the refrigerator. He opened the door, studied the interior, and reached to adjust a knob. The refrigerator shuddered and died. "It will work better when you get some food in it."

Maggie felt guilty. He was just a cook who took time to run and keep in shape, and he'd steered her to free food and a good place to stay at a cheap rate. She forced herself to speak. "Thanks for the coupon. The food is good."

He closed the refrigerator door and scanned the room, noting the changes she'd made. "The best. Watch the freezer. It needs defrosting sometimes."

"Okay. You can go now."

Nick didn't move. Those black eyes flickered just once beneath that heavy set of eyelashes, and she had the impression that he could only be pushed so far. "I'm supposed to help you carry up your things. Mom said your pickup looked full and you looked too tired. Had a long trip?"

Maggie didn't answer that question. She'd learned a long time ago that small talk led to big problems, and she preferred to keep her life private. "I can manage. It sounds busy downstairs. Don't you have something to do?"

He tilted his head as though he were settling in to take his time with her. "It's a slow night. It gets busier a little later in the season. Have you got a thing against people helping you?"

In the past few years, Maggie had discovered a new fact of life: If people helped you, they wanted to be involved in your life, or they wanted something, and either way Maggie didn't need the complications. "Yes, I do. You can leave now."

"Am I making you nervous?" Both arrogance and charm were present in his deep voice, nudging her into an admission she didn't want to make.

Maybe she was just too tired to deal with him, or maybe she was right to be wary. In either case, she wanted him gone. Maggie took a deep breath and leveled a stare at him. "Because you pointed my way to this apartment doesn't mean you've got squatter's rights. The friendly conversation is over. Now get out."

He wasn't budging, but the muscle moving rhythmically in his jaw said he'd taken offense. His hand opened, broad palm turned up and waiting. "Keys to your pickup."

The calluses on his hand surprised her, but the arrogance that said he usually got his way did not.

Sensing tension, Scout moved between them. Scout's instincts had locked onto Maggie's fears, the way they poured from her. One movement or sound or look and the dog was on instant alert. Nick glanced down at her. "She's protective. Any special reason?"

Maggie needed a job, not problems. And Nick looked like

a king-sized problem. "Okay, you can help. But no more questions."

"I'm not usually interested. But if you're in trouble, I'd rather you didn't bring it to Mom and Pop's."

She resented the inference that she might bring harm to the friendly Alessandros. "I am not in any trouble. I just like to be left alone."

"There's usually a reason for that." His dark eyes were too solemn, watching her. When she refused to give him any insight into her life, he said, "Okay, have it your way, but I've got orders to help you. Coming?"

A few minutes later, she followed him back up the stairs. Her large worn duffel bag was slung easily across his shoulder, and he carried her cardboard box, filled with mementos of Glenda and their parents—a few framed pictures, albums, a bit of inherited jewelry—beneath his other arm. Maggie lugged up the picnic cooler, placing it on the table.

Nick put the duffel bag and the box on the bed, then picked up her empty plate and fork with the air of a waiter cleaning a table for a good tip. Maggie resented the thank-you she had to give him, because she hadn't asked for his help. "Thanks. I'm not tipping. I didn't ask for your help, and I didn't need it."

His head went back as though he'd taken a slap, and those eyes narrowed, his nose flaring slightly. He nodded and then closed the door after him.

Scout tilted her head and whined softly, pinning her eyes on the closed door.

"You're so easy. I'm the one who pays for your vet bills and dog food. There's this thing called loyalty, you know," Maggie grumbled as she opened the cardboard box and placed the framed photos of her family on the dresser. She ran a fingertip over the one with her sister and herself, grinning into the camera, arms looped around each other.

In another photo, Glenda's young sons, Seth and Cody, just six and three, had sat on their mother's lap, each kissing her cheek . . . and a slice of pain went through Maggie. She missed her nephews, missed seeing them grow. She wanted them in her arms, safe and alive and warm.

But they reminded her too much of Glenda, and she couldn't bear to see them. Travis, their father, was a good, loving man, remarried now to a woman who loved the boys. At times, Maggie had seen his shielded look at her, taking in the pale complexion and sleek reddish brown hair that had matched Glenda's. Maggie was only a reminder to everyone of the pain in their past and the uncertainty of her place in their future.

Her hand automatically went to hold the small locket at her throat; it held a picture of her sister, who was always with her, always in her heart. The chain Maggie had chosen was perhaps too heavy for the locket, but she didn't want to lose this part of her sister—*Glenda*. . . .

"Not a sound from Maggie," Rosa Alessandro said at eight o'clock as she prepared to go upstairs to her own apartment, leaving the younger members of the family to deal with the restaurant's closing and the balancing of receipts. Like a mother checking on her children at bedtime, Rosa placed her hands on her generous hips. She surveyed the restaurant, eyeing each red-and-white-checkered tablecloth, the candles in the empty wine bottles, the chunky shakers of crushed red pepper and cheese. Vic Damone's crooning over the sound system added to the Italian-style setting.

In the off-season, the restaurant had regular, steady customers, year-round residents who knew where they could get good food and warmth. Right now, a few couples sat at the round wooden tables, a tired family in a large booth where the baby was fussing. Newlyweds who had been holed up at the harbor's hotel snuggled in another booth. They were so busy with each other that they didn't mind waiting for the takeout order that Nick's oldest brother, Tony, was preparing in the kitchen. Because Tony's wedding anniversary was tomorrow, he was likely to be too generous.

The dark wood of the tables and booths shone with years

of varnish and use and held three generations of warm, good memories. The main dining room was enough for the off-season crowd, which held a high percentage of relatives. The other smaller rooms would be opened during summer season for overflow and parties.

An active, early sixty-year-old, Nick's mother had raised three sons and moved with the ease of a younger woman. She wanted to travel when possible, and the large house that Nick had grown up in was now filled with his brother Tony's family. Hair that was once dark now held waving fingers of gray that slid into a neat bun at her nape. Despite her usually happy temperament, her husband and her sons knew when she meant business.

Rosa watched Nick roll silverware into red-and-white-checkered napkins. She automatically moved in to help him. "Maggie is a poor little bird, so quiet. She's so stiff in my arms. You'd think she never had been hugged. So what if she has a dog in the apartment? It looks like a good dog and she looks like she needs a friend. You boys always needed Benny when you felt bad. Nick, you'll see that the tablecloths are washed tonight, okay? The stack of clean ones in the back room is getting low."

"Go on up, Mom. It's a slow night." Nick had grown up in this restaurant, listening to stories on his grandfather's knee and twisting spaghetti onto a fork. He had hoped his children would do the same things, but that wasn't going to be.

"Did you finish bottling wine today?" she asked. "You shouldn't come here after working so hard at your own business."

"We're done bottling. The vines are pruned and looking good. The vines are breaking dormancy. The trellises are all strong, posts and wire, and the vines have been tied. We'll be thinning blooms in another five or six weeks, then if we don't get another frost, we'll be picking nice fat grapes by the end of September. You remember how good my wine is when you think about buying more," he teased.

"You make good wine. You should be making good babies . . . I saw Lorna in here earlier."

Nick frowned slightly as he remembered Lorna Smith-Ellis's visit. An only child from wealthy parents, she was spoiled, twice divorced, and seemed deadly certain that she was going to have him. Maybe he was lonely, but he'd enjoyed the brief flirtation, the company of a woman, the way she smelled and moved and dressed. But sex with Lorna wasn't in the mix. "We dated a little bit and that was it."

"I thought so. I don't think she is a bad woman. Lorna has had to fight to get the love her father withheld—that evil, stingy man. She only knows that she has to win every challenge and you would be that . . . Your cousin, Vinnie, still wants her after all these years, after her two marriages. I see it in his eyes. They have something between them. I can feel it. But he doesn't think he is good enough for her, a poor workingman wanting a rich, spoiled woman. And I wonder if you dated her a little to make him jealous. But still you are a man, and I know that you miss—"

His mother didn't finish, looking away. Nick understood that she ached for him. After twelve years, he still missed Alyssa. Would he ever ever stop seeing her crumpled on the pavement, after that motorcycle accident? Ever stop seeing the bloody stain that had been his child spread from her? Ever stop seeing her on life support?

How could he forget? It was his fault—and he'd been the one to sign the release to stop the life support . . . that monitor's little line going straight and flat and lifeless . . .

His mother spoke quietly and leaned close to him. "See that your dad doesn't eat any more meat. His cholesterol is up again. Do not let him put that hot bacon dressing on our spinach salad. I made him some nice munchies—celery and carrot sticks. Tell your brothers. They let him have his way too much."

Nick automatically lowered his head for his mother's good-night kiss. The girl upstairs bothered him. The heavy watch on her wrist wasn't feminine, it was functional, a stop watch, and she had a folded massage table in her pickup. From the way she'd run with her dog, she was in shape. And at first acquaintance, the dog had been protective. Maggie had resented his visit upstairs, and earlier there had been tears in her eyes, a contrast to her tough-loner attitude.

Where was her family? And why was she so alone?

Just then, he could have hugged her himself—but then the Alessandros were a hugging family.

Dante, Nick's divorced older brother, let out a burst of laughter as he refilled wineglasses for the Fergusons. Dante's laughter concealed an ache shared by the Alessandros—he missed his three-year-old son, a boy now frightened of him. His ex-wife had used the boy for leverage in their divorce to hurt Dante. The aching need to recover his child was reflected in Dante's expression each time he held a child. He feared placing his child in a free-for-all, revealing court battle. But when the time came, he would fight for his child.

The Fergusons lifted their glasses in a toast and admired the meal before them. To round off their *filetti al pepe verge,* or beef fillets with green pepper, they'd chosen a Pinot Noir from Nick's winery, aged just right in his underground cellar.

Three years ago, a light frost had claimed a good portion of his grapes, but the wine from that year was passable, even good, mellowed in sturdy oak.

Nick slid a bottle of last year's bottled Chancellor into a brown sack, stuffed that into a larger white one with paper handles, and added an assortment of plastic forks, knives, and spoons with foil packages of Parmesan cheese. He handed the sack to Bobby, a young cousin who was home from college and working at the restaurant, clearing tables. "For the honeymooners."

On his way to the kitchen, Bobby passed Nick's father, Anthony, and dismissing the difference in their ages, they did a playful you're-in-my-way dance.

Stooped a bit by age, Anthony had given his three sons their over six-foot height and broad-shouldered build. In his late sixties, with thick, black, waving hair and only a bit of gray, he enjoyed life. The slight bulge of his midsection said he enjoyed his family's restaurant. "He also enjoyed teasing his wife. He winked at Nick as he passed, carrying plates of veal Parmesan. "Your mother works me like a slave all day long and then forgets that I am a red-hot lover by night."

"Papa, don't speak like that in front of the children," Rosa admonished sternly as she made her way to the table with the small children. They were strangers; the young parents were tired and the baby was protesting, rubbing his small fists against his eyes. An expert with children, Rosa soon held the baby, who slept draped over her shoulder. From his mother's expression, Nick knew she was recommending a good, reasonably priced motel up the street.

Anthony visited with the veal Parmesan customers and the office supply store owners, and came back to watch Nick hang the clean wineglasses bottom-up on the overhead rack.

"How's the girl upstairs? I saw her go out, taking her dog for a walk. I told her that she could use the washer and dryer in the storeroom. She doesn't say much. It's a good dog and no mongrel, either. Something is wrong with the girl. I came in from the kitchen too quick while she was going out the back door. She didn't see me, and she jumped, flattened back against the shelves. She's scared, Nicholas. It's a terrible thing when a woman is alone and scared."

And sad, looking as if she were haunted, Nick thought. When she answered the door the second time, those shimmering dark green eyes, the soft tremble of her lips belied her warning keep-away frown.

Nick didn't want to know about her shadows. He had enough of his own.

Attuned to the dog's tense movements in the bed beside her, Maggie awoke easily. Yet the dregs of the nightmare clung to her, the watery image of her father reaching out to her and then disappearing until only his hand could be seen beneath the waves, and then it was gone. Then another man's face appeared—this man had had an affair with Glenda and had ruined her life. As Maggie surfaced, blurred images of Glenda, drugged and used, slid by her.

"I don't believe he tried to rape you," Glenda has slurred in her drugged haze. "He said you flirted with him, and he's only a man, after all. You're just trying to take him away from me. You probably invited him there, to find you in that bathtub. And stop hounding me and his friends. They're my friends, too. I like how I live and what I do. Brent is all that matters, and so what if he wants me to do favors for his friends. It's nothing, because he loves me and you can't stand that, can you, Miss Perfect High and Mighty?"

Lying in the dark apartment above Alessandros Restaurant, Maggie's fingers latched onto Scout's pelt. "He's not going to get you," she whispered to Scout.

The same man who had ruined Glenda's life had hurt Scout . . .

The dog stared at the apartment's closed door while Maggie adjusted to her new surroundings, tearing herself again from the past.

She would make a new start in the morning . . . she had to . . .

At ten-thirty at night, muted sounds of a restaurant kitchen seemed almost reassuring. On the stairway, a man's low, indistinguishable rumble blended with a woman's softer tones. The wood steps creaked beneath their passing, and then opposite Maggie's apartment, the Alessandros' door opened and closed softly.

A burst of male laughter carried up the stairs and then the sounds were muted again, and Scout settled her head on Maggie's chest.

"This is just temporary, Scout," Maggie said firmly as she rubbed the dog's ears. "If I can just pick up enough work to get some money, I'm going to get my own business and settle down. I've had enough of running. You'll have your own fenced-in yard. I am going to make this work. Someone in this town has to care about their physical fitness, otherwise there wouldn't be that small gym down the street. That's all I'm qualified for, all I know."

She'd once lived her life for her ex-husband, believing in the dream world of working together, then having a family.

She'd stopped crying a long time ago. The images and arguments were three years old and still painful: She'd been attacked by a man she hated, and Ryan hadn't believed her. He didn't want her to bring charges . . . the man was too important and could help them build their business . . . Her husband thought more of his own safety and business than he did of Maggie . . .

Determined to rest for the job in front of her—getting clients and therefore money—Maggie turned on her side and wrapped her arm around Scout. The street lamps sent a soft glow into her second-floor apartment. It was only April, cool and fresh with spring and the scent of daffodils, and a new start. "We're going to be just fine. I'm just not used to a big meal. I shouldn't have eaten all that—it hit me hard and I fell asleep too early."

Because she knew she couldn't sleep easily now, Maggie eased out of bed and dug through her duffel bag, found a lavender-scented candle, and lit it. With her CD player's earphones in place, she sat on the floor in yoga position and began a slow, relaxing meditation. She focused on the sonorous Asian tones of the woman, the bells tinkling lightly in the background . . .

In the cluttered workroom of her tiny yellow house, Celeste Moonstar poured melted wax into stocky candle molds. Her shop, Journeys, was not quite as well inventoried as she would like for the approaching tourist season. She critically studied the red wax, disappointed that she had missed the delicate pink shade she wanted.

But her mind had been elsewhere, on how she felt earlier, fingers of fear gripping her, holding her as she locked her shop's door. She'd hurried for the safety of her home, and the fear seemed to slither after her.

Celeste frowned as a stream of bloodred liquid wax ran down the side of the mold and spread on the counter. She listened to the tiny wind chimes on her porch and the scraping of a small branch on the window. As a psychic with some talent, she recognized the wary restlessness within her—as if her senses were about to tell her something.

On the counter, the spilled wax hardened and lost its liquid shine as though fate had been cast and couldn't be changed.

Celeste ran her hand over it, testing the heat, and found the impression of her fingerprint. Not all the fingerprint had taken, just the half crescent that formed a long C. An eerie chill rose up her nape, and the flowing scarf around her throat seemed to tighten.

She smiled tightly, dismissing whatever prowled in her mind. She was overworked, a little upset by the strange sensations she'd felt outside her shop, nothing more.

The wind chimes tinkled again, and Celeste turned to her inventory. Sometimes the wind carried other's sensations to her that she'd never know or experience. It was best to dismiss her uneasiness for now.

At seven o'clock in the morning, Alessandros' kitchen was busy again, and aromatic scents of bubbling sauces began coursing up the stairway. As Maggie came down, passing through the kitchen storeroom on her way out the back, two men were vehemently arguing the worth of making and packaging Alessandros' own pasta against the commercial grade. On the family dining room table sat a battered pot of coffee, along with two plates of sweet rolls, and a number of half-full cups of coffee. A massive bundle of fresh herbs bundled in damp newspaper lay on the plastic tablecloth next to a menu that had been heavily marked with black pen. The sound of television's morning news cruised over the spacious, homey room.

In the customers' dining room, Dean Martin's "That's Amore" provided another layer of sound, adding to the family's energetic mixed exchange of Italian and English.

Anthony waved to Maggie, bidding her to come to him. When she did, he wrapped his arms around her, lifted her off the floor, and playfully waggled her. He kept his arm around her as he poured coffee into a new cup. "So you're hungry this morning, huh? Sit. Have a sweet roll and some coffee."

Uneasy with the friendly familiarity, she moved away from him. "I'd better not. I'm still full from last night."

As soon as she could, Maggie was hitting a grocery store and stocking up on healthy food—celery and carrot sticks, black beans and lentils, and tofu and sunflower seeds.

The sweet roll was oozing with frosting and smelled like fresh-baked cinnamony heaven. At one time, her weight had ballooned with fragrant comfort food; she'd eaten, but not to satisfy her hunger. Ryan's disgust for her sexually had only added to her need for comfort food.

"Have some coffee then."

"Thank you, but I don't drink coffee."

He peered down at her. "You look healthy. What's wrong with you? You don't sleep so good, do you?"

When had she ever slept through the night? Maggie avoided the question with a light smile. "I'd better take my dog for that run now. She's been waiting. I need to pick up a few things. Is there a health food store in town?"

He straightened and sniffed elegantly, clearly offended. "And just what's wrong with the food at Alessandros Italian Restaurant?"

In the end, to erase her offense, she ate the sweet roll and drank a glass of milk, and wished she could snuggle back into the comfortable bed upstairs.

On her way out the back door, she held the screen door for a huge, beefy man with a friendly face and a mop of black, waving hair. The box in his arms held several white paper bundles. "I'm the butcher—Marco Alessandro. Got a fresh delivery here—veal, the best. Hold the door, will you?" he asked.

He edged through the door sideways, carrying his box. "Heard Anthony had a renter with a dog. I'll start leaving a good beef knuckle bone now and then. Looks like a good dog. Maggie is your name, right?"

She nodded slowly. Apparently news traveled fast in Blanchefleur, and when he looked curious, she said, "Thanks. I'll pay for the bones."

Inside the door now, he looked back at her through the mesh screen. "Nah."

His look was too intense. Maggie, adept at sliding away from conversations that might reveal too much about herself, nodded again and hooked Scout's leash to her collar. While Scout stood, sniffing and locked dead center onto the smell of meat, Maggie did her usual warm-ups. She'd run as far as she could from bitter truths and a battle she couldn't win, and now she had to start—today, she had to start creating a life for herself.

If she needed anything it was a home with a kitchen and her parents' old furniture around her, a little garden to plant and watch grow. She needed to drape it all around herself and heal, to fill the emptiness.

By eight-thirty that morning Maggie had already taken Scout for her morning run. She braced herself and started making her rounds—first the small gym, Looking Good.

Behind the dirty windows, the two-story nineteenth-century building had little equipment, a couple of ancient treadmills, a weight bench, and an assortment of yard-sale health-type gizmos and floor mats. Next to a set of workout tapes, a perky newscaster was busily chatting on the old black-and-white television set. A disinterested teenage male playing with an electronic game lounged behind the battered desk. His mottled complexion said he probably liked too many french fries and hamburgers.

He glanced at her, then did a double take at her only presentable jogging suit. His eyes slid up her breasts to her face, and the electronic music said he'd just clicked off his hand-held game. His "Hi, there" held a warm, sensual invitation.

"Hi. Where are your customers?"

He shrugged and puffed up his angular tall body a bit.

Head tilted to one side, eyes narrowed, his pose was all ma-cho. He considered the arm muscle he was flexing. "The name is Jerry Russo. I just work here. Ole Longman owns the place. Some customers just left—the early-morning set. There's usually a little break before it gets too busy."

"I see. Please tell Ole that I'm a personal trainer, just set-ting up business. If he has anyone who wants one-on-one, I'd appreciate them being sent my way. Just put a note in my mailbox at the Alessandros Restaurant back door. There's a ten percent referral fee for you and Ole, and I'll steer some work over here. How does that sound?"

"Depends. Ole might just go for it. Better stop by and talk to him later." He leaned over the desk to peer out of the win-dow at the street. "Where's your dog?"

That jarred Maggie's protective instincts. "How did you know I have one?"

"New woman in town and not a tourist. Word gets around. Heard Nick gave you a coupon for a free dinner and steered you onto that upstairs room. Nick Alessandro is my cousin. We're family," he stated proudly.

"Nick Alessandro? As in Alessandros' Restaurant?"

Maggie stood very still. Nick had said the apartment needed filling . . . it came with one meal a day . . . he'd felt sorry for her.

He'd given her charity and everyone knew it. And just maybe he wanted something in return.

Okay, she was suspicious. In the past few years, she'd been in enough situations to be wary of anything that looked too good—and Nick was exactly that.

# THREE

Jerry flexed his biceps and studied them. "Yeah. He works at the restaurant when he can, but mostly he runs his vineyard and the winery. They just finished bottling, so he's got some extra time, I guess. He and his brothers and some of the cousins help his parents a lot. It's a family business with good food. Shoot, in the tourist season, the customers line up on the street, just waiting to get in. He must have liked you, or they wouldn't have rented that room to you. It's just for the summer help and when family visits."

While Maggie was running through what to say to Nick, Jerry spotted Scout sitting, tied to a street bench. Scout was listening attentively to whatever the elderly woman in a wheelchair was saying.

"Is it a deal?" Maggie pushed, worried that Scout might try to play and jump, hurting the older woman.

"Yeah. Hey, are you doing anything later, maybe tonight? I can show you around town."

"Some other time."

"Oh, yeah. You're trying to get a business started. That

personal training stuff. Tell you what, why don't I advertise for you, and you can give me a little personal one-on-one training?"

The boy not only had big ears, he had big ideas, Maggie decided as she smiled and hurried out to untie Scout's leash.

"Nice dog," the elderly woman said. "We're having quite the conversation about you, all fit and perky in the morning. You're new around here, aren't you? Come on down to the beauty shop and I'll introduce you around the blue-hair set."

By five o'clock, Maggie's sleepless night was telling on her, but she'd picked up an elderly customer interested in regular walking routines. She'd stopped by the Looking Good gym again and talked with Ole Longman, the owner. Once a champion weight lifter, seventy-five-year-old Ole was still spry and set on physical health. According to Ole, he'd hit a streak of bad luck—mostly due to ex-wives and managers on the take. The Looking Good and a few trophies were all he had left. "Have a soda," he'd invited.

"No, thanks."

"It gets real busy in here," Ole had said, eyeing her as she unzipped her jacket. In her T-shirt, her upper arms were defined, her abdominals tight. Used to angling for tradeoffs, she'd sat on the weight bench and did a few arm curls with a ten-pounder, just to show Ole that she knew proper form. Ole nodded and took off his cotton shirt to reveal an undershirt over a nicely defined torso. He did a few weight lifter poses, flexing to show off. "Not so bad, huh?"

After an hour of taking turns bench pressing and discussing technique with Maggie, Ole agreed to let her schedule six women's fitness hours, three days a week, morning and afternoon, in his gym. Ole slyly let Maggie know that he would appreciate a Mrs. Dee Dee Hopper, an attractive widow, attending classes. Apparently Ole was ready now to settle down to a good woman and Dee Dee was a shy sixty-eight, but "one heck of a lalapalooza" with a fine, prime backside.

So much for raging teenage hormones, Maggie had

thought as she took Ole's pulse and blood pressure with an old arm wrap monitor that had seen better days. She agreed to call Dee Dee's number—quickly supplied by Ole—and invite her to classes.

But angling on Ole's needs, she had hinted that women liked cleanliness, washed windows, and a clean bathroom. When Ole blinked as in shock, Maggie had offered to help clean.

One look in the ladies' dressing room and bathroom, and Maggie had decided to wait until morning.

After talking with Jerry, she had bigger things to do than clean bathrooms—namely setting Nick Alessandro straight. If one more person insinuated that she was under his protection, his girlfriend, or needed charity, she'd explode.

Fifteen minutes later, Scout sat in the passenger seat as Maggie drove out of town. She drove northward, a distance away from but parallel to the lake. She passed a few houses, small and modern with well-trimmed yards, and a few roads leading from the blacktop. Signs for Jake's Tulip Farm and Dutch Clogs R Us invited, and a small farm's "Wagon Ponies" grazed in a fenced field. A distance down the road, a small camper sat in an overgrown yard, marked by a No Trespassing sign; a sprawling marsh of cattails lay behind the site.

Following Ole's directions, Maggie took the winding dirt road to Alessandro Vineyards and Winery. Just up and away from the shoreline, the vineyards sprawled out like patchwork, the bald vines evenly spaced between the posts. A sign marked the direction to the winery, a rough wood building. A tractor sat outside a large garage, and a battered station wagon was the only vehicle in the visitors' parking lot. A small, bent, aged man wearing a vivid Hawaiian shirt struggled to unload grocery sacks and laundry baskets from the back of the station wagon.

Maggie pulled to a stop and got out. "Let me help you with those."

His weathered face changed, wrinkles shifting into a big

grin beneath his 1930s-style hat. "Any time a pretty lady wants to help, that's fine with me. You're new here, aren't you?"

"Uh-huh." Maggie reached for the grocery sacks and hefted them into her arms. "I'm looking for Nick Alessandro."

He lifted the laundry basket of neatly folded clothing. "He lives down the road, in the Frenchman's lighthouse. It's not really a lighthouse, more of a brick tower where the old Frenchie's ghost is supposed to roam, looking for his sweetheart. I'm Eugene, by the way. I live and work here. We've got plenty of help, but we're needing someone to work the showroom and to help with wine festivals later on, just parttime, during the real busy season. I can show you around if you want. Nick's a good guy to work for . . . I got good insurance because of him . . . Nice dog. Did you come to apply for a job?"

"No, thanks. I'm trying to get my own business started. I just need to talk with Nick."

At her side, Scout had that I-want-to-run look, staring at the rows of stark grape vines fingering up to grasp the wires between them. "No. Don't you dare," Maggie ordered quietly.

Eugene's grin widened, his eyes twinkling. "If I was a young woman, Nick would be first on my list, too."

"It's not like that."

"Maybe not for you. Nick may still be wrapped up in losing his wife, but he's not blind."

So Nick's wife had left him and he was out to score, and Lorna wasn't taking any play and so-longs.

She followed Eugene into a side door of the weathered board building. The room was big and dark, lined with new shelving and a counter. "This is going to be our showroom for visitors and tastings. Lately, Nick has been working on some promotional brochures, in the office—it's back there above those big tanks. He likes to separate his living space and work. I stay here year round and watch the place. There's an intercom thingie hooked up to Nick's house if I need anything. I live in here—"

The apartment was small, neat, and cheery, and Scout immediately began sniffing the perimeter and everything in it. Maggie placed the grocery sacks on the red Formica and chrome table. "How do I get to Nick's?"

Eugene gave her directions and then winked. "Should I tell him you're coming? Or do you want to surprise him?"

"I think I'd rather surprise him."

She noted Eugene's pained frown as he bent to place the laundry basket on a stool. "Is there something I can do to help?"

His smile apologized. "I'm almost eighty and my pieces are worn. It's my hip and back. I've got pain pills."

Maggie had already noticed his limp and the way he favored one side. "Let me see."

She placed her hands on Eugene's shoulders and studied him. "I think you've got one leg shorter than the other. That means the other side has to compensate, the longer leg doing the work. You could get orthopedic insoles to correct that."

"The doc gives me pain pills," Eugene said firmly.

Maggie was used to resistance and mindsets. "Next time, ask him to check the length of your legs. It's worth a try. If you need help in therapy, maybe strengthening the weaker side after you get an insole adjustment, contact me down at Ole's Looking Good."

"Can't. Won't step foot in the place. Ole is trying to make the moves on Dee Dee. He called me a 'raisin.' You know, a shriveled, dried-up—" Eugene's mulish look said he wasn't budging.

Maggie tried not to smile; unknowingly, she'd already given Ole the edge by inviting Dee Dee to his gym. "I think you're good-looking, and a few wrinkles give a man not only attitude but an interesting look."

Eugene flashed his oversize false teeth. "I ain't no beefcake like Ole."

"Women like other things. Concentrate on what you might have in common with Dee Dee."

"She loves soap operas. No self-respecting man would watch those things."

"Start," Maggie advised, before taking the narrow winding road toward Nick's house.

She passed a huge garden spot, recently tilled, and a few small outbuildings, and stopped near an odd house. Just past the knoll where the house sat, the lake gleamed like a blue ribbon, and a few seagulls hovered white in the sky, making the most of the winds. Built square and laid with shingles, the weathered clapboard was topped by a jutting brick tower.

If there was a ghost haunting the tower, he was likely to be disturbed, because Maggie wasn't feeling peaceful—she wasn't Nick's rumored "new girl" and she didn't take charity. She parked next to a well-kept old International pickup laden with brush and trimmings.

Released from the pickup, Scout was already running around the house, through the yellow patch of daffodils. Just rounding the house, Maggie saw Nick, standing against an expanse of sky. In worn, dirty jeans, boots, a frayed sweat-shirt, and standing in what must have been an herb bed ruled by tarragon and garlic, he stared at her. Nick leaned the shovel he'd been holding against the house. "Hello, Maggie."

His welcome was quiet, as if he'd been expecting her. But then Eugene had probably called to give him a heads-up.

"I want to talk with you," she said while Scout was busy leaping on him and he rough-played with her. Barking happily, Scout ignored Maggie's order to sit; instead she ran like a puppy around Nick and then leaped at him. Nick chuckled and pushed Scout down, only to have her leap at him again with power that would have knocked Maggie to the ground. "I want to talk with you," Maggie repeated more loudly as she tried to grab Scout's collar. "Scout, stop."

But the dog had found a new playmate and lunged again, breaking free of Maggie's grasp. In a heartbeat, the dog was racing along the slight path down through the dunes and grass from Nick's home to the wide open sandy beaches.

"Now, see what you've done. She's excitable—" Maggie started after Scout, only to be brought short by Nick's hand around her upper arm.

"She's a retriever. She sees water and she wants to play. It's natural with her—"

Maggie shook with fear for her dog and anger at the man challenging her. She tried to jerk her arm away, and Nick held firm. She stared up at him, furious now. Another man had held her like that, as he was telling her that her sister was beyond help. Ryan had wanted her to "cut her losses and let Glenda destroy herself," but Maggie couldn't; she'd kept trying and nothing had helped her sister's decline. "Let me go."

"I saw how you acted on the beach yesterday, as if you were afraid for your dog, as if you were afraid of the water. Why?"

This time, he did release her. How easy life was, she thought, for him, a man who had been safe within his family.

There amid the clear blue sky and the hovering seagulls, she felt twelve years old again. She felt the sucking power of the waves on her life jacket, heard Glenda—just a bit younger and terrified, bobbing in her orange life jacket and reaching out to her for help. By habit, Maggie's hand clasped Glenda's locket, all that she had left of her sister. Now she had only Scout, who was racing happily across the sand. She had to save her. . . .

Nick watched Maggie tear down the slope of sand dunes and grass, falling and sliding in her panic to reach her dog. With her ponytail sticking from the back of her ball cap, her body in flight, she looked more like a boy than a woman.

He shoved his hands into his pockets. Oh, she was a woman, all right. One look at those dark green eyes and that bit of a nose and that generous mouth, and his nose was sniffing for female pheromones, his body tight.

He picked up the shovel, put his foot on it to dig, and

changed his mind; he couldn't resist following Maggie. Since she was already furious with him, he might as well go all out.

On the wide expanse of brown sand, she looked small, crouching to hug her dog. Nick walked slowly to her, appreciated Scout's welcoming bark, and ignored Maggie's frosty look. "Go away."

Nick sat near her and scanned the white sails of a small ship headed for Blanchefleur's harbor, putting in for the night. The ship was small and light, a classic wood frame, well tended, a fast-runner, just like the woman with fear written all over her face.

"You're on the run. Why?"

Maggie's quick, blank look, her ponytail feathered by the light wind as she whipped to stare at him with that flash of anger, said he'd struck truth. "You don't know what you're talking about and you ask too many questions. Now leave me alone."

Nick was already wading in deep, murky problems she didn't want disturbed—and he wanted to help. "She can swim, you know. Probably better than you. The water is smooth. Let her go. She needs this, Maggie. She's bred for water, and you're holding her from what nature gave her."

She continued to hold Scout close, staring grimly at the water as if it were her personal devil. "Shut up."

Nick slid a cool look at her; Maggie wasn't only furious, she was stark white, fighting panic. That quick swallow, her fingers digging into the dog's coat told him everything—she loved the dog desperately, as if the animal were her only friend. "What did you come here to tell me?"

"I came to tell you that you can butt out of my life. I'm not a charity case, and I could have paid for my meal and the room. Now everyone in town knows that—"

"So you're moving on, afraid to face a little gossip?"

Those witch's eyes cut at him and narrowed. "I've had worse."

He wanted to hold that hair in his fist, to feel the life and thick silk in his grasp, the sunlight catching the red highlights and coursing down the strands to flick fire at the ends.

Her chin went out, those eyes dark emerald and gold now, striking at him. "I've got work. I'll be around awhile, and you're not in the picture. Half the town thinks I'm already your girlfriend and the other half—your relatives are telling me all about what a great guy you are, a real marriage prospect."

Nick couldn't stop his grin; he was used to family and friends touting potential girlfriends to him. "They mean well, Maggie."

"Leave . . . me . . . alone," she ordered tightly.

"Lady, *I* didn't come to see *you*. You're the one who turned up here, all full of spit and fire. I'll bet you get plenty of clients with that friendly attitude."

Scout squirmed and whined in Maggie's grip. "I do okay."

He reached to brush a bit of sand from her cheek, and her skin was smooth beneath his fingertips. She stiffened and he jerked his hand away. "Don't touch me."

Nick knew her walls were up, pasted with big flashing warning signs. She'd been hurt badly, and by a man. "Let the dog go, Maggie. She loves the water and wants to play, but she loves you, too. You're really upset and shaking. Your fear of water isn't ordinary. Is there some way I can help you?"

"No." In profile, Maggie's face lowered, a tear dropping from her cheek as she whispered, again gripping that gold locket, "She's all I've got. I couldn't bear for anything to happen to her."

"I know. I won't let anything happen to her. Just let her go into the water."

Maggie's pale, capable hands tightened on the dog's thick coat. "No."

If he couldn't help the woman, he could help the dog. Nick slipped off his canvas loafers and stood. He walked to a small stick; he was taking a big chance, he thought as he sailed it out onto the water.

Immediately Scout started barking excitedly, struggling to free herself from Maggie. Finally twisting free, Scout ran full speed into the water and with a leap, started swimming for the stick.

"You idiot!" Maggie was on her feet, running toward the water. She stopped abruptly, just inches from the lapping foam of the waves. "Scout, you come here this minute!"

Scout had the stick in her mouth and was swimming back to shore.

Maggie turned to Nick, her cheeks pink with wind and anger. "You idiot."

"You already said that." For a man whose temper rarely nudged him, Nick was starting to feel the burn. "Look, I've offered to help you with no strings attached. Are you always in a bad mood, or is it just me?"

The answer shot at him like a bullet. "It's you. I get along fine with most people."

"So do I. In fact, most people think I'm likable."

"They're mistaken." She watched him walk to the stick Scout had dropped. He stopped to pick it up, and Maggie ordered, "Don't you dare."

With a look that said he would, Nick dared, and Scout was racing out into the water, leaping into it. She swam to the stick, retrieved it, and returned to shore, carrying it directly to Nick. After a small tussle, she released the stick to him, and he threw it once more. When Scout was swimming, Nick turned to Maggie, watching her.

She was stubborn and a fighter, and that fear was still in her eyes, her hand clasped on that locket.

Nick wasn't going to ask any more questions and get another verbal slap. But he wondered about that locket—to whom it had belonged, who had given it to her, and what rested inside.

He could almost feel Maggie's heart gallop with fear, and that was a terrible thing. This time, as though sensing Maggie's fear, Scout dropped the stick and ran to her, leaping happily on her.

Maggie went down with a soft cry and Scout was all over her, playfully licking her face and ignoring her orders. Nick hurried to grab Scout's collar and haul her back. Amid the dog's prints in the sand, Maggie lay quiet, breathing hard as she frowned up at Nick. Sandy dog pawprints ran across her T-shirt where her sweat jacket had opened. She blew sand from her mouth and ignored his extended hand as she got to her feet, brushing her clothing.

In the fracas, her nipples had hardened, thrusting at the light cloth. Nick's throat dried suddenly and his body became sensually taut and locked onto her curves. He wanted to brush her body, feel that softness flowing beneath his hands, ease that damp, muddy T-shirt from her and—and from the blaze of those green-gold eyes, he was likely to have a hard time of it.

"Maggie is in a bad mood," he said to Scout. "Let's behave."

The dog whined softly and stared longingly at the water.

"So she likes water and she can swim," Maggie stated grudgingly. "You've proved your point."

"Didn't you know that when you got her? Hunters use Labs for retrievers."

"I know exactly what they use them for—showing off what a high-priced dog can do for their buddies. But if that dog is untrained and too young and—"

The dark, bitter leap of temper surprised him. "So you rescued her."

"Someone had to." Her fists were tight now, her color high and her eyes lashing at him.

"It takes a lot of patience to do rescue work. Sometimes the dog is too far gone, but you've done a good job."

"You don't know anything about it."

The bitterness was there again, simmering just beneath the surface. "I'm listening. Tell me."

When Maggie frowned and looked away, Nick knew he'd hit a nerve; he'd come too close to her life and the secrets she wanted to keep. She walked to Scout's stick, hesitated as if the decision came hard to her, then picked it up and threw it into the water. With an excited bark and ready to play, Scout leaped into the lake.

Nick stood still, admiring the woman from the back. Her ball cap had tilted, her ponytail was coated with sand, and the wind pushed her loose jogging pants against her body. He admired the curve of her bottom, and when she turned, he served his best innocent smile. "Looks like she'll be at that awhile."

"Don't you throw another one. She's my dog. If she needs something, I'll do it for her."

"Fine." Nick settled down on the sand and watched Maggie kick off her jogging shoes, dump the sand from them, and then peel off her socks. She stuffed them into her shoes and began rolling up her pants.

He wondered how those slender pale feet would feel on his calves, bracing as her hips lifted in lovemaking.

He sighed roughly. It had been a long time since he'd made love.

Maggie glanced at him, anger simmering around her. "Don't you have something to do?"

He could have watched her forever. Maybe it was his fate to meet a foul-tempered woman with witch's eyes and fire in her hair, and to want to take her, right there on the sand, and never let her go.

And maybe bottling wine and working at the restaurant for fourteen-hour days had made him a little crazy. Maybe it was that he needed a woman's body again, his own coming to life, shocking him. "Not really. It's not often that I meet a real mystery woman and want to know everything about her. But then, I'd just be wasting my time if I were to ask more questions, right? You must love wallowing in your own secrecy, making people wonder about you. Maybe it's a game with you."

"It is not a game. You're prodding and pushing. Try someone else. It's my life and my business, not yours."

Nick's easy patience said he could outlast Maggie's walls,

and he deliberately nudged her. "Well, then, maybe you're just a moody woman and this is the wrong time. If there is a right time, I'm available. Something has happened to you that's made you distrustful of everyone. I'd say you need someone to listen—unless you just like being a sourpuss."

Maggie's dark look at him and her silence, those lips firmly pressed together, ended any further conversation.

After several more runs, Scout began to tire. She carried the stick not to Maggie this time, but to Nick, where she did her dog-shaking-water thing. Scout plopped onto the sand beside him and stared at the lake.

"Let's go, Scout," Maggie said as she picked up her shoes and began carrying them toward the path up to Nick's house.

The dog remained, tongue hanging down as she panted beside Nick, a new friend.

With a tired sigh, Maggie returned to sit on the other side of her dog. "Whenever you're ready, Scout, just let me know."

With the dog between them, Nick and Maggie settled into silence and peace. Nick liked the feel of that, the feel of the wind, telling him that he was alive, the sense of peace that water always brought, and the sense that something was happening with this woman. Maybe he was just a romantic, but the odd inner calm told him his life had changed and that something waited for him—with Maggie.

"That's a strange house," she said, her voice flowing over the sound of the waves breaking on the shore. "With that brick tower on top."

That was something, Nick thought. That quiet remark showed a woman's curiosity working, stilling the brief bitterness. "It's supposed to be a lighthouse, or at least the Frenchman's version of one in another century. He built the house on the highest point of land—built it around the lighthouse, and his fiancée was to join him. Legend has it that her ship sunk just out there, and that he still haunts the place, waiting for her. My brothers and I used to go there with Dad and hunt for treasure that might have washed ashore from Monique's shipwreck."

*He wanted to smooth her hair, to feel the warm burn of it on his skin.* Instead, he brushed sand from her shoulder and caught the quick wary tension of her body. "My grandfather bought this place because he thought it would make a good vineyard. We worked together out here when we could. We got the grapes going—he wanted only reds—selling them to buyers, until we got enough to start the winery. He never saw the first bottle out of it, though we made some home wines."

"That tower makes quite a statement here on this knoll."

"Oh, what's that?" But from the way she turned away, he knew that she hadn't meant the words to come out as they did. Some men drove expensive mechanical penis symbols, but *he* had chosen a lighthouse.

Nick considered the suspected jutting monument to manhood. "Maybe."

"I meant that you like the solitary life." Her blush delighted him, soft and rosy and sweet beneath the crust and the fear. He had to know more of what ran beneath the surface and why she hoarded it.

Maggie removed her ball cap and dusted the sand from it. Nick watched, fascinated, as those deft feminine hands removed the band confining her ponytail, her fingers winnowing through her hair. It caught the wind, and sailed in a dark red storm around her head, unwilling to be captured—just like the woman.

As if she felt him watching her, Maggie turned slowly, and their eyes locked for just that heartbeat.

"Hello, Maggie," he said again, more softly this time, as his heart hitched just that half beat.

She shivered as if sensing what ran between them, and then stood. "I'd better go. Scout?"

At the top of the knoll, Maggie glanced at the house, and Nick wanted to keep her with him longer, to know more about her. "Would you like to see the house? I work on it when I can. The view from the old lighthouse is something."

"No, thanks. I'm leaving."

Nick tried again, justifying his lie with his need to be with her. "Give me a ride into town, will you? My pickup is dead and I've got to work tonight. Someone could come get me, but that would take more time."

That hesitation said she was wary, that she wasn't used to sharing. "I didn't ask you to throw sticks for my dog. If you're late, it's not my fault."

All defensive bristles, he thought, until she feared for her dog and clasped that gold locket. Then cracks in that brittle façade revealed a woman's softness and pain. What had happened to her? Why did that locket mean so much? Why was she so scared of water? And why was she alone and afraid? "Do you ever laugh?" he asked abruptly, and wondered what she would look like if she were happy.

Her fierce scowl held a big warning. "What's it to you?"

"Don't get all touchy. Look, you can either drive out of here and leave me stranded—" Okay, Nick decided, so he'd learned a little something about guilt trips from his mother. "Or you can take in the fantastic view from the old lighthouse while I shower and change. On a clear day, you can see Blanchefleur's red lighthouse, and there's a gray bump way out on the horizon that is a tiny island. Supposedly Monique, the Frenchman's fiancée, drowned near there. We call it Monique's Island."

He watched Maggie weigh options as she glanced up at the brick tower-like structure. It really was a hell of a symbol for a man living alone, he thought, amused.

"How long before you're ready?" she asked.

"Long enough."

Maggie was dying to go up into that old lighthouse and look out, scanning the lake. She didn't often go in for romantic notions, but the idea that the Frenchman haunted the structure was irresistible. How could a man love a woman so much that he still waited for her through time? "Make it fast."

Inside the home that had been built around the lighthouse, Nick indicated the doorway to the Frenchman's tower and then disappeared. Smooth with age and use, the winding wooden stairs led upward, the bricks gleaming from the sunlight shafting from the top. The tiny enclosure provided a fantastic view of Lake Michigan, a sprawling beach, and in the other direction—toward land—naked grapevines in neat rows flowing across the land.

A wooden Adirondack-style chair dominated the small space. An empty jam jar sat on the chair's arm, a bottle of Alessandro Cabernet Franc on the rough plank floor beside it. The only other things in the room were a table containing an album, and an ornately framed picture of a bride and groom, cracks splintering across the glass. Young and carefree, Nick smiled down at the woman he held in his arms, her black hair in a curling froth around her pixieish face, the white bridal gown draped to the church steps.

Her face turned to the camera, the young bride smiled wistfully; another woman from another time, she seemed to stare right into Maggie's eyes.

Maggie had been a bride just like that once, believing that the world waited for her.

Ryan was in her past; he had sided with the man who had led Glenda to her death.

The windows were new, and on impulse, Maggie slid one open, needing the relief from the heavy nuances in the room. Nick's wife had left him and he brooded over her in this room. A fresh wind swirled inside, lifting the hair on her nape almost like a caress. The breath of air held an earthy spring scent, tinged with new beginnings and hope.

The feeling was so strong, Maggie felt as if she could reach out and grab it in her fist and make it come true.

Instead she traced her finger over the new caulking on the opened window. Were the quiet vibrations, the feeling of expectations to be met Maggie's own hopes for a new start? Or the dreams of the Frenchman long ago, in love and waiting for his bride-to-be? Or was it Nick's longing for his wife that seemed to soften the barren room?

\* \* \*

Wind, Earth, and Fire milled around Celeste's long flowing skirts, their tails high, rubbing against her as cats do when seeking selfish attention. But just now, Celeste was intent on the restlessness within her. She'd tried to push it away, but still it came coiling back, wrapping around her.

Turning in the breeze, a pewter earth goddess like the one outside Celeste's shop made her rounds within the wind chimes' silver tubes, producing a relaxing melody. With bare breasts and flaring hips and arms upraised, the goddess in different styles was a favorite of Celeste's and her customers. In the goddess, they recognized the woman within, an earth mother, life giving, and sensual. In the universe, each person played a part, and Celeste liked to think that goddess defined and brought sensuality to women who had forgotten their role.

She smiled slightly. The goddess's spinning movements mirrored Celeste's own restlessness.

The dying day had been sunny and warm, enough to liven the lavender growing around her small yellow house. Perched on a hill overlooking Blanchefleur's Main Street, the cottage had once been a summer home to the wealthy, abandoned for the sleeker, upscale models more popular now.

Celeste raised her face to the chilly April breeze. She could smell tourist dollars in the air, those bored rich wives coming to her shop, their soft hands manicured and gleaming with rings. When the bell over the shop's door tinkled, she would be fattening her checkbook.

She wrapped her shawl around her, felt the fringes brush sensually against her skin. She enjoyed the sunset before she settled in for a relaxing night of labeling her specialty lotions and ordering supplies for her soaps.

Mary Lou Ingeborg, Iowa farm girl, was in her past, and she had become Celeste Moonstar, Blanchefleur's resident psychic. Her specialty ran to tarot cards, because they never lied to her. *She* might lie to clients, giving false hope and dreams because they wanted them so, and there was really nothing she could do to change what would come.

She shrugged lightly and smiled. She couldn't change the future, or their lives. So long as her clients were happy, her bills were paid. She carefully worded her assessments of their futures and problems so that they fell into a quasi-zone of how the clients wished to translate them.

But when the police called on her in murder cases, she saw awful things, the darkness that lived in humans, the need to hurt and kill. The sensations of the victims as they met death made her ill, and it sometimes took weeks for her to recover.

The wind chimes tinkled musically, and that wave of restlessness stirred in her again. On the end of her chain, the goddess turned slowly, her slender nude body silvery in the light, and then in shadows as dark as death.

Celeste bent to run her hand over the fur of her cats, treating each one equally, and each sat, twitching its tail, watching her.

Did they feel it? That strange unsettling of the air?

The cats on the porch strolled in separate directions. One sprawled on the boards, another leaped to the wooden swing, and the third sat by the troll, hunched and clasping his knees, his ugly cement face grinning at her.

"You feel it, too, don't you?" Celeste asked her cats quietly, and time flew back to when Mary Lou had been an odd little child, bothered by the cold, squeezing feeling inside her that hadn't stopped until her grandfather died.

There had been others who'd died, too, always after that same sense of waiting. Then, with increasing certainty, Mary Lou's senses began to whisper to her. She tried to ignore the foreboding that came before a death, but learned she could not.

Out on the street, the new woman's pickup appeared, gleaming white as a ghost. Celeste smiled. Everyone knew of the new woman renting the apartment above Alessandros Restaurant. When one of the Alessandro bachelors took a woman under his wing, gossip flew like wildfire.

When the pickup came closer, Celeste saw three heads in the cab. The woman drove, the companion-dog she was never without sat in the middle, and Nick Alessandro filled the rest of the space.

Celeste lifted her hand to wave. At fifty, she wasn't too old to appreciate a good-looking man with soulful eyes and a body—well, a very nice body that stopped women's thoughts as he ran by.

But today Nick wasn't jogging into town or driving his own old beloved pickup. He was riding in the new woman's passenger seat, and it was just possible that he was interested in her, a male staking his intentions.

*Nick Alessandro.* Beneath that easygoing surface was a dark guilt he couldn't escape.

Celeste smiled at her musing, half trusting her senses, and the Iowa farm girl half disdaining to believe. She lifted her face to the wind rattling the leaves of the tall trees, coursing down the streets, bending the daffodils into yellow waves—

Just then, when the pickup drove by Celeste, the woman and the dog turned at exactly the same time to look at her. The woman's face was shaded by the cab and her ball cap, and everything within Celeste froze. It was the same feeling she'd had when she'd locked her shop's door last night.

This woman had taken a terrible journey, and that struggle would end in Blanchefleur. *Whoever the woman was, she brought death.*

Shaken, Celeste hurried into her house to lay her tarot cards, her hands trembling. She laid them again, changing the pattern, and again, fearing to believe.

The death card could mean a change or an end of an old life. But when Celeste got that feeling, it meant someone was going to die.

Just like her sister, Maggie would tell him she loved him before she died.

Brent Templeton placed the collection of worn notes on the hotel room's table. They were in Maggie's handwriting, thumbtacked to bulletin boards in an assortment of gyms, spas, and health food stores. For a year after her divorce, she'd tried to find work and then she'd disappeared. At first, he'd methodically called all the numbers on the old notes, but new voices had answered, not Maggie's slightly husky, low tones.

He needed to hear that voice as she told him she loved him.

With care, he replaced the notes in a small envelope and called Maggie's ex-husband. Once Ryan had bowed and scraped to get favors from Brent, but now his voice was curt. "I told you not to call here anymore. I'm remarried and I don't know where Maggie is."

"I helped make you what you are. I helped get you those connections to make your gym a success. You'll do as I say and have Maggie tracked down. Call Judge Jones and—"

"No one wants anything to do with you now, Brent. You've pushed your weight around for the last time. Call Jones yourself. I'm certain he'd like to know where you are, since you still owe him money. That's the deal, Brent. Leave us alone, or someone comes after you and it won't be pleasant. I hear you've already had a taste of it. Take it or leave it. If you're obsessed with Maggie, that's your own problem. None of us ever wants to hear from her again—or you. You're both just plain trouble."

"Your damn wife started all the trouble, not me."

"Everyone has moved on," Ryan stated fiercely, and the line clicked off.

Brent shook with anger, but meticulously replaced the receiver on its base. He would find Maggie, punish her, and then return to punish them all.

He'd hold that bright penny-colored hair in his fist as he watched fear leap in those hazel eyes. He'd take her out in the water she feared and—

In the way of a predator whose hunger needed satisfaction, Brent thought of the girl at the health food store, the one with soft hazel eyes. She'd been compassionate and helpful, and perfect to tell him that she loved him.

She'd have to die later, of course. Just like Maggie.

# FOUR

**M**aggie looked at the man sitting next to her. Nick had beautiful, expressive eyes, and they told her that he was curious.

Her senses told her that he wanted to touch her. He was too big, taking up too much space—and her air. Every time she breathed, she caught the enticing scent of a man who had just showered and shaved.

His hair was damp and curling at the ends, long past the snip of a barber's scissors, and Maggie pushed down the impulse to smooth it.

Nick quite simply made her feminine senses jump—and that wasn't good. Maggie had to focus, to keep her priorities. He'd pushed her too hard, asking questions she didn't want to answer.

"I'm not into small talk," she said abruptly, down-shifting to prepare for a stop sign. "Just leave me alone and we'll do fine."

"And if I don't?" There was steel beneath the easygoing, lady-killer smile, just enough challenge to raise the hair on the back of her neck.

In the past few years, she'd learned how to send out verbal spikes. "I'd think you'd have enough to do with Lorna. Or with that sweet young thing you married. I saw the wedding picture up in the old lighthouse and the album open on the table with the empty bottle of wine. Instead of drinking and pining, you might go after *her* and apologize for whatever you did."

"Is that what you think? It's too late for apologies. My wife is dead," Nick stated grimly. "She died almost twelve years ago. And yes, I should have done something and didn't. Instead, I lost Alyssa and the baby she had just told me about. Strange, the things a man will let pass when he's just been told he's going to be a father—like letting his wife ride behind him on a motorcycle without a helmet . . . just to let the wind play in her long hair."

She stiffened, hit by surprise; Nick's wife hadn't left him—she'd died. Maggie hadn't expected the bitter Keep Off sign, the sudden chill in her pickup cab, or the silence.

*He was still grieving. . . . He'd lost his wife over a decade ago, and he still missed her.*

Maggie knew about grief. She'd had a lifetime of it, and now she'd just stepped into Nick's. He'd been grieving the day she'd come to town; while he jogged, he'd been fighting the past, and still bristled against what he couldn't change when he came down to the beach.

She struggled for something to say, smoothing her mistake. "I'm sorry" wasn't enough, not when one loved deeply. "Look, just don't push me and everything will be fine. From what I hear, in another month or so, the summer people will be coming back. I'm hoping to pick up some business from them. By the end of the summer, I should have what I want and then I may move on. Or I may stay. But in either case, my life is my own."

She sensed that Nick was a patient man, one who wasn't going to stop at her fences. His next statement proved her right: "What do you want, Maggie Chantel the woman, other than a paycheck?" he asked.

More than anything, Maggie wanted her sister to be alive and happy, she wanted to see her mother cuddling her grandchildren. . . . She wanted to paste everything in her life back together the way it had been, but that was impossible.

"I want to be left alone," she replied firmly, pulling into the parking spot behind the restaurant. When she stepped out of the cab, expecting her dog to follow as usual, Scout hopped down on Nick's side of the pickup.

Rosa waved from the back porch and moved down the steps, holding a big soup bone in her hand. Scout took the present without hesitation, flopping down for a good chew session.

Nick's mother hugged Maggie. Unused to open shows of affection, Maggie stiffened. Nick was quick to notice, his eyes shielded with those black lashes. "I'll just go up to my room now," Maggie said.

"Oh, you must be so tired. I heard you were looking for work—everyone is excited about the women's classes at Ole's. If you're going to be up and going so early, we need to feed you breakfast. Go on up, and I'll have one of my boys bring you dinner, a nice salad and walnut bread."

"Really, Mrs. Alessandro, I don't need any more to eat—"

"Call me Mom or Rosa. Of course you do. Is something wrong with your pickup, Nick?"

Nick hesitated, looked at Maggie, and holding her stare slowly answered, "No."

"Ah."

That "ah" had a lot of understanding that Maggie didn't want to know. But she did. Nick had wanted to ride with her, to spend time with her, and he couldn't lie to his mother.

Another tall, dark, and obviously Alessandro male came down the steps to loop his arm around Rosa and Nick. "Hi, Maggie. We haven't met. I'm Dante, Nick's good-looking older brother."

When another tall male appeared wearing a chef's apron splattered with tomato sauce, Dante added, "That's Tony. He's married. I'm not."

Tony draped his arm around Dante's shoulders, and the Alessandros stood smiling at her, a close, loving family.

Maggie pushed away the offer, the haunting loneliness. Warm, friendly invitations usually meant questions, and she couldn't afford their curiousity.

Dante's survey of her body said he was definitely interested. Tony's grin was open and friendly, an older brother type, well satisfied with life and his wife, and aware of his brothers' interest in her.

A little on the plump side, Rosa seemed small beside the brothers. In the dappled, shaded parking lot, they were tall, lean, and gorgeous. Dante's elbow was digging into Nick's ribs, and they shared a slow look. Rosa watched her two single sons intently, and Maggie sensed she was the object of a silent mother-to-sons conversation.

She didn't want to be the object of any family discussion. "Nice meeting you. I'd better go. I have a lot to do. Come on, Scout."

Scout continued to gnaw loudly on the bone, ignoring Maggie's command.

Anthony appeared at the back door, wiping his hands on his apron. "Hey, you lazy kids, get back in here."

Then with a big grin, he came outside and walked to Maggie, enclosing her in a big hug. "So you're settling in, huh? Getting used to us and the town?"

She wasn't used to being waggled playfully. The arm that remained around her shoulders, holding her close, as Anthony grinned at his wife, made her uncomfortable. "You take the boys. I'll take the girl."

Rosa came to stand on tiptoe and kiss him. "Pay no attention to him. He's an old man, dreaming of when he was young."

When Rosa went up the stairs, Mr. Alessandro's fond smile followed her. "What a woman. Look at what she gave me, three fine sons."

He winked at Maggie. "I should go inside now and try to steal a kiss before it gets too busy."

When he left, Maggie automatically tried to isolate herself from the family scene that had just enfolded her. As a loner, protecting herself, she was wary of easy friendships. All she needed was her dog—

Too late. Dante and Tony were already rough-playing with Scout, just as she loved. She barked and jumped on them; they held her front paws as they danced. Dante tossed a ball obviously left by a child, and Scout was running after it happily.

"I'm going to be a dad again—our fourth. Sissy is two months along," Tony announced proudly. "We can always use another baby-sitter."

"That's nice. Congratulations." Maggie had lost all control of the situation—of keeping her distance from this family. Suddenly she saw too clearly how much Anthony loved Rosa, and Tony's happiness over his family and wife. She saw how much the Alessandros loved one another and what could have been in her own family. And she was too tired to fight the pain, concealing it, and Nick was watching her with those dark shielded eyes, taking her apart, searching for answers. People usually left her alone, taking her hints for privacy, but apparently the Alessandros did not.

"I'll show you around town, if you'd like. I own that little boatyard across the harbor. Maybe you'd like to go for a sail?" Dante asked, tossing the ball to her.

Her fingers dug into the red plastic. *A sailboat.* Her parents laughing and in love, sunlight golden on the waves, beads of water glistening on the varnished cherry wood. Her younger sister excited. A sudden wind becoming a storm, and then she and Glenda were alone, her mother struggling toward them.

*And her father's hand slowly fading beneath the water.*

When Nick frowned, looking at her hand, Maggie realized the locket was in her fist, the edges biting into her palm. She forced herself to release it. "I'm sorry. I can't go sailing with you. I'm busy getting set up."

"Maybe when things slow down a bit," Dante offered easily.

"My wife wants to meet you," Tony said. "We live in the folks' old house, the big white one on Schooner Street. We all grew up there. You can recognize it by all the toys in the yard and on the front porch. Drop in any time."

Maggie didn't answer and gave a passable, but unconfirming, light smile. The Alessandros were too friendly, and if she was right, Dante was definitely interested in her. She toyed with the idea, because it had been a long time since she'd felt like a woman—and Dante had the look of a man who knew how to please.

Who was she kidding? She had loved one man all her life, and he had betrayed her for his own gain.

Her smile died when her eyes locked with Nick's solemn, dark, assessing ones. He had asked too many of the right questions, and he'd seen her fear when Dante offered a sailboat excursion.

While Dante might offer a pleasant, light diversion, Nick was far more intense. He was patient, and he wanted answers from her, and she didn't want him inside her life.

"Come down for a glass of wine later?" he asked slowly. "I could use a ride home."

She didn't spare words. He'd maneuvered a ride with her and she wasn't giving him another. "No."

He wasn't backing down, those dark eyes narrowing, the easy smile gone. "Too bad. I was counting on it."

Dante's offer came with a quick teasing grin. "Nick, I'll be glad to give you a lift."

This time it was Nick's shoulder bumping Dante and none too gently. Dante bumped back, and Rosa opened the back door to warn firmly, "Boys. Stop. You know, Maggie, when this bunch was growing up in the old house, they would start wrestling and shoving and I'd end up with something broken."

"I'd better be going. It was nice to meet you, Dante . . .

Tony," Maggie managed before she patted her thigh. "Come on, Scout. Let's go." She wanted to be away from the Alessandros, from the family that threatened to engulf her with their warmth.

Scout picked up her soup bone and plopped down by Nick's side.

"Let's go, Scout," she repeated, more firmly, and Scout didn't move.

"Come on." Nick patted his thigh and began moving up the steps into the restaurant. Scout trotted after him. Nick held the door for the dog and then for Maggie, forcing her to pass close to him. She hesitated just that bit, then forced herself to move, her head lowered, avoiding those intent dark brown eyes. Too aware of his height and scent, Maggie edged back.

"I'm not going to hurt you, Maggie. And I'm sorry that someone did. Trust is difficult to give again, once it's broken, isn't it?"

She hadn't asked for his understanding and he wasn't giving up. "Just leave me alone."

"If that's what you want." He was still at the bottom of the stairs, watching her, when she opened her door.

Nick wasn't going to be dismissed easily. She closed the apartment door, shutting him away.

That night, Nick settled in the Frenchman's lighthouse with a bottle of his best velvety, rich Pinot Noir and the sensual beat of Peggy Lee's music curling up from his living room speakers. Sprawled in a chair that overlooked the moonlit lake, he poured the wine into a glass jelly jar. Out of habit, he lifted it with his grandfather's favorite toast to good health, old friends, and the enjoyment of fine food and wine. "*Cin cin.*"

The label on the bottle reflected their shared dream, the old man, bent by work and age, and the young boy at his side, loving him. With a peasant background, Roberto Alessandro had preferred to drink wine from glass jars rather than wineglasses. He loved to sit in the shade of the vineyard's shed and view the vines that were just leafless sticks shipped from a friend in Italy. Roberto would sip the wine he'd made for his family and dream of healthy, lush vines filled with fat, rich grapes, mirroring those of his homeland.

Nick had taken that dream and made it his own with the help of mortgages and backbreaking work and love of the land. With many failures and a few strong successes, the Alessandro Winery was beginning to draw faithful customers who trusted Nick's notations on his wines. Even the cellar clearance wines, slightly defective in the blend of fruity aromas and bouquets of fermentation and wood, sold well; buyers appreciated the reduced prices. At the last barrel tasting in March, a few new buyers had arrived, previewing the upcoming wines for their shops. Two buyers were unexpected, representing wealthy clients with private wine cellars.

He inhaled the unique scent and took that first sip, appreciating the slow roll in his mouth before swallowing. That year's almost navy-colored grapes created full-bodied wine, low in tannin, moderate in acidity, with the typical Pinot Noir flavors of cherries, raspberries, and smoke, complemented by the American oak barrel's vanilla tones.

Perhaps his Italian blood leaned toward the red wines, but the stainless steel barrels of crisp, ripe apple character Chardonnay whites would be bottled and selling well in another two years.

Nick's thoughts veered from the chance of frost and summer's temperatures and rainfall and sugar content of the grapes to the woman he'd just met.

A woman who capably handled a stick shift like Maggie Chantel wasn't easily forgotten. Nick's body had clenched every time she changed gears, those slender fingers tightening on the stick shift, her legs pushing the clutch and brake, working them with ease. Even with the wet dog between them, Nick had been aroused, his body tightening each time she shifted.

Downstairs, the telephone rang. His message machine picked up, and the line clicked off. Earlier, the message from

Lorna hadn't been sweet, but sizzling with jealousy. It had been a mistake to think that another woman could ever make him forget Alyssa's sweetness.

With another sip, Nick settled back into his thoughts, and memories of his wife came floating gently into his mind. He smoothed the ornate gold frame holding their wedding picture. His high school sweetheart had just become his wife. Alyssa, wearing a traditional wedding gown, had laughed up at him. They'd had their whole lives waiting for them. In a temper, his rage against life's pain, he'd thrown the frame, cracking the glass, but he couldn't change fate.

He closed his eyes and laid his head back on the wooden lawn chair, thinking of her.

Another woman had driven her pickup beside him, intruding into his pain, and now her face, those dark green eyes with the gold flecks, the burst of fire in her hair came back to him.

The telephone rang again, and distracted, Nick automatically picked up the cordless unit. "Yes?"

Celeste asked pointed questions about Maggie, the same ones as he had asked. Nick had no answers about the mystery woman, but he asked one of his own—"What's wrong, Celeste?"

The psychic brushed him off, but there was something in her tone that stayed. Celeste had never asked him about anyone, and now for some reason, she was uneasy about Maggie.

Celeste wasn't the only one that Maggie had stirred. Restless now, Nick refilled his glass, and for once discounted the aromas. He wondered why Maggie Chantel haunted him so, why his body stirred with just one glance of those eyes that could be green as new leaves, or tinged brown when she was brooding. Did she remind him of Alyssa?

But Alyssa's eyes were blue, and she was sweet and innocent, and something in Nick told him that Maggie had lost all illusions about life, that she trusted no one.

He shoved his hand through his hair, leaned back in the chair, and found himself wanting more of Maggie—the sound of her voice, the way her hips swayed. While he appreciated how women looked and acted and smelled, Nick had never felt that sharp jerk of lust, the need to reach out and capture those hips, to draw them back to him. But then, when a woman handled a stick shift as Maggie did, a man started having ideas.

When she had passed close to him, he could almost scent her fear, and he'd been angry that she'd been hurt, wanting to protect her. The image of her going up the stairs would keep him awake all night.

The telephone rang again, and this time a woman's indistinguishable, soft voice left a message that could wait—because it was Lorna.

The wind coursed softly around the Frenchman's lighthouse, whispering of a woman in another century who could not come to her betrothed—and of a young wife, gone too soon.

Yet again, Nick's thoughts pivoted back to Maggie. Her face had paled at Dante's offer of sailboating, and she'd instantly gripped the locket at her throat. Why? Who was she trying to hold on to? To remember?

What ghosts haunted her?

He closed his eyes again, his body needing rest and his mind traveling over what he knew of Maggie. He saw her eyes again, dark green tinged with earth brown. Before she became friends with Nick, Scout's defensive position said the dog sensed Maggie's fears.

*Who had hurt her, and what did she fear?*

Brent would use Maggie Chantel's fear of water to torture her.

He rented the same room she had, lay in the same cheap hotel bed she had used over a year ago, and thought about how he would tell Maggie everything about Glenda—how she had said she loved him, how she begged for the needle, how in the end, just nine months after he'd tried to rape Maggie, nothing else had mattered, not even her children.

Glenda had been weak, but Maggie's strength would prove her worthy of him.

Brent rose from the bed and dressed neatly for the night. He'd visit the local gym fishing for tidbits about Maggie, spend time at the local email pub researching her, and telephone his sister.

Cheryl Ann was late with her payment—the one that kept him away from her oh-so-very-special family. She'd do anything to protect them, and the money was easy enough for her to get from her husband.

Because Cheryl Ann knew exactly what he was capable of, and she feared him and the secrets he knew . . .

But if he ever discovered that Cheryl Ann was withholding information about Maggie's location from him, he would destroy his sister.

Where was Maggie? How could she just disappear?

He had to find her, to hurt her . . .

Maggie did her stretches and then began walking quickly, warming up for her early morning run in the fresh, cold air. On her third day in Blanchefleur, dawn had turned the windows on Main Street a silvery pink, almost like the inside of an abalone shell, the cobblestones catching the color.

Last night the cobblestones had gleamed beneath the streetlights. Maggie had just been preparing for her evening run when Lorna had stepped out from the shadows. "Leave Nick alone," she'd said. "Or I'll run you out of town."

Maggie had been harassed, unable to find work, and fired from positions before—and it wasn't going to happen to her again. "Try it," she'd challenged briskly. "Maybe you've got reasons to be so obnoxious, but don't try the tough stuff on me. You're a typical spoiled brat, with nothing else to do but cause trouble. I don't care what's between you and Nick, but just maybe you can't buy what you want this time. Back off."

Lorna's threats had slid into the night as Maggie set off on her run. But she didn't miss the way the woman had reached to Scout, affectionately scratching her ears. And the elderly in Blanchefleur credited Lorna with her donation to the Senior Center, and to a shuttle van to help them with town travel. Lorna wasn't all spoiled brat; she was probably a woman with a painful past—just like Maggie.

At five-thirty this morning, the streets were deserted. At eight, Maggie would work with George Wilson, an elderly man who needed to exercise his legs and depend less on his wheelchair. Because his daughter's family were working and busy, she had hired Maggie. George was an outrageous flirt, and she enjoyed his company.

By ten o'clock Maggie would be at Ole's, cleaning and scrubbing and praying that women would sign up for her classes. It was a start, Maggie told herself as she settled into run, Scout at her side.

Determined to quell her fear of water, Maggie ran down the highway leading to the beach. High on a side street to the right of her, the woman in the yellow house watched her as she passed, but then Maggie had moved through enough towns to recognize curiosity.

She had a grip on her life and it would get better; a flattened checkbook had narrowed her options. She'd work hard to get the home she needed for her parents' furniture, and for Scout and herself.

At a sound, Maggie turned to see Nick running easily beside her. "Get lost, Alessandro."

"You don't own the highway. I usually run into town once a day, depending on when the folks need me. And try not to hurt my feelings, will you?" In a sweat-damp T-shirt and jogging shorts, he was breathing easily, matching her shorter stride.

She snorted at that, moving up the pace to lose him. Nick wasn't falling behind. Instead he was grinning at her as he both ran and played with Scout, who was tongue dangling, dog-happy.

"You're getting all sweaty. I hear things are going good for you." Nick's look down her body lingered and appraised. He had a way of touching that wasn't physical, rather it raised her senses and they started jumping.

She refused to answer, digging her shoes into the firm wet sand of the beach. She was almost a quarter mile down the beach before she noticed that Scout wasn't with her.

Maggie resented the run back up the beach, where Nick was bent over Scout, pushing her bottom onto the sand. "Sit. Sit, Scout."

She braced her hands on her hips. "I've had enough of your interference with my dog."

He stood and grinned down at her. "She likes me."

"Listen. Your friend Lorna Smith-Ellis caught me on my run last night. She made it clear that you and she have something going. She thinks I'm trying to get you—which I'm not—and she was very unpleasant."

Nick's smile died. "I'm sorry she did that. I'll talk with her. We dated a couple of times and she had big ideas about marriage and—"

"She's obsessive about what she can't have, and you're still in love with your wife. Until Lorna, you hadn't dated. Amazing the things I've learned about you in a short time. That's why the Frenchman's lighthouse appeals to you so much, because you like to go up there and brood about your wife. That's where you should be now, isn't it? Why the sudden interest in me? Do I remind you of her?"

Nick studied her critically, tilting his head a bit. "Not a bit. Alyssa had blue eyes and a mop of curly black hair."

"Act like her?" she pushed briskly.

"No," he said more gently as if remembering his young wife. "Alyssa was very sweet."

Maggie sighed deeply. "Look, I like being alone. Really. Some people don't, but I do. I'm fine with it. So don't try to play big brother with me, or anything else."

He reached out a hand to her face and Maggie reacted instantly, gripping his wrist and hooking her leg behind his. Off balance, Nick went down heavily in the sand with a surprised "Uh!"

Before she could move, his hand circled her ankle and he was studying her bare legs with that dark, intent look that sent warning bells clanging in Maggie's head. The gripping sensuality was all hungry male, and her body was responding to that, an excitement running through her that she hadn't expected.

"I'll talk to Lorna. She won't bother you again."

His thumb was warm, caressing her skin. "Maggie," he added softly as if testing her name on his tongue. Those black eyes were saying things she didn't want to know, like how he wanted her, to move with her, in her—

Then Nick released her, his arms going behind his head as he lay easily on the sand. "You're trying to face your fear of water, aren't you? That's why you chose a lakeside town."

Scout flopped her chest and paws over Nick's stomach and watched Maggie. She forced herself to break away from the sensuality of Nick's gaze, his big body sprawled on the sand below her. He was trouble, and lots of it, and he wasn't going to keep his distance.

Maggie wanted to hurry away, to protect herself. Nick already knew too much, her fear of water and her need to face it. "Come, Scout."

The dog didn't move, whining softly. Then slowly, as if resenting leaving a new friend, she rose to follow Maggie.

Because Nick had upset her, Maggie chose to run toward town and away from the beach, pitting herself against the slope, faster and faster, Scout keeping at her side.

When she returned on the highway, the woman in the yellow house high on the right side of the valley was holding a cat, almost as if she had been waiting for Maggie. And the wind chimes' musical notes floated on the morning air following her. . . .

Freshly showered in his parents' apartment and ready to help in the restaurant, Nick pulled on his jeans and a shirt, stepped into comfortable loafers, and opened the door.

His mind was on Maggie: how it felt to touch her skin, the

way she looked down at him with the blue sky behind her. He'd barely kept his hand from sliding higher on her leg, over that smooth, gleaming skin, the muscles beneath that tightened at his touch.

His body told him to tug her down, to hold her beneath him. His hunger for Maggie rode him, the need to taste that sassy mouth, to hold her tight and close, fitting her to his body.

Maggie was fighting her desperate fear of water, trying to adjust to it. And she trusted no one.

But her recognition of the attraction between them had been there, brief but true, and Nick realized that he had begun a journey he could not stop—to know more about Maggie.

To know how she felt in his arms.

To know the scent of her body, the hidden hollows and the sounds . . .

He shrugged, his body still damp within the clinging cotton shirt and jeans. Maybe he could forget her if she moved on. More than likely he wouldn't forget a woman with witch's eyes and silky copper-colored hair.

But if Maggie stayed, he intended to have answers.

With his hands on his jeans' unbuttoned snap, he stepped into the hallway landing between the two apartments.

Just then, Maggie's door opened and she moved into the doorway. At the same time, Scout barreled past her, leaping on him. Off-balance in her dog's wake, Maggie started to tip toward the stairs and with a small cry, hovered on the edge of the first step.

Nick reached out to her, snagged her upper arm, and holding his breath, drew her back to safety.

Maggie sank against the wall, breathing hard. "Thanks."

Nick couldn't move or speak because she was looking at his chest, his shirt unbuttoned, with a woman's awareness that couldn't be ignored. He followed the swallow down her throat, took in the way her lips softened in that heartbeat. Trapped in that moment, the same as he, she looked helpless and warm and feminine and sweet. There were little damp tendrils clinging to her neck and in front of her ears. He breathed her fragrance, rich and fruity, sweet and new, with just a touch of herbal bite.

He mocked himself, a vintner, comparing a woman to the finest reserve wine, but then, unguarded and vulnerable, Maggie Chantel was a very desirable woman.

Nick leaned closer, lowering his face to hers, catching the aroma of woman and shampoo, and her eyes widened. He'd thought they were green, but instead they were the color of new earth and lush, dark grass, capturing his reflection.

He heard her indrawn breath as he bent to brush her lips with his. Soft and sweet, they moved just that bit in a welcoming, knowing, womanly response, rich with layers of interesting character.

Maggie's hands went to his bare chest, fingers open to push him away, but instead she held very still, watching him with those green-brown eyes as he kissed one corner of her mouth, then the other. Summer moved through him then, sweeping away the coldness of spring.

"I don't play games, Nick," she warned huskily.

"Neither do I." This time he sank into the kiss, fed on it, searched for her hunger and found it, simmering and soft.

He tasted the smoothness overlaying the sweet fruity nip, wanted more, but caution made him pull back. Like a fine wine that should be savored once again, her taste remained after their lips parted. Breathing hard, Maggie flattened against the wall and watched him.

"Is it me that you're afraid of, or you?" he asked gently.

"I'm not afraid," she whispered unevenly.

"I think you are." He eased a reddish tendril onto his fingertip and smoothed it with his thumb. In the dim light, fire danced across the ends, unexpected and exciting, like the first blend of rich, sweet grapes, aged in fine oak, the taste rich and mysterious.

She shook her head.

Nick hadn't expected the shimmering tears in her eyes, the way her head tilted, shielding her expression from him. Her hands fell from his chest to her sides.

In the shadowy landing, with Scout sitting and looking up at both of them, with Maggie's scent twining around him, Nick ached for her. "That locket means a lot to you, doesn't it, Maggie?" he asked gently.

Her hand instantly clasped the locket on her chest. "It belonged to someone I loved very much."

"Who was she?"

" 'She'? I never said it was a woman."

"Only a woman would wear a locket like that."

Then she was in movement, her ponytail bobbing as she raced down the stairs and out the door.

When the door slammed, Nick braced his hand against the wall that still held her body's warmth. He'd wanted to hold her, to make her feel safe, and to trust him.

And just like Celeste, who had called him about Maggie, he wanted to know more . . .

Maggie rubbed her hands together as she walked quickly down the street toward Ole's. She could still feel Nick's warm chest, his heart beating heavily, kicking up in pace.

She briskly rubbed her palms on her hips, trying to dislodge that lingering sensation. He had smelled so good— soap, spicy aftershave, and just that bit of man. She'd wanted to smooth his wet hair, to feel those sleek waves, the way it curled at his nape.

She'd wanted to slide her hands down to that unbuttoned snap of his jeans.

She'd wanted to arch up and take his mouth, holding him. So she wasn't sweet and innocent. She'd been married and knew the hard, mind-blowing impact of good sex, and then later when sex was a task, an empty routine, quickly finished.

But earlier, she'd wanted to back Nick Alessandro up against the wall and take.

Quick pick-me-up, take-the-edge-off-tension sex wasn't for her.

Nick looked like one big package of trouble, and she'd had enough problems dealing with her bitterness about Ryan.

To avoid Nick, she'd have to find another place to live, and right now, Ole's ladies' room needed an energetic scrubbing. Bleach and sweat would definitely take the edge off any sexual tension.

Deep in her thoughts, Maggie smiled briefly at the woman unlocking the door to the Journeys shop. She was the woman who lived at the yellow house.

"Hello, Maggie. I'm Celeste," the woman said softly, her voice blending with the tinkling of the wind chimes outside the shop's door. In the center of the wind chimes was a slender naked woman of metal, her hands held over her head, her legs pressed together, a deep indentation between them indicating her sex. She turned slowly in the morning sun, first bright and silvery, and then dark with shadow.

"Hi, Celeste." Maggie didn't question how Celeste knew her name; word got around in a small town, especially when she was trying to promote a business.

She needed a lot more clients, if she was going to find a place where she wouldn't run into Nick. *He'd gone into her, separating and dissecting each expression, those dark eyes seeing more than they should . . . taking in her body as if she were ripe fruit, waiting to be picked and pressed . . . That look was unsettling, and so was his body, the wide tanned expanse of his chest . . .*

"Come inside and have a cup of tea with me," Celeste offered softly. "You look like you could use it. You seem— tight."

"Do I? I've got a lot on my mind. I'm trying to get a business started—I'm a personal trainer, but right now, I'm doing fitness classes at Ole's." Maggie tried to release the tight ball of energy in her, the feeling that Nick could relax her in really good hot sex—not that she was buying.

And she didn't need the tenderness he seemed to offer, either. "My dog might be a problem in your shop. She's not that graceful and her tail can be pretty destructive."

"True. If you have a leash in that backpack, maybe she wouldn't mind sitting by the street bench while you relax.

Now, how about that cup of tea? Just a little calming before you start work?"

Scout safely tied to the bench, Maggie followed Celeste into the shop. For a big woman, Celeste almost floated toward the curtain at the rear of the store. "I'll be right back. Look around."

Celeste was just a friendly woman trying to make a living, Maggie decided as she watched the crystals hanging in the window catch light, dividing the sun into spears of pink and blue. Bottled lotions stood on a shelf, the Journeys logo pasted to them. Jars of loose tea, books, rocks, and various candles cluttered the shop. A glass case held jewelry—bracelets of jade, onyx, and more mixed with pendants and earrings of silver and semiprecious gems.

Celeste returned to the shop and began placing fat pastel candles with bits of fragrant rosemary and lavender caught in them on her counter. "The hot water kettle will be ready in a minute. I really must remember to order more ribbon and raffia to wrap my new candles and soaps. I wonder if I might give you a welcome gift—a bar of lavender soap, my specialty, all sinfully stuffed with nice expensive glycerine? I know. Let me read your tarot cards. I charge tourists a nice fat fee, but it's free for you."

Maggie glanced at the clock. She had a good forty-five minutes before class, and the way she was feeling now, she needed to wind down, not that she believed in fortune-tellers. The diversion might take the edge off her taut nerves; she didn't need to start her first class in a dark mood. "Maybe I could trade you."

Celeste moved to the door, locking it. "I wouldn't hear of it. Now, come on, let me read your cards. We'll have that tea later."

When Maggie had gone, Celeste didn't move, but sat trembling and cold in the shadows.

She forced herself to move to the window, watching Maggie's fast athletic walk down the street, the dog at her side. Maggie stopped to talk with a small boy admiring the animal. There was a sadness in her smile as she watched the child pet the dog. Her hand reached out for the boy's head and then stopped, almost as if Maggie were remembering another time and another boy.

The dog understood the woman, knew her fears and gave her friendship. They moved together as one. Somehow they were linked in another time . . . and they brought death . . . Celeste's hand went to her throat; she could almost feel the life being squeezed from her. The death Maggie and her dog brought to Blanchefleur was Celeste's . . .

As a forensic psychic occasionally helping the police, Celeste didn't doubt the cold clammy feel of death, the jumble of images in her mind, but this time *she* was the victim . . .

Celeste had lied to Maggie, giving her a tall, dark, and handsome truth—because Nick Alessandro was definitely interested. But the cards hadn't lied. The shadows from Maggie's past were closing in, and the locket she wore held the reason for everything. Death of loved ones was in her past, and Maggie was poised on a dangerous brink.

The dog, Celeste thought frantically, the dog and the locket held the answer and she had to know more . . . She hurried back to her tarot table, smoothed the green cloth edged by crystals, and quickly began laying her cards. "Tell me more, tell me more. If I'm going to die, tell me why," she chanted feverishly.

The cards told her that the answers lay inside Maggie, who wasn't aware of the danger prowling, hunting for her.

Brent Templeton carefully aligned the bills by value, easing them into his wallet. Cheryl Ann's monthly payment wasn't much, but then a good negotiator knew when not to press too hard—and when to apply pressure.

The fat slob of a detective he'd hired when Maggie first disappeared a year ago had taken too much money for too little work. He'd provided only the places that Brent already knew about, the places from which his "brotherhood" had Maggie fired in the previous year.

Maggie's credit cards had been cancelled and her checking account closed. Because Brent no longer had the help of his powerful friends, he couldn't trace where she had worked in that year since she'd vanished by her social security number.

On the move to expand his search, Brent had gone to Mayfair. The town south of San Francisco was small but elite, filled with fitness buffs. Brent walked to a jogging path that led into the park's wooded area. He liked to watch the women jog, but none of them was as smooth and graceful and powerful as Maggie.

He'd sit on a bench, pretend that his leg was hurting miserably, and question those who came to help—maybe they knew of Maggie.

And maybe he'd find a woman who reminded him of Maggie, a woman who would eventually tell him that she loved him.

# FIVE

Maggie awoke to her own scream, her mind caught by the sight of her father's hand beneath the water.

The nightmare clung to her as she forced herself into reality. Beside her, Scout whined softly, and Maggie locked her hand on the dog's thick pelt.

The bedside clock read ten o'clock. Her late afternoon nap had lasted five hours, the days of traveling and sleepless nights catching up to her.

The soft knock at her door was followed by Rosa's "Maggie? Are you all right?"

"I'm fine. I just—" What? How could she possibly explain the nightmare, the terror that she kept locked inside, until her dreams freed it? "I'm fine, really."

The voices behind the door were muffled, and then Anthony said, "You haven't eaten yet. You come down and eat something. You'll feel better. It's a slow night and we closed early. Come down and have a little bite to eat with us."

She didn't feel like facing anyone, panic still racing inside her. "I've got something here, thank you. I didn't take Scout for her walk. I'll be going out later."

"Do you want me to come with you?" Anthony asked. "Maybe I can keep up."

She needed to run out her panic, but the kindly offer brought tears swelling to her eyes. How easy it would be to turn to the Alessandros. How awful for them to know the truth of her life.

"You're not disturbing us, dear," Rosa said. "But if ever you need us, we're here. *Buonanotte*."

"Good night." Beneath her apartment, the restaurant was quieting. Maggie lay quietly amid her tumbled sheets, her T-shirt damp with sweat. "This isn't working. I can't do this to them."

A few minutes later, Maggie let Scout out of the back door and began walking down the street. The night was cold and mist tingled on her skin and she wanted to face her fear of water, the demon that pursued her.

Then a big man moved out of the shadows and Scout ran back to him with a happy, excited bark. In the pool of a streetlight, Nick played with Scout. Then he walked to Maggie. The light caught the angles of his face and made them hard; nothing about him seemed like the man who had kissed her on the landing, first with gentleness and then with hunger.

"The folks were worried. They're afraid something will happen to you."

It already had. And she had survived. "I'm just taking Scout for a walk. We don't need company."

"Mom—"

"I know. You always do what your mother tells you to do."

"Don't you?"

She didn't answer; she missed her mother, who had died ten years ago—and Glenda—too much.

Nick was silent then, moving beside her as she began to walk away quickly. "You've got a big chip on your shoulder, Maggie."

"They say Blanchefleur is safe. I don't need a bodyguard."
To evade Nick's question, Maggie began to walk quickly.
Along the way, she searched the streets crookedly leading
upward to the hills surrounding Blanchefleur. In the night,
the windows of the houses caught the moon in silver squares.

Then, just two blocks down Main Street in the direction of
the lake, she found what she needed, a substitute for gym
step equipment: a series of steps leading up a hill. She took
the steps at a run, pushing herself. Intended for the walkers
residing in the cluster of poorly tended houses, the concrete
steps were old and worn, almost overgrown by brush.

At the top, she fought for breath, and scanned the back-
yards of small houses, the rubble of junk and trash cluttering
them. She turned to see Scout sitting beside Nick, looking up
at her from Main Street.

The sound of bushes being disturbed caused Maggie to
turn back to the row of small houses. The shadows stirred
and a girl moved from the back of a house. In the dim light,
she was young beneath the paint and the tousled, long,
bleached hair. Her black bra showed beneath her tight white
sweater, a tattooed rose revealed by the low cut, and her
ankle-length jeans were skin-tight. She blew smoke from her
nose and took another puff of the cigarette. She smelled of alcohol, but there was something about her eyes—

Glenda had had that same too bright, edgy look when she
was high.

"You're the new woman in town, huh?" the girl said as she
blew smoke again.

"Beth!" A man's harsh voice cut the night and the girl's
tough look changed to fear.

"You've got to go," the girl whispered desperately. "Ed
doesn't like me talking to anyone when he's in a bad mood.
He took the night off so we could be together. I live with him
sometimes—when we're not arguing and I can stand him.
Sometimes he goes with his old girlfriend, Shirley, and she's
not happy about me. He runs the bar where I work and I don't
want to get fired. The tips are good in the summer and I owe

him. So don't get me in trouble. I'm talking too much. I do that when I'm scared. Go away." She shrugged and tossed her cigarette to the ground, grinding it into the cement.

In her mind, Maggie saw Glenda again, used and bruised. She grabbed the girl's arm. "Don't let him hurt you. I'll help you. Come with me."

She thought she saw hope in the girl's face, soon covered by that hard look. "You've got Nick Alessandro with you. He's waiting down there on Main Street. I saw Nick and you from the window and that's why I came out, to warn you away from here . . . and Ed. He's in a mean mood. The last time Nick tried to help me, I let him down, but I owe him . . . I've got to stop talking. Mind your own business."

And then she was gone and Maggie started after her. Beth stopped and turned. "I hate do-gooders. If I wanted help, I would have asked for it."

*How many times had Glenda said the same thing?*

Maggie breathed deeply, trying to quell the rage in her. One man had ruined Glenda's life, and Maggie had been helpless to stop her sister's decline . . .

Bracing herself against her anger, Maggie ran down the steps, then back up, hoping that Beth had changed her mind. But the landing was empty, with just Beth's crushed cigarette as a reminder that she had passed.

Taking her time, Maggie came down the steps. "I don't want to talk," she said to Nick, who was standing there, his head tilted, hands on his hips.

Her fight to save Glenda had been futile; she'd take Beth's advice and mind her own business.

Once Maggie had needed someone on her side, believing in her, and no one had been there. She started to run, picking up speed, and when she turned, Scout was at Nick's side as he walked slowly behind her. She flattened against a brick wall, breathing hard, and waited until he came to stand near her.

"I'm supposed to see that you get something to eat."

"No, thanks," she stated flatly and realized that her heart

was racing not only from running, but from the memory of his kiss.

He nodded slowly, watching her. "You still have to eat. If you're finally done running off steam, or that nightmare, I'll fix you something in the kitchen . . . Tell me about your nightmares, Maggie. Maybe I can help."

She shook her head; she didn't want any more complications or people in her life. "No, thanks. You sure don't give up easy, do you?"

"Some people think that. I still want to fix you something to eat . . . Come on. I haven't eaten, either." Nick walked beside her back to the restaurant, and it was an odd feeling, a silent companionship she hadn't expected.

He moved expertly in the large family-style kitchen, apart from the restaurant's, opening the refrigerator, scanning the contents, and removing a large covered casserole. "Ah! Perfect. Good old vegetable lasagna. Most customers take the meat sauce, so vegetable is usually the leftover. Sit down. This will be ready in a minute."

He lifted out a square of vegetable and pasta mixture, placed it on a plate and set the microwave to working while he prepared the next plate. Then he began to make a salad. With an artistic movement, he poured vinegar and olive oil from the matching cruets onto a small saucer and sprinkled the mixture with chopped herbs.

Dipping a piece of crusty bread in the oil and vinegar and herbs, Nick talked about his vineyard, the dream his grandfather had started. Forty acres of vineyards kept him and a few family members busy—with Pinot Noir, Cabernet Franc and Chancellor selling steadily and hopes for his white Chardonnays and Rieslings, and a few special blends.

Nick paused and frowned slightly. "I made a bad decision after I lost my wife and sold off part of the land—it was sixty acres of vineyards. I had medical bills to pay, and at the time, nothing was making sense. I was thinking of selling entirely, and leaving—running away. And Lorna's father was a good salesman. Lorna owns those twenty acres now, and she's not selling. I work the land because my grandfather loved it. Every day, I think about how much he loved that land and how he had saved for his dream, how hard he had worked. But I wasn't listening to anyone back then. I was wrapped up in lost dreams, I guess."

Maggie remembered Lorna's threat. "I imagine you could get that land very easily."

"It isn't worth the price. Lorna will eventually realize she can't buy everything. She's just messed up because of her childhood." His tone was stormy as he placed the plate in front of her. Clearly more than money was involved in the return of the vineyards to Alessandro ownership. The lasagna square looked and smelled delicious. Nick added the garlic bread he had just heated. "What to drink?"

"Water, please. But I can get it myself."

He snorted at that, his hands on his hips. "Sweetheart, wine goes with Italian food. What do you prefer? Maybe a nice blend, my Smooth Blue? It's dry and fruity, good with pasta and sauces."

He walked to a well-stocked wine rack, considering the bottles. Nick turned to Dante, who had just come down the stairway. "Go away."

Dante yawned and stretched and playfully hit Nick's shoulder with his fist. "Fell asleep while I was watching movies with Mom and Pop. Hi, Maggie. Make sure you come by the boatyard, okay?"

The flirtatious warmth in Dante's voice didn't match Nick's frown. "You've already eaten."

Dante grinned and said, "I know, and I'm ready to eat again. Fix me something, will you, bro?"

Nick coolly eyed him. "Sure. You can go now. I'll bring it to your place over at the boatyard later."

Dante sniffed lightly and reached down to waggle Maggie's head in a brotherly gesture. She swatted at him, and he grabbed her hand, kissing the back of it. Dante stooped to shake Scout's paw. "Smells good, huh, Scout?"

When footsteps sounded on the stairway, Dante's grin widened. "Mom and Pop are coming down."

Looking rumpled and sleepy, Anthony shuffled into the kitchen. He grunted and looked at his wife, who was wearing a faded cotton housedress. "Your sons are eating my lasagna. You made it special for me. Tell them to stop."

"They're still growing, Anthony."

"They eat all the profit," he grumbled and bent to hug and kiss Maggie. He sat beside her. "Eat. My wife's lasagna is the best. She learned from my mother—"

"*My* mother's recipe, Anthony." Rosa bent to hug Maggie and then set about warming the food. "This is nice. So you had your walk, Maggie? It's a nice night, isn't it? Anthony, get that bone Marco left for Scout. Nick, pour some good Alessandro wine. Dante, set the table. Maggie, fix the salad, will you, dear?"

When the meal sat on the worn red and white checkered table cloth, Dante raised his wineglass to Maggie. "To this girl, Maggie. May she feel a part of our family."

While they settled down to eat and talk adamantly about the current political fracas, Maggie traced the rim of her water glass. The Alessandros' late night snack was a full-blown meal, and she didn't care. After a routine of peanut butter and jelly sandwiches, the lasagna was a treat.

It was only when Maggie lay full and relaxed in bed that she realized her glass had been refilled. She hadn't been in a warm family atmosphere for years, and was surprised at how she enjoyed the simplicity.

Nick had looked mildly surprised when she held the wineglass by the stem to prevent the heat of her hand from influencing the taste, that she rolled the wine on her tongue before swallowing, that she inhaled and appreciated the bouquet.

But then, she'd had to learn to appreciate wine. As entrepreneurs starting a business, Maggie and Ryan had had dinner parties, entertaining clients and business associates. She'd learned enough to present good wines, and then Ryan had introduced her and Glenda to a powerful businessman.

Even with his rich wife on his arm, the man's eyes spoke of darkness and lust . . .

His first move had been on Maggie, and when she refused, he'd turned to Glenda.

Glenda, who had eventually lost her marriage and her children.

The girl Beth haunted Maggie, reminding her of Glenda . . . Maggie turned on her side and wrapped her arm around Scout. Maggie's own husband hadn't believed her— no one had believed her, not even Glenda, and now her sister was dead. *Glenda*. . . .

Maggie couldn't fight or think any more; she simply gave herself to sleep.

Brent couldn't sleep, the need to punish Maggie ruling him.

He needed her to say she loved him.

He needed to see the terror in her eyes before she died.

He needed to find her.

Brent eased from the bed and turned to straighten it. He could not bear an unmade bed. His knee ached from walking, from going into every gym and spa, from visiting health food stores and jogging paths.

And it was Maggie's fault. It was her fault that he'd lost everything. That his friends had turned against him, friends who didn't want their vices known, and he'd provided for those vices.

He'd provided Glenda with what she needed more than drugs at first—praise, just meaningless words. Stupid, infatuated Glenda, who always knew she was second best to Maggie.

With the meticulous care of the businessman he had once been, Brent sat down at the shoddy room's lone table, and organized himself as if he were still at his desk. He began methodically to call any gym that might be open at night, hoping for a lead.

Oh, Maggie would pay for his trouble, she would indeed.

\* \* \*

Nick sat in the Frenchman's lighthouse, thinking of how delicately Maggie had handled the stem of the wineglass, of her familiarity with fine wines, to taste and appreciate. With good food and wine, she had relaxed and softened just that bit, that small knowing smile at Dante when he flirted with her.

Maggie's nightmares were enough to wring that terrified scream from her, and she was wary of letting his family—or him—get too close.

Who had wounded her so badly? Who had taken her trust?

Impatient with himself for needing to know more about a woman than she wanted to give Nick tossed down the dry Chancellor of three years ago, instead of appreciating it. His wife still held his heart, but Maggie wasn't a woman to be forgotten easily.

He rubbed his lips on the glass jar, thinking of Maggie's warm mouth, the way she'd smelled . . . like the earth in spring when he stood between the rows of vines, like a vanilla-spice aroma, sweet and yet with unexpected bite. Her kiss had a smooth, supple entry and moved into the round character and velvety texture of good Merlot.

Nick stood abruptly and rubbed the scar on his side. What was he doing?

He and Alyssa had planned to raise their children in this house, and now . . .

He gripped the jar and hurled it onto the stone floor, watching the shards fly and burst with light. Just that quickly, Alyssa's life had ended—and he'd been to blame.

Celeste had come to Nick just a week before the accident, warning him to be extra careful with Alyssa. Like Maggie, Celeste stayed within her own parameters, but she had a nose for trouble and was more than a little successful when working murder cases.

He should have listened.

He picked up an unopened bottle of reserve wine and smoothed the label with his thumb. He'd had high hopes for Alessandro's Alyssa, a sauvignon blanc blend and a tribute to his wife. Now the twenty cases rested in the shadows of the cellar, and he was as unable to part with them as he was the memory of Alyssa.

Two days later, Maggie stood inside a small camper trailer two miles outside of town, on the same road that led to Nick's vineyard. From her new home, she could easily jog the three miles into town, if she wanted. The tulip farm was on one side, and a marshy expanse leading to Nick's house on the other.

The camper had been George Wilson's getaway from his daughter's family. But now, confined to a wheelchair and needing a caretaker to remind him of his regular medication, he no longer used the tiny retreat. In return for George's regular exercise program, his daughter was more than happy to let Maggie live in his beloved camper, rent-free.

At five o'clock, Maggie, dirty and sweaty, had worked in Ole's gym—cleaning it, arranging the equipment. She was looking forward to relaxing in her new home, and she was happy with the exercise class of five ladies. The overcast day had turned to a light rain, which had made a welcoming sound on the small camper. It looked like paradise where she wouldn't fear disturbing the Alessandros with her night-mares, where she could find the peace she needed. And away from the Alessandros, she wasn't likely to meet Nick in a too-close situation.

She opened the camper's windows, letting in the fresh, rain-scented air. There was a tiny bedroom at its one end; in the middle was a minuscule bathroom, a kitchen with a two-burner gas stove, and an apartment-size refrigerator; and at the other end lay a small living space. It was like heaven, de-spite the cobwebs and dust. She tested the water faucets and the stool, which George had had a handyman reconnect and service, and they worked. With the exception of a few light bulbs that had to be replaced, the electrical systems were okay. A small heater and the oven would afford enough warmth on chilly days, and the air conditioner in one window would serve in the summer.

While Scout explored the small overgrown yard, Maggie began to clean.

She had to mind her own business. She couldn't take Beth under her wing, trying to reshape her life, trying to give her what she needed. Beth wasn't her younger sister to protect. She had to forget Beth.

But she could never forget Glenda . . .

Nick looked up to see a big black dog bounding across the marsh, running toward his house—and Maggie trudging behind, none too happy as she swished the cattails from her path.

In mid-May's late afternoon sun, the dog's coat gleamed, and while worried that she might startle a rattlesnake in the marshes, Nick admired the picture of Maggie, determined to reclaim her pet. She was a strong woman, ready to fight for what she thought was hers, and if she did cross a rattlesnake, the snake would definitely lose.

*Why did she wear that locket, favor it when she was troubled?*

The dog's thrust through the marsh grass and cattails had flushed mallard geese. Distracted, the retriever cut a swath in their direction, ignoring Maggie's angry shout. Then Scout was running toward Nick with Maggie working her way through the muddy marsh down the hill, between George's camper and Nick's vineyard.

In the two weeks since Maggie had moved into the camper, Nick had kept his distance. If she wanted privacy, that was her right.

If she wanted Dante, that was her right, too.

Nick's brother was working overtime, trying to connect with the elusive Ms. Chantel. He'd taken an Alessandro carryout dinner to Ole's, and he'd brought one of their mother's favorite amaryllis bulbs to Maggie's camper. Nick's mother had whispered of Dante's aching muscles after he'd run with Maggie, how he could barely move.

Nick knew exactly how Dante could move . . . fast.

Maggie called to Scout, who was between the vines now, running fast, hell-bent for Nick. With a fair amount of dirt and weeds and cattail fluff clinging to Scout's coat, she barked and leaped onto Nick. He waggled her head and pushed her down playfully, and she leaped at him again, licking his hands as he held her paws away from his bare chest. He pushed her down and Scout ran between the bare vines, circled him in a fast run, and then came to stand beside him, tail thumping Nick's jeaned calf as they watched Maggie come up the slight incline between the vineyard's rows.

Her sweatsuit was mud-splattered, bits of debris clinging to the mud on her pants and covering her shoes. The late afternoon sun caught the fire in her hair, that dark burnished red, and in the distance, her frown found and locked onto him.

Nick folded his arms over his bare chest and enjoyed the view. Maggie was breathing hard, and that bounce to her breasts said she wasn't wearing a bra.

The sensual jolt hardened Nick's body. Maggie was all woman, raw, sensual woman, all curves and movement. He could feel the hot beat of his blood, the throbbing that he'd almost forgotten—

Beneath the spots of mud, her face was pink and sweaty, tendrils clinging to her cheek. She frowned up at him and tried to catch her breath. Nick couldn't stop his long, slow look down her body. "Hello, Maggie. Nice of you to drop over. There are rattlesnakes in that marsh. You're lucky you didn't meet one of them."

"You whistled for my dog, didn't you?" she accused, her hands on her hips. "That's exactly what your brother did, and I wouldn't put it past you."

"Did you tell him off, too?" Nick didn't shield his irritation, and didn't like that slip of jealousy.

"I tried. But Dante is likable."

"Most women think that." Dante appreciated women like Nick appreciated good grapes, sweet with the right percentage of sugar content. But then, looking at Maggie, clearly hot and bothered, Nick changed his mind. He preferred a good bite in his wine, the lasting aftertaste, filled with character.

"You're wearing Scout's mud on your chest." Her hand was on Scout's collar and the dog had lowered, paws braced, digging in for a pulling match. Maggie blew the strand of hair back from her face. Then she noted the wide scar on Nick's side and ribs and frowned slightly.

He didn't want to explain the details of the motorcycle wreck in which his wife had died. "So how's business?"

"I've got a class going at Ole's and a few clients on the side, just regular walkers. Not enough business to make me rich."

"Celeste Moonstar?"

"Yes, how did you know?"

"Word gets around." Celeste obviously wanted to know more about Maggie; she was interested enough to request fast walks down by the water. Only Celeste walked with Maggie by the lake; Maggie had other walkers in a group, but their path included the city streets.

While Nick had asked questions outright, Celeste was working in her own way. The psychic would pick up on Maggie's fear of water, and her goal to overcome that fear. Celeste was foraging for answers to Maggie's silence. Why?

Now Maggie cursed softly as Scout tore free and ran toward Nick's house. While Maggie shouted and ran toward Scout, Nick walked slowly behind, enjoying the view, just that slight feminine butt jiggle.

Scout was barking happily, Maggie shouting, and Nick rounded the corner to see Maggie pulling on one end of his bedsheets and her dog at the other. "Scout, bad dog. Bad dog."

Nick's white T-shirt fluttered, the only piece of laundry still on his clothesline. The rest of his clothing had been trampled with mud. So much for wanting the scent of fresh air on his clothes, Nick thought. With a happy bark, Scout made a leap for the remaining T-shirt, tore it free of the pins, and ran down the embankment toward the lake.

When Scout had released the sheet, Maggie had fallen back, sitting abruptly on the ground with the sheet still in her hands.

Nick couldn't help laughing and she frowned at him, ignoring his outstretched hand. She struggled to her feet. "This is *not* funny."

"Depends on your point of view."

She began gathering up his laundry. "I'll wash these and return them. I'll pay for anything torn. Right now, I've got to get my dog—"

Nick picked up a dirtied towel, shook it, and brushed it over his chest. "She knows where you are. She'll come back when she's ready."

He flopped the towel over a clothesline and reached for a washcloth. Holding Maggie's face and ignoring the efforts she made to avoid him, Nick mopped her face just as he would his nieces' and nephews'.

Because he wanted to keeping touching her, he tilted her head, studied her ear and carefully wiped away a drop of mud. His finger and thumb lingered to smooth her earlobe. Silky and delicate beneath his touch, it fascinated him.

Maggie shrugged free as though his gentleness upset her. "And just how do you know so much? How do you know she'll come back? I could lose her."

Nick tapped her nose with his finger. "Because she loves you."

He wanted to keep Maggie with him a little longer; she looked so frustrated and feminine and cuddly . . . "I've got a washer and a dryer. I just use the clothesline sometimes. You could take care of that laundry tonight and wash your own clothes."

He watched her scan the beach where Scout was flopping the wet, muddy T-shirt in the water. On impulse, Nick lifted his hand to brush back a tendril from Maggie's cheek, and couldn't resist tugging her ponytail. "Looks like today I should have chosen the dryer. You can clean up meanwhile. I'll fix dinner—"

Her eyes were clear and dark green. "You're lonesome, Nick. I can almost feel you ache. I'm not filling any vacancies left by your wife."

The sudden, defensive walls-are-up sign surprised and nettled him. "Did I ask you?"

He walked into his house, leaving her standing with his laundry in her arms.

That muscled, stiff back said she'd offended him.

Maggie sighed and decided that he hadn't done anything but offer to make life easier for her. Scout was racing back up the sand dunes, dragging the muddied T-shirt. She plopped it at Maggie's feet and sat, tongue hanging down in a doggie grin.

"Don't try to make friends with me," Maggie said sternly as she dumped the laundry onto the wooden porch and dried Scout's wet coat. She took off her canvas shoes, tried to scrape the mud from them, and gave up, placing them beside Nick's on the front porch.

She used the towel to wipe the mud from between her toes. "It's your fault we're here, and I've just put my foot in my mouth. Now we have to go in there and make nice with Nick. I have this laundry to do, and there is no way I'm carrying it home and washing Nick's clothes at the Wash and Dry. The whole town is wondering which Alessandro brother I'm picking."

At the Alessandros' late night dinner, she'd learned there was more to Dante than flirtation and good looks. Dante ached for his child, a boy only three years old. He'd thought the boy better off with his ex-wife, and now his son feared him. He worried that the child would be harmed in a custody suit and he worried that he wouldn't be the parent the boy needed.

Maggie knew about trying to fill a loved one's needs. Now she couldn't allow herself to substitute Beth for Glenda, to try to correct the past by salvaging another woman. Yet inside, Maggie knew that if Beth needed her, she would fight as fiercely for the girl as she had for Glenda.

So much for not becoming involved in other lives.

Scooping up the wash, Maggie tucked her chin over the laundry, and holding it in one arm, opened the screen door to Nick's house.

Previously intent on the view from the Frenchman's lighthouse, she hadn't noticed the shadowy, darkened living room. Ceiling to floor book racks were filled; a beautiful book displaying wine bottles rested on the low blocky-style coffee table. A framed picture had been placed facedown on the table beside a small fruit jar and a bottle of wine. Clothing had been tossed over a man-size chair made in the same heavy wooden style, but with leather cushions. A matching sofa was just as big, dominating the room, and the indented pillow and rumpled blanket said Nick had slept there.

Various family pictures, some old black-and-whites and even some tintypes, hung on the wall and stood on the fireplace mantel. The picture of an old man, bent by age and using a cane, caught her—the man's other hand held that of a small boy as they walked down a row of grape vines. The picture reminded Maggie of the Alessandro Winery logo.

Uncertain of what to do, Maggie called softly, "Nick?"

But Scout was already running through the darkened house, leaving Maggie to follow. The kitchen was small and neat, and Maggie dumped the soiled laundry onto the floor in front of the obviously new washer and dryer. Bedrooms were clearly down a hallway, and the large bathroom by the kitchen looked like heaven.

Maggie found Nick on a backyard wooden deck, at work over an oversize smoking barbecue grill. His glance at her wasn't friendly. "I'm grilling chicken and having baked potatoes. Yes, I get tired of Italian food. There's enough for you, if you're hungry. If not, fine. I can take you home, or you can drive my pickup. I'll get it in the morning."

He closed the lid to the grill, sprawled in a redwood deck lounger, and sat. He ignored her and surveyed his kingdom while Scout sniffed around the weathered picnic table, making herself at home.

Maggie decided that if he wanted to brood, he could do it alone. "I'm doing this laundry. And then I'm walking home and taking my dog."

"You just do whatever your little heart desires." *Just leave me the hell alone.*

"Fine." Maggie left Scout with Nick and went back into the house. She jammed sheets into the washer, added detergent, and watched the tub fill and agitate. She decided to use the bathroom meanwhile and turned off the washer, leaving the sheets to soak.

In the bathroom, a heap of towels lay in one corner, layered with jeans and T-shirts and shorts.

Nick stood at the door, barbecue sauce bottle in hand, just as she stood in front of the sink, washing one foot in it with men's heavy-duty hand soap. He frowned at her. "I said you can take a shower if you want."

He left for a minute and came back to toss a towel, a man's clean shirt, and a pair of jeans onto her head. She pushed them aside and they fell to the floor. "You'd better save these. From the looks of this place, you might need them. And maybe if you asked Lorna real nice, she'd come out here and do your laundry. It looks like someone needs to. You apparently didn't do everything."

"Have it your way," he said. "I've been looking after myself for a long time."

"So have I. And if you don't watch it, these clothes will mildew. You should hang your bath towels to dry when you're finished."

Nick's unshaven jaw hardened. "It's my house. I do what I want."

Maggie reached to close the door in his face. She finished washing her other foot and decided since they were on such good terms anyway, she might as well take advantage of that king-size shower. She'd stay just to irritate him and then she'd walk home when she was ready and . . .

Her dark mood gave way under the shower's luxurious spray. A big serviceable bar of men's soap wasn't up to Celeste's fragrant, bubbly soap, but right then it was heaven. Maggie heard herself crooning in the shower as she used Nick's masculine shampoo, lathering it into her hair.

She tried finger-combing her hair, and when that didn't work, used Nick's brush. She could have stayed in the bathroom forever, pampering herself, but keeping in mind Nick's bad mood, she decided to finish the laundry quickly.

As she sorted the clothing from the towels and washcloths, Maggie decided she missed having her own home with her own washer and dryer and the things other women took for granted. The chug of the washer, the whir of the dryer, the warm, soapy scents were relaxing. Once started, she gathered the laundry from all over the house, stripping the two bedrooms.

Cleaning was automatic, and maybe it came from inside herself, to wash away—Maggie shook her head, forcing the past away. It was Nick's house, and he'd disappeared—probably to sulk upstairs with the Frenchman's ghost. She hesitated, weighed the right and wrong of her actions, and didn't care. It wasn't a crime to clean, and Maggie dismissed her doubts as she whipped through the rooms.

The larger bedroom hadn't been used, and Maggie automatically opened the windows to the fresh cold air. Beneath the layers of dust, the room held a woman's touch, softer shades of mauve and tans, the layers of pillows with shams on the bed. A tumble of women's clothing lay on the bed, next to an opened box, as though someone had tried to put them away and couldn't.

*The shadows seemed to stir quietly as if dreams had died there . . .*

A picture had been turned facedown, and when Maggie righted it, she saw it was of Nick seated on a motorcycle, dressed in a black leather jacket and jeans, grinning at the camera, a young girl holding tight behind him. The frame's glass had been shattered.

Maggie ached for Nick's wife, for the children she would never have, for the dreams torn away.

Glenda's two children, Seth and Cody, were two sweet little boys that Maggie ached to hold. They would soon be playing summer ball and soccer and diving into swimming pools, and she missed them desperately. But one look at Maggie and they would remember their mother, and probably not the pleasant things either.

The smaller room was where Nick slept—if not on the well-used couch. Maggie stripped the bed and gathered the clothing on the floor, dumping it in front of the washer as Nick passed, carrying a platter of barbecued chicken and foil-wrapped potatoes in one hand and a barbecue fork in the other.

He stood, boots on a towel, and stared at the mountain of laundry she had collected. "You're on a cleaning bender," he said with the doomed air of a man who had lived with women.

She poured stain remover onto the knees of his jeans, rubbing the cloth together. "That master bedroom smelled of must. I opened the windows. Don't forget to close them—"

Nick's dark eyes were taking in her damp hair, the way his overlarge shirt hung on her, the rolled up cuffs above her bare feet. Still holding the platter and the fork, he leaned toward her. "Hi, Maggie," he whispered softly.

Maggie knew he was going to kiss her, and she leaned back against the chugging washer, the heavy beat matching that of her heart. Nick's eyes closed, and his lips fitted gently over hers. She couldn't move as a current of sweet hunger danced through her, and then his lips slanted to the other side. He moved closer, his body pressing against hers. "Nick?"

He didn't move, watching her. She could refuse or she could take.

Nick placed the platter and fork down, and then his hands were braced beside her hips, the washer chugging behind her. "You smell like bleach," he said huskily.

There was so much of him, dark and sensual, and Maggie's senses started to quiver and warm. "Your sheets and towels really needed it. You'll need to get more fabric softener."

She couldn't breathe, couldn't move, as Nick slowly lowered his head for another kiss. "Okay. Anything else?"

This time her lips were parted and she needed more than a taste of him. "I can't think of anything now—"

He kissed her again, this time slow and thoroughly, as if he were learning the shape of her mouth. "That's good. Neither can I."

He was tasting her, she thought distantly, as his lips brushed and teased and floated over hers. When she wanted more, just that nip of hunger, yet of beckoning gentleness, turning toward his lips, he'd move again.

Nick nuzzled her cheek, an erotic male brush of rough skin against her own. His face rested in the cove of her shoulder and throat and the gentle flicking of his tongue surprised her, sending a chill up her nape.

She turned to meet his kiss, and he moved to the other side of her throat, tantalizing her with his lips and tongue. Maggie had to have just one firm, long satisfying kiss, and the gentle pressure of Nick's aroused body between her legs had set her body aching.

His light kisses trailed across her lips, ever avoiding full contact. "You're really warm . . . really warm," he said as his lips started to tempt her earlobe. "And you're shaking. Why?"

She trembled, fighting the need to capture him, and the need to escape to safety.

"If you're going to kiss me, do it," she stated finally.

"I'm getting all the good flavor, the bouquet, that balance of aroma and taste and—"

She reached for his head, framed his jaw with her hands, and kissed him hard, finding the essence of his hunger and heat and danger. His arms went around her, lifting her up against him, pressing her close, one hand open on her bottom, cupping her tight against him.

He dived in for more, and she met him, arching against him, her fingers digging into his hair, then those taut hard shoulders.

Nick lifted back, just that fraction, and she came after him, pressing his head toward hers, and the low, ragged sound in his throat said he approved.

Not that she cared. Maggie was too busy taking, feeling like a woman, feeling soft and feminine and desired. It had been so long—

She broke away, leaning back, and Nick's dark intent look traveled across her lips and slowly, slowly downward to where her breasts pressed against him. He moved his hand on her back up and down in a caress, and then ever so slowly, meeting her eyes, he unbuttoned the shirt, revealing the tops of her breasts.

He breathed raggedly as he looked downward, and his body trembled, a dark flush running beneath his tan. Nick eased back from her, and this time, Maggie trembled as she gripped the washer behind her. She wanted more, wanted to take and satisfy and be free once again.

Nick slowly reached for a sweatshirt and drew it on. Still looking at her, he lifted the platter beside her. "Dinner is ready. Sorry, no salad."

*No sex.* Maggie held very still, her heart racing. She realized that her face was flushed, and when Nick's gaze touched her lips, her tongue tasted him again. She felt as if her skin were shimmering, alive with sensation, needing more of—

His big hands hadn't touched her skin and she needed that, his hands on her flesh, stroking her . . .

"I've been married," she said suddenly, surprising herself. "It didn't work."

What was she doing? She didn't need to explain anything to Nick.

"Okay," he said softly, watching her. "Do you want to eat at the kitchen table or outside?"

"Outside." The night air would cool her cheeks. *I can manage this, a little flirtation, a free meal, a little relaxation. No strings attached.* "I'll be out in a minute."

"Bring plates and silverware, and don't forget the butter and sour cream from the refrigerator."

She turned back to empty the dryer, dumping the clothes into a laundry basket. When she stood, preparing to transfer a load from the washer, Nick's lips were at her nape, his breath warm against her skin.

Electrified, Maggie held very still. It was a playful kiss, soon ended, with just that nip at her earlobe, and enough to make her senses quiver and heat.

Her hands shook as she removed the plates from the shelves, and when she went outside, Nick was sprawled in his lawn chair again. "You forgot the tea. Sun tea, on the counter, and don't tell anyone that I like iced tea and barbecue. It's not good for a vintner's image."

"I brought the plates and silverware. I don't drink caffeinated tea."

"Drink water. I cooked."

"I'm doing your laundry."

The lines beside Nick's eyes deepened with humor. "My soap, my electricity."

She fought the smile inside her; the argument was friendly, easy. "I'll tell everyone you drink iced tea, probably beer, too, right? There's a six-pack in the refrigerator."

"Okay, you have me there." He rose and stretched, and Maggie's senses leaped again. She looked away into the marsh, the sun setting over it just as peace had somehow settled for a moment within Maggie.

It was gentle toss-and-toss-back play, not an argument. She could handle this—an easy evening, sharing a few hours.

When Nick came back, he carried a tray of glasses, bottled water, and a pitcher of iced tea. "Here," he said, tossing a light jacket to her.

It was just that simple. No questions, no responsibility, just companionship. After dinner, Maggie leaned back in her lawn chair, snuggled down in Nick's coat, and closed her eyes, inhaling the fresh, damp night.

She'd come so far, fought so hard, and now, totally relaxed, she dozed.

* * *

In the chill of the night, Celeste sat on her porch. She rocked within the warmth of her shawl, holding Earth's warm body close to her. The cat purred loudly, boldly pushing against Celeste for more. The rest meant little, but her cats had given her comfort. She should make arrangements for someone to take them after she died.

Celeste inhaled the fresh scents of her herbs and thought of her family's farm in Iowa, the rev of the big John Deere tractor coming out of the massive barn, the corn stalks in the field growing high over her head. Strange how approaching the end of her life, she remembered the beginning so clearly. Every breath meant more, the colors more intense, the smiles more welcome, a child's laughter more delightful.

No matter how she laid her tarot cards and ignored her inner senses, the answer was always the same. She would die soon. But Celeste depended more on those flashing images in her mind, including the shadowy figure of a man reaching for her throat.

The cat's warmth and purr relaxed Celeste as she settled deeper into her thoughts. She had accepted her own death; what would come, would come. But perhaps by knowing more, she could save her friends.

In the scheduled walks she took with Maggie, Celeste had hoped to learn more. She kept the conversation light and flowing, adding personal tidbits about her life, hoping to find an opening to talk about Maggie's life. A loner, Maggie was holding her past, fighting it. The shadows beneath her eyes said she had sleepless nights, perhaps nightmares.

If only Celeste could hold something of Maggie's, something from the past, then she might have the answer to her own death . . .

She eased her cats inside and gave herself to the night, walking toward the call of the harbor, the river walk, now quiet. No one questioned her now, the odd times that she strolled through town.

But tonight, the answers did not come—only the sense that her time was short.

# SIX

*If he found Maggie Chantel, he would kill her.*

*He'd had everything and she'd ruined his life. No one respected him now, his power was gone, and he would make her pay.*

A foghorn sounded in San Francisco Bay, its cry punctuated by the loud jukebox music in the small tavern. Brent Templeton circled the glass rim of his drink, the neon light advertising beer over the bar flashing on a face that had once been handsome. Facials and manicures were in his past; he could no longer afford pampering.

He sneered at the waitress and with the arrogance of a lord, he lifted his empty glass for a refill.

He sank back into his brooding silence, and the side long look he gave the waitress caused her to pale and shrivel back into safety. In the short tight skirt, her legs weren't as nice as Maggie's, the barbed wire ankle tatoo not to his taste.

The man hunched over his drink and raked the men at the bar with one narrow-eyed glance. His mouth curled bitterly as he let his hatred for one woman churn and fester and grow.

Once he lived for his power, for what it could bring him, and now he lived to kill Maggie Chantel.

Not too quickly, taking days perhaps. Perhaps he would destroy those she loved first, making her watch and beg for mercy.

He'd practiced with the pretty young hitchhiker along the Interstate.

Then because he couldn't stand the nagging slanted picture on the wall any longer, he stood to straighten it. He ignored the people watching him as he rounded the room, straightening the other pictures.

Everything had an order, he decided, as he straightened the stack of menus on the counter. He understood the rules of that order, and soon Maggie would, too.

She was on the move, and not in the vicinity. The message service she'd used had been closed for a year.

Maybe one of the men she'd confronted about using Glenda had already taken care of Maggie—Brent pushed away the thought. He could feel her out there, waiting to be punished for ruining his life.

Where was she?

"Tell me you love me," he whispered as he walked out into the night. "Where are you, Maggie, dear?"

In the alley, he found someone to make him feel strong and in command again. The sleeping drunk huddled beneath newspapers died beneath the savage beating.

Maggie awoke to Nick crouching at her side and gently shaking her. She was tucked beneath a blanket, the pillow under her head resting on the lawn chair. The night was cold and damp, stars sprinkling the sky.

"Hey. Sleepyhead. Wake up. Time to go home."

"Hi," she said as Nick brushed her hair back from her face. Whatever had nagged her in her sleep slid into the night as Scout nuzzled her hand. Maggie could feel the remnants of stark fear, and yet she hadn't dreamed . . . She petted the dog, and rested momentarily beneath the familiar safe weight of Scout's head.

Nick seemed so familiar, and she remembered how gently he had first kissed her, and then how hungrily. She could still feel him hard against her, the press of his hand on her bottom, urging her closer.

There was tenderness in him, and so much sadness, and now something else bothered him. "Your hair is still wet. You'll catch cold."

She lay looking at him, snuggled beneath the warmth of the blanket. He seemed so safe. "Hi," she said again and smiled sleepily.

Nick frowned and stood suddenly, his hands in his back pockets. The moonlight painted his hair silver and outlined the taut, edgy look of his body. "Do you want my pickup, or do you want me to drive you home?"

She wanted him to carry her into his house, to . . . Maggie stretched and squirmed beneath the blanket. She felt so good and warm and safe. Most of all, with Nick, she felt safe.

All angles and broad shoulders, his face in shadow, he watched her. "I'll drive you home," he said unevenly, his voice raspy and deep.

"Well, that was fast," Maggie said when Nick bundled her in the blanket and carried her to his pickup. "I left my shoes."

"I'm in a hurry. I'll bring them by," Nick stated roughly. It was a wonder he could talk. Ever since he'd heard her in the shower, her sounds of pleasure like those of a woman having a long, slow orgasm, Nick's body had been humming. Those kisses at the washer, the way she responded, arching up to him bowstring-tight, hadn't helped.

If he'd taken more than a taste, they'd be in bed right now.

Or not. Maggie was independent, the kind of woman who moved on when she decided.

Nick preferred to take it slow and let the flavor ripen between them. She didn't trust him yet, and he wasn't too certain about himself. Quick sex could only complicate both their lives.

On the other hand, his body protested the lengthy abstinence, needing relief.

Then Scout, lying on the deck, had come to lay her head on Maggie as she slept. The dog's senses were right, because Maggie had started to squirm beneath the blanket he had placed around her.

Her face had been so vulnerable, soft and open, all the usual defenses wiped away. And then she'd frowned, her expression sad, then angry, then fearful. Her hands clawed at the blanket, fighting—and he couldn't bear to see her locked in a nightmare.

When she awoke, all sleepy and snugly, he'd started thinking about how she kissed, hungry and hot and sweet, and how he wanted to wake up to her in the morning. But he suspected Maggie was like fine wine, better when understood and given time to ripen, and to come to her own rich flavor.

"I'm wearing socks," Maggie stated in surprise as Nick opened the pickup's passenger door.

"Your feet were cold." He slid her onto the seat and motioned for Scout to leap up beside her.

When he slammed the door on the driver's side and revved the pickup, Maggie studied him. "You're mad. Why?"

"Just leave it, okay?" She wasn't ready to trust him, and that nettled. Or did it hurt?

"If it's because of the laundry, just stop the pickup and I'll finish it."

Nick shifted and drove toward her camper. He wasn't ready to talk, and he knew Maggie wasn't answering questions. "You're not wearing shoes. I'll carry you—"

Maggie opened the passenger door, and Scout hopped out. "What's with you?"

*What's with you? Who hurt you?* he wanted to ask. But instead Nick said, "Look, we're both tired. Let's call it a night, okay?"

Then, because he had to, he gripped the blanket at her throat, tugged her to him, and kissed her before she could say anything else. There was lots of soft, curved, fragrant woman beneath that heavy blanket, and he wanted her. But it wasn't that easy, not for him, and he suspected not for her. He placed her away before his hands started wandering and filling and taking. "You need to trust someone, Maggie. Whatever is eating you isn't going away."

"And you would know so much, would you?" Her tone was bitter and frustrated.

"Yes, I do." Nick's guilt wasn't going away; he never should have let Alyssa ride without a helmet.

Maggie shrugged free of the blanket and scooted out of the cab. She hopped on one foot while she took off one sock, and then the other, tossing them in his face. "I don't think I like you very much."

Her borrowed shirt had come unbuttoned and the curve of her breast quivered as she moved. Nick's body locked in a painful knot, and before he knew it, he was out lifting the truck's bumper to ease the throbbing lodged low in his body.

Taking a deep breath, he stood upright and frowned at her. At first her expression was blank, and then she began to smile, and then she was laughing. If the sound hadn't been so good and honest, he might have been angry. Instead, he smiled at her. "Good night, Maggie. I'll bring by your shoes in the morning. Eugene said you'd be good for the part-time job, working for me. Think about it."

"I really did need this exercise program. Just walking to the shop and back home and a few times between wasn't really stretching my legs—or my walks at night. That's what walking should be, easy, slow, thoughtful. Not the pushing the limits hurrying you make me do. Hills are made to walk down, not up, Maggie. Didn't anyone ever tell you that? I appreciate you taking me as a client, Maggie, but my rear end and legs hurt like heck," Celeste said.

"I like to hear you complain. That says I'm doing my job. Did you do those stretches before we started? It's really important to lengthen your back and legs, Celeste."

"I'm lengthened, I'm lengthened." It was Celeste's right to gripe, she thought moodily. Clearly she wasn't a morning person, yet here she was amid the disgusting morning people, actually smiling and enjoying themselves—their minds had to be numb or maybe they were daylight zombies.

She breathed in the fresh cold air and wished she were still in bed amid her cats. The morning fog layered over the concrete walk down to water, softening the hard red of the lighthouse at the end of the pier. The tall clumps of grass stood eerily in the sand dunes.

She wanted to know all about Maggie, but the young woman was a loner, used to keeping her life private, and she didn't talk about herself. Celeste had worked with several law officers, and she could have tracked Maggie's life by using those resources. But the past could muddle her inner mind with too many facts, and she preferred using her senses to feel through the danger Maggie carried with her.

The flashes that ripped across Celeste's mind came more frequently when she was with Maggie; so did that tight feeling in her neck as if it were being squeezed. Celeste didn't dismiss these sensations; she clung to them, trying to arrange the puzzle into a meaningful picture of how and why she would die.

This morning Maggie was walking very fast, as if she were trying to work free of a problem.

Nick and Dante Alessandro would be enough problems for any woman to handle, Celeste thought as she tried to match Maggie's stride. Scout moved between the women, big and definitely protective.

*The dog and the locket . . .*

Celeste panted, her pulse racing, her mind churning. If only she could hold something of Maggie's past . . . "Maggie, I hear you moved into George Wilson's camper. I've never been in it, but I'd love to see it. I hear it's so cute and compact."

"It's nice." But there was no warm invitation to visit Maggie's home.

On their usual path, Celeste worked to keep up with Maggie, the street's incline steep and layered with modern multicolored executive-style houses on either side. They usually belonged to "snowbirds," those going South to avoid Michigan's harsh winters.

"What do you know about a girl named Beth?" Maggie asked suddenly as a paper boy surged past them on his bicycle, tossing rolled papers onto lawns of the vacant houses.

The question surprised Celeste. Maggie didn't ask questions about other people, and Celeste suspected her trust was low; keeping to herself was Maggie's protection. "She comes into the shop once in a while. She works at the bar, waitresses at summer parties sometimes. Sometimes she lives with the bar's owner, Ed. She's in her early twenties and has had to make her own way. People have tried to help her, but she's determined to be independent."

"Or kill herself. She was using when I saw her," Maggie stated abruptly, and in profile, her expression was fierce. The shields were gone, her eyes flashing with anger. "Where does she live?"

"Where she wants. I asked her if she wanted to stay with me, just to help her get on her feet. She did, worked a few days in the shop, and then was gone when summer came and she had more money. I tried to help her. She has a hard life, but she's not dependent on drugs. I'm certain of that. She comes for dinner once in a while and stays overnight, but she's like my cats, very independent, choosing her own way. I like her."

Maggie smiled automatically at Dante's broad grin as he jogged down the opposite side of the street. "It won't be long before she loses all respect and then it gets worse."

Just that bitter edge of her voice told Celeste that Maggie

grieved for someone like Beth. Was it a younger Maggie? Or someone else?

"Beautiful morning," Celeste said, forcing herself to go slow when there were so many questions leaping to her mind. Maggie was interested in Beth, a tough young girl scarred by life. There was strength in Beth, though, if she'd use it and her sharp mind. Someone had damaged her a long time ago, and Celeste suspected it happened early in life. Beth had said little about her mother, and said she didn't know her father. "You'll be having more clients than you can handle later on."

Maggie wasn't distracted from her dark mood. "Maybe. It's sure not too busy now. Try to lengthen your stride, swing your arms."

Celeste had to play for time. "Maggie, would you mind checking my pulse, please? I feel like my heart is racing right out of my chest."

She had fifteen seconds to reach gently for Maggie's ever-present gold locket; Maggie would be multiplying that quarter minute by four. When Maggie held Celeste's wrist and studied her wristwatch, Celeste slowly touched Maggie's locket. It wasn't expensive or special in any way, and yet Maggie was never without it.

"This is lovely," Celeste said to cover her need to search for answers, to see the pictures. Under the cover of inspecting it closely, she held the locket in her hand, felt the white-hot burn of anger, rich and boiling. She sensed grief so deep that it chilled her, taking away her breath. There was more lurking behind those emotions, so much more, a tangle of happiness and pain.

The clear sunny morning started to fade, and in her mind, Celeste heard children laughing, two happy little girls with coppery hair having a tea party. They looked alike—sisters!

Maggie frowned slightly and moved away, studying Celeste. "Your pulse just leaped and you're pale. We discussed your medical history before we started. Are you certain you don't have a heart problem?"

Celeste forced herself not to look at the locket. It still burned her hand, and it was the link to Maggie and the man in the shadows. "I had my checkup and I'm okay. I'm just feeling a little off today. Sometimes when I'm making candles, the scents are too strong in my house overnight, and morning's fresh air hits me like this."

Maggie was pure business. "Watch that, okay? It isn't good publicity for me if a client collapses while in my care. When you see Beth again, tell her I'm looking for her, okay?"

Later, Celeste would look at her hand and see the locket, hear the girls laughing, the sisters who looked alike. What had happened that caused Maggie to seem so alone? And why, suddenly, would she step out of her safe shell to ask about Beth?

She'd already tried to stop one woman's freight train ride to hell and failed. The agony of that experience should have taught her something. She shouldn't be doing this, getting involved with Beth, Maggie thought as she opened the camper door to the young woman's knock.

In the third week of May, Beth appeared at Maggie's door. Her open leather jacket revealed a lacy crop top, a belly button ring on her bare midriff, and low-slung, worn, tight jeans. The platform shoes looked as worn as the battered car parked near the camper. Beth's hair was naturally blond and boy-cut, her eyes heavily painted.

Beth hitched up her small leather backpack on her shoulder and looked at the small wind chimes Maggie had hung outside the door. "Yeah, so I was wearing a wig when you saw me. Some men like blonds with big hair. I have a wig. Celeste said you wanted to see me. Why?"

"I thought we could have dinner and talk, relax a bit." *I made too many mistakes with Glenda. I was so righteous . . . Glenda was doing the best she could . . .*

Beth checked her watch. "Yeah, well, not too long. Celeste

said you were lonesome, or I wouldn't be here. I owe her."

What did Celeste see in Beth that gave her hope?

What had Maggie missed in Glenda?

"Come in. I just made a tuna casserole. Nothing too fancy."

Beth entered slowly. "I used to stay here when I needed to hole up. The lock is easy to pick. You should get it changed . . . What's this?" she asked as she picked up a red ceramic frog. "It's ugly."

"It's a feng shui three-legged money frog. He's got a Chinese coin in his mouth and is sitting on more. It's supposed to bring money."

"I could use one." Beth took in the Native American leather and feather beaded ornament hanging at the window. "What's this thing?"

"A mandella. It's supposed to bring good luck. Do you believe in good luck, Beth?"

"No. I believe you have to take what you want." Beth plopped her backpack down on the couch and sprawled beside Scout, petting her. "Nice dog."

Easily swayed, Scout placed her head on Beth's lap. "What do you want?" Beth asked as she petted the dog.

Maggie began to set the tiny table. Why did she so desperately need to help Beth? To replace Glenda? "I could use a friend."

"I'm not listening to any preaching, so get that straight right away. And besides, you've got Celeste and the Alessandros, Ole and Eugene—I like old Eugene—and the women in your class think you're something. I don't know why you need me."

Edgy, wary, on alert, Maggie decided as she slid into the small booth opposite the couch. "It's just a dinner, okay? Don't make more of it than it is."

"Sure. Smells good." Beth looked at Maggie as a car slowed and pulled onto the gravel area by the camper. "Expecting someone?"

"No, I'm not." Maggie got up to open the door to Lorna.

Her late-model BMW contrasted with Beth's dented mini-car and Maggie's practical light pickup. Lorna's denim jacket and jeans were designer and expensive.

Lorna glanced past Maggie to study Beth. "Well, well, well. I thought so. Lesbians," she concluded. "Sorry to interrupt your romantic dinner. I'm Lorna—"

"Lorna-bitch," Beth muttered. "You know we're not lesbians. You just like to toss stuff around and see what trouble you can make. Vinnie Alessandro is too good for you, babe. Why don't you let him off the hook? Maybe I'll help him see what a real woman is about—"

"I don't know what you're talking about."

"I see him look at you. And you look back, even though you were married at the time. Now you're after Nick, because you know he's someone you can't have, and your sick mind works like that—you want what you can't have. And you're too good for Vinnie, who just runs an auto supply store and works as a mechanic, aren't you?"

Lorna flushed. "You're a fruitcake. Talk about trying to start trouble."

"What can I do for you?" Maggie asked briskly. She sensed that Lorna and Beth had battled many times.

"Lay off Nick. You picked this place to be closer to him, and he's already taken."

"By who?" Beth asked sharply. "You? He's smarter than that."

Lorna smiled coldly. "I'm not bothering with you. You're not worth it."

Beth was on her feet, crowding Maggie from the back. Maggie braced herself, blocking Beth's advance on Lorna. "You've delivered the message. Now you can go."

Lorna's blue eyes narrowed. "Okay, let me put it like this. I can help Nick, you can't. He may want to play a bit, but he needs big money to turn that tiny vineyard into a paying proposition. He needs someone with class. In the end, he'll come back to me. I'm on my way to see him now.

There's a buyer for a private client coming into town and I'm going to arrange a meeting for Nick. He'll want my help."

"You just do that." Maggie didn't want to think of Nick holding Lorna, kissing her in that sweet, hungry way he had kissed Maggie.

With that, Lorna walked to her car. She leveled a cold stare at Maggie and burned rubber as she left.

"Bummer," Beth muttered as she dug into the casserole. She plopped a hefty amount of salad onto her plate and poured half of the small oil and vinegar cruet mix over it. "Just because Lorna inherited Big Daddy's money, she thinks she's hot stuff. She won't lower herself to date Vinnie, and he's really a nice guy. Watch out for her. She has a thing about getting what she wants."

"Put some sunflower seeds on that." While Beth spooned out her second serving, Maggie sat and closed her eyes. She tried to cleanse her mind of all anger, to enjoy the meal with Beth. She didn't succeed and ended up pushing her food around on her plate. She didn't need to be involved in anyone's business but her own, and here she was thinking that she could help Beth, and on the bad side of a woman who wanted Nick.

She wanted Nick. Or sex. Somehow the two mingled together and were difficult to separate. His black eyes carried sultry messages that turned the air steamy between them, and tiny motors within her body had started humming at the sight of him.

When Beth had cleaned her plate, she leaned back on the couch and studied Maggie. Scout sat beside her on the small couch, and Beth slung an arm around the dog. "She got to you, didn't she?"

"I don't like being attacked in my own home, for something I didn't do. Nick isn't on my agenda."

"Liar, liar, pants on fire."

Maggie couldn't help smiling. "Smarty pants."

"What a nice way to say 'smart ass.' But then you've got a lot of class. It shows."

Beth grinned, looking very young beneath her makeup. She settled back with the bottled water Maggie handed her. "Nick is hot stuff. So is Dante. Nice, you know. Good guys. Not for me. Nick is still in love with his wife. If Lorna got a piece of him, it was because he was messed up at the time. I know about stuff like that—that missing someone who died, or who left you, can make you reach out for the wrong things. You try to fight it, but you're human, you know? And you make mistakes. Oh, maybe not you, but me. I make mistakes."

"I make plenty of mistakes." *She hadn't understood Glenda's pain; Maggie had been so righteous . . .*

Beth's head tilted. "So what's the deal? You've got class, enough to match Lorna-bitch, and no one knows anything about you . . . except maybe Celeste, and she's not talking."

"There's nothing to tell."

"I saw you run the other day, working it, sweating, fighting something inside you. I'm not much, but I can listen. And if you want to get in the running with Nick, try looking like a girl. Loose sweat suits and grubbies don't cut it when it comes to men. I can loan you something if you want." The quiet, heartfelt offer was atypical of Beth's reported hardness.

Maggie smiled at that; she'd wanted to help Beth, and now the girl had turned the tables. She scraped the remainder of the food into containers and placed them on the table. "Take those. Come by and see me now and then. If you hear of anyone needing a sports massage or personal trainer, tell them about me, okay?"

Beth's hard, knowing eyes were solemn. "I mix with the summer crowd after the bar closes. Ed thinks it's good for business. There's good money to be made on those private yacht parties. But some of the guys might think the massage bit should include extras, you know?"

"No extras provided," Maggie stated flatly.

"Your call. Gotta go. Got an appointment. Thanks for the dinner."

At the door, Maggie touched Beth's arm. "Listen, Beth, if ever you need someone, I'm here. You can crash here when you want. I'll make up the couch."

"Yeah, right. See you."

Maggie couldn't let her go just yet. She couldn't bear to think of Beth being used as Glenda had been, dying of a drug overdose. She gripped Beth's shoulders. "Don't let him beat you, Beth. It isn't worth it."

"He doesn't mean it. He was raised rough. It doesn't happen that much and I owe him. I've been with him a long time. He took me in despite Shirley's squawling—she was his girlfriend for a long time, and maybe some nights she still is. They go way back . . . Listen, you're all worked up. Did that happen to you?"

The nightmare of Glenda's descent tore by Maggie. "To someone I knew. I don't want it happening to you. And stay off drugs."

"They can lighten the load. I'm not a regular user—"

"Don't," Maggie stated fiercely. "Look, I'd offer you a job if I could, but I can't. Isn't there something else you can do? They're looking for help at Nick's winery."

Beth shrugged, that hard, determined look on her face. "I'm not qualified for anything that pays good, and I don't want to screw up Nick's business. I'll be around, but it won't help your business to be seen with me. I know about class distinction and money making. And you look like you could use some money. Take it easy."

"Beth?"

"Hmm?"

Maggie stuffed the feng shui frog and the mandella into Beth's backpack. "For luck."

Maybe she should have given her sister more support of any kind, instead of condemning her for her affair. Maybe she should have understood how a predator could fasten onto Glenda's insecurities and use them. Never strong in her self-worth, Glenda was perfect for the seduction that ruined her life.

Maggie couldn't deny her feelings for Beth—to protect and help, and just maybe to love as her own sister.

For a moment, Beth's youth and softness slid through the hard look. "Are you sure you want to give me these? You might need them for good luck."

"I'm going to be okay. I had to start a new life, and yours is waiting there for you, too."

Stark pain washed across Beth's face. "I've blown it. My life is crap."

"No, you haven't. I know. And Celeste thinks you're wonderful. So there's the two of us. How many do you need to believe in you?"

"How many to turn a dumb blond's light bulb, right?" Beth asked sadly.

"We can do it, Beth. All of us together. In my way, I need you." *If I couldn't help Glenda, maybe I could help you and then myself . . .*

When Beth was gone, Maggie sat down to hold Scout and allowed the tears to come. "I miss Glenda so much, Scout. I shouldn't try to make Beth into my little sister, and yet I can't help myself. What if I would make the same mistakes again? Is this about what she needs, or about what I need, another chance to save someone like my sister and to do it right this time?"

Maggie cared more for others than for herself. To harm them first would make a payment on what she owed him . . . to make her know that she caused their deaths . . .

Far from San Francisco, on a long stretch of Interstate, Brent tightened the garrote on the prostitute. Now tied to the bed and squirming beneath him, she'd been easy enough to spot at the Interstate's truck stop, so easy to get into the motel, so eager to feed her drug habit. He'd needed to get away from the city to feed his own personal habit, practicing the murder of Maggie.

"Tell me you love me," he ordered, angry that she wasn't Maggie—or someone Maggie knew.

How often had he played this game with Glenda and others?

But pseudo-Maggies never really completed the game. No woman's voice had ever matched hers, their bodies not as sleek or powerful.

*He had to be careful and not let his obsession rule him too soon, controlling his need to punish Maggie.*

He fought himself and yet when the prostitute croaked that she loved him, sex rose and consumed him. When he returned to control, the woman lay dead and limp beneath him.

Garbage, not like Maggie at all, he thought. Maggie would have fought more, given him more pleasure. This woman was low-life garbage that he had to manipulate into the trunk of his car, driving to an isolated place to dump her.

"Maggie, this is all because of you," he whispered cheerfully later, as he drove away from the woman's shallow grave. "You're out there. I feel you breathing. It's your fault if others die because of you."

Nick took his time in the shower; he was sweaty and tired and restless. The sap was moving in the grapevines, warming to the sun, and he wasn't exactly certain that the same thing wasn't happening to him—kissing Maggie, holding her, had only made him want more.

He tried to turn his mind to business. The mortgage was due, and despite himself, he wanted to meet the buyer for the rich client as Lorna had offered. With the wine-tasting festivals and the fall fairs coming up, he might make a few connections, but satisfied wealthy customers who bought by the caseload were the best promotions.

But Maggie kept coming back to his mind. He tried not to remember the way she had crooned as she bathed, a feminine symphony of orgasmic sounds that haunted his nights.

He dried, tugged on his boxer shorts, and slung the towel around his shoulders just as he heard a dog's excited barking. He opened the back door and Scout raced in to jump on him.

Nick shoved the dog in play, and Scout raced around the house. "Hey, she's not going to like this."

Maggie's pickup pulled beside his; she slammed the door and then walked to him. "Scout ran away. I let her out before going to bed, and she took off."

Nick opened the door wider to reveal the laundry baskets behind him, knocked aside with clean clothing tangled on the floor. Scout came to sit on the clothing, her tongue dangling in a happy dog smile.

"I am sorry. Come here, Scout. Let's go home."

"So I hear that you had a visit from Lorna."

Maggie patted her jeaned thigh, a gesture that Scout should come. "Beth told you, no doubt."

"It was quite the sight—Beth in those wobbly wedgie heel things, trudging across the vineyard at night. She wants to protect you. Her lecture to me was pithy, to say the least. Apparently my talk with Lorna didn't register. I'll try again."

"She doesn't bother me. I've been through worse . . . Nick, can you help Beth? I mean, get her a job and out of what she's doing?"

Nick wondered about the "worse." "I tried. That toughness is just her way of protecting her low self-esteem. She doesn't believe how good she really is."

"I don't want anything more to happen to her," Maggie stated firmly.

"Neither do I. You seem focused on Beth. She's the first person you've asked about. There's something in her that you respond to. But what about you? What happened to you that could make you want to protect Beth more than any other woman? Does she remind you of someone?"

Maggie looked up at him, her expression guarded. "Come on, Scout," she repeated. "Let's go home."

"Okay, once more you've effectively shut me off—this time. You don't want to answer questions and you're not sticking around if I ask more. But Maggie, I have just one more—is there some reason you are not looking lower than my face?" Nick asked and reached out to touch her flushed cheek.

"You're big and you're only wearing boxer shorts. You haven't shaved. You look tough. There's water on your shoulders. That scar goes straight down the side of your thigh."

The sensual tug went straight to the area beneath Nick's shorts. "Anything else?"

"I want my dog."

*Take it easy*, Nick warned himself as her eyes darkened, and that funny little quiver moved through her taut body. If he reached for her, took her mouth beneath his—

Nick reached for a T-shirt and tugged it on. The jeans that followed helped confine a heaviness that needed easing. "So how's business?"

Maggie seemed to relax a bit. "Slow."

Keep it light, Nick thought. "It will pick up. People here are cautious. You'll find there's a difference between summer people and the ones who have lived here a long time. I'm getting ready to watch an old movie. Care to watch it with me? I'll pop some corn."

"I have an early morning client. I'd better be going. Thanks."

When Scout moved toward Maggie, Nick knew his time was short. "Mom and Dad's anniversary is in a week. You're invited. They're closing the restaurant for the night. Come if you can. Bring Beth and Celeste. It seems you've made good friends with them. They like the food."

She hesitated and nodded. "Maybe."

"Maggie?" Nick asked as she turned. "There's just one thing more."

Her lips were smooth and warm beneath his, slightly parted and sweet. The gentle taste of hunger caused him to linger to savor the rich-bodied flavor just beneath—vanilla and blackberry spice, he decided, mellow yet with just that nip to add character . . .

"What do you want from me, Nick?" she asked against his lips.

"To know you."

The woman in her was wise. "You want more than that."

"Yes," he answered honestly, smoothing back the tendril that brushed her cheek. All the questions that he needed answered were carefully, momentarily placed aside. "Yes, Maggie, I do. I need someone with your laundry talent," he added to soften the need deep within him. "I'll cook and do the dishes. You do laundry. Yours, too."

She smiled at the invitation, just a bit of entrancing warmth curling around her lips and eyes. "Ask your mother to help you. Let's go, Scout."

Nick watched her leave into the night. "Run, Maggie, run. I'll see you tomorrow."

Why was Maggie so curious about Beth, wanting to help her? She seemed more interested in ways to help Beth than herself. Did Beth remind her of someone dear? Was there a link between that someone and the locket that Maggie held when she was troubled? And how did Beth fit into Maggie's past and her closed doors?

One thing was certain and could not be placed aside—his need for Maggie despite all her mysteries.

The nightmare churned around Maggie, clawing at her. Glenda sobbing, aching for her children, needing money for her habit . . . Glenda high on drugs, or hungover and beaten in a sleazy hotel . . . Glenda, cold and pale on that morgue bench . . .

A man's bitter words tearing at Maggie, hurting her . . . betraying her. Another man laughing at her, the men together—two friends, her ex-husband and another, keeping her away from Glenda. Maggie reached for Beth and found her sister, sweet and caring, a loving mother—Scout was barking . . .

Then Maggie was drowning—

She awoke to her own scream and Scout barking at the camper door to the loud insistent knock. Out of breath, Maggie lay for a moment, listening to Nick's voice. "Maggie? Open the door!"

Over the sound of her heartbeat, birds were chirping and

dawn pried at the thin curtains. Maggie struggled out of the tangled sheet, stood too quickly, and bumped her head on a cabinet. She rubbed the pain and sat down on the bed. "Scout, stop barking."

The door rattled and Nick called again, "Maggie?"

"I'm fine. Just a minute."

"You'd better be fine," he said darkly when she opened the door. His hands were on his hips and he was dressed for running. "That scream said you weren't. I was running into town and I could hear it clear out on the road. It sounded like you were terrified, like you were being attacked. What's wrong?"

She rubbed her head. "So I have nightmares and I talk in my sleep. Who doesn't?"

Nick's expression was grim, his black eyebrows gleaming with sweat and a scowl. "Not like that."

"Leave me alone. Just get on with your run. You didn't have to stop anyway. I've been taking care of myself for a long time." She started to close the door, only to have Nick hold it open.

"You're driving me nuts," he stated as his gaze slowly took in her T-shirt and bare legs.

"Likewise." Maggie continued rubbing the pain in her scalp.

"Let me look at your head. What happened?"

He reached for her and pushed her head down, inspecting the area she had been rubbing.

She felt like a sullen child—admonished and inspected for a bruise she could have avoided. "I know how to take care of myself."

Nick lifted her head with his hand, turning her face side to side. "I'm used to taking care of my brother's kids. You're acting like one. So who is Glenda? You called out her name and you've been crying."

For just that instant, Maggie wanted to slip into his arms and feel his strength. Her affection and fear for Beth had triggered the awful past and Glenda's horrible path to destruction. "You can go now."

Scout was pushing out the door, leaping on Nick. Nick smiled and waggled the dog's head, pushing her down. Scout barked and ran in a circle, then leaped on Nick again.

Maggie closed the door and sat on her couch, trying to adjust from her nightmare to the man outside the camper. In a few minutes, the door opened and Nick ordered Scout to get in. When he spoke to Maggie, Nick's voice was rough with anger and sarcasm. "Have a nice day, Maggie. Mom and Dad are wondering about you. Drop in if you can."

After Nick left, Maggie sat, petting Scout, who looked hopeful. "Okay, I like him, too. But you can't go over there when you want. We can't get involved. There's this man-woman thing going on with Nick, and he's just a nice guy who misses his wife. Let's just not get tangled up in that, okay? It wouldn't be good for anyone. Don't you go to his house anymore, do you hear?"

*Nick.* Easygoing, nice-to-look-at man who was still in love with his wife. Neither one of them needed complications—

Nick smoothed the side of an oak barrel, then ran his hand over its bunghole. He appreciated the cool, dark aging cellar, the few barrels upon which he hoped to build a fine reserve wine. Almost two years ago, the grapes' sugar content had been perfect for the wine that Nick wanted as his trademark specialty, good enough to take to the international competitions.

On the other side, boxes of various Alessandro bottled wines ready for shipping held his dreams of a major competing vineyard. The wines would be judged by experts at fairs and universities, at culinary events and regional competitions. Placing in the competitions raised the profile of Alessandro Winery, and building his business to an international level would take time.

Patience and time with Maggie was something else; the leash on his sensual need was close to breaking.

He'd tasted the woman beneath the protective exterior and

he'd seen her tears, that shattered, helpless expression when she'd opened the camper door.

*Glenda.* Maggie had cried out the name, a terrified call, without anger.

Nick had wanted to tug her into his arms, to hold her safe.

But then, he just might be confusing her with Alyssa, and that wouldn't do at all . . .

# SEVEN

"If you leave now, I'm leaving with you." Maggie reached for Beth's hand when she felt the girl start to draw back.

"Well, that would ruin my chance for a fun time with my friends," Celeste said.

In contrast to the usually quiet and candlelit Alessandros Italian Restaurant, the dining room was alive with light. Dean Martin's voice crooned over children's yells, men and women talking. Rosa and Anthony were busy at a table of food, while Dante had his arms loosely around two women as they swayed to the music. Tony had a child up on his shoulders, with his wife, Sissy, snuggled up to him, clearly in love.

Beth's words mirrored her dark, resentful expression. "It's an anniversary, for crying out loud, a family 'do,' grandparents, parents, and kids—babies, Maggie. *Kids and babies.* I've got no right to be here. I let Nick down—"

Maggie wondered briefly about Beth's comment, but the blast of noise and people in the restaurant wiped the thought away. For once, Scout sat by her feet, not resisting the leash.

She tried not to look for Nick, but her quick scan of the crowd said he was busy, behind the bar, laughing as he re-filled wineglasses. Framed by the dark polished wood, the glittering hanging wineglasses, he was big and gorgeous and heart-quivering masculine. Under the bright lights, his hair gleamed, waving neatly, the black long-sleeved sweater matching his rugged look.

Marco loomed in front of her, cutting off Maggie's view of Nick. "Hey, girls. Glad you're here. I've got a good knuckle bone for Scout in the back, if that's okay, Maggie. I'll just take her out the front door and around the back. This crowd is thick and vicious, packed with kids and sticky hands and women in high-heeled shoes."

When Maggie looked at the bar, Nick was gone and her friends were talking.

"Beth, you talk too much, and I'm hungry. Maggie works me like a dog. I deserve this and if you're part of the pack-age, you're coming with us," Celeste said easily and from be-hind the girl, nudged her forward into the filled and noisy restaurant.

Beth refused to budge, staring at the dining room of peo-ple. "Bossy old biddy—"

Celeste laughed at Beth's resentful tone. "Okay, do it for Maggie then."

Maggie squeezed Beth's hand. She didn't understand her need for Beth, but it lay there, sweet and tender, easing the uncertainty inside her. "I want you both here. Rosa made a special point of coming to Ole's and inviting me. The Alessandros have been nice to me and I won't offend them."

"I still don't get why I have to—"

"Because we're all the family Maggie has," Celeste stated quietly.

Beth gripped Maggie's and Celeste's hands. "You got me into this. You stick by me or I'm leaving. That's the deal."

Rosa was making her way toward them, her smile warm and happy, her arms outstretched. She hugged each one of them. "Welcome to our home, our family. I am so happy you are here. Come eat. Drink some of Nick's wine, and share with us. We are so lucky—Anthony and me, so blessed."

She turned to her husband, who was carrying a tray of food. "Anthony, come welcome our guests."

Maggie barely registered his greeting when across the crowded, noisy room, she found Nick. He was wearing black jeans that matched his sweater. He held a sleepy, black-haired toddler in the crook of his arm, rocking it with the sway of his body. When the child nestled against his chest, he kissed its black curls with the ease of a man who gave affection easily.

*He was a family man, meant to have a wife who fit into his life, and children . . .*

As though drawn by her stare, he looked at Maggie, and his laughing smile slowly died. From across the room, the searing heat in his eyes caught her, held her, and closed away the noise of the room.

The primitive jerk of her senses told her that he wanted her right then, hot and raw and hungry to satisfy them both.

Maggie forced herself to breathe, to lick her suddenly dry lips. She couldn't look away from that hot, dark intensity that said nothing could keep him from her.

Pinned by his look, now shielded just a bit by his lashes, Maggie trembled, feeling as if his hands were already on her, big and slightly rough, but very certain of what he wanted, what he would demand.

What *she* would demand was more frightening—mind blowing, forget everything for that moment, and take. Her body was already warming, softening, moistening—and he hadn't touched her.

There was no promise of tenderness in his grim expression, nor of a seduction. He intended to claim her, possess her. It would be no easy, forgettable passage, but filled with hunger and demands and very, very slow and thorough . . .

*Nick would take his time, and there would be no quick release from that passion . . . He would taste and savor and*

*take only what was given, returning it with an intensity that
would brand her—*

Maggie had never felt such a primitive sense of a man's
desire, not even in lovemaking.

Lovemaking? That wasn't what Nick was offering. It was
deeper, darker, more terrifying—because she wanted just the
same, a surrender to honest passion.

When a middle-aged woman laughed and reached to hug
Nick, his eyes didn't leave Maggie's. Instead, they flickered,
and his slow, genuine smile down at the woman was warm as
she eased the baby from him. And just that easily, Nick
turned from Maggie as though he'd never seen her.

No longer riveted by Nick's look, Maggie slowly realized
that her hand was on her throat, and her other hand was gripping Beth's.

"You're killing my hand," Beth muttered. "It's supposed to
be me who's scared, remember?"

Dante moved toward the women, and Beth's indrawn
breath hissed by Maggie's ear. "How do I look?"

"Sweet," Maggie said, glancing at Beth's loose cream
sweater, denim skirt, and fringed, knee-high suede boots.
With her naturally blond short hair and scrubbed face, she
looked like a teenager.

"I should have worn all my makeup. I feel naked. You
shouldn't have made me take it off," Beth grumbled.

"That's just self-protection, your armor, like a knight going
into battle. You don't need it when you're with us," Celeste returned in a distant tone, as if her mind was somewhere else.

Dante's slow look down Maggie's green sweater and
slacks—the only good outfit she'd managed to keep—was
pure male appreciation. He held her away just a bit to look
down at her high black strappy heels, a purchase from the local thrift shop. "Nice. Saucy. I love a woman in heels," he
said in a deep voice that held a hint of sensual attraction.

"You look nice, too," Maggie said, returning the compliment.

With ease, Dante moved between Beth and Maggie, his arms around their waists. "Sorry, Celeste, no room for you," he teased.

Celeste had turned pale and Maggie touched the other woman's arm. Beneath the flowing mystical caftan of moon and stars, Celeste's body was rigid and her eyes glazed, fixed on Maggie. "Celeste?"

The psychic shook her head as though trying to clear it. She smiled briefly, but her eyes were still searching Maggie's face. "I was thinking about food and how much you'll make me do to work it off."

"Get your hands off me, Alessandro," Beth was saying.

But Dante had turned his attention to Maggie, his finger lifting her chin until they stood close and intimate. "I'm glad you came. Don't let the kid spoil your fun."

"Hey, Alessandro. I was forced to come."

"You'll live through it," Dante responded easily.

Someone called out for Nick to pour another tray of wine, and Dante looked as if he'd just been reminded of something. "Oh, yeah. Nick. Listen, Maggie, I'm the much better deal. Let me fix you a plate of spaghetti and I can tell you how wonderful I am."

Beth snorted and crossed her arms, looking off into the party as if disinterested.

"Come on, Beth," Maggie urged, sliding her arm through the girl's. "Let's get that free food."

As Dante moved them through the crowd, Maggie turned to see Nick leaning against the wall, his arms crossed, grimly staring at her. Seemingly unaware of Nick, Dante pulled her closer to whisper in her ear. "When you're ready, I'll take you out on the lake. The relaxation would do you good."

Maggie smiled and eased away slightly from his intimate pose. "Thanks. Not yet."

He leaned closer and flicked the tiny round beads of her earring until they danced. "I like you. But I'm getting a little tired of seeing my big brother wonder about you. I'd like to kick up his action a little bit. He moves too slow."

"I'm not interested in action, but you definitely don't move slow," she said, teasing him.

He smirked a little, charming her. "Can I help it if I'm every woman's dream?"

"Try that on someone else, okay? But thanks for the interest. A girl needs that once in a while." Dante was a friend in a good mood, and Maggie intended to enjoy the night. For the first time in years, she felt feminine and light and certain of herself. She'd enjoyed dressing for the evening, and being with Celeste and Beth. They were almost family, surrounding her with warmth, teasing, and understanding without questions.

Jerry moved close to her, taking his time to admire her clothes. "I'm still available, beautiful. Anytime."

"Thanks. You're looking good, Jerry. Did you notice that girl in the corner checking you out?"

Jerry looked at the girl, and it seemed as if his whole body had locked onto her. "Debra Morales. She just moved into town and came with my cousin Mary. I've been trying to date her. Better go. Sorry. See you."

After Jerry left, Maggie ran her fingers through her hair, enjoying the sensual brush against her skin, and suddenly the room seemed to quiet as her eyes locked with Nick's dark intensity.

Then a child laughed and ran by her and Anthony was giving her a big hug, lifting her off her feet, and she gave herself to enjoying the night.

Dante's attentions continued through dinner and introductions to an extensive family, including Tony's children. Sissy, Tony's petite wife, took Maggie's arm. "If you only knew how good it is to see Dante and Nick on their toes. Usually women are running after them. I hear you are wonderful at Ole's. I'd love for you to drop in at nap time and give me some pointers on exercises—I'll pay, of course. Maybe we could set up regular sessions."

"I'd love to." It was Maggie's first real offer as a private trainer, and she was thrilled.

Still smiling and happy, she turned to see Nick and Dante, standing side by side against the wall, considering her. The double jolt of prime masculinity—all dark waving hair and expressive eyes, the height and strength—startled her.

"Aren't they gorgeous?" Sissy whispered. "If you only knew how many women are jealous of you, including Lorna."

"You know, Lorna could have another reason for wanting Nick to be interested in her. It's an old game. Maybe there's someone she wants to make jealous."

Sissy shook her head. "No one that I know."

Nick raised his wineglass to Maggie in a toast, and her fingers trembled. From across the room, the sensuality between them stirred into life. He wasn't flirting as Dante had, he was merely giving her notice that the hot, simmering tension between them waited to be fed.

Maggie enjoyed the next hour, the simple talk, Dante's open flirtation. Beth relaxed slightly. Celeste, while pleasant, seemed too quiet, almost alone in the crowd, as if she were trying to fit pieces of a puzzle together.

When the crowd waited for the Alessandros to speak before cutting their cake, Nick eased beside Maggie.

"Having a good time?" he asked against her temple.

Dante's games—to make Nick react—didn't matter, because when Nick first saw Maggie's reddish hair loose on her shoulders, that clinging green sweater and slacks, he'd wanted the woman beneath the clothing, beneath the mystery.

He amended the thought: He wanted her dressed in nothing but those sexy high heels.

Because he was a methodical man, he couldn't rest until he knew what ran behind those changeable green-brown eyes, beneath the recognition by a woman of the man desiring her.

The impact of her body softening and quivering had hit him from across the crowded room. Without touching Maggie, he knew how she would feel beneath him, how hot and tight—he could almost feel her against him, moving as smoothly as the lake's waves, or in hunger, a tempest, strong and hungry . . .

But he wanted more, a lot more. He wanted to know why nightmares plagued her, why she was so alone, and more than that, he wanted her trust and her friendship. He didn't like the lick of dark anger within him, the questions that were left unanswered, even when she had responded to him.

"You look nice."

"Thank you. So do you."

*Small talk,* Nick thought, *keep it rolling.* Maggie looked easier tonight, as if she'd temporarily packed away her shadows. "How's business?"

After a hesitation, Maggie said, "I'm hoping it will pick up."

Nick nodded, pacing his questions while his parents spoke of the happy, fun years between them.

"It's crowded in here. Care to step outside?"

Maggie's dark green eyes turned to him. "Exactly what business did you have with Beth? She's only a girl, Nick. Very young and vulnerable despite her years."

The direct hit surprised him, as though Maggie's anger had been brewing in the last few minutes. "I like Beth."

"How?" The word was another hit that nettled.

Nick took Maggie's arm and maneuvered her through the crowd to the family kitchen, which was full of children seated at a table, their dinners monitored by hovering adults.

When Nick released her on the back porch, Maggie turned to him, and there was nothing cold about her anger. Her arms were wrapped tightly around her. "Don't . . . ever . . . manhandle me again."

Women certainly had their moods, he thought, contrasting the sensual sparks earlier against Maggie's temper now. "What's this about Beth?"

"She said she'd let you down. Exactly how did she let you down, Nick?"

No woman had ever made him account for his actions. But then no other woman was Maggie, all wound up tight and passionate about protecting her friend. "Take it easy, Maggie. She's a good kid. I tried to help her, that's all. Dante has too—he's actually paid her to come down to the boatyard, trying to get her to learn bookkeeping."

A car slid by, hard rock blaring in the night, then dying. Maggie looked off into the night, holding her bitter suspicions away from him. "Did you have sex with her? Did you pay her?"

That she should question his motives and his honor raised Nick's temper just that notch. He was passionate about his wines and his family and little else, except this woman. "What's it to you?"

That locket was in her fist and shadows swept across her face. She turned to watch moths circling the back porch light, drawn irresistibly to the glass fixture's enclosure, which would be their death. "I've seen it all before. Man takes a young girl, tries to mold her into something she isn't. Painful for the girl, destructive. Sometimes he moves on. Sometimes the girl doesn't know who she really is when it's over."

Nick's head went back as if he'd been slapped. "What gives with you? What do you think I am?"

She sighed tiredly, as if she had just run through scenes that disgusted her. "I think you miss your wife. Don't ask Beth to replace her."

"What are you asking Beth to replace for you?" He hadn't meant to ask the question nettling him, but there it was, stark and cutting in the air between them. "Who is it that you're missing, that you see in Beth?"

Maggie paled, and her hand gripped that locket.

"And whatever you feel, it's tied up with that locket. I said I'd listen and I will, but don't start throwing accusations at me that aren't true."

Nick had reached his limits. He tugged Maggie into his arms and held her, despite her struggles. "Give it up, will you, Maggie? I'm not whoever you're fighting, whatever he's done to you."

"You haven't answered me," she said breathlessly as she blew a strand of hair from her cheek.

Maggie wasn't giving up until she had her answers, defining what ran between Nick and Beth, and he sensed that she would fight more fiercely for her friend than for herself.

"I never touched Beth, not in that way. I tried to help her. Yes, I gave her money. Beth was thinking of leaving Blanchefleur, of taking work on the docks in the city. She deserved better, but it didn't work out. She disappeared for a few days when she tried to find her mother. She came back looking like she'd been to hell. Her mother never wanted to see her again. But Beth did what she had to do. I get the feeling she's a lot like you in that. End of money. End of story."

He'd given Beth a full mortgage payment, saved from money he'd earned moonlighting for another winery, and then he'd asked the bank for an extension, working until he dropped to make double payments. Because Beth was worth it. Because evidently Maggie thought so, too—enough to leave her safe, quiet, lonesome harbor and come out swinging for her friend.

Maggie was studying him again, this time intently, searching his face as her hands spread on his chest. "I never touched her, Maggie," he repeated more softly. "Not in that way. I haven't wanted a woman for a long time. And I'm sorry someone hurt you."

Her expression changed, softened, and her smile was slow and shy. "Nice party."

He could have held her like that forever, enjoying the night and the softness against him. Her scent was that of spring, when the blooms filled the vines, the promises of sweetness and depth and tomorrows—

He could have held Maggie closer, kissed her to find the hunger he knew she controlled, freeing it.

Instead, Nick savored this soft trusting from her, that rare, shy smile of the woman inside. He released her, then slowly smoothed her hair, enjoying the silky feeling against his skin, the way it ran through his fingers. "Been working Celeste hard, have you? She was grumbling through her second help- ing of spaghetti, wondering how much you'd torture her."

Maggie's smile changed from shy to impish. "She likes to groan and whine."

"She does a lot of walking—at odd hours in the night—a slow, thoughtful sort of walk. We're used to it, but she's doing it more often since you've come to town."

"She doesn't like it when I push her, trying to get her heart rate up. She prefers those slow, easy walks, stopping when she wants. They're not exactly a cardiovascular workout. Maybe she's just reclaiming herself from me."

"Now why would anyone want to do that?" Nick asked softly.

She didn't answer, but that little uneven breath said Mag- gie understood the sensual undertones of the question. He noted that Maggie's fingers stayed open on his chest, the easy softness of her body against him.

Against his promises, he leaned down to kiss her, just that brush of flavor that he had to have, the smooth, soft aftertaste to remain with him—

Maggie sighed and moved closer, her lips parting slightly to allow him to taste her. Because Nick couldn't trust his con- trol, he drew back when he felt the gentle suckle of her mouth, the slight restless movement of her hips. "Let's go back in, shall we?"

In the shoddy room above a bar, Brent didn't look at the pros- titute as she hurried out the door, her footsteps racing for safety.

Women, he thought, disgusted by their weakness. Auto- matically, he straightened the room, such as it was, placing his polished shoes neatly next to the door, smoothing the crease in his slacks as they hung over the back of a chair. And always, the pictures in the room had to be straightened.

He lifted the bottle and let the cheap whiskey burn his throat, the hatred of Maggie Chantel burn his mind.

He lined up the glasses provided by the hotel. Three matched and one didn't. He automatically tossed the unmatched glass into the trash.

*Disappear from him, would she?*

"Well, Maggie, dear, you left an unpaid bill," he crooned, licking the bottle he had thoroughly washed, as he planned to taste her skin.

In the cracked mirror, he studied his broken nose, a gift from a strong-arm collector. Of course, he couldn't repay the loan—because Maggie's persistent harassment had made him lose everything: money, business, friends who could send fortunes his way.

Friends. The word turned sour on his tongue. They were all gone now, fearing to associate with him, fearing to loan him money, disdainful of his poor fortune.

He hurled the whiskey bottle against the wall, scorning the cheap brew when once he'd had the best.

That's what he was, the best. And Maggie had ruined him, running from his wrath.

Tacked to the cheap stained wallpaper were pictures of her, because he never wanted to forget. He wanted to fuel his hatred. "Selfish witch. You didn't even come back to see your nephews. When I find you—"

He paused to draw the hunting knife's sharp tip down Maggie's face, glossy and smiling on a brochure. "You won't be smiling then, will you, honey?" he crooned. "Where are you, baby? Come to Daddy . . ."

Then, because reality beckoned to him, Brent picked up the telephone and dialed his sister's number. "Cheryl Ann, I need more money . . . I am being careful . . . Don't make me tell your husband your little secrets, just send the money as usual. And I want to know if you hear anything about Maggie Chantel—What? Hurt her? No, I just want to repay her for something."

His sister would cooperate, financing his full-time hunt for Maggie. Because Cheryl Ann knew what he was capable of doing.

* * *

The hanging line of colorful plastic lanterns someone had strung across the room swayed and Celeste felt the room turning. It was supposed to be a festive night and she tried to push away the slithering, tightening, shadowy coils that came for her. She wanted to resist them, to give herself to the music and life and joy, but the whispers that came as lightly as her cats' paws wouldn't release her.

As she leaned against the restaurant's wall, the flowing purple paisley caftan slid cold as a shroud against her skin.

She took her mind to a spot above the noisy room, above the lanterns. The Alessandros were a caring family. Would they give her a wake? she wondered distantly.

Or would they be giving a wake for one of their own?

Because fainter, less certain danger also stalked the Alessandros. Celeste could feel it pulse around her.

Her fingers pried loose the scarf she'd tied at her throat, a frivolous last-minute addition. It was red paisley and silk, her favorite. She'd always loved scarves long enough to flow the length of her caftan, circle her throat, and glide down her back. Vanity, perhaps, but they seemed to make her more slender.

*Now, her scarf seemed almost alive, choking her.*

She watched Nick and Maggie rejoin the lively crowd, and there was a softness about Maggie that hadn't been there, a relaxing of those taut shields. What was her past, and how did her trail lead death to Celeste?

Or to Beth? What kindled warm and sweet within Maggie as she looked at Beth? What ran between them, the bond so close to love? Would that deadly trail lead to Beth?

Or perhaps to Maggie, Celeste added sadly, as another dark wave slithered over her. She would have to wait, to know more, because tonight it seemed as if Maggie had forgotten whatever haunted her.

Outside on the street, a car prowled over the cobblestones. Lorna's Lincoln was easily recognizable. Celeste circled the wealthy, spoiled woman, hovering uninvited outside the restaurant. Lorna wanted Nick, and he was too smart for her games. Or did she really want someone else, someone who wouldn't play her games?

Vinnie, Nick's cousin, watched the car from the window and quietly lifted his glass in a mocking toast to Lorna. Framed by shadows, her face was rigid and pale, then the Lincoln shot into the night.

Celeste saw inside Lorna's bitter, lonely anguish. She was terribly lonesome and covered her scars with brusque attacks. Her father had demanded too much from her, withholding his affection until he'd fashioned her into a seemingly emotionless female shark. Then he'd manuevered, rather sold, her into two consecutive bloodless marriages.

Lorna was doing the best she could, and beneath that brittle exterior, she was just a woman wanting someone to love. Love lay within her like a shriveled bud, waiting for sunshine and nourishment.

Celeste watched Maggie take a glass of wine from Nick, their eyes meeting over the rim. His hand reached to smooth her hair, and Maggie's smile at him was shy.

*Oh, Maggie, I want so for you to live, for you to be happy . . . please, please let me see . . .*

But the images wouldn't come, because Celeste saw flashing pictures of what happened before the victim's death, and the only death she could predict for certain now was her own, and Maggie had brought it to her.

Did she hate Maggie for that? No, it was only as fate would have it. Celeste needed answers, and Maggie couldn't give them to her—because Maggie didn't know. . . .

Nick damned himself for the need he couldn't help, and knocked on Maggie's camper door. He'd stayed to clean up after the aniversary party and should have gone straight home, but the ache to see Maggie again was too strong. She'd been so relaxed, laughing at Dante's jokes.

Dante needed to lay off, Nick thought darkly, because when it came to Maggie, he was very selfish.

Inside the camper, Scout barked excitedly and Nick answered Maggie's cautious "Who is it?"

She opened the door slightly and Nick fought reaching for her. She'd relaxed tonight, leaned slightly against him, the soft curves had stayed with him. Nick reached down to pet Scout. "I forgot something."

The door opened wider and the light behind her created a halo of reddish soft hair, the towel she held in front of her shielding the over-large T-shirt. Her bare legs were slender and long and gleaming smooth—

Inwardly Nick groaned, because he wanted to run his hands over those legs and upward and over and in; he wanted to be the cause of those soft crooning sounds she'd made in the shower.

"What did you forget?"

"This," he said, giving way to his need to feel her against him. Nick moved very slowly so as not to frighten her. He placed his hands on Maggie's shoulders, sliding them down her arms, and gently enfolded her hands with his. The towel dropped to her feet, and Maggie stood still, watching him.

Nick studied the fit of their hands, the way the bones felt strong and lasting beneath the skin softer than his. They were good hands, callused and unpampered, smaller than his, the palms more square.

"Enjoyed yourself tonight, did you?" he asked as he brought her hands to his mouth, cruising his parted lips over her knuckles.

Her yes held just the right amount of breathlessness to stir him on, not too fast, he cautioned, but enough to satisfy just that bit.

Nick turned her hands, opened them, and placed his face within their cradle, wanting her to feel inside him, to trust him. "I did, too."

"You're not coming in," Maggie said huskily.

He'd needed that, to know that she hungered for him and recognized his own hunger. Nick slowly looked down her body, the curved silhouette, the flaring of her hips revealed by the light behind her. "No, I'm not."

With a tug, he brought her out of the doorway, catching her against him, holding her feet off the ground. It was enough for now, he thought, as her eyes darkened and her arms loosely rested on his shoulders.

He closed his eyes, pleasured by her fingers slowly toying with his hair, one prowling around his ear. Her fingertips skimmed his brows, his lashes, his cheekbones, and slid down his nose. The curiosity was there, the woman testing him each step, wanting to be certain of him.

When they trailed over his lips, he kissed them and settled into a sense of well-being. The late spring night was fragrant and new, and he was with the woman he wanted.

"You're a lonely man, Nicholas Alessandro. I can't be her."

"Did I ask you?"

Her lips brushed his so lightly he feared they hadn't. "I'm not lonely. I've been too busy trying to survive."

"Mmm," his tone was all male appreciation.

Maggie smiled against his lips. "Your hands are wandering."

He moved her slightly against his body, already hard and aching. "I'm just testing your muscle density. You're in good shape. You feel so good. I wonder if I need a private trainer."

"You can let me down now, and there's not an ounce of flab on you and you know it."

He leaned his head against the hand smoothing his cheek, enjoying the gentleness that lingered between them. "No, you're staying put. This is nice. You know, I'm a much better guy than Dante. You sat on his lap. Now everyone thinks you're his girl. You could have sat on my lap."

She smiled at that. "He's very charming, and there wasn't anywhere else to sit. And I didn't think his lap was danger-ous."

Nick didn't allow his smirk to show—when a woman no-

ticed a man's lap, that gave him hope. "And I'm not charming? Okay, maybe I'm out of practice. I'll try harder." He intended to give her something to think about, lowering her to
her feet, and taking her mouth, devouring it, flying with her.

Instead, Maggie's hands fisted his hair, her mouth open beneath his, tasting of hunger and storms and heat. He slowly
slid his hands down her body, from beneath her arms, to her rib
cage, to that indentation of her waist to the curve of her hips,
and ran one finger around the elastic waistband of her briefs,
lingering where he wanted to take, and cupped her bottom.
"You are a fine-looking woman, Maggie Chantel. Can you
blame me?" he asked wryly.

Her laugh was sultry and knowing and feminine. "You're
on the make, Nick. I'm just the closest and the newest game
in town."

"I'm wounded," he returned, moving into the friendly
tease, enjoying Maggie without her defenses.

She patted his cheek, and Nick lifted her in his arms, placing her safely inside the camper. "Good night, sweet
princess. You can do my laundry any time."

She laughed outright at that, and Nick closed the door, and
the temptation that was Maggie, from him. The encounter
was friendly and tender and enough—but he wanted much
more.

Celeste raised her arms to the moon, calling to the winds,
asking them to show her more.

"That's creepy," Beth said behind her. "I don't know if I
should stay the night or not. You've been in a strange mood
lately."

The winds tugged at Celeste's caftan as she tried to see inside, where the darkness hovered, expected, and warned.
"Do you like my house, Beth?" she asked, loosening her
long hair to flow in the wind, twining with her scarf almost
sensually.

"You know I love it."

Celeste liked the idea of Maggie and Beth sharing her

small cottage, tending the herbs. Maggie had linked with Beth in some unexpected way, and the younger woman had settled in Maggie's presence, trusting her.

Beth would survive, but Maggie—there the whispers doubted and ended, because Maggie had closed herself to Celeste. But in the psychic's mind, the dog and the locket were bound to Maggie, and there lay the danger . . .

Strange that Maggie had no sense of danger, and yet it slithered after her. But then too many images filled Maggie's mind, not letting the danger in. What were those images? What was the link between Maggie and her own death?

Celeste closed her eyes, and beneath her hands, her heart skipped and leaped and stopped. "You'd take care of my cats, wouldn't you, Beth? If something happened to me?"

They were her family, and so was the girl, and now Maggie.

As a child, Lorna had sought refuge from her father in Celeste's arms. Perhaps Lorna-the-woman didn't want to remember those times when she'd needed love so badly. But the attachment was there in a soft look, or the way Lorna stopped by the shop now and then, for no special purpose.

Celeste would never live to see the good Lorna would do, never see her come into a woman's happiness. But Celeste knew that Lorna would find her path and in giving, receive more than she had ever hoped . . .

"Jeez, you're creeping me out, old woman." But Beth stood beside Celeste and held her hand. "Nothing is going to happen to you. Don't say that again. I don't want to think about it."

But Celeste had to think and wonder and prepare, because her death was coming closer. "I'm going for a walk. Alone. But I'd love for you to spend the night."

"I'll come with you—"

"No, it's my time to think. I need the night at times. It holds me close and whispers. And I listen."

*But I can't hear what it says about Maggie—only that she brings my death and maybe her own . . .*

# EIGHT

Maggie sucked in air and knocked on Nick's back screen door. The rippling, cool jazz music coming from within the house did not soothe her, nor did mid-June's evening fragrances. After sunset and an evening of doing yard work at the camper, the fast walk to reclaim Scout was not welcome.

She swatted at the moths fluttering against the yellow porch light and impatiently brushed away the bits of grass clinging to her tank top and cutoff shorts.

Maggie hadn't talked to Nick for two weeks and she liked keeping her distance. He had pushed her too hard for answers she didn't want to give. Was her affection and concern for Beth so easily read?

Was she actually trying to substitute Beth for Glenda? Was she obsessing about salvaging Beth when she couldn't save Glenda? Or was it about reclaiming herself?

Maggie forced herself to release Glenda's locket. The habit was too telling, leaving her vulnerable for speculation and questions.

Nick was patiently working her for answers, but he was disturbing on a sensual man-woman level.

When he wanted, Nick could send a dark look that sizzled the air between them. In passing, Rosa had said Nick was thinning the blooms on his vineyard, working long hours outside, and also in the winery, contacting customers and working on his bottling supplies and inventory. It was obvious that Nick's mother wanted Maggie to know that he was very busy, but Rosa's broad hints were unmistakable. He also came into the restaurant for meals at exactly eight o'clock at night, and if Maggie wanted to drop over for a meal, there would be no cost because the Alessandros liked her.

Rosa had added tightly that her son was not in love with Lorna, who hadn't resolved the issues her father had created. Maybe she was looking for a strong man like her father, maybe not. "She does things to get attention from men, and she has to have what she can't have—I think that is why she has chosen Nick. It's rumored that she has a boyfriend, but no one knows who he is. She actually paid some gigolo to romance her and she likes to shock people by the things she says, getting that attention she should have had from her cold father. What Lorna needs at times is a good spanking, but most of all I just want to hold her like a poor little lost bird," Rosa had said.

Maggie frowned as she heard footsteps inside Nick's house. She wasn't befriending a woman like Lorna; she was already too deep into Beth's life and couldn't seem to back away. Lorna had her problems, and Maggie had hers.

Scout's direct run toward Nick's house indicated that he was home tonight; Maggie's dog seemed to have radar where Nick was concerned.

Nick opened the door; a background trumpet wailed softly, curling around her, and Scout appeared to sit beside his feet. The kitchen light behind him framed his body, and other than the towel around his hips, all Nick wore were the glittering drops of water on his shoulders and in his hair.

As yet uncombed, the thick black waves were plastered to his head; the curls at the ends almost touched his shoulders and dripped slightly. Without the softness of those waves, the jutting masculine planes of Nick's face caught the light, the hollows in shadow. Those thick brows were locked in a frown, his lashes spiked over narrowed eyes, and a muscle moved beneath that stubble-covered jaw, a pulse throbbing in his muscled neck.

One drop slid from his ear to his shoulder, gleaming on his dark skin. Then it slowly trailed downward to match the others beading the hair on his chest. From there, the single dark line narrowed until it reached his navel, and the white border of flesh where the towel had slipped said Nick wasn't completely tan.

"I want my dog," Maggie stated abruptly, to stop the big vibrating warning of you-haven't-had-sex-in-years awareness of her body.

He took in her sweaty face, the bits of grass clinging to her chest and arms, the worn tank top, cutoffs, and bare legs. She fought wiggling her toe in the hole Scout had chewed in her cheap canvas loafers.

"Bad day?" he asked softly, picking a twig from her hair, and his expression slid into darkly sensual.

Maggie tried not to inhale too deeply; the scent of masculine soap and man was definitely erotic. "Yes. My battery is dead. I've been mowing and cutting George's hedge and cleaning out his old garden. Then I had to walk the two miles to your house to collect my dog."

She decided to move quickly out of Nick's sensual appeal. Maggie patted her thigh. "Come on, Scout. Let's go."

Scout whined and disappeared into the shadows of the house.

"I would have brought her back. She was here, barking, when I got out of the shower."

Maggie kept her eyes firmly on Nick's face. It was just one of those days when nothing went right, including the leap of her senses, the need to slide that towel from Nick. Her personal battery seemed to be well charged.

She looked up at the ceiling and hoped she wasn't drooling.

"You're all sweaty," he said huskily and Maggie's skin started a different sort of heat, the kind that ran clear through her, staking her soles to the wooden planks of his deck.

"Hi," she managed, quite a brilliant statement for her lips to make when her mind wasn't working. In shocking contrast, her body was revved and already in nipple-contraction mode and it wasn't chilly. The sudden alert had surprised her; she didn't consider herself a woman whose sensuality was at the fore. But it had certainly leaped at the sight of Nick.

"Hi," Nick returned, and bent to brush his lips over hers. "You smell sweet, like fresh-cut grass."

"You smell like soap. I smell like sweat," she corrected automatically. But while her mouth spoke, her mind had seemed to stop turning. When it did, she envisioned a cartoon of herself—tongue unrolling to the floor, eyes popping, and heart leaping out of her chest to pound madly.

He chuckled, those velvety black eyes flowing warm upon her. "Nothing like a pragmatic woman. It's girl sweat, sweet and warm and sexy and arousing."

"I'm really tired, Nick, and not that happy with my dog." She didn't want to discuss her sweat with Nick. The damage she did to George's overgrown yard, heaps of trimmed brush, was a result of taking an in-depth look at her thin finances. Scout's regular checkup at the veterinarian's office had been costly, so had the replacement for her pickup's bald tires, and now it needed a battery.

Longing for a real home, she'd just splurged on women's magazines, an expensive treat for a woman with a flatliner checkbook—but just possibly they could fill her mind enough to keep the nightmares away.

"I can help you jumpstart that battery. But it would be pretty easy to drop one in tonight."

"Everything is closed tonight. I walk most of the time anyway." Tonight, after destroying a major overgrown hedgerow and leaving mounds of brush, she couldn't manage walking back—not unless she curled up on the roadside somewhere and rested. "I would appreciate the ride. I'll pay you back. I'll clean or something . . . laundry, maybe?"

"A little ride isn't worth that. But come in. I'm about to have a sandwich. Want one?"

Food wasn't something she'd thought about in her snit. Now her stomach cramped slightly and she remembered that small carton of yogurt she'd had for lunch.

Nick's fingertip slid between her brows. "You're thinking too hard. You're always thinking too hard. A little relaxation wouldn't hurt you."

While she was balancing her hunger and bone-tired fatigue against his favors, Nick's hand found hers. He tugged her into the kitchen, closing the door against the moths that had begun to circle the porch light. She was just like them, Maggie thought as Nick's close study sent her a sensual message strong enough to take her back against the wall.

On that broad chest, a muscle shifted beneath the tanned skin. His nipple jumped, startling her as he reached to steady the small decorative wall plate she'd bumped with her shoulder. His hand remained to slide the band from her ponytail, to run his fingers through her hair. He picked a blade of grass free and tickled her nose. "I've missed you."

"It's nice seeing you again," she managed, very properly, and smiled when he laughed.

"You can cool off in the shower if you want. Or I can take you home now," he added as he turned to walk to the kitchen counter. That damp towel left little to her imagination.

He began to make sandwiches, leaving Maggie with a mouth-watering view of his backside and a powerful thigh that she wanted to caress—okay, maybe dig her fingers into a bit.

"I want to go home now," she whispered and wished her voice didn't waver.

That look over his shoulder, that cocked eyebrow challenged her. "We could eat on the beach and Scout could have a dip."

She crossed her arms and dug her fingers into her flesh, because if that towel slipped another inch. . . . Her hands could almost feel those hard buttocks. . . . "I'd better go home now."

"It's a nice night, not too cold."

"I'm tired," she lied because every muscle in her body was locked onto those broad shoulders, that waving wet hair—and she definitely was primed, not tired.

Nick sliced through the sandwich, cutting it in half with one deft movement. He placed the knife aside and turned to her, his arms crossing his chest. "Afraid?"

"Of what?"

That lazy expression turned grim and hard. "Of me. Of you. Of what might happen. Relax, Maggie. It's only a friendly offer. I'm not going to jump you. But someone has, and maybe some day you'll trust me enough to tell me about it."

She rubbed her forehead, trying to ease the headache brewing there, and leaned back against the wall, closing her eyes. Just a thread of pride was holding her upright, and any minute she'd crumble. What did her admission matter now? "You're right. I have had a bad day."

"Get in the shower, Maggie. I've seen the one at the camper, and it's not big enough for a child. You'll feel better," Nick offered more gently.

"I don't think I can move." Every muscle in her body had locked, aching from the ladies' class, a fierce angry stab at her own extreme aerobics to siphon off some frustration, and then a battle with her finances, the yard trimming, and the walk to his house.

The sound from Nick was rough and impatient, a contrast to the soothing blues coming from the other room. His hand took hers. "Come on, Maggie. You'll feel better after a shower and some food. I'll heat up some of Sissy's vegetable lasagna. I doubt that you're a pastrami and salami kind of girl."

She smiled weakly. "You're right."

"You're working too hard, pushing yourself. And it isn't all about money. Something is going on inside you and it's all coming out, despite you trying to hold it back. Beth is some kind of trigger for you, and you're fighting yourself too hard. Your fear of water—did someone you love, who reminds you of Beth, drown?"

So much had happened—Maggie slowly opened her eyes and found his concern. She shook her head. "I've been on a long trip, trying to figure out my life, Nick. It costs. I'm just trying to find a place for myself and Scout."

The toll on her had been heavy, because she couldn't find what she was seeking, a sister that would never come back to her—she couldn't find that simple peace that would allow her to rest . . .

"Take a break for tonight. We can eat when you get out of the shower, okay?"

With Scout curled beside her later on Nick's couch, Maggie felt the tension slide away, the effects of soothing music, delicious food, and a walk along the beach, allowing Scout to swim and retrieve. It was only a moment, and then she'd leave, she thought sleepily as she nestled her head against the pillow he'd used, catching Nick's scent and wrapping it safely around her.

She awoke to the sound of Scout's excited barking. Terror streaked through Maggie, bringing her to her feet, her heart pounding. Following the sound, Maggie stepped out onto the porch, searching for her pet.

In the predawn's pale light, Nick stood on the beach, playing fetch with Scout. Maggie waited for her heartbeat to settle, and suddenly she was so tired, as if she'd wandered too long and had finally come to a place where she could really rest.

For now, she thought, as she snuggled back beneath the

light throw on the couch, for now she could rest and let the world slide past . . .

Brent's anger rose as he listened to the voice on the other end of the phone. The attorney was once one of Brent's old "brotherhood," a top social set who helped one another. Daniels had needed help in getting the right dominatrix—classy, firm, painful—just like dear old mom.

"I've already given you payment," Daniels stated roughly. "I'm not helping you locate Maggie Chantel. She left the area a year ago, and I don't ever want to see her again. Same goes for you. You're both nothing but trouble—she actually confronted me about her sister, right in court. If Judge Jones hadn't been my friend—well, Sam shut her up, and we all managed to close her out of any work near here. You'd do well to leave the area, too. You should have been a lot more careful in who you selected—someone without a bulldog of a prying sister. After Glenda overdosed, Maggie really set to work making trouble. Hell, it took a whole year of her hanging around, trying to get work and make more trouble, before we got rid of her. You've been tracking her all over the gyms and spas where she might be working—oh, yes, your activities are easily tracked without the slightest effort. If you call me one more time for anything—money or information—you won't like the results. I hope you both rot in hell. You will, if you call again."

With a curse, Brent slammed down the telephone. It bounced from the cradle and tumbled to the floor, the dead line hissing metallically.

He pulled his anger back into him where it could be nurtured until he found Maggie—the woman who had ruined him.

He carefully picked up the receiver and placed it on the cradle. Everything nice and neat. Everything in good time. "You'll tell me you love me, Maggie. Wait for me."

At one unexpected thought, his indrawn breath hissed around the cheap motel room. If Maggie dared to take a lover, that man would also have to die very slowly—in front of her—because she should wait for her punishment.

After a sleepless night, Nick stood in the shadows, his hands in his jeans pockets, watching the woman on his couch. She slept deeply, almost too deeply, unstirred by the nightmares he'd seen creeping onto her earlier.

She gave him nothing of her fears, her shadows; she didn't trust him, and that nettled. Frustration wasn't an easy burden, either sexual or in friendship. He wanted to carry Maggie to his bed, just to hold her close.

She was running too hard—and from him, from the sexual attraction that had snapped and heated between them earlier. He'd wanted to taste that sweat between her breasts, feel the slick softness of her beneath him, and the strength.

Nick sucked in air, remembering the incredible sounds she'd made in the shower. Another minute and he might have joined her.

Maggie would probably explode when she discovered that Nick's cousin, Vinnie, at Vinnie's Automotive had made a late-night call to her pickup, replacing the battery. Vinnie hadn't needed keys and while he was under the hood, he did a few minor fix-ups, replacing the hoses she'd taped.

Nick smiled slightly. Vinnie looked tough and bragged about his "time in the joint," but he was a soft touch; he'd always loved the image of being a knight in shining armor—or Santa Claus. Out of respect for Vinnie, none of the family pointed out that his tough jailbird image came from protecting an abused child from her parent. Maybe he'd chosen the wrong way, letting the woman know how it felt to be slapped, and hard.

Was that what had happened to Maggie?

Is that why she always stepped back from what ran between them? Fear of abuse? *From him?*

"I'm back with my special cucumber, pore-tightening mask. I've added seaweed. Then you're going to have a real treat—

my new moisturizer, packed with chamomile and E and all good stuff, including ylang-ylang. You're the first to try it. I want to know what you think." Celeste eased Beth's shoes, if that's what the bits of leather straps could be called, off the coffee table. Amethyst, citrine, and other crystals in abalone shells ranged across the walnut, a pretty display, catching the candle's light. Between the shells were Celeste's best teacups, decorated with delicate sprays of light green Queen Anne's lace.

After a salad dinner in Celeste's tiny kitchen, the three friends sat in her living room. She'd chosen the herbal tea carefully, a blend of chamomile, to relax her friends. She wanted to lessen the interference of their shields because she wanted to prowl through their thoughts and emotions. Impressions and sensations might give her more.

Celeste had purified her home with sage; she wanted none of her fears to touch them: Beth, caught by life into less than she could be, merely needing a helping hand to create a new life; Maggie, obviously caring for Beth and unaware that danger stalked her, and that Nick's desire for her was so intense that he would wait through time.

"Guinea pigs, that's what we are. But you're a genius, Celeste. I'm in heaven." Beth's face ran smooth beneath Celeste's hands as she applied the mask. The young bones were strong and good and pure beneath her experiences. Her face lifted like a child's to Celeste's gentle ministrations, the girl craving love that she'd never had. *Soon*, Celeste thought, *soon he will come to you and do not turn him away, Beth* . . .

The girls' night at her home was paying off. Her cats were purring, snuggled tight against Beth. She would need them to find her way, and they would need her as a champion.

Maggie watched the candle's flame, locked in her struggles with the past, the locket in her hand.

Celeste couldn't pinpoint the danger, because Maggie didn't know it existed. Whatever was causing those shadows beneath her eyes said she wasn't at peace. It didn't take Celeste's psychic powers to see the ache in Maggie's expression when she looked at playing children, to feel the chilling fear of water, to know that the locket had special meaning to her.

*Why was Maggie in danger? Why did it seek her? Why would Celeste die?*

Maggie settled back on the lavender-scented pillow, allowing Celeste to spread the relaxing mask on her face.

When she touched Maggie, Celeste almost gasped; the gripping sense of her own death was stronger.

"Is something wrong?" Maggie frowned slightly, watching Celeste.

"No, of course not. I was just thinking about the mixture and the scent, how to improve it. How does it feel?"

Maggie leaned back, once more relaxed. "Lovely. I've never had anything like this. You're a genius, Celeste."

"You're working too hard, Maggie, if you can be swayed by a bit of beauty butter. How's business? And where is Scout?" The dog was always present, always protective.

Celeste saw a puppy, tethered to a stake and lying down in the mud. She saw a hand ready to strike—

"She's with Nick and Dante on the beach. Don't ask me. Boys and beer and bratwursts on a beach, and my dog happy as can be, running into the water to fetch sticks. She runs off to see Nick when she can."

"What girl wouldn't?" Beth drawled. "So is that why you're down there so much? To retrieve your dog?"

"Smart mouth. Yes, I've had to go after her a few times. I don't know why I put up with you," Maggie said after a moment.

But Celeste did. The link was immediate and deep. Beth was changing, her self-respect growing, and part of the reason was that she wanted Maggie as a friend. Beth had taken a part-time job at Celeste's and was staying with her more nights than not; the harsh makeup had softened and the sexy tight clothing had slid into T-shirts and jeans.

In return, Maggie had found someone in Beth whom she had loved and lost.

Celeste forced herself back to the girls-only night, needing to see how the two women reacted to each other—her heirs and her family. Her cats would need them, and perhaps the little cottage, too, for comfort with its herbs and fragrances, the soft sounds. Perhaps because she knew her end was near, Celeste held these two friends more closely, wanting their happiness more than her own.

They would eventually circle Lorna and draw her into their warmth, freeing her of shadows, just as the loving woman captured inside Lorna deserved.

Beth and Maggie were comfortable in Celeste's home, moving easily in the kitchen. Even now, Beth had left some clothing in the extra bedroom where she had begun to stay. Almost wistfully, Maggie had weeded the rue and lavender before dinner, as though she wished for her own home. Her hand had skimmed Celeste's furniture, the mark of a woman who loved tending her home and beloved possessions. Where were they? Those possessions that Maggie needed?

Maggie had come from a terrible journey; her life hadn't been perfect.

Celeste pieced the facts she knew of Maggie's life—she'd lost her father, been raised by a loving, strong mother, loved her younger sister who had passed away—ah, there, there was friction and torment that tangled with a marriage Maggie had wanted desperately to work, and it hadn't. That much was easy to read: When one is betrayed, the bitterness remains in the turn of the mouth, the wary shadows of eyes. In the month and a half of their friendship, Celeste had gathered bits of Maggie's life and stored them away. The images of the two young girls with copper-colored hair were very strong, just as powerful as ones of the mistreated dog.

Perhaps Celeste's abilities gave her more cause to listen closely to Maggie, to find small nuances within her words and to draw from them:

"My mother was a good role model—she had to work too hard after Dad drowned," Maggie had said. "Mom never recovered from losing him, but she forced herself to go on for my sister and me. Mom died when I was twenty-one."

Bitterness came slipping through with her comment. "I thought I could count on a man once. But, put to the test, I wasn't that important to him."

Then at a different time, Maggie had said, "I wish my sister could see me actually stand in water and try not to be afraid. She was younger and a good swimmer. She's gone now, but she understood. I miss her so much."

The locket was part of her sister; Maggie's habit of touching it came more often when she spoke of a younger sister.

Her father had drowned—that explained her fear of water, that pained look as Maggie gazed out onto Lake Michigan . . .

A betrayal, a mistreated puppy . . .

But there were so many unanswered questions about Maggie, the pieces of the puzzle unmatched and bothersome.

On the porch, the goddess wind chime tinkled slightly, warningly, rhythmically, counting down to Celeste's time to die . . .

Again, Celeste pulled herself back, focusing. She wiped her hand on the towel around Maggie's throat and couldn't help the shudder passing through her—the locket gleamed on Maggie's chest.

The connection leading to Celeste's death came from the locket and the dog—but how?

Whatever stirred inside Maggie, Celeste would be the key to unlock it . . .


In his wine cellar, Nick ran his hand over the bottle's surface, critically studying the slope of the shoulders and the punt, or raised indenture at the bottom. He placed the bottle—an expensive reserve red—on its side in the rack. In time, he would strive for a more distinctive style and upgrade the label with a frame of gold. He ran his thumb over the Alessandro logo—the picture of a man with a small boy at his side, bending over a row of small grape vines, just as Nick remembered being with his grandfather.

Outside, the early July sun was bringing the sweet harvest,

and in late September the grapes would be fat and lush.

Maggie had said she was busy tonight with a client, and he missed her. He'd grown to expect her chasing after Scout, eventually helping him prepare dinner, then taking Scout down to the beach. It was a time to know and wait and let the flavors of friendship ripen and deepen.

The desire pressing him made waiting difficult, because the scent of Maggie, the look of her could make him ache instantly. Even the thought of her could distract him. One look at her jogging, her breasts bobbing gently, the sheen of sweat on her skin, the muscles of her body moving in a rhythmic push-up was enough to stop his mind completely, and his body shot into full hard alert.

He turned to the shaft of bright light coming through the open door of his cellar. Eugene and Beth stood at the doorway to the stairs, then Beth was flying down to him. Her footsteps echoed eerily in the large cellar, her face pale and terrified as she collided with him.

He held her away and watched her fight for breath. "What's wrong?"

"It's Maggie. She has an appointment with a customer at his house—it's that rented Evans place on Lakeshore Drive. I heard it in the tavern just now. He's one of them—the summer people—and has his own boat. It's tied up to the Evans's private dock now. He's not sweet and I don't think he's really wanting a sports massage. At the bar, I just heard that he's got his buddies coming in later for a little dessert—I know of a girl who got hurt awful by them down the coast. I took off early and Ed didn't like it, to tell you. Oh, Nick, you've got to get her away from there."

Nick tried to leash his panic. His hand trembled as he replaced the bottle in the rack and tried to balance his fear for Maggie with how much she wanted to start a good business. Her excitement had been happy, bursting over the telephone lines to him. "Nick, I've got a favor to ask. Is it possible for you to keep Scout tonight, just until I can pick her up? I've got this great appointment—if it works out, I'll have a really good client who can provide referrals. I've been working piecemeal, but this could mean a step up to my own exclusive clients. He says he's allergic to dogs, or I'd take Scout with me."

Nick had driven into town to collect Scout, and when she was seated beside him, Maggie had leaned into the window, lightly kissing his cheek. She was riding on excitement, and when he turned slightly, the kiss lingered and tasted, and hungered. Impetuously, she'd reached into the pickup cab and held his head as they kissed, each seeking the other, satisfied for the moment. "Thanks," she'd said.

"Come in here, and we'll go for a ride," he'd invited when he could talk, because Maggie's quiet reserve had slipped for once, allowing him into the woman.

She'd laughed knowingly and playfully ruffled his hair. "You want more than to take a ride."

"Some other time?" he offered, steaming and feeling quite rosy himself. But she had run into Ole's, waving back at him. That slight jiggle of her butt had left him with the hard knot of desire that even hard work in the vineyard wouldn't ease.

"Nick?" Beth was urging as she and Scout followed him up the stairs.

Terror wrapped its ugly fist around him; Maggie could be—"I'm on my way."

Eugene held open the outside door. "Beth told me. I just called Old Reno. He fishes down there by the Evans place. That thirty-footer, high-class outfit just took off down the harbor, out to the lake. The guy was helping a woman into the boat. She looked like she needed it. Said she was a red-haired woman. Maggie—"

"I know. Tell Old Reno that I need to borrow his boat, okay? And call Dante, tell him to meet me at the boat."

"Sure. Don't let anything bad happen to Maggie, Nick. She's not like that party crowd we get in sometimes."

"Nothing is going to happen to her, Eugene," Nick said and prayed that he was right. "Come on, Scout."

Nick rammed the vehicle into gear and spun out of the parking lot. If Beth was mistaken, all that could happen was a little embarrassment for him. If Maggie was in danger—he didn't want to think further and focused on racing to the harbor. She was terrified of water, but she just might have overcome that in her desire for a new client base. *Or not.*

Maggie couldn't shove the haze in her head away. She remembered Leo Knute serving her an iced cola, which she drank as he asked about her background and skills, if she had any family in Blanchefleur. It seemed an innocent thing to do, chatting with a client over a soft drink, getting him to relax and become comfortable with her. From the boat moored at the dock and the luxurious interiors of the house, the way he dressed, he seemed to have money and friends. A connection with wealthy friends who could—

Maggie's stomach churned as the floor seemed to shift and the lush interior of his home became the varnished, plush cabin of a cruiser.

A powerful motor hummed, the night sliding by the windows, and Maggie couldn't shake free of the fog in her head. She remembered the man helping her walk, his arm around her, easing her down the ladder. Dimmed fear of the water lapping against the boat had kept her moving to his command.

Now she was on a sprawling round bed, gripping one side as she eased upright. A wave of nausea hit her and she closed her eyes. Her head spun, trying to put the pieces together, and then the motors cut and she heard water slap against the boat.

Not even her fear of water could shove away the fog in her head, the heaviness of her body.

Summoning all her strength, Maggie eased to her feet and Leo opened the cabin door. His shirt was unbuttoned and he held a bottle of whiskey. "Hi, honey. Ready to play?" he asked, leering at her. "I knew you were fully packed and all woman. Now let's see just how much."

He moved toward her, and still Maggie couldn't push herself into fast-forward. Her hand was too heavy to push him away. His hands were on her, hurting, his mouth wet and open on hers as he shoved her against the wall. "Let's have a little action before the rest of the guys get here, honey. Let me see what you've got."

"Get off me." But she was too weak to push him away.

"I like a little fight. But not too much," he warned roughly. Leo ground his body against hers. He smelled of alcohol, his eyes glazed as he held her hair painfully, his tongue licking at her cheek like an animal preparing to feast on its victim.

She knew how to defend herself, but now her body was too heavy, her moves were too slow.

"You're fighting it, honey. You need a little drink with a little go-power in it—"

"No." Her lips felt rubbery, her tongue swollen and dry.

"We're going to have a party. You'd better warm up some. The rest aren't as nice as me," he warned roughly, gripping her upper arms painfully hard.

"Let . . . go."

She'd fought a man before, managed to protect herself, but now she couldn't. The burn at her throat and the sliding of the chain from her said she was losing Glenda's locket. She couldn't lose Glenda, not again.

*Where was Scout? Where was she?*

*Nick, take care of Scout, please. She's all I have of Glenda. And Beth. Please help Beth . . .*

Tears burned her lids, not from pain, but from helplessness, watching herself become what Glenda had become, knowing now the realities and the shame from experience.

Leo cursed as he began pushing her toward the bed.

He was over her, and still her hands couldn't rise to push him away.

Then a crash sounded in the foggy distance and Leo was torn from her, flying into the wall. Scout was barking and snarling, the sounds indistinct and primitive, then Nick's face was over hers, his hand pushing away the hair on her damp face.

Men were growling, the primitive male sounds of threats served and returned. Dante asked, "Is she hurt?"

Nick was too silent, his face slashed by a brutal contrast of light and dark, his hair tangled as if by wind, his eyes burning down at her. It was a cruel face, wrapped in rage, capable of—"Yes, she's been hurt."

Then his expression softened; there was a tenderness in his touch as he cradled her cheek, inspecting her face and taking the pulse at her throat.

She was ashamed he could see her like this—helpless, tears oozing from her lids, trailing down her cheek, and she turned away from him. This was what Glenda had become, what she had experienced. "My locket—"

"What?" Nick demanded roughly and turned from her, leaving her with the need to hold her locket, to know that it was with her.

"You can't just break in here and—" Leo was saying. His body hit the wall with a thud and he grunted.

"You put your hands on her," Nick was saying in a low, uneven tone edged with violence.

Scout snarled, and the storm was in the cabin now, harsh and loud.

"Get that dog off me!" Leo screamed frantically.

"Nick, Maggie needs you. I'll take care of this mess," Dante warned, somewhere in the haze that floated outside her body.

"Scout," she managed to whisper. Immediately, the bed dipped, the big dog coming to her, lying chest and front paws over her.

But the storm continued, terribly, frightfully, hard, abrupt, and then Nick was bending over her again, his expression savage. "Come on," he said roughly, picking her up and carrying her easily.

"Mmm—" She couldn't leave her locket, couldn't lose Glenda.

"It's in my pocket. Your locket is safe. Did he . . . ?" Nick's question slid into oblivion as Maggie gave herself to the beckoning darkness and the safety of his arms.

# NINE

In flashes of heat and power, Nick's anger ricocheted off the tile walls of the shower; his dark mood trembled in his hands, reflecting his struggle to control it. Yet he handled Maggie carefully, firmly beneath the stinging shower. She tried to twist away but couldn't.

She'd been in Nick's pickup, held tight against him as he drove, and she remembered answering the questions he'd demanded. What were they?

She had weakly batted her hands at him as he slid away her wet clothing. "Let me look at you," he said grimly.

With streams of water pouring down on her, Nick turned her head to one side, found the burn at her throat where her chain had been torn away, and cursed. "Your locket is safe, Maggie. Let me see about the rest of you."

She wanted to crumple into a fetal position, to protect herself. Was this how Glenda felt, not only bruised but demeaned as well?

Nick's big, callused hands ran lightly over her nude body, slick with soap, and paused over the bruises on her arms. His breath hissed by her in the steam, filled with rage she hadn't suspected him capable of having. Nick had wanted to take her to the clinic, but she couldn't stand anyone looking at her, touching her . . . no one but Nick.

"You've got to file charges, Maggie. Dante is holding Leo now, waiting for you to decide."

She shook her head and covered her breasts with her arms. But fully understanding her sister's shame overrode all pain.

Maggie gasped as Nick gently worked shampoo into her hair, rinsing just as carefully. She had kept her eyes closed, not wanting to face him with her shame, and now Nick cradled her jaw between his hands and whispered roughly, "Open your eyes, Maggie. Look at me."

"No, I don't want to."

"You've done nothing wrong. Open."

The stinging shower had flattened his hair to his head, water dripping from the waves, a veil of steam softening his harsh face. His thumb lightly crossed her jaw and his eyes burned through the steam, pinning her.

She recognized the silent question and shook her head. "I don't think so."

"I don't either. You're too aware of your own body and the changes in it. You would have known. Can I hold you?" he asked, smoothing her shoulders and her back. "Just hold you . . . I need that," he added shakily.

He looked as if he'd been to hell and needed comfort, and Maggie couldn't deny him. When she nodded, Nick slowly, gently, folded her against him and rocked her. "It's going to be okay, Maggie. Everything is going to be okay."

Nick was strong and naked against her, and careless of their bare bodies, all sensuality gone now, she needed his strength, his tenderness.

"It's so awful," she whispered against his throat, the raw reality of what had happened to Glenda making her ill.

"Yes," Nick eased her closer, the shower steaming around them. "Yes, it is."

Nick's cold anger was almost terrifying, contrasting with his gentle treatment of her. But his set expression, the tight press of his lips, and that thunder and lightning flash of those black eyes spoke of a dark, dangerous storm within him.

He wouldn't let Maggie go to sleep when all she wanted to do was to sink into oblivion and forget. He rolled up the cuffs of the shirt she wore and placed a cup in her hand. Sitting on the coffee table opposite her, Nick's jeaned legs framed her own bare ones. The press of his legs against hers insisted and Maggie frowned at him. "I hate coffee."

"Drink it," he ordered, urging the cup up to her lips.

The sip of coffee was hot and fragrant, jolting her, and she handed the cup back to him. "That is pure mud."

Violence ran beneath his soft tone, as if he wanted revenge, as if little kept him from returning to Leo. "Think of me as your mother, giving you cod liver oil. You'd take that, wouldn't you? Think of coffee as a payback for not taking you to the clinic when I wanted. But oh, no, I let you talk me out of that, so you owe me. You should be watched for the drug's effects, to see that it didn't leave any lasting harm. But oh, no, you wouldn't have that. So drink that coffee and shut up, or we can pack up and go to the clinic right now."

"Boy, you're in a bad mood," she managed.

"I've got a right to be. I'm not a doctor, and what if something happens to you, stubborn woman. Now drink that coffee."

Maggie took the cup he handed her and sipped the dark, fragrant brew.

Her ex-husband should have shown that much emotion, but instead he hadn't believed her, that Brent Templeton had tried to rape her, that Brent had come into their home while she was in the tub bathing and had attacked her. Oh, no, Ryan hadn't wanted to believe her—because Brent was an influential man and could ruin their business. She was just imagining the attack, maybe she'd fantasized about Brent, and so on, anything to save the lucrative business with Brent. She wasn't worth her own husband supporting her, believing her. But then, after all, she had a prostitute and a drug addict for a sister, didn't she?

Maggie moved the shirt's hem over her bruised thighs, because after a glance at them, Nick's scowl said his anger roamed too close to the surface.

The cold anger eased just that bit, and warmth curved his lips. "Stop pouting. I bet you were a difficult child and probably spoiled rotten. By the way, Celeste called the gym and your appointments and canceled them. Dante retrieved your bag and massage table from the Evans house, too. So all you have to do is be a good little girl."

"I think I hate you," she said darkly.

"Then you're feeling better. I love it when you snarl. Finish drinking that."

"You're not the boss of me." Admittedly, the remark was childish, but the only one she could summon.

That brought his grin. "I am for now."

"Just wait," she threatened. "I am not going to forget how you bullied me."

He walked her then, his arm around her, Scout pacing at her side. And the more the haze cleared, the more she saw his silent anger, the determination for revenge. She couldn't let him unleash that terrible rage. "Don't leave me, Nick."

His silence wasn't reassuring. If she fell asleep now, he could return to Leo and Nick's whole life could be ruined by a wealthy man set on revenge. The power of money and law sometimes wrapped together, and Nick was struggling to put his life right, to grow his business. "Stay with me, Nick," she asked, turning to hold him. "Stay close."

Whatever happened this night would set the wheels of her death in gear, Celeste acknowledged sadly as she packed her herbs and creams into a wicker basket. She looked at Maggie, curled beside Scout on the bed, and whispered, "It's a natural sleep now, Nick. You've done a good job. She's exhausted. Let her sleep and heal. Make certain to keep that salve on her throat—it won't scar to remind her. If you have any questions about the herbs I've left, just call me any time."

"I will." In the shadowy bedroom, Nick's hands were in his jeans pockets, his chest bare. With stubble on his jaw and angry lines cutting his face, Nick looked raw, like a man barely controlling himself and poised to spring into action. The hollows of his face seemed haunted and desperate, his lips pressed tightly together, the cords bunching in his jaw and down his throat to those powerful shoulders.

Then his fists were tightly knotted at his side, a big workman's hands that could kill—Maggie had been right to make him promise to stay with her.

Leo wasn't worth Nick's life. Only the woman on the bed tethered him, her plea to stay with her. "I'm afraid to touch her. Put her locket on her, will you? She asked about it when he— Dammit, he tore that chain off her. It cut her throat."

"The wound will heal well. Yarrow is amazing. I grabbed some fresh clothing from her camper—she'd already given me a key. Get rid of her other things. They'll be a reminder." Celeste bent to slide the repaired chain around Maggie's throat, and as if sensing comfort, she turned and snuggled closer to the dog.

Nick's gaze had never left Maggie. "She should have had an examination and a rape kit. Then, I was only interested in getting his touch off her, and waking her up. She didn't think she had been raped, and she's an athlete, pretty aware of her own body. I recognized the prescription bottle that was in Leo's pocket as one for muscle relaxers. I had no idea how many he'd given her. What if they'd killed her? Or he'd put something stronger in the bottle? I should have taken her to the clinic, no matter what she wanted, but she was crying, begging me not to. That guy should be in jail right now."

"You did the right thing. She didn't want medical help, or the questions that came with it—somewhere in her life, she's had very bad experiences with that. He didn't rape her, Nick."

Those narrowed black eyes pinned her, staking her with

the angry violence that Nick had leashed. "How do you know?"

Celeste didn't often share her powers with someone else, but this was the exception. "I would know. I knew when I put my hands on her. Her pain is more from the journey she's traveling now, blending with the past."

The unexpected release of Nick's violence went hissing, slithering around the room, startling and nipping at Celeste. She hadn't expected the depth and the fury of his rage.

"He was set to give her other drugs to stimulate sex and he'd invited his friends. Maggie won't prefer charges. She's been through something like this before, Celeste. She told me she didn't trust the law, and wouldn't go to them. She tried legal charges once and they laughed at her, told her that she'd be slapped with harassment if she didn't stop. No one believed that she'd been attacked in her own home, not even her own sister. They told her she was imagining it, that she had a 'thing' for the guy, and when he wasn't playing ball, she charged him with attempted rape. She's been attacked before and no one believed her. No one helped her."

There was one more piece to the puzzle that had been missing. Maggie had been attacked before—by whom? Why? The questions circled Celeste, the bits she knew of Maggie leading her on like a bird following a trail of seed. But the trail ended abruptly, because Celeste didn't sense that Maggie had been abused—at least not physically. "She told you this?"

"She told me—she doesn't know . . . on the way coming home. Her sister was a prostitute and now Maggie knows how she felt. I think she cried more for her sister—Glenda was her name—than for herself. Glenda left two kids— boys—and Maggie can't stand to look at them because they remind her of her sister. I never want to hear a woman cry like that again—like her soul was being torn from her."

*Click.* The pieces fit into place. Maggie was on the run

from her past, from her disillusionment with the law and her life. Maggie's interest and affection for Beth, the way she looked at children, that locket.

That information whirled around Celeste: The women were linked, fitting the trail of bits to lead to Maggie's sister. A loving woman, Maggie would naturally miss her sister's children. Her sister had been a prostitute, and if Beth's path had continued, she was likely to be one, too. Maggie had done everything in her power to sway Beth. *Click. Click.*

Nick's fists were at his side, the grazed flesh strained white against the knuckles. "Do you think Maggie's ex-husband beat her? Attacked her?"

"No. Until now—this attack—she wasn't a victim of physical abuse—I think the pain from her ex-husband was deeper than that. Without the use of drugs, she's pretty capable of defending herself. Very capable. She's been teaching Beth basic self-defense. They're close, you know. Like sisters." *Click.* No one had believed Maggie, supported her, not even the sister she loved. The other logical person she would seek support from would be her husband. They were divorced. He hadn't stood beside her. Why?

Nick's struggle to control his need to avenge Maggie stormed around the room, battering Celeste. His beast was close to the surface, snapping at the leash, but Nick was a strong man and mindful of Maggie's wishes. "She doesn't want Beth to see her now."

"I'll take care of it. Beth knows something happened, because of Leo luring her to the boat, but she won't question why Maggie is staying with you for a couple of days. She'll just think that you and Dante headed off trouble—or that's what we'll say, if she asks." Beth, the little sister Maggie wanted to protect . . . the sister she couldn't protect. The links were growing stronger and bringing Celeste closer to her death.

If only she could protect Beth and Maggie. . . .

\* \* \*

In San Francisco, Brent ran through his daily routine of calling for new telephone listings; no Maggie Chantel turned up. He began calling major cities, keeping methodical notes on dates. An Internet search had proved useless. There was no way she could escape him. Sooner or later, he'd find her, and nothing could stop him from punishing her—and those who were keeping her from him . . .

"Eat, and stop looking like you've done something wrong. You haven't." Nick placed the plate of eggs and toast on the table in front of Maggie.

She wasn't talking; she wasn't looking at him. Maggie had cut him away from whatever was going on inside her. One thing was apparent—Maggie felt guilty about not being able to save her sister.

He knew the feeling of helplessness too well: first with his wife on life support, still and unable to climb back into life, then with Maggie, who had slept all night and all day with the aid of Celeste's herbals.

Leo and his friends wouldn't be back; Dante had seen to that. The law had let her down before, and she'd fought a futile battle with no one believing her. She was adamant: She wasn't going through that humiliation again, convinced that the law would do nothing but give her a hard time. If Maggie changed her mind and decided to press charges, Leo could be found easily enough. But Nick wanted more, his need to avenge Maggie festering as he sat in that dark bedroom, watching her. Celeste's herbs and poultice healed magically, and little could be seen of Maggie's trauma.

Except for the shadows hovering around her, a sister she mourned, and there was more—the guilt of a survivor, and Nick understood that very well.

Nick sprawled in the chair next to Maggie. Sunset crossed through the windows and that red fire leaped to her hair. If she didn't want to talk, he wouldn't pry—the hell he wouldn't. "Talk to me. You've been crying. Your eyes are all swollen."

"I'm going home." Her voice was quiet and firm, slamming that door closed to him again.

Nick's anger slid into indecision. A stubborn woman, Maggie couldn't be pushed too far. Leo could circle back, and one good jerk from an intruder could pop open the camper door. "I'd like you to stay here until you're up to talking with people."

"They'll be gossiping about us. They'll say we're living together." Her voice had changed to flat and empty. Her sister had probably put her through the hurtful bogs of gossip and somehow this was about Glenda—the name she called in her nightmares—and not about Maggie.

"That's good. At least they won't be feeling sorry for me anymore," he said lightly, hoping to persuade her to stay. *He* needed Maggie safe, to know that she wouldn't be attacked again. The thin line on her throat reminded him too sharply of how she had looked, sprawled on the bed, half undressed and vulnerable.

Maggie had drawn inside herself, shutting him out, and that hurt, squeezing him ruthlessly, painfully.

He couldn't think of anything to do but to take her hand and bend, brushing his lips over hers, telling her that he cared and he waited . . .

*Keep it light*, Nick told himself for the hundredth time. "Scout and I are going down on the beach. She's stayed close to you, but the exercise will be good for her. We'll be close enough to hear you call, or blink the porch light. Is that okay with you? Or do you want me to stay?"

*Ask me to stay. Tell me you need me . . .*

But Maggie nodded and slid her hand away, folding it with the other in her lap. "I don't want you feeling sorry for me, Nick. I've managed—"

Her withdrawal from him hurt. Her distrust included him. Wide open and flat, his hand hit the table and he stood, wanting to tell her that she wasn't alone anymore, that he cared. "Stay here and wallow in it, if you want. Come on, Scout."

Ruthless? Maybe. Nick didn't trust the emotions nudging him, the need to hold her close.

On the beach, tossing sticks to Scout, he saw Maggie standing up on the porch, watching them, her arms crossed around herself. Then the porch was empty, and Dante was walking down the beach. With an excited bark, Scout ran to meet him.

"How is she?" Dante asked, playing with Scout.

"She's a strong woman. She's working on it."

"Are you? I've known you all my life and I'd never seen you like that with Leo. For a moment there, you scared me and I've fought with you over Sarah Brown."

Nick smiled thinly, briefly, the humor not reaching his eyes. "Third grade. Pink hair ribbons. Classy in lacy socks and black patent leather shoes."

Dante's gaze skipped up to Nick's house. "Maggie is up in the lighthouse. What do you suppose she's doing?"

"Thinking." Nick looked up to the solitary figure silhouetted by the light. He knew well enough the time that thinking required; that was where he'd spent hours, prowling through the might-have-beens. "She's got a lot going on besides Leo and his boys."

Dante hurled a stick out into the water and Scout waited, leaning forward, but not moving. When Dante gave the hand command "Go," the dog leaped into the water, swimming toward the stick. He watched and then spoke to Nick. "Let me know if I can help."

"Okay. I'm not going anywhere." Nick studied the woman in the old lighthouse. If Maggie needed him, he'd be near.

It was dark when Nick and Scout returned to the house, which was brightly lit, the squares of light pouring out onto the ground. He paused at the front door, listened to the vacuum's roar, and stepped over the mound of throw rugs. The front door wouldn't open easily, and fearing for Maggie, Nick muscled it open.

He stepped around the barricade of stacked furniture and hurried into the kitchen where the dryer and washer were in full blast. Maggie stood on a chair, reaching down into the bucket of soapy water on the counter, revealing the panties she wore beneath his borrowed shirt.

Nick took a chair from on top of the table and placed it on the floor. He needed to sit badly. He'd left a woman vulnerable and wrapped in pain, and now Maggie frowned at him as if he were a trespasser. "You didn't come in the front way, did you?"

"After I got past that stack of furniture. Yes, I did."

"Look. I just mopped. Why do you think I put the chairs on top of the table?" She pointed to the damp trail of his footprints leading from the living room.

"Oh." Nick had been proven guilty. Maggie was in top cleaning form, and he was the intruder. He considered his options and came up with an uncertain "Where do you want me?"

"Out of my way."

"Oh." Nick thought the word was brilliant, considering he'd made the leap from protector and friend to offender.

"Don't you ever polish your furniture? I can't find any polish."

She sounded desperate, as if the polish were an anchor to her reality. Maybe it was—routines offered safety. "Um . . . I don't think I have any."

"Good furniture needs care, Nick," she lectured briskly as she squeezed the soapy water out of the rag and began scrubbing the cabinets. "Wood dries out with heat and air conditioning."

"Okay. Is that something your mother told you?" he asked slowly, and tried to adjust from the injured woman fighting her past to Maggie, her hair tied with an old bandana, dressed in his shirt, and standing on a chair and working furiously. He noted the iron he'd never used standing on the old wooden ironing board with a sheet pinned around it for padding. His freshly laundered clothing hung above the ironing board. "I didn't know I had so many shirts."

"They were everywhere, balled in drawers and closets.

Yes, my mother always kept the furniture polished. I used to love helping her. We—I have what is left of our family furniture. It's in storage."

He wanted to ask more, but decided against pushing Maggie now. She seemed tethered to cleaning by an invisible line, as if it were a familiar task that kept her moving away from the darkness.

Assorted buttons and thread from his junk drawer cluttered an area of the countertop beside a mound of his shirts. Nick studied the clothing on the floor and picked up a pair of his favorite shorts—worn and comfortable despite the holes—and his good-luck T-shirt, just as worn. He carefully placed them with the other clothing, protectively shoving them beneath the rest. There were limits to Maggie's cleaning, after all.

He eased to the living room, taking a better look, and then walked down the hallway. Everything was stacked and pushed aside and stripped as naked as he felt. Somehow she had managed to turn the mattress against the wall, the beds stripped and moved, windows bald without the lined curtains, closets emptied. Nick shook his head at the strength of women locked in emotional battles and returned to the kitchen. "Do you need me for anything?"

"Yes, I do. I haven't thanked you for helping me. Thank you, Nick." Maggie tossed the rag into the bucket and stepped down from the chair. She paused, wiping her hands on the shirt, then looked straight at him. "Thank you, Nick," she said more softly. "A little cleaning is the least I can do."

"You don't owe me anything."

*But she did.* Maggie knew Nick was offended, bristling sensations coming off him in waves. She gave way to the tenderness wrapping around her for a man who had held her close and whispered away her nightmares when they came creeping after her. He'd held her like a child in the shower, making her feel so safe and clean. Somehow he'd known that the cleansing away of Leo's touch was more important to her than anything else. He'd been careful to retrieve her locket, all that she had remaining of Glenda.

Maggie came to him, studying the goodness in him, the safety and the power. "I hope you don't mind. Cleaning is therapy for me. I'm sorry if I've offended you."

A quick wash of emotions crossed Nick's face, first startled, then hungry and then that tightening. "Clean away. Let me know if you need anything."

He walked out of the kitchen, and the door clicked shut a little too hard. Maggie opened it and found him out on the deck, his hands braced on his waist as he looked up at the stars. "This isn't easy, Maggie," he said when she touched his shoulder. "I want to go after that guy and—"

"Don't. I'm sorry."

"You don't have anything to be sorry for." Anger rumbled in his deep voice as he pushed his hands through his hair. "I want to help. I don't know how. There's a lot more to this than that attack. You could have been killed, Maggie. Just that easy. Or overdosed and spent the rest of your life like a vegetable. Where's the anger? Where's the need for revenge? You didn't even want the guy arrested. 'I just don't want any trouble,' you said. 'I can't take any more.' I don't undertand not turning in some scum that will probably hurt other women when he can. I don't understand how you can just mop and wash clothes and iron and pretend that nothing happened."

"Life goes on, Nick. I'm trying." She tried to keep her tone even, not to show all the emotions gathering in her, the regret that she didn't understand Glenda's downfall better. Maggie had been so certain, so righteous, so unaware of the depths of Glenda's pain. *She hadn't understood* . . .

Nick turned on her then, furious and dark and primitive. "You should deal with it. You should want to pin his hide to the wall, see that he is arrested, and make him pay."

"Money goes a long way in making people *not* pay. It wasn't worth the trouble for everyone, including you and Dante. I found that out the hard way."

Nick's hands braced on his hips, then one pushed back his hair. "I get that idea. You don't trust anyone but yourself. Let me get this straight: You wanted to protect me and Dante from some jerk who needs a lesson on how to treat women. Have you thought about yourself? Have you thought about what might have happened? That he intended to let his buddies have you?"

"Please don't lecture me, Nick. I've been attacked before. I managed then, too. I know how to take care of myself. What I need to do to survive."

His blank look changed to fury, his voice so quietly sarcastic that it shook the kitchen. "Oh, that's real nice. I thought you might tell me about that, but I really don't know anything about you, do I? Lock me out. That's a pretty damn helpless feeling, Maggie. Thanks. Just feed me bits, but not the whole story. I got a little bit of the picture when you were still drugged. Don't let me get too close. Arm's length is fine with me."

Maggie tried to force the bitterness out of her tone. "It isn't a pretty picture. There's nothing to tell. It's over. I was in the bathtub. A man broke into my home and tried to rape me. I stopped him. He was injured. I wasn't. My sister was too caught up in her own world by then. My ex-husband didn't believe me. Ryan preferred to think that I'd misunderstood a 'business partner and a friend' dropping in unexpectedly. And he didn't want 'conflict of interest' in their 'profitable arrangement.' He wanted me to forget the 'misunderstanding,' as he called it. Ryan didn't want me to make trouble. I did, but it didn't help. Men in power have a way of making problems disappear, including me."

Maggie shook her head. "My sister died—overdosed— just eight months after that. I'd made enough trouble trying to salvage her by that time, and for a while after she died. I wanted revenge and made even more trouble. The police weren't listening to me at all. I tracked down her . . . customers and the men who used her, and created scenes wherever I could find them—at work, at a party. A troublemaker is bad news for business, so no one would hire me. Then I divorced Ryan, struggled around for a year trying to find steady work, and eventually moved on with my life."

Nick's hand slapped the countertop. His emotions were all out there—the frustration, the anger, and the caring. "Clean away. The house could probably use it," he said finally as if defeated, and turned his back on her. "What do you need me to do?"

"I need you to . . ." Maggie hesitated, forming her thoughts. She needed Nick's tenderness, the way he held her in the night and day, soothing her. She needed the honesty of his passion and hunger. She needed to feel his strength—and her own—and she needed to give him what she couldn't express with words. "I need you to make love with me."

His body tensed, and it was a long time before he spoke; she counted each second with racing heartbeats. "Payback?" he asked in a deep, uneven voice. "No. I don't want that."

"No, because I need you. I haven't needed anyone for a long time, Nick. I haven't wanted anyone in my life. And now there is you."

He was silent, her heart beating so loudly it sounded like a drum. Then he said very softly, "You'd better be certain about this, Maggie. I'm not too steady right now."

She tried to keep her answer light, when she wanted him desperately, the safety and the passion burning the air between them. "I'm certain. I'm taking a shower now. I could use company. But I'll understand if you don't want me."

If he didn't want her, she'd be even more empty than before, Maggie thought as she tilted back her face to the shower's spray. Because now she cared for him.

Celeste stood in the shadows of her front porch. She needed the quiet night and the warmth of her home and animals. She held Earth close to her, stroking the cat's fur and listening to the pleasured purr. Celeste thought of her father, the way he squirted milk from a dairy cow into a waiting kitten's mouth, the way he was always safe, big hands holding her from danger.

At her side, the goddess wind chime moved within her silvery pipe cage, the musical sounds blending with the soft scents of summer.

She could only wait for the man hovering around Maggie, coming to harm her and bringing Celeste's death.

The uneven rumble of an ill-kept motor announced the arrival of a van pulling in front of her home. After the slam of a door, Celeste studied the powerful man moving toward her, anger cut into the grooves of his face.

He brought the smell of whiskey and anger, but the big fists knotted at his side, the rage on his face didn't frighten Celeste. It wasn't her time to die; he wasn't the man from Maggie's past.

She thought of her father's gentleness, her good, sturdy Midwestern upbringing and yet how the fates had called her here, to where her trail would end.

"Hello, Ed. Nice night, isn't it?"

"Beth moved out. She's here, isn't she?" he demanded roughly, and within Celeste's arms, Earth stirred and tensed, her claws digging in slightly.

Beth had come to Celeste for sanctuary, crying and worried about Maggie—and furious with Ed. "She's here and she doesn't want to see you, Ed. She knows that for a price, you put those men on to Maggie, giving them the impression that she would party with them."

Time had twisted Beth's emotions and she'd been vulnerable and alone when Ed had come into her life. Beth now fought her allegiance for the man who had rescued her from teenage prostitution. But Ed had betrayed her trust, had broken the final straw between them.

Strange, Celeste thought, because Ed did truly love Beth, in his way—with a sick mix of pride and possession and obsession, but something else deeper and more tender. He would die for her, if need be. But he'd brewed his own dark fate and wasn't the one Beth would come to love.

He moved toward Celeste, and Wind and Fire leaped from their cushions, sitting in front of her, their tails twitching slowly as though they were studying a mouse and waiting for it to move.

The night wind churned the wind chime goddess and stirred in Celeste's long loose hair, sending it in a storm around her, churning in the hem of her long gown and catching the tinkling charms at her wrist. Theatrical—perhaps. Her peers would have sneered. But Celeste knew how to stir effects, how to use them, and now she focused on terrifying Ed with that intense, close look, as if she could see into his soul.

Ed stopped suddenly, his eyes widening fearfully. "Witch woman," he muttered.

With a growl, he turned and took two furious steps away; then Celeste spoke quietly. "Ed, if you're thinking about finding Maggie—"

He turned, his face puffed and red, fists white knuckled with rage. "She's the cause of this, telling my girl to leave me, mixing in our business, giving Beth high and mighty ideas. Her mother was a tramp and so is she."

"Ed, go home and sober up. Shirley loves you. She's stayed with you all these years, even though she knew you were unfaithful, even though she knew you'd replaced her with Beth. Make some kind of a life with Shirley, Ed, or someone other than Beth. She's working for me now and she's making a new life away from you. She's paid for what you've given her, more than enough. Maggie is staying with Nick Alessandro, and if he finds out who put those men on to her, he'll come calling. As it is, you'll be lucky if he doesn't find out."

She read the indecision and the fear quivering within Ed, scurrying around like a mouse seeking a hiding place. Nick Alessandro wasn't a man to challenge, and Ed knew it. Just to make certain Ed understood perfectly, Celeste focused on him. She would protect those dear to her, and summoned her power and wrapped it around her. "Don't cross me, Ed," she said quietly, and with a small movement of her wrist caused the charms to tinkle eerily. "It's true. I am a witch. If you ever want to have sex again, just don't cross me. What is tiny could be even smaller and very, very limp."

His face turned white as he backed away. Ed hurried to his van and shot into the night. The wind chime goddess turned slowly within the silvery, musical pipes, and Celeste breathed quietly, waiting for another man, powered by fierce hatred and fury.

She lowered her face into the cat's soft fur, taking what pleasure she could of life. "My fate is sealed, but how can I protect Maggie?"

The answer came in the wind, playing in her gown and lifting her scarf as Celeste walked into the night. It came in the silvery goddess, imprisoned within her musical pipes as completely as Celeste was trapped within her fate.

In meeting her past, Maggie would meet her future—it was for her to decide.

The San Diego night, colored by neon lights and traffic sounds and bawdy laughter, slid by Brent's hotel window. The reflection in the glass was that of a scarred man, eyes burning bright within the hollows of their sockets, hair thin and limp over a skeletal face, the scrawny neck within a too large collar.

Maggie was out there, somewhere, and he'd find her.

None of this was his fault; she'd taken everything, betrayed him.

He folded his clean socks and put them into plastic bags, placing them on top of others in his suitcase.

She was his obsession, the woman who had ruined his life.

When she was under his power, his luck would change—he would make it change.

Maggie owed him, and when he found her, she would pay.

He turned back to the almost specterlike reflection in the cheap hotel's window. "It's only a matter of time, Maggie dear. There are always people to help me, because I have the power over them, just as I will have over you. The right person, that's all I need to find you. Just one person will lead me to you."

# TEN

"Do you have any idea what it does to a man, just to listen to you taking a shower? Those—those noises you make? To distract myself, so I wouldn't get in there with you, I put all the furniture back and made the beds. Do you have to sound like you're making love?" Nick demanded rawly when Maggie came out of the shower.

She knew him for a patient man, taking his time, setting his limits, pacing himself. But right now Nick looked just perfect—at the end of his leash, his body tense and desire etching the bones of his face.

He looked like a man uncertain of his control, and that suited Maggie perfectly. She reached to adjust the towel wrapped in a turban around her head and purposely allowed the one tied around her chest to slip a bit.

Nick's stare locked onto that damp towel, knotted between her breasts, and her confidence to seduce him inched higher—because she needed him badly, the tenderness and safety that was Nick to wipe away the feel of being unclean and used. He would touch her in just the right way, taking his time—and at the moment, his patience was a problem.

"I enjoy the shower's space. You're right about the camper being tiny. It was sheer luxury. Have I upset you?" she asked, moving toward him. Maggie enjoyed the rare feeling of being a female predator, set on capturing a wary male. She slid Nick her best flirtatious look, and his expression darkened. She enjoyed seeing the battle within him, lust fighting his control, that step-by-step assurance, that muscle twitching on his cheek, the searing burn of his eyes beneath those long black lashes. She strolled a fingertip down his cheek and circled that locked jaw. "Isn't making love to me now in the rules, scheduled in your personal timetable?"

Nick leaned back against the counter, breathing deeply and crossing his arms over his chest. "I'll bet you were the kid who couldn't wait for dessert."

Maggie slid the towel from her hair, rubbing it over the wet strands. She watched Scout pad into another room as if she were bored with the humans. "Sometimes dessert is better when it's first."

"Let me have that," he said roughly and took the towel from her hands. "You jiggle in all the right places when you do it."

"Mmm," she crooned, giving herself to the luxury of his gentleness, breathing in the scent of his body and the hunger that filled it.

"Stop it."

"Make me."

His hand was in her hair, fisting it, and drawing her face up to his. His gaze burned, traveling over her skin, taking in her features. "I don't want you to regret this later, Maggie. To blame your trauma for what might happen between us. I will not take advantage of you."

"In this, I know what I want. You. What happened doesn't change that." His body heated hers, the desire written starkly on his hard-boned features. She moved her hips against the thrust of his body. Her need was primitive and simmering. "This just kicked up the pace a bit, because you were taking too long."

"I thought I'd let the situation ripen a bit. Get to know each other better. Make you trust me."

Once she'd been made to feel undesirable, less than a woman and more like a machine. She needed to feel now, to leap into the current of heat between them. To take and to give, to know that she was a woman and alive. "Dating? You want to date? The situation is here and now. Stop talking."

Nick closed his eyes, his expression grim. He shook his head. "I had planned quite the moment, seducing you. Watching your eyes turn that dark color of rich summer earth. You are a very earthy woman, dear heart. A physical one."

"Talk . . . talk . . . talk . . ." Maggie smoothed his shoulders, found the taut resistance there, digging her fingers in slightly, because he wasn't getting away. She stood on tiptoe to briefly kiss his lips. When she lowered, Nick's gaze locked onto her breasts against him and his breath caught.

The hunger that she needed was right there, simmering hot and potent in his eyes, the taut lock of his body. She smoothed his chest with her open hands, his heart pounding, racing beneath her palm. "I am ripe, Nick. I've been bottled and aged. You can seduce me later."

His grunt said her humorous allusion to his precious grapes had surprised him.

Maggie traced the hot flush of his cheeks, stroking the stubble of his jaw. "Love me now, Nick. Don't think. Just—"

"I haven't been with another woman since my wife. I'm not certain I can be gentle—"

She stood on tiptoe to kiss him, and his arms tugged her tight against him. His mouth was hot and hungry on her own, the edge of his teeth nipping erotically. His tongue tempted and seduced; his unsteady deep sound telling of a hunger that ran trembling down his body.

Maggie sighed inwardly, savoring the pleasure and the anticipation. Nick knew exactly where to put his big hands, open on her, drawing the towel away from the back, firmly, gently, until her body pressed against him.

Those hands cruised her body, cupping, heating, sensing shape and softness, and smoothing.

With a rough, deep sound, he slanted the kiss, fusing their lips together, and she tasted his passion, the demand, and the gift—but gentleness ran there, too, in the trembling of his hands as they cupped her breasts, finding the taut peaks.

Big and magnificent and so hot, Nick vibrated with life, hunger, and passion—and she was as greedy for him. Then the big hands beneath her bottom lifted her easily, and he continued to kiss her as he walked toward the bedroom.

She framed his face, started to go deep into his flavors, and stopped. "Nick?"

He was staring at her breasts, then his mouth closed over her nipple, searing it, and Maggie cried out, caught by the riveting heat leaping through her. "Nick . . ."

"You are truly ripe and sweet and you smell so good—" He nuzzled the hollow between her breasts, one hand edging deeper, intimately, sending a liquid jolt through Maggie. She hissed, her body taut as the constriction hit her, throwing back her head as pleasure went ripping through her.

In a soft, warm haze, she realized he'd passed the master bedroom and had entered a smaller one.

In the shadows of his room, he lowered her carefully upon the bed, standing over her. His eyes locked with hers as he ran his hand down her body, skimming the curves and hollows, the ridge of her hipbone and lower, to the inside of her thighs. "You're quivering."

His expression darkened as his hand rose to cup her, stroke her.

"Now is not the time for patience, Nick," she managed breathlessly as she caught his hand and tugged hard.

He resisted just that moment and then stood to tear away

his clothing. He eased down on her, lodging full and hard over her, bracing his arms by her head, smoothing her hair on the pillow.

"I know," he said softly, unevenly, at her slight frown. "But right now, your aroma and bouquet are incredible."

She drew her nails down his back. "Action, not appreciation, okay?"

His nuzzle on her neck was playful and told her that he understood. Nick reached into a drawer by the bed.

"I had hopes," he whispered rawly, explaining the condoms. Then he was back, easing gently into her.

Her body tightened, remembering trying so hard to have sex when the emotions weren't there—

His back flowed beneath her palms as he began to kiss her, deep, long soft, drugging kisses that soothed and warmed.

"You taste so good," he murmured against her throat, nuzzling her as his body shifted slightly, welcomed by hers.

She closed her eyes, pleasured by the fullness deep within. Then Nick began to move and the storm began whirling around her, mixing shadows with heat and breath and scents and sensations. Textures and strength and gentleness all blended into smooth movement growing faster, running ahead of Maggie, and she had to catch it—

In the distance, she heard the sound of Scout barking, as if she wanted attention.

Nick's body tensed at the same time the riveting constrictions took her higher and tighter and burst, leaving her high keening sound and his deeper, raw one mating in the shadows.

Maggie closed her eyes and floated, cradling Nick, soothing them both from the summit, his face pressed against her throat.

The bed suddenly depressed with Scout's weight and she nuzzled Maggie's face, seeking reassurance. Maggie stretched out a hand for her pet, but when Nick would move away, kept him close by gently biting his ear. "Don't go anywhere. She sleeps with me. She's worried you're hurt-ing me."

He tensed and raised to frown down at her, a storm of fear and concern mixed in those wonderful eyes. "Did I? Maggie, it's been so long for me that I—"

"For me, too. No, you were very careful. You didn't hurt me." In that moment, it seemed as though she had a fam-ily again: Nick, who had gone from a friend to a lover, and Scout, who had seen her through so much. In just those few safe, warm, pleasured heartbeats, she wasn't alone or afraid. It seemed that the tension she'd known for years had slid away, allowing her to drift and relax. She smiled softly, know-ingly, because Nick's hands were already wandering over her, soothing and gentle.

"You made the bed." Maggie wanted more, but Nick eased her beneath the sheets. They were deliciously smooth, a con-trast to the volatile lovemaking of moments past, peace after the heated storm. She settled into the sheets with a luxurious sigh.

"I had hopes of just holding you tonight. But apparently you don't believe in taking too much time for the flavors to ripen." A smile ran through his deep tones, but she was too tired to open her eyes, sleep weighting her. She managed to reach out her hand and smooth his face, taking in the heat and the dampness and the truth between them. His kiss warmed her palm as she slid into a sleep she hadn't had for years.

She was still sleeping when Nick came to spoon around her back, drawing her closer. "Scout is fine. Go back to sleep. Stop wiggling your bottom, or—"

"Promises, promises," she whispered, turning to him. With a sigh and a smile, she gave herself to him, reveling in his body, already taut and hot against hers, his breath un-steady, his heart beating hard against her own, solid and de-pendable, those big, strong, and gentle hands moving over her, just like the man . . .

\* \* \*

In Los Angeles, hatred pushed Brent Templeton from health spa to gym, shoving the picture of Maggie at anyone who might have known her.

A cockroach slid along the battered table in his cheap room as he poured another drink. Brent leaped to his feet, brushed the insect away with a newspaper and stomped it. Using rubber gloves, he cleaned the area meticulously and used disinfectant. It was Maggie's fault that he'd had to use cheap rooms, cleaning before being somewhat comfortable in them.

One of Brent's calls had paid off, an upscale gym manager remembered Maggie working for him. Then one day a real estate magnate had come in, recognized Maggie from San Francisco, and had pressured the manager to fire her. The manager received several calls from prominent San Francisco clients who added pressure, and he'd let her go. She had acted like she was expecting it and did not object.

But then, Brent had had a hand in ruining her career and her business, too. From his motel window, he looked at a woman jogging down the street, hoping—but the woman didn't have Maggie's rich chestnut hair.

His finger circled Maggie's snapshot. "Glenda looked like you, but I much prefer the real thing, not a substitute. I wonder how you'll look when I tell you that I gave Glenda that last shot in her arm. She welcomed it like a lover, begging for it, and in my way, I put her out of her misery."

He picked up a picture of Maggie and Glenda, young women hugging each other, the same bright, penny-colored hair. "I'm a hunter and I'll find you. I'll find you," he repeated confidently.

His face loomed in the mirror, not a pretty sight. "In the year and months since you disappeared, they put me in the hospital a couple of times, and I don't have the resources I once did, but I'll find you. Please don't be dead. That would ruin the pleasure of killing you—slowly."

Then with the air of the methodical businessman he'd once been, a fast-moving entrepeneur, Brent picked up the telephone and began calling gyms and spas, looking for information.

He would find Maggie and when he did, she would be punished.

Nick fastened the locket's gold chain at Maggie's neck as she stood in front of him.

So much for taking his time and earning Maggie's trust. Their lovemaking had been pure released hungry lust, and they'd burned themselves into exhaustion.

Shocked? Yes—at himself and at Maggie's wide-open giving and demands, devouring both of them. And it wasn't enough.

She'd startled him, a physically strong woman needing a desperate, mindless release. Nick damned himself for his lack of control, making love with Maggie when she had just been through a trauma and fighting the past. He could only wait now, and try to set an even, steady pace between them.

Maggie had been full and ripe and bursting with all the right flavors, and the aftertaste only added to his desire to sip again.

In the early morning, with dawn skipping through the kitchen's window, Nick mocked his plans for dating Maggie, gently easing into the friendship he needed, perhaps as much as the sex.

But then, after three times last night and another this morning, he wasn't certain about anything—except he knew little about Maggie, about her nightmares, about her distrust of people coming too close.

When he opened the shower curtain to step in with her, he could see her fear, fear she'd kept at bay earlier. Now, although Maggie had struggled valiantly to be casual, her smile was wobbly, so Nick had taken a brisk shower and stepped out, leaving her alone.

What had happened to her, other than Maggie's love for Glenda and the pain caused by her sister's decline? he wondered.

Time, Nick cautioned himself. Give yourself and Maggie time.

But, hey. He'd already stepped into the fire too soon, hadn't he? Unable to stop, to think, to do anything but feed on their hunger—and it still simmered between them—until he'd heard those incredible sounds and had stepped into that shower . . .

Even now, with Maggie in front of him, her hair damp and fragrant, he wanted to slide his hands beneath the shirt covering her and feel her body, the curves and the strength all covered with incredibly soft skin. He'd tasted her passion, and he wanted more . . . far more. He wanted her trust and her friendship.

"I feel awkward," Maggie admitted as she moved away from him.

"If it helps, so do I. I haven't made breakfast for a woman in a long time."

He rubbed his hands roughly on his jeans, trying to push away the need to feel her skin, her body beneath his fingers. The shaving cuts on his face were from seeing his stubble in the mirror and realizing how it must have chafed her. His hands had trembled then, and the razor had nicked him. He turned his hands now, studying the width and strength and callused roughness. There in the shaft of sunlight a vision of her breast pale in the cup of his hand seemed to turn, tightening his gut and lower, with the need to have more—to carry her back to bed.

A man who had abstained for twelve years had indeed been bottled and cellared long enough to reach ripe maturity. So ripe that he couldn't resist Maggie's impatience to make love.

So much for his control and taking steps one at a time. Maybe he was feeling unsteady and vulnerable, and those were emotions he didn't like at all.

Maggie scanned the clutter in the kitchen, the contents of shelves and drawers heaped on the counter and table. The rest of the house looked much the same, the aftermath of

Maggie battling her emotions. Now those earth-green eyes were troubled, Maggie fighting too many battles alone. "I got carried away. But I don't regret anything."

"Neither do I." He loved when she got carried away, forgetting everything but him. Nick didn't want to remind her of her passion just now. Not when she looked as if she would bolt at any minute.

Just as his best wines benefited from cellaring for years, Nick wanted all the generous layers open, the rich, soft depths that came from finesse and maturation of a trusting relationship. On another level, Maggie seemed so alone, fighting wars in which he couldn't help—and feeling helpless wasn't pleasant.

She turned to him, and time slanted and hovered and breathed with possibilities and warmth. "You look so grim . . . You're upset."

"We can't undo this, Maggie. I was planning to spend more time getting to know each other. Now we're here and now I'm wanting you, not exactly thinking straight. I didn't intend to go after you like a starved man. I'm sorry that I didn't know you'd be scared when I stepped into the shower with you."

Her eyebrow hitched up as she studied him. "I'm not a bottle of wine. You were planning to let the flavors mature, weren't you? Now you're upset because your schedule is messed up. You were planning to seduce me, weren't you? Dinners, dating, that sort of thing? You did have protection ready," she reminded him.

He wished the irritating warmth wasn't rising in his cheeks. She made him sound inflexible and old-fashioned. Maybe he was. He needed courtship and the sweetness that came from discovering each other. "Something like that. This is new to me, too. So is my hunger for you. I didn't know it could be so strong."

Nick lifted her in his arms, watching her. Surprised, Maggie tensed, but she didn't hit him. He considered that a good sign, because last night, he had learned that in her hunger, she was a very, very strong woman with an appetite that surprised him. Right now, his own raging hunger frightened him.

He felt her putting distance between them, reclaiming whatever she'd given him in those burning storms, and he couldn't have that. If sex was all they had, then he would take what he could get. "Are you going to pull any of that self-defense stuff on me, like you did that day on the beach?"

He adored that smug curve of her lips. "You went down like a brick building."

"All I want to know now is, yes or no."

"Yes." This time, the game had changed, Maggie thought distantly as Nick carried her to the bed and lightly tossed her onto the rumpled sheets.

He moved with certainty, touching her just right and then claiming her so fast that her own aftermath left her breathless and stunned. He took her quickly, hungrily in that storm, and caught in it, she sensed his frustration. She managed to turn her head on the pillow and look at Nick, her hand over his still-racing heart.

Those sultry, heavily lashed black eyes returned her stare, a muscle tensing in his jaw, the set of his mouth tight and grim. Then he was off the bed, big and strong and jerking on his jeans. "I'm taking Scout down to the beach. Do what you want."

He stopped and looked down on Maggie as she drew the sheet over her body. His hands went to his hips, and the leaping fire of his anger shot into the cool shadows, quivering and hot. That deep voice was uneven and low, sizzling the distance between them. "So here we are. And I don't know that much more about you than when we met. I don't know why you shut doors when I come too close. Apparently, I have no resistance to you, but I'm not paying for the man who hurt you. I didn't do it, Maggie. You're all tangled up in something I can't understand and yet it spills over to me. You don't want to talk. Fine. Don't."

Maggie sat up slowly and drew the sheet around her, taking her time. Nick had laid out his mood for her, no holds barred. He wasn't threatening her. Caught between the afterglow of a storm of lovemaking and an obviously frustrated man seeking answers, Maggie fought for balance.

"I don't like being pushed. I should be going," she stated cautiously.

Nick's hand slashed the air. "Fine. Go. Hit and run. Run away. What's the matter? Hasn't anyone ever asked you why you're on the move? Why you haven't found a place that suits you? Have they asked what you're looking for?"

No one had. She hadn't allowed anyone close enough. While Maggie struggled with how to answer calmly, keeping her past locked inside, Nick shook his head. "You just turned pale, and those eyes are big and haunted. It's right there, Maggie, whatever you're running from. I'd like to help."

Ryan's betrayal pounded her and she swallowed, unable to speak.

Nick frowned at her a minute as an icy wall slid between them. "I guess that's my answer."

After Nick left the room, Scout sat looking at Maggie. "Go on. Go with him. I'm fine. I'm always fine."

But she wasn't. And she'd hurt Nick.

*Beth's smirk said she knew.*

In the shadows at Journeys, amid the soft scents and clutter, Maggie turned her face to hide her blush and pretended to sample the lavender foot and leg lotion. "What are you gawking at?"

"You and Nick. You're all lit up and rosy and jumpy. You had sex with Nick, didn't you?"

Maggie turned to burn a stare at Beth and found Celeste's gentle, knowing smile as she served herbal tea in her best china cups—almost as if she were celebrating. "She doesn't know what to do with him yet. He'll not take the sex without wanting more. It's the more that she fears."

Beth's derisive snort raised Maggie's temper a notch. Did

the whole world know she'd made love with Nick? "Stop it. He helped me out. That's all."

"I'm glad that Nick and Dante turned up before Leo could put the moves on you. Celeste said that Leo was planning a private party and wasn't happy that they'd ruined it. She said she thought it was a good idea for you to stay with Nick for a while. Ed had a hand in it. Celeste won't tell you, but I will. Ed came to her house for me—I'm staying there now. He backed right off when Celeste told him that you were with Nick. But don't trust Ed. He's thinks you're the reason I left him, and maybe you are," Beth stated earnestly.

"Thank you for telling Nick about what Leo might have planned," Maggie said, glad that Beth did not have the complete story.

Fire nudged against her leg, and automatically Beth reached down to collect the cat, holding her close. "Maybe you're the reason I started thinking that I might be a real person and that I was worth fighting for."

Maggie noted Celeste's approval as the other cats came rubbing against Beth's legs; crooning softly, Beth sat to gather them all up into her arms. The easy affection was there, for Celeste and for her animals, and in a pretty short print skirt and a black vest, Beth looked young and fresh. The scent of light spring flowers had replaced the heavy musk perfume Ed had preferred.

Celeste put her arms around Maggie. "I want you both to remember that I'll always be with you," she said gently.

Beth rose to her feet and frowned at Celeste. "She's weirding me out, Maggie. She says things like that, like she knows something we don't. There's all this weird stuff about Lorna, like someday she'll realize that she is a good person and to give her a chance. Sometimes Celeste looks at me and she's sad. And she keeps telling me how to tend her gardens and her shop."

"It's a thing a mother tells a daughter," Celeste said easily.

"It's truly weird," Beth groused. "I don't like it. And I don't like her roaming alone all hours of the night, either."

Maggie returned the squeeze Celeste had just given her. "It's a wonderful gift, Beth, that she cares."

"You're the element that has changed our lives, Maggie—that will change our lives."

Maggie studied Celeste, and the psychic returned a sad smile. "It's just time, Maggie. There's a time for everything. We three will always be together—and Lorna, too. Fate has joined us. Four pieces, maybe more, all women, of our private puzzle, complete when joined, and very strong—remember that."

Beth's curse hissed around the room, and Celeste smiled knowingly. "Get over it, okay? You'll see."

"It will be a cold day in hell when I think that Lorna is okay. She's sneaking around with some man now—everybody knows it, they just don't know who. Probably some married guy."

But Celeste just smiled.

Maggie wouldn't like it, but he had to know she was safe. Images of her helpless on that ship's bed had haunted his morning.

Nick crossed the street to where Scout was tethered to a park bench, her head on Mrs. Friends's lap as the elderly woman petted her. "'Morning, Nick."

"Mrs. Friends. How's the arthritis?"

"Better now that the summer is here. Thanks for plowing my little garden. Dante came and helped me work it. Maggie is looking very pretty this morning. Different and bright as a new penny."

He cleared his throat and bent to pet Scout. He hoped he sounded casual, when he hoped he was the reason Maggie seemed "different and bright." He needed all the encouragement he could get. "I can help you with that climbing rose trellis, if you want. It could use a little sturdying up."

"Thank you, but Eugene came early this morning and worked on it. He said you were feeling chipper for some reason." She patted his head, taking him back to the third grade.

Her smile was kind and knowing. She'd seen him court his wife and lose her, and now she hoped for the best. "Bring Maggie for tea sometime, will you?"

Eugene was never one for keeping secrets, Nick decided, as he stood and looked through the Journeys window to find Maggie's pale face. So, she would give him sex and nothing more, would she? His anger and frustration, bright and crisp, licked around him like sparks of fire in the early morning sun.

"She's in the shop," Mrs. Friends said gently.

"So she is." Then Nick found himself strolling through the open Journeys door, trying to look casual, when every nerve he possessed had focused on the woman who'd shared her body and not herself with him. He skipped pretending to study the bottles on the shelves and turned to Maggie. The worn T-shirt did little to hide her curves, and the frayed hem of the cutoff shorts only emphasized the length of her legs, legs that had wrapped around him last night, cradled him. Nick could still feel the sweep of that reddish hair along his chest, the soft way she panted for breath. He could still hear the high keening sound of her pleasure and with the memory of her taut body squeezing his, he heard his own frustrated groan.

Amid the layers of gentle scents, he found the one that was Maggie's and locked onto it. The scent of her flesh, sweet between her breasts, in the hollow of her throat and the inside of her elbow. The fragrance clung to where she was hot and moist and tight—

Was she so untouched by their lovemaking? Was he so easy to have that his cork could be popped that easily? That she could come strolling out of the shower, hips swaying, eyes shadowed with mystery and hunger, and have him with only a few words between them?

Aware of his size in the diminutive, feminine shop, Nick nodded to the three women, standing close together, watching him—the man who had had Maggie. Who had been had by Maggie.

" 'Morning, girls," he said casually, and wondered if he

could play her game, if he could be delectable and tasty and leave her drooling, just as she had left him.

He didn't care for Beth's saucy grin and turned to Celeste. "It seems I need a good furniture polish. What can you recommend?"

Her smile told him she knew what he really needed— Maggie's kiss to take the edge off his uneasiness, to let him know that she remembered their lovemaking. Nick turned to Maggie and hooked his hands in his back pockets to keep from reaching for her. He saw no need to talk, because the night, hot and stormy, had just leaped between them. Nick noted the pulse in Maggie's throat, the skin fine and slightly marred by his last night's stubble. The softness of her lips parted and the flick of her tongue knocked aside his plans for revenge.

She met his stare boldly, not denying what had happened between them, but not giving him more, either. She'd flattened his plans for dating and letting their relationship ripen, and gave him nothing of herself. The wound stirred within him, as well as the bitterness that she could hurt him so deeply and yet seem unaffected.

Celeste seemed to flow across her shop and returned to hand a bottle to him. "Beeswax and more. Rub it on and then wipe it off."

Without releasing Maggie's stare, Nick said, "Thanks. There's one thing more—"

He tucked the bottle beneath one arm and raised his hands to frame Maggie's face. He breathed in her surprise, taking the token of their morning-after warfare as his prize and fused his lips to hers, ruthlessly taking what he needed, a taste of Maggie.

Only when her lips softened and her body leaned toward his did he release her. A narrowed glance at her flushed face and parted lips, those drowsy witch eyes upon him, and Nick knew she wasn't unaffected.

A silly victory, he mused, as he nodded to Beth and Celeste. He struggled with the aching hot pit of need in his belly and forced himself out of the shop. Only when he was on the street did he release his breath and realize he was strangling the bottle of polish, that his palms ached to hold more than glass.

He tried to appear casual when he dragged air into his lungs, his hands sweating and shaking as Mrs. Friends smiled up at him, her blue eyes twinkling and knowing. All those years ago, when he'd been a boy, disgusted by a girl's kiss, Mrs. Friends had been right—a girl's kiss was something he could manage.

At least he'd left Maggie speechless and hungry, and that small thing soothed his ruffled pride.

Nick leaned back against Maggie's pickup and watched her carry a box from the camper. He'd handled the situation too roughly, emotionally, and he'd pushed Maggie too far, prying into the dark corners of her life. Frustrated and angry with himself, he made no attempt to hide his emotions. "So you're leaving. You're running away. That's what you do, isn't it? When life doesn't suit you and someone comes too close, you just pack up and go."

In the afternoon sunlight, overcast by heavy rain clouds, her face was pale, shadows beneath her eyes. She'd finished cleaning his house, and had left him with a sleepless night.

George Wilson had called Nick. Maggie had dropped by to talk with George and make arrangements for the return of the camper key. She'd brought Beth, who'd evidently "spilled a tear or two," and had showed her how to massage George's legs.

Eugene's call was next. Maggie had stopped by to tell him she was leaving and to instruct him on exercises. The old man was furious with Nick, telling him he was letting "one in a million slip through his fingers."

Nick didn't offer to help Maggie heft the box into the back of the pickup. He kept his arms folded across his chest because if he didn't, he'd reach for her, just to hold her against him once more. "I think you owe me an explanation for leav-

ing. I'm not asking for anything else. Was it that bad between us?"

Maggie still gripped the box in her hands, her knuckles
white, and she didn't look at him. "You know it wasn't. I'm a
hard luck story, Nick. I don't want you involved."

"This isn't personal. It's business. You need money, and I
need help at the winery, especially when we open the tasting
counter at the vineyard. I've got a wine festival in August,
and I'll need help manning the booth. I should sign up for a
couple more. They're only for a few hours, but are pretty intense. Eugene is better off resting that day."

"Ask Beth. She's trying to start a new life away from Ed."
Maggie looked at Nick, her eyes bright beneath the shadow
of her ball cap. "I want you to see that nothing happens to
Beth, that Ed doesn't hurt her. She's staying at Celeste's now
and helping with the shop. Celeste seems bothered and
seems to need reassurance."

"Does she know you're leaving?" Odd, Nick thought, that
Celeste, a woman who held Maggie's friendship dear, hadn't
called.

"Yes. I wouldn't leave without talking with her. She's distracted, but didn't seem concerned, almost as if I weren't
planning to leave. I'll send Vinnie's Automotive a check for
the battery when I have some money."

He wanted to hit whoever had hurt her so badly. "You can
work right here."

Her body stiffened, her head went back, and those dark
green eyes narrowed, the gold flecks catching the light, as
she looked directly at Nick. "I don't need your charity. I've
managed."

Nick fought for the right persuasive words because
Maggie was clearly offended. "Maybe I need you—for my
business—to help me with these first shows and to work the
showroom this first season. It's an important one for the business, the first big step out into competition. Hopefully that
big road sign and our brochures will bring in tourists who
will buy. In tourist season, it's hard to get help, even from

relatives—they've got their own businesses to manage. I really need someone this first season, Maggie. Someone to help with brochures and mailings and taking calls. You had a business and the experience we need."

"It's hard work, promotion and developing a clientele."

"That's exactly why you would suit the job." She lifted her face to the drops of rain and Nick held his breath, waiting for her to decide. "You can keep up with George and Eugene and your job at Looking Good, just by shifting your hours around a little. The pay isn't that much, but I'm hoping you'll stay."

Blanchefleur's gossip traveled fast: According to Dante, Maggie had visited Ed at the tavern. The timing placed her visit just after Nick's morning kiss.

Nick could only hope that Maggie was working off the frustration he'd given her when an hour earlier she had tossed Ed on his dirty barroom floor; she'd sat on his back, twisting his arm and making him promise to stay away from Beth.

She'd faced a man twice her size and had flattened him, and hadn't asked for Nick's help. *She hadn't even told him.*

Things would have to change, Nick thought darkly as his frustration stormed him afresh. Independent, Maggie moved on her own, careless of his need to help her. But with Maggie on the verge of leaving, he could wait to make his point. And he'd always been a patient man.

She turned and stood on tiptoe, leaning into the pickup bed, and the hem of her cutoff shorts lifted over a round cheeky softness that he had held the night before. Nick tore his stare away to look up at the gray rolling clouds. He corrected his thoughts—*before* meeting Maggie, he had always been a patient man.

Finding a woman he wanted had a way of confusing big plans. Maggie was definitely a physical woman, enjoying the challenge of lovemaking, and giving as well as taking. If that's all there was between them—

"Think about staying," he said abruptly, fearing that he would say more and humble himself entirely. "If not for a job with me, then for Celeste. Something is going on with her.

She's visited my cousin Dom, who's an attorney. He's not talking, but it's like she's putting her life in order."

"Yes, I know," Maggie agreed softly. "It's there—a sadness and an acceptance."

"Think about it, Maggie," Nick said again and hoped she would. "It's only part-time, but if you're free, it's work and a paycheck."

She leaned a hip against her pickup and reached a hand to pet Scout's head. The gold flecks swirled in her eyes, and he caught that bit of heat from her temper. She hadn't mentioned the kiss in Journeys, but it simmered between them. "On your terms," he added slowly. "Friends or something more. I'd prefer the more, but it's your choice."

Her finger traced his lips, and Nick regretted the softening in him, the nip he took at the tip.

"Your choice, Maggie," he stated firmly and knew his voice was raw with need, curling out of his gut. In another minute, he'd be having her on the ground—if she'd have him.

"If I stay, you'll pay for that kiss today."

"I can only hope, sweetheart. Inviting me into the camper, are you?"

"Not a chance. You mess up my thinking—you're a complication, Nick."

Her admission was some comfort, he decided as he managed to place his aching body into his pickup. Through the windshield, he held her look, sultry with a challenge that only a woman could give a man. Then she turned, leaving him with a mouth-watering view of the denim, tight across her swaying bottom as she moved toward the camper.

Nick's hands shook as he shifted into reverse, and he didn't look back as he drove away. He wasn't certain he could withstand Maggie on the prowl.

# ELEVEN

Maggie awoke to her own scream. The nightmarish vision of her father's hand reaching out to her, Glenda's lifeless face staring at her, faded into the silent night. Damp with sweat, Maggie kicked off the sheets and lay listening to the racing of her heart. Why couldn't she sleep without the dreams? Why were they stirring so furiously? Was it because she wanted to run from the pain and memories inside her and couldn't?

She automatically let Scout outside, then stepped into the cool, star-filled night. The moon and stars reminded her of Celeste's favorite caftan.

She hadn't wanted attachments, yet since she'd arrived in Blanchefleur, she'd seemed to gather friendship whether she'd wanted it or not.

And Nick's lovemaking wasn't exactly a forgettable experience. After a long sexual drought, it should have relieved some pressure—instead, now she wanted more. Nick wasn't an easy man. He wanted answers and had the patience to get them. He wouldn't stop pushing. She rubbed Scout's ears. "He's got that macho thing going . . . wants to protect and gets all emotional and frustrated when he's not invited to help. I didn't need him to handle Ed. We could stay longer . . . What do you think, Scout? Do you like it here? I know you do—but I can't make any promises."

Maggie looked up at the stars and shivered. "I dread going back to sleep. Let's stay outside awhile, okay?"

She thought of Nick roaming the old lighthouse, missing his wife. Maggie pushed away the urge to go to him, to burn Alyssa away. Sex was one thing; a complicated man like Nick was something else.

She knew she should leave town. But she could use the extra cash, and she wanted to stay in Blanchefleur for a while— just until she was certain that Celeste would be all right, Maggie told herself as she followed Nick in the wine cellar the next day. A new employee, she listened to his explanations and noted that his open hand caressed the oak barrels and tanks as if they held his life and dreams.

Maggie tensed, her body remembering the gentle skimming of that big hand on her body, the roughness of calluses and controlled strength, and admitted that Celeste's distraction wasn't her only reason for staying.

"We started with a well-insulated one above ground, but use this cellar now. I've shown you the fermenting vat and the crusher-destalker. We're only doing estate wines, the grapes grown on Alessandro Vineyards. The skins are left in the vat, and they rise to the top of the fermenting must. This 'cap' has to be continuously mixed back into the juice as it ferments. After fermentation, the first run of juice, the 'free-run' comes naturally. After the free-run is off, then the 'must' is squeezed for 'press wine.' The waste, or 'pomace,' is returned to the earth. Depends on the year, but sometimes we blend with the free-run. Our best red wines need barrel time to let the flavors harmonize."

Nick's pride and love mixed with the shadowy cool room.

He lifted a bottle from a large rack of others, studying it, cradling it like a baby in his hands. "This was a good year. Some years aren't. That's important, Maggie, to know the year—they're all different, the sugar is different, the weather, everything is a factor. We're small, tight, and good, varietally correct for our grapes. Michigan's even climate and close distance to the lake is good for Rieslings and Pinot Noirs and others."

He moved to a smaller rack, frowning as he picked up a bottle. "Not so good. A drought year, small grapes, lots of skin and not enough pulp . . . too tannic. I planned to enter competition that year, but decided not to. Still, we have a special order customer in Chicago who likes it, and more so as it ages. We'll be showing two- and three-year-old wines in competition, nothing younger."

He smelled of fresh air and the blooms he'd been thinning when she arrived, of the earth that he'd bent to clasp in his hand, letting it drift through his fingers. In the shadowy musty cellar, he smiled at her like a boy showing off his favorite toy, and her heart stopped, turned, and quivered, and finally settled. She pushed herself into thinking about her new job and asked questions as they walked toward the steps leading to the showroom.

"You're right," Nick answered. "We do have alternatives. Over there are the sparkling juices—nonalcoholic. We recommend a few years cellaring for most of our wines. We only made a few cases of that free-run, and are limiting the purchases."

With a gallant sweep of his hand, Nick said, "Ladies first."

Maggie knew by his grin that he would be watching her bottom. She added a little sway to torment him, and maybe herself. At the top of the stairs, Nick was suddenly all business, moving behind the rough wood counter and explaining her new job.

But then, she'd already felt the heat of his body, that storm of hunger swirling around them, and noted the thrust of his body against his jeans.

The jolt of her own reaction stunned her, the driving need to leap upon him, rip off his clothes and hers, and feed.

She wanted to leave him mindless and hungry, just as he had left her at Journeys, weak-kneed and grasping a chair for support. Beth's bawdy, knowing laughter had taken a few moments to register and nettle.

Maggie toyed with a wineglass, not the best quality, but good enough for some heavy-handed tourists. She lifted it to the dim light and turned it, finding better quality than she supposed.

She tilted her head and studied Nick, whose bland, innocent look covered whatever he had planned for her. And just maybe she was a little miffed that he treated her like an employee when they had been lovers. So he was determined, was he, to torment her sexually? To be methodical and cool, waiting for her to take the first move? she wondered with an irritated flick of her hand to her loose hair.

Nick caught her left hand and turned it, running his thumb over her third finger where Ryan's wedding ring had circled. Brooding and dark, an accusation lay in his deep voice. "You dated him, your ex-husband."

He moved too fast, leaping into her emotional trails, shocking her. She gave him the truth as she had no other. "Yes. For years before we married—through high school and college. I thought he was perfect, the other part of my heart and soul. I loved him desperately. I trusted him completely. I thought I knew him. But I didn't. And now, I don't know myself, who I am and what I really want. Here I am, thirty-one years old, a professional in my field and it's really *his* field. I lived my life for Ryan, and now—"

Maggie stopped, the bitterness still echoing in the room. She hadn't meant to free her resentment, yet it nipped in the air between them. "I take responsibility for my own life. I'm not looking for pity. I did it. I lived it."

Nick's dark eyes roamed her face, considering the emotions she held safe from him. He'd slipped inside her emotions, dissecting them, exposing her. "He didn't give you what you want. You gave him everything and he hurt you. That's what you have locked inside you. You're afraid to give too much again. I know how that feels."

He'd seen too much, and Maggie drew her hand away, rubbing it on her jeans. She'd lived and breathed for Ryan, for his dreams and hopes, and he'd betrayed her when she needed him most.

Of all, the betrayal of her trust was the worst cut; she'd believed in him completely, believed that Ryan would stand beside her to avenge Glenda. He hadn't.

"What else do I need to know?" she asked, pushing herself out of the past and into her new part-time job.

"Just this." Nick's breath curled on her palm before his lips rubbed it lightly. He lifted her hand away from his face, studying it. "I like your hands. They're good, strong hands—capable."

With a tug, she was in his arms, and he was smiling down at her. "I like them on me."

His change of mood startled her, and was just what she needed. Maggie returned his smile and stood on tiptoe to nip his bottom lip. "You are certainly unpredictable, Alessandro."

"Mmm." Nick was busy nuzzling her throat. He back-walked her into the shadows, his hand busy at her back, unhooking her bra. "I knew practicing with Mom's old bra would pay off someday."

With a laugh, she kissed him hard. "Are you as good at garter belts?"

He froze, still holding her in the air. Nick sounded startled, amazed, and eager. "Do you wear those?"

"Not today, not for a long time. What are you going to do with me now?"

Nick looked mildly disappointed, then he was smiling and easing her to her feet. "Give you something to think about."

There in the cool, dark shadows of the cellar, Nick's hands smoothed her body until she ached, holding him tight. Then with one touch, he sent her soaring, quivering and hot and bursting.

Maggie gripped his shoulders for an anchor, felt the burning of his skin, the heaviness of his body against hers, the pulse beating deep within him, and let herself fly—

When she surfaced, Nick held her limp body safely against him, his hands soothing and gentle.

"If I could move, I'd hit you," she whispered raggedly against his rapid heartbeat. "You did that deliberately."

"I want you thinking about me. I'm selfish that way." He bent to give her a mind-blowing kiss, and when her hips started moving against him, Nick's big body shuddered. He eased away from her, and with a satisfied, arrogant nod, he turned and started walking from her.

Maggie could have killed him. He was deliberately playing her, making her want more. Instead, she managed to take off her canvas shoe, and threw it at him. It hit Nick's back, and he stopped for a heartbeat before going up the stairway.

"Well, he's certainly right," Maggie whispered raggedly as she jammed her shoe back on and shakily straightened her clothing. She wasn't thinking about Ryan anymore. She was thinking about revenge. If Nick wanted to play games, he'd picked the wrong woman.

Brent Templeton hurried to pack—at last, he'd found Maggie.

His time spent searching in gyms and spas had paid off. In San Francisco, a man named Leo Knute had come to brood and to beat the punching bag with his fury. He'd seen Maggie's picture pinned to a bulletin board, and had called Brent's number written beneath it. Over dinner and drinks, Leo's face bore the glazed marks of an ungloved fist, and he moved stiffly, quickly downing the alcohol as he described "the bitch" and her friends. "Saw her up in Michigan. We were all set to party when two big guys moved in. I could have taken both of them," Leo had bragged, "but they used sucker punches. One of them was her boyfriend, and that dog she has was a devil. Big and black and mean. It belonged to the woman from the way she held it."

"Dog?" Brent's mind had turned to the high-priced, pedigreed Labrador who had shamed him in front of his friends, fearing the sound of gunfire, cowering in the marshes when she should have been retrieving. She'd cost him a five-thousand-dollar bet. Evelyn, his ex-wife, had told him that the dog had run away that night, but instead, Maggie had taken her. *Maggie had stolen his dog.*

Once that five thousand dollars had been little to him, and now he couldn't raise money to go after Maggie.

But then Leo Knute had slapped a thousand dollars into Brent's hand. "I'd give a lot to pay the Alessandros and Maggie back. You look like you're down on your luck and it sounds like you'd like to get your hands on her, too. Check it out and call me when you've got something. There's more in it for you if you can set something up privately."

Brent had managed a humble, grateful attitude, but inside he hated Leo's arrogance and casual payoff. The man was a slob who didn't polish his shoes.

On the other hand, Leo could be useful to a man much smarter than he; Brent was that man. He knew how to take the weaker and use them, play upon their needs until they were in his grasp and playing his game . . . Yes, Leo could be very useful indeed, but there would be others, and he would use them all to get Maggie . . .

After a fitful night, Maggie's only compensation was the fact that yesterday, in the cellar, Nick's body had been very hard against hers, his body hot and heavy and throbbing with sexual need. She wanted to see the night's damage in his face, to know that he'd ached for her as well.

She rapped on his back door and shivered in anticipation. She admitted that after Ryan's coldness, Nick's hunger gave deep inner satisfaction, in more than one way.

Maggie waited for Nick to come to the door, and it seemed only right to place the potted mound of salmon-colored impatiens on the board railing circling the deck. At dawn, she

shushed Scout and let the cool mist layering Nick's overgrown yard curl around her. It rose upward to the tower, caressing pink shades upon the glass windows.

Had Nick gone there to brood last night? Did Alyssa still
hold him in the midnight hours, when he sprawled big and
warm and drowsy in his bed?

Maggie's stomach tightened with the sensual punch, and
she sniffed lightly, wishing Alyssa away into the dawn. She
retrieved a bag of cookies from her bike's basket and set to
enjoying the fresh scents, the dew dripping from a spider's
web like a trail of diamonds in the morning light. She tilted
her head, studying the effect of splashed color on the dark
wood, and, satisfied, turned to knock on his door again.

Her hand met warm flesh and Nick, rumpled from sleep
and needing a shave, stood, legs apart in his boxer shorts.
Sleep fogged his eyes, or was it dreams of Alyssa? He rubbed
a shaggy length of thick, wavy hair and eyed her owlishly.
"What's up?"

Was she jealous of a dead woman? Maybe. Maggie
braced herself against the full blast of Nick-in-the-morning.
She crossed her arms and slowly took in his body—aroused
and hard. She could have leaped on him. "Been dreaming of
anyone?"

With a low growl of disapproval, he eyed her warily. Then
he eyed the earthen bowl of impatiens as though the flowers
were somehow encroaching on his territory. He frowned at
Eugene's old bicycle that she had used to pedal to his house.
"Why are you here? And why are you happy?"

*So he hadn't slept soundly . . .* The fact that he was
equally unsatisfied—perhaps even more, because he hadn't
had release the day before—brought a smile to her lips.

"You're smirking," Nick noted darkly, warily. "Why?"

The day was glorious, promising, and for the first time in
years, she felt bone-warming happy. She didn't want to dis-
sect why; she just wanted to accept and enjoy. "I'm running
into town. Care to match me?"

In the morning, Nick's responses apparently ran to grunts and growls. But the look in his eyes said that five minutes of those slow, deep kisses, and she'd be in his bed. "Come in."

If he'd come from sleeping, dreaming about Alyssa, to wanting Maggie . . . the thought nagged a bit as a shadow crossed the glass on the tower. It was only a bird, flying in the pink dawn, Maggie knew, yet she preferred not to replace Alyssa in Nick's bed. "No, thanks. I'll wait."

"What's that?" Nick pointed to the pot of impatiens as though it were the invading enemy.

"It's from your third grade teacher, Mrs. Friends. So are the cookies. She told me how you were mortified when Mary Jo Frasier kissed you, and you hid up in a tree until she told you kissing girls wasn't so bad."

"Depends on the girl. She had a tongue like a lizard," he muttered, and looked beautifully disgusted at his notorious past in the third grade.

"Cookie?" She lifted the plastic bag up to his nose. Nick took them, jammed a hand inside the plastic, and retrieved one. He looked adorable, all drowsy and sweet. Maggie's heart did that quiver thing, as she thought about how Nick might have looked as a little boy. "She bought too many impatiens and I've already done pots for outside the camper. I thought your deck needed some color. It wouldn't hurt to weed your herbs, either. The garlic is everywhere."

Nick looked at her as if she'd stepped down from a space ship, one gold eye in the middle of her head and all eight green arms waving. He ate another cookie, eyeing her. "So?"

She almost felt sorry for him, waking up after a night with Alyssa. "Are you up to running or not?"

"Just keep that cheerful stuff out of my face," Nick said, closing the door between them. He scrubbed his hands over his face, trying to leap from a sleepless night into the morning.

Maggie smelled like freshly baked cookies and *woman*. Before his defenses were up, the combination was lethal.

She thought about color on his deck and he thought of her in his arms, of him in her, of—Maggie was driving him nuts. Nick stumbled over one running shoe and went rummaging for the other beneath the bed. He was a pitiful excuse for pride, when with one look, he wanted Maggie in his bed, when he'd spent the night tossing and forcing himself not to go to her. To wake up from an erotic dream of her, only to find her on his doorstep, was a dark test, separating the dream that had flowed under him, silky soft and yet strong, to the woman looking healthy and strong and awake and fresh.

He didn't feel fresh. He felt . . . hard and aroused and frustrated. She wasn't sharing her past with him. She didn't want to date, and if she knew his plans for her, she'd probably run. They were good plans, not a thing wrong with them. Conventional he-she stuff.

At least yesterday, he'd wiped the thought of another man from Maggie—even if he'd had to pay painfully. That good long, yowl at the moon had eased his frustration a bit.

Nick stopped brooding in the middle of tying his shoe. Uncertainty wasn't for him. By the time he reached the deck, Maggie was bending over the old herb garden, pulling weeds. The pretty picture of a woman dressed in a too-large sweatshirt and cutoff jeans, her legs gleaming and smooth, took the huff out of Nick. He admired the sight for a heartbeat and then vaulted over the hand railing, perhaps to show off a bit, to impress a woman he wanted.

"First things first," he said huskily and sealed the surprise on her lips with his kiss.

On the sandy beach, Celeste looked at the moon, the silver trail across Lake Michigan spearing straight toward her. Somewhere out there, the beast had quickened, breaking whatever leash held him, and he would be coming to kill her.

She had to summon her power, controlling and nourishing it as she had never before. When the time was ripe, she would give it to Maggie and pray that it would protect her.

Maggie's nightmares told her the truth; and deep within her, hidden so deep that she didn't consider the danger, was the knowledge that her past would come after her, and that whatever had begun long ago must be finished.

With Celeste's inherited power, Maggie just might survive.


"Live with me." Nick watched Maggie dress, and in a few minutes she'd be gone for the night and he'd count the minutes until he saw her again.

A solid week of Maggie in his bed hadn't dimmed his need of her. She was always very careful to return to her camper for the night.

That camper had become both a challenge and a symbol that Maggie held him outside her life.

Maggie's fingers hesitated as she buttoned her blouse, then she shook her head. "I can't."

Nick was on his feet, prowling around the room, careless of his naked body. He braced his hands on his hips. "Why exactly can't you? Tell me again. The last time, I had my mind on just how fast I could get us undressed and on this bed. We're lovers, Maggie. We're adults. There's not one reason why you have to go back to that camper tonight, or any other night. Stay here, with me. You see this as a temporary thing, don't you? That you'll be moving on as soon as you feel the need."

Across the rumpled bed where they'd just had mind-blowing sex, Maggie shook her head. "That's not it. You're a traditional man. I'm not ready to move into what you need, what you're meant for—marriage and children."

"You've had your shot and it didn't take, right? So therefore I don't qualify to date or as a housemate." His hand swept toward the bed. "Is this it? Nothing more?"

"You're emotional. I don't like dealing with you when you're like this." Maggie's icy barriers shot up, angering him more.

"Tough. So everything has to be on your terms, does it? No obvious dating, you pay your own way at restaurants. We've been lovers for over a week, and we still haven't had a date. I need a date, Maggie."

"See? You're traditional. You go from A to B to C. And you're angry. I don't like to deal with you when you're angry."

"Oh, well, maybe I am upset." Nick jerked on his jeans. She'd nicked his pride. He was good enough for her bed, but not for her life. "I don't like hiding how I feel."

"You kissed me right there in the restaurant, in front of your folks. It wasn't any friendly little kiss, either—one of those long, slow, melting ones. How do you think I felt then?"

He leveled a look at her. "Very good. I like you when you're all warm and pink and flustered. You're cute like that."

"You stood there grinning like a little boy who had just pulled off a major coup and I was your brand-new toy. I was embarrassed—you made it seem as if we were . . . I'm not setting up housekeeping with you. Give me a break. Stop pushing me, Nick. Things are fine as they are." Across the room, her hand shook as she smoothed her hair. Maggie kept her emotions close and guarded, and he loved tugging them out of her, watching that fine rosy blush move up her throat and cheeks.

"Says who? You?" Nick realized his tone challenged, but he felt raw. "I don't like sneaking around."

Maggie bent to tie her running shoes. "I'd hardly call that kiss sneaky. I'm a private person, Nick. I don't like people to know my business—"

Nick turned his back. She'd hurt him, keeping herself from him, setting up fences every time he came too close. He heard her move through the house, the quiet closing of the back door, and he was alone once more. Only the rumpled bed said that Maggie had been there, leaving her scent—their scents combined.

Nick fought going to her, and instead drank a beer on his deck, contemplating his non-appeal.

So he was sulking, his feelings bruised, he admitted the

next afternoon in his office. Maggie was waiting on customers at the new tasting counter, her voice sultry and warm, floating up to him in bits of easy laughter.

Nick slashed across the close-out offer on his new brochure. He should have inventoried the stock before taking the brochure to the printers, but his mind had been filled with Maggie.

She didn't want to date. She didn't want to stay the night. She didn't want to move in with him. What the hell did she want?

"Okay, she wants sex and that's all." He slammed a file drawer a little too hard and it crept back out to mock him. Another shove and the drawer returned again, a pile of paperwork on top of the cabinet beginning to slide to the floor. He dismissed it and stood to look down on the tasting room. Maggie was behind the counter, laughing with a male customer as she poured wine into his glass.

And then into her own.

Nick frowned as she pointed to the wine list, and a ripple of her laughter nudged his dark mood. Fine. Attempting to keep his mind on business, Nick called a bottle supplier late in delivery and was sharper than he intended. Then because he was rather enjoying his nasty roll, he dialed Lorna and made another offer for the twenty acres that had once been Alessandro land. He could survive the dinner date she suggested if it meant getting back that land and keeping his mind off Maggie.

Downstairs, Maggie was still entertaining the customer, and four of Alessandro's best wines were lined up at the cash register. She came around the counter and slowly walked to the display of nonalcoholic juices. Nick didn't blame the man for watching that slow sway of her hips in those worn tight jeans, those long legs.

She was free to flirt up a storm if she wanted. He wasn't jealous. Okay, he was, but he wasn't running after her. He was setting his own terms from now on. With determination, Nick settled back into his dark, brooding mood.

* * *

Maggie felt wonderful. After a sleepless night, disturbed by the commitment Nick wanted, she'd been uncertain of him. He'd clearly avoided her, sending Eugene down with messages.

Now, with a massive order from a customer with a private wine cellar, she couldn't wait to share the news with Nick. The customer's buying representative was tight on time— just passing through on his way to a convention—but he would call Nick later. Don Raleigh was easygoing, and she'd enjoyed the light conversation. With the fantastic order tight in her hand, she hurried up the stairs to Nick's office. She'd be professional and deliver the news calmly, waiting for his boyish grin, the way his eyes lighted when he was happy.

Seated at his desk, Nick was big and sexy and cute, scanning his computer and making notes, a little bit of cellar dust on his shirt and his jeans. He looked all bothered and in need of petting. Nick would be thrilled with the order, and she couldn't wait to see his expression.

Maggie moved to his side and placed her hand on his shoulder. The sudden jerk of heavy muscle told her that he knew she was there, but he kept scanning the computer.

He hadn't ignored her last night. He'd been intense and powerful and sensitive to her pleasure, taking his time.

She wanted his full attention before showing him the order; bubbling with excitement, she anticipated his surprise and reaction. "Hi."

His grunt wasn't exactly welcoming.

The order was burning her hand, but she waited for him to notice her. "Hi," she said again, and with a jolt, realized that she'd come to celebrate her victory with him—her friend and her lover.

"Nick?"

He stood up and frowned at the computer. "I've got to check the cases in the cellar. I thought we had more of the Pinot Noir for that year."

Nick brushed by her, and Maggie gripped the paper in her

hand, her anticipation of his reaction to her sales falling flat at her feet. She hurried after him and found Nick crouching on the cellar floor, inspecting the notations on the side of a box and marking them on his pad.

She wanted his full attention as her excitement slid into frustration. Nick could be very irritating and bullheaded. He was deliberately ignoring her, making her run after him, spoiling her thrilling news.

He stood suddenly, almost knocking her aside. "Don't flirt with the customers."

Maggie stared at him blankly. "What?"

Nick moved behind a skid loaded with wine cases, and she followed him. "You heard me," he said briskly. "The guy was all over you. You were leaning toward him and nibbling those crackers like you'd like to . . . It's a wonder he could walk out of here. Did you set up a date with him?"

"I got the order. Here." She shoved the crumpled paper into his chest. Ignored, the order fell between them and with it, her thrilling victory, the one she wanted to share with Nick, her friend and lover—the ill-tempered, surly man in front of her, a taut muscle moving in his cheek. "You're in an evil mood."

"I get that way when I make love to a woman one night and see her flirting with another man the next day."

"He was friendly, easygoing, and fun. We made a deal. You're ruining it. He'll call you, by the way. He represents a major buyer who's impressed with your wines."

"Or with you." Nick's head tilted, his expression challenging. "So am I on your list tonight, or do you have other plans?"

He should have known better than to push Maggie—with a cold stare, she had turned and walked away from him.

His telephone call to Celeste's was met with Beth's "Maggie is busy now. She's painting my toenails and then we're watching movies—*High Noon* with Gary Cooper. You goofed, chum. Boy, those nightmares she has are freaky."

Nick's early morning run past Maggie's camper had proven that she hadn't returned. However, her pickup was parked in front of Celeste's house. His quiet knock at the door started Scout barking, and soon the dog was charging out the door, leaping on him. While the dog was happy to see him, Maggie frowned at Nick and shut the door. She didn't answer his next knock.

"Unless you have any objections, sweetheart, I'm taking Scout." He had thought she'd open the door to that, but it remained closed.

While Scout was making her friendship rounds in Blanchefleur, visiting Marco at the butcher shop to carry her bone reward to the Alessandros, Nick brooded about that firmly closed door over coffee and a slice of his mother's *torta alle nocciole*.

Dante arrived, and after eating a hefty slice of the chocolate and hazelnut-filled cake, settled back to make his assumptions. "Scout is making her rounds. I just saw her go into the beauty shop. Ethel likes to put a bow on her, and Scout doesn't mind the brushing. It's a good thing Maggie doesn't know how many treats her dog gets on her visits. . . . I know that look. You're right and you know it, but maybe you aren't. You shouldn't have done whatever you did, and now you don't know how to back up, right?"

"Something like that. Mom said to leave the cinnamon rolls alone." Then Nick reached for one—he deserved a dessert of *some* kind.

Dante licked a cinnamon roll's frosting from his fingers and grinned. "So does this mean I have a chance with Maggie?"

Nick glowered at him, and Dante shrugged. "Guess not. Let's go move that dresser for Mom."

Carrying one end of a big mirrored dresser his mother wanted moved into the empty apartment, Nick backed into the room. Dante, at the other end, pushed hard, jolting him. "Pay attention, Nick. We drop this thing and Mom isn't going to like it."

Dante looked down at the street. He tossed his pickup keys to Nick. "Maggie's pickup is headed out of town. Now might be a good time to corral her."

Maggie's pickup wasn't at her camper; rather it was parked in his driveway. Nick entered the back door cautiously. The washer and dryer were humming, and Maggie—

Maggie was at the kitchen stove, dressed in black lacy lingerie over a bustier, thong panties, garter belt, stockings, and high heels. Her hair was piled on top of her head and little spiral curls played around her face. She turned off the stove, placed one hip against the counter, and folded her arms across her chest, staring at him with those dark green eyes.

When Nick could lift his eyes from her breasts, all pushed up and soft and gleaming, he cleared his throat and tried for a brilliant statement. "What's up?" came out.

He knew what was up and very hard.

One wrong move and he could lose what he hadn't gotten.

"I like you," Maggie said slowly.

"I like you, too."

"I'm changing. I don't quite know myself, but I'm learning. You already know yourself. Just don't push me. This is something I have to walk through by myself, becoming me," she said firmly.

Then Maggie's tone softened, curling around him, and before she turned away, he caught the color rising into her cheeks. "I like being a woman and I like being sensual. It's new and a little awkward. But I thought I'd like to try this on you, if it's okay."

"Just exactly what are you trying on me?" Nick didn't want to make any more mistakes.

Her hand swept down the creamy skin contrasting with black sexy lingerie. "This."

"We can do that. It's fine with me," he managed to say.

"And don't push me. I've been pushed a lot and I'm going to react defensively. I'm just saying that a happy balance might be possible. Watch the arrogant and overbearing stuff.

It's definitely a push button with me. I like your honesty, but sometimes you're just plain overpowering."

Despite his body's arousal, Nick knew that Maggie was struggling desperately with herself and her past. She was negotiating with him, trying to retain herself, but give him what she could—where once she'd given too much. The tenderness for her rose and swelled and filled him. "Anything else?"

"It's a front-hook bustier. I haven't had one before and it's a loner from Beth. When I think back, my life has been pretty uptight and some of me is just now coming out. I want my own visions, but I want to be reasonable, too."

"You're being very reasonable."

"You said you'd practiced with a bra. Did you ever practice with a garter belt?"

He shook his head, and Maggie smiled seductively and lifted one leg to brace it over a chair, revealing the garter strap down to the black stocking. "Now's the time to try."

In the bright morning sunlight, Celeste felt the fingers of icy shadows curl around her. Her hand gripped the old brass doorknob of her shop, locking to it as if it were safety. She lifted her head and smelled the late July air, soft with a blend of dew and raindrops and flowers. The cobblestone street seemed to slide into the lake's waves, a little rough, white caps forming in the distance.

The wind chime outside Journeys turned, silver and shadows, and in one breath, everything seemed too still.

On the opposite street, Maggie and Nick were jogging easily, their strides matched, Scout a few paces behind. Maggie was laughing up at Nick, challenging him, and suddenly he stopped, his hands on his knees, the picture of a man sucking in badly needed air.

Concerned, Maggie returned those few paces to him and bent, her hand on his back. Nick straightened, and with a grin sailed by Maggie, heading for the beach.

The lovers' race should have brought a smile to Celeste, but the chilling stillness remained, waiting . . .

Hearing the bump of car tires on cobblestones, Celeste shaded her eyes as she looked toward the morning sun—and the late-model, navy blue sedan that kept rolling toward her, *bump, bump, bump*, the sound terrifying and familiar, like the sound of death coming closer.

She couldn't see the driver's face; she didn't need to, because it was the man for whom she had waited—her killer. Hatred bristled, almost alive in the air, snaking around her ankles, winding around her chest and throat, tightening slowly, painfully. Bitter and strong, it held Celeste immobile, chilling her flesh.

Her hand over her racing heart, Celeste forced a smile for the Joneses, an elderly couple taking their morning walk. When she turned, looking for a license plate, the car had cruised over the hill and disappeared.

With shaking hands Celeste unlocked her shop and hurried inside; she stopped, wrapped in the safety of her shadows and scents, just for a moment. Then with her heart racing, she closed the shop again and hurried home to her cats, needing their comfort. Her little yellow house nestled in the shadows of towering trees, a jumble of brightly colored flowers circling it. Caressed by a slight breeze, the herbs sent her their scent, the hunched ceramic troll smiling a welcome. Home, Celeste thought, inhaling the sunlight and the scents, wrapping them around her, if only for this short time—

Inside her house, Earth, Wind, and Fire leaped from their window perches, milling around her skirts, wanting their treats. "You'll miss me, won't you?" she asked, consoling herself, though she knew Beth would take perfect care of her cats.

Celeste had just finished filling their bowls and settling down for a game of catch-the-catnip-filled-cloth-mouse, when her front door ripped open and Beth stood, hands on hips, calling out to her. "What the hell are you doing home this morning?"

So much for quiet and thought. Celeste tossed the mouse once more, smiled at the sight of her cats scrambling for it, and then walked into the kitchen. "I live here, remember? And I'm the boss and I can take off if I want to."

"Yeah, right." Beth slammed the door behind her. "What's wrong with you? I take George Wilson for his stroll and see you tearing up the hill to your house. Don't tell me you forgot cookies in the oven."

"Wax," Celeste corrected as she lifted the metal pitcher from the pot of water on the stove.

Beth's curse would have made a longshoreman proud, searing the quiet shadows and the windowsill's potted herbs. "I want to know what's wrong with you."

Celeste tried to sound normal, to protect Beth, her heart's child. "I think I'm going to die."

Beth stared at her blankly, then her expression crumpled and tears came to her eyes. "And you weren't going to tell me? What makes you think so? How do you know?"

Celeste welcomed Beth's shaking body into her arms, rocking her. "It's a natural cycle, dear. Birth, life, dying. I've made my peace. When my time comes, I want you to make yours and go on, caring for yourself most of all, but then, if you find it in your heart, my dear cats. You've got a good start now and you've got a good head for business, and you'll be fine and you'll have a wonderful husband and enough children to keep you running."

She kissed Beth's bright hair and felt the girl's fingers dig in, clinging to her. "Tell them about me."

"Can't the doctors—?"

"No. I choose to meet my fate as I will."

Beth jerked back, tears streaking down her face. "That is absolute bullshit."

Celeste nodded and dried Beth's tears with a linen handkerchief. The cloth was warm and damp, and Celeste knew that she had left her mark in life, that Beth was capable of enormous love. In time, she would be able to accept and like Lorna.

She ran her thumb over the soft wrinkled cloth. Maggie had loved very deeply, and she'd been hurt. Whoever came after her was part of that pain. "But it's my bullshit. Haven't you told me that often enough? Open the shop this morning, will you? I love you, but I want to be alone."

Celeste wanted to think of Iowa and wind waving through the cornfields, of her parents and the big white farmhouse— and how to protect Maggie.

Along the way, Celeste decided that her cousin's son, a good sturdy farm boy with a clean mind and a loving heart, would be perfect for Beth.

All in order, Celeste thought, pouring tea into her best china cup. Lorna was already in love, and Beth would be. In her heart, Maggie was already Nick's, and he was hers. Together, and with Celeste's power, the women were strong— they would have to be.

Celeste traced the shadow of her finger behind the delicate finish. Now she could only wait.

# TWELVE

Seated in a car, parked in the small grove of trees, Brent Templeton tipped the monogrammed silver whiskey flask high and swallowed. He let the searing burn of the liquor match his hatred, the need for revenge boiling in him.

On Blanchefleur's wide beach, Maggie's wind-tossed hair caught the sunlight. The tall man she was with tugged her to him. Her arms went to his shoulders as she moved against him, returning his kiss. The man's big hand swept down her back possessively, stroking her, smoothing her bottom as he gathered her closer.

Watching them, Brent tapped the scarred tip of his cane on the dashboard. He should have been tired from the flight from San Francisco to Louisville, Kentucky, and by the drive in the rented car to Blanchefleur—but he wasn't. He'd wanted to set up a misleading scenario for anyone who might be curious about his whereabouts. And the drive from Louisville had given him time to temper his fury, because everything had to be perfect. He'd waited too long to punish Maggie Chantel.

She hadn't been playing nice when she'd injured his kneecap. He intended to use the cane on her, just as he had the dog, that worthless female Labrador afraid of gunshot and feathers.

What kind of a Labrador feared gunshot, feathers, and birds? The breed was supposed to hunt and he'd paid well for her.

The first time he'd taken her hunting with the club, she'd shied and made a fool of him by refusing to take the mock bird in her mouth, by bolting at the sound of gunshot. His friends had laughed at him and he'd become the club's joke. . . .

Maggie had stolen his dog and the income Brent could make from breeding her over and over. It was nothing like what he once considered income, but from that, he could start building his return . . .

Maggie didn't move away from the big man, rather she simply melted into him, her hands gripping his thick, shaggy black hair.

Fury rose in Brent as he glanced at the rearview mirror and caught his own thinning limp hair. He couldn't afford implants or stylists now and it was *her* fault.

Maggie had refused him and now she'd taken a lover, her body moving into his, his hands caressing her.

Brent's headache pounded, because Maggie should have been his, just as Glenda was. Women had always been his, fascinated by his power and money and status. Now he had nothing—because of *her*.

"You'll pay, damn you," he muttered and stopped, held by the sight of the man hurling the stick into the water, the dog waiting for a hand signal and then leaping into the waves to retrieve it.

The dog shook a spray of water from herself, then came to the man, who rubbed her head. He gave a hand signal, and the dog sat at his side. When he walked, the dog heeled perfectly.

That man had Brent's woman and his dog—the one Maggie had stolen.

Maggie had ruined him, going to his high-powered friends and accusing him, before and after Glenda's death. They'd protected him just long enough to get out of range and then they'd forced him out of that tight, elite circle. Because of Maggie Chantel dogging him, going to his rich wife with evidence that he'd had an affair with Glenda, Evelyn and her battery of attorneys had made certain he couldn't come near her fortune, or their children. The pittance she'd given him had only served his needs for a time. "That damn prenup—"

Now he'd lost everything, and Maggie would have to pay.

He saw a boy on a skateboard and signaled him to the car. Brent held out a five-dollar bill. "Hey, kid. Here's a fiver. Who's that down on the beach?"

Cautious of strangers, the boy took the bill, stepping back quickly. "That's Nick Alessandro and Maggie and Scout. Everybody knows them. His folks run Alessandros Restaurant up on Main Street. You want a coupon for their specialty, spaghetti? I get paid for handing them out to tourists."

"Yeah, sure. I'd like that. Thanks."

"Hey, don't take whatever is bothering you out on me," Beth ordered as she stepped from Maggie's path.

Her arms circling a box of brochures, Maggie crossed the winery's showroom to arrange them on the counter. She adjusted a glass on the overhead rack, critically studying the pictures on the rough wooden wall. She'd chosen copies of the pictures, those of Nick on his mantel, a small boy holding his grandfather's hand as they walked through the rows of vines. One day Nick would do the same with his son. His future lay ahead of him, while she had yet to understand herself. "I'm not bothered. I have a lot of work to do."

Beth picked up a bottle of limited free-run Pinot Noir, and seemed to study it as she said casually, "Nick is in town, having lunch at the restaurant with Lorna and some private client's buyer."

"Word must be getting around. Nick seems to have a lot of private buyers."

"Yeah, well, they have wine cellars and show off what they know at parties. If a wine grower gets popular and has a good product, they're all over him."

Maggie didn't intend to shut the cabinet door quite so hard, jarring the glasses in it. She lifted a bottle of three-year-old Chancellor from beneath the counter and set it down too hard. She wasn't upset. She wasn't jealous. Who Nick met was none of her business.

"Lorna is wearing a low-cut number and a high-cut skirt."

"I care less. This buyer has a private cellar and wants it well stocked for his yacht and parties. I hope everything goes well." Her tone was too edgy and she disliked the temper flash that could only be labeled as jealousy. Lorna was set to push Maggie any way she could—Nick was only the *objet d'push*.

Maggie retrieved cheese from the small refrigerator behind the counter and sliced it, plopping it and crackers onto a paper plate for Beth. "Eat."

Beth munched on the crackers and cheese and eyed Maggie. "Lorna's hands were all over him."

Unfamiliar little fiery edges spiked inside Maggie. Lorna would know that her setup scene would be gossip-channeled to Maggie. "I do not care."

Beth's arched eyebrow mocked Maggie. "Sure."

"So how is Celeste?" Maggie asked to distract Beth.

"Worried. Odd. Spooky. Taking a lot of time with everything, like she's absorbing it for the last time. She says she's feeling fine. But she's walking alone a lot at night. She says it gives her peace."

"I'm worried about her."

"I am, too. Maggie, she told me she was going to die. She wouldn't tell me why, but she's accepted it."

"I'll talk to her."

"You'd better schedule ahead of time. She's moving right through her checklist. While you were busy with Nick, Celeste decided that Eugene needed a little old-fashioned sexual tune-up. She ordered an overnight delivery of some sexy stuff, including a ruffled bib apron, which is all she wears when cooking for him. It's disgusting, but she's already vamped him. Jeez, she's half a century old and he's maybe two hundred."

Celeste sipped her mint tea and smiled at the album's picture of a young farm family. "My sister. She had five boys. That one is Jeff. He's perfect for Beth. I've invited him, and he should be here any day. When the time is right, I want him to take me home, to Iowa. I miss the cornfields and my family."

Maggie leaned back in the kitchen chair. As Beth had said, Celeste seemed to be putting her affairs in order, including matchmaking for Beth. "Celeste, I'm concerned. Why do you think you're going to die?"

"Because it's my time. I feel it. There's a time for everything, Maggie, didn't you know? Beth is going to have beautiful babies, and she'll be a perfect mother. She'll be good for Jeff . . . keep him from getting too set in his ways. He has the stability and ethics to ground her, and I want her protected. The first part of her life was too dark and harmful. She should have brightness and love surrounding her. That's what I want for you, too. And Lorna. That is only a game she's playing with Nick, to push you—like that restaurant scene. Like you, she's battling what she could not change. But she will."

Maggie took her friend's hand. "Celeste, we're talking about you. What's wrong?"

The older woman's expression closed with a bland smile and a shrug. "I want you to move in with Nick. I feel a darkness now that includes you. If there is trouble, he'll protect you."

Nick would agree with Celeste. To him, living together was natural. To Maggie, it held uncertainty. "I'm struggling to find myself now, Celeste. Nick is . . . overwhelming. He's emotional, and I've never dealt with someone like him."

"He cares. He wants you in his life. Is that so bad?" Celeste asked gently.

"I've got so much baggage. Trust is difficult for me on that level. It wouldn't be fair."

"Give yourself a chance and time. You're learning to trust again. You're finding yourself, and you're not who you were. You're a whole new, beautiful person." Celeste was quiet, toying with her china teacup, a finger prowling over the painted roses. "Is there anything I should know to help you? Is there any reason someone might be following you? Someone tied to your sister and Scout? Someone who might—might be dangerous?"

"No—yes. I don't know. My sister was on drugs. I exposed her pusher and upset a lot of powerful people who were . . . using her. But I don't think any one of them would take the time or energy to follow me."

"Think harder, Maggie. Your nightmares are trying to tell you something. They're running beneath the surface, erupting in powerful scenes. You're blocking something evil, and it's unfinished. Your subconscious knows that. Could it be your ex-husband?"

"Ryan? He wouldn't care. He was glad when I left the area, rather when I was driven out, and he helped. I'd become a liability to him, because everyone knew we'd been married. I think he was active in getting me fired or maybe not hired in the jobs I tried to work. Why are you asking?"

Celeste stilled; she sensed she'd asked the last question too soon, sending Maggie down the wrong path, away from the danger to her. "Because I wondered, nothing more. You are in danger, Maggie, and from someone in your past. Please be careful."

Troubled by Celeste, Maggie managed her aerobics class and walked toward Journeys. Ryan had been glad to be rid of her, and though she couldn't erase her bitterness for his desertion when she really needed him, he would never want to come near her again. Their agreement was unstated; he left her alone, and in return, she did not expose the shoddy equipment and deals he'd arranged with the help of Brent Templeton.

*Brent Templeton.* The name seared her. His furious expression sailed out of the past to chill the beautiful day. He had everything he wanted. Wealth, a rich wife, good old buddies who played the same brotherhood game. He was protected by his powerful friends in San Francisco, and she'd made scenes with all of them, a futile effort to avenge Glenda's death.

As a successful entrepreneur, Brent would have too many deals—real estate, equipment scams, trade-offs, the parties and appearances of his social set. He wouldn't endanger any of that, or invest any time to find Maggie. Evelyn, his wife, hadn't believed Maggie, and Brent wouldn't risk his high lifestyle by following her.

Judge Jones? He hadn't liked her emotional courtroom exposure of his seedy life, or his legal friends. At the time, she didn't know their games, and it was a hard lesson to learn. She should have never burst into his courtroom. His veiled message in his private chamber came through loud and clear—any more trouble and she not only wouldn't be working in the area, she'd be very dead. The remark about her two nephews, specific information about them, had reminded her of just what he could do when tested.

She hadn't pursued any of them after that. There would be no reason now for someone to come after her, to take time away from his wealthy life to seek her.

Maggie caught the delicious scents flowing from the Alessandros Italian Restaurant and pulled herself back from the past. She heard a window scrape above Ed's Place and automatically glanced up to catch the flash of a mirror behind the old curtains.

But concerned about Celeste, Maggie dismissed the sound and entered Journeys, where Beth was ringing up a purchase and scowling at a customer. Once the door closed behind the woman, Beth turned to Maggie. "Women with her hips should never wear tight pants. It looked like two watermelons with cellulite back there . . . You know that Celeste has invited some bumpkin here for me to meet. He's a gee-shucks farm boy, for gosh sakes. I knew she did some match-making on the side, but I didn't think she'd zero in on me."

"He might not be so bad."

"He's used to taking care of cows, not women." Beth shuddered elaborately, then asked, "You talked to Celeste, then. How is she?"

"Very quiet and not saying much. She says I'm in danger."

Beth inhaled sharply and leaned forward. "Then you are. Celeste feeds a lot of crap to tourists, but she doesn't hand it out to us. Okay, she usually doesn't—except for the farmboy part. What does she mean—you in danger?"

Maggie remembered the threatening calls from influential men who were involved with Glenda the prostitute, Glenda the user. "A few years ago, I made trouble for a social set. They didn't want their private lives exposed. But I can't see any of them coming after me. They were threatening mouth-people, but not actually backing up their threats. I was a pariah at one time, and they just wanted to get rid of me. I was killing myself, battling everyone, and no one was listening. They cut me out of any work by pressuring the owners, so I just moved on. I did my best to make life rough for them and in turn they did a pretty good job of running me out of town. I haven't been in contact with anyone there, and no one has tried to contact me."

She glanced out at Scout, who was tied to a bench, listening intently. In front of Journeys, Ole, Dee Dee, and Eugene, in that order, were seated on the bench, and each man held one of Dee Dee's hands. Mrs. Friends stopped, chatted, and sat down by Eugene. He edged away from her slightly. Then he moved back and casually placed an arm around her.

Dee Dee frowned and glanced at Eugene, whose returned smile was innocent.

"I'm worried," Beth stated. "For both of you."

"I'll be fine, but I am worried about Celeste. I love her."

"So do I. But I'm not baby-sitting for some farmboy from Iowa. That's asking too much. Shudder. His hands would have touched those cow-milk thingies, teats or tits or whatever. And I'm looking for a man for Celeste. Someone younger than Eugene. Getting laid might distract her—if it doesn't break a hip or something. It sure changed you."

"If you don't lay off me, Beth honey, I'm going to hurry the farmboy's visit."

"That's all I need, some yokel hick, and stop laughing."

Maggie made her usual rounds, enjoying the sunshine and her friends: George Wilson, for his therapy, and Mrs. Friends, because she enjoyed visiting with Nick's elderly teacher and listening to the tales of the three Alessandro "scamps." She had been helping Mrs. Friends paint her sunroom. But today Mrs. Friends was miffed, saying, "That hussy Dee Dee is making a play for all the handsome, eligible bachelors in town. She actually has Eugene discussing those trashy soap operas." Maggie left the older woman mulling Dee Dee and briskly dusting and replacing her miniature animals to their tiny wall boxes.

Maggie found herself by the harbor, watching the boats glide, the tourists milling on the concrete walks bordering the water. They seemed to fall into two categories—those wearing the sun-washed natural khaki and T-shirts with logos, or those wearing Hawaiian prints.

A child raced after a ball, and Maggie's thoughts raced as well: Celeste was certain of her death and certain that Maggie was in danger—but who would want to follow her across the country? To invest that time and energy and money in locating her?

Brent Templeton had been vicious, furious with her. She'd injured his knee when he'd attacked her in the bathroom. His wife hadn't believed Maggie's story, and neither had Ryan. Brent was in San Francisco, wrapped in his vices, his wealthy powerful circle, and his wife's money. He was probably glad to see the last of Maggie.

Ryan definitely had been glad to sever their marriage ties as quickly as possible.

Nick had shown her more compassion in the brief time

they'd known each other than Ryan had shown in their whole marriage. She'd loved him too much, given too much. Nick was right about her low trust level, and he didn't deserve the backlash from Ryan's treatment.

The waves licked at the channel's concrete seawalls and on impulse, Maggie decided it was time to meet her nightmares—

In the harbor at the end of the channel, she found Dante at his boatyard, listening intently to a high-priced cruiser's inboard motor. Looking up and shading his eyes against the sun, he grinned. "Hi, stranger. What brings you here?"

"I thought I'd take you up on that sailboat ride. Whenever you have time."

"Sure. Let me finish up here and close shop. I thought you were afraid of water."

"I'm working on that."

Out on the water, Maggie worked so hard that afternoon that her hands ached from gripping the sides. Though the lake's sunlit air was cool as the sailboat glided over the waves, fear lodged in her throat every minute, and her skin beaded with sweat.

Concerned, Dante had checked on her frequently and she'd forced a tight, sick smile. "I'm fine."

He reached a hand to waggle her head playfully. "A little seasick? You'll get your legs soon enough."

She nodded, but every molecule of her body was locked onto that day, the sudden squawl, flying off into the water with Glenda. Then her mother had struggled toward them— and her father's hand had sunk beneath the water.

Holding Scout close, she lifted her face to the wind and let it take her away until only the sound of the breeze in the sails and the creaking of wood melded with the easy flow of the waves. Maggie held her locket and let her mind sail back to happier times, the birthday parties, learning how to ride their bikes, their father running alongside, helping steady the wobbles. They were good times and ones locked in her heart.

As they glided into the harbor, she looked at the tourists and found a man with a cane. The man's hair was thin, wisps catching the wind, his face narrow and pale, his body hunched beneath the worn brown raincoat. But deep within their bony sockets, his eyes had locked onto her, and the shock had squeezed and dried her throat. It couldn't be Brent Templeton. He belonged to another time, another place. When she looked again, he was gone.

That man wasn't Brent Templeton. Brent was a big man, strapping and fit from hours of working out, his hair thick and groomed and his clothing immaculate. Shaken by the burning look that had sailed across the harbor to her, Maggie gripped the railing, looking down into the dark water.

The man was only a passing stranger. Celeste's uneasiness was spreading, washing over Maggie, and yet the man couldn't be Brent—

When Dante helped her up to the dock, he scanned her sunburned face and whistled. "Better put some lotion on that. But . . . beneath all that pink, you still look scared. You did fine, kid. You were afraid, but you met it. It will get easier, you'll see. And if Nick says anything about me taking you out, he can take it up with me."

"I'm fine," she lied shakily and hurried from Dante's worried frown.

Then, because he cared and because life had treated him ungently, she turned and hurried back to him. Maggie stood on tiptoe and kissed his cheek, smoothing it with her hand. "Thank you. You should go get your little boy and bring him home. He needs the love you have and that of your family."

"Thanks. He's afraid of me now. It's not that easy."

She didn't mind being gathered against him, his face buried in her hair. "I failed my little boy, Maggie. I thought she would be better for him. Motherly love doesn't apply. Brenda needed him for child support, and now that she's getting married, she's tossing him away . . . Maggie, he doesn't know me. The last time he saw me, he was terrified. It was like a piece of me was being sliced away. I didn't know what to do. I handled it badly, reaching out to him, but I wanted to hold him so much, to keep him safe, you know?"

"I know. We want our loved ones safe and can't always do the best for them. But you're going to be wonderful, Dante. If you need someone to go with you to visit your son—just for support—I will. I . . . I used to do a lot with my sister's boys."

"And you miss them."

That painful knot inside her twisted. "Terribly. One day, the youngest called me Mom—my sister and I looked alike. I couldn't step into her place . . . I couldn't remind them of—well, the things she went through before she died and what she put them through. Yes, I do miss them."

"You could visit."

Maggie shook her head. "No. I'm afraid they remind me of their mother, too, and it breaks my heart how they look at me."

"That's rough. . . . By the way, I'm going over to baby-sit at Sissy and Tony's tonight. Scout would be a real help with those wild animals. Can I borrow her?"

"Sure."

Someday she'd visit Cody and Seth—when she was ready, Maggie promised herself as she pulled in front of her camper. Lorna's big shiny Lincoln was waiting, the hard rock music throbbing out of it. It died when she rolled down her window to speak to Maggie. Her wraparound silvery sunglasses mirrored Maggie's face. "I've been waiting for you."

"How may I help you?" From the look on Lorna's face, the conversation wasn't going to be pleasant.

"Stop messing with Nick. He's mine. If you can't understand that, I'll have to make you understand."

Maggie had dealt with stronger threats than Lorna's. "Is that a threat?"

"I'm merely telling you that Nick and I have an understanding."

Maggie had had her share of bullies, and Lorna fit the obvious profile; however Celeste saw more in her, and according to Rosa, Lorna had been fashioned into what she was by her father. The woman beneath had yet to emerge; meanwhile, Lorna would test herself against anyone in her way.

"Celeste seems to think that you already have someone you love. You might ask yourself why you're pushing Nick, and if he's who you really want. Or if you're using him to get whoever isn't playing your game right now. Whatever the case, exactly what would it take for you to return that land to Nick?"

Lorna's laughter was brittle, erratic in the quiet day. "More than you'll ever make in your lifetime, unless you get serious about playing with summer—"

She clamped her lips closed and looked away, her face red and furious beneath her sunglasses. The bright day hovered and turned and Maggie wondered, "Summer vacationers? Men with boats who want to party? Lorna, you know something about Leo Knute, didn't you? Did you have Ed fix it?"

"That lowlife? Beth has already jumped me with the same accusation. One thing I have to say about Beth, she doesn't pull her punches. Hey, maybe I even admire that. Ed told me there was trouble. He was trying to get me primed to take you out. I pull some weight around town and he knows that I'm not happy with you moving into my territory—namely Nick. And no, I don't have anyone on the side, but I would if I wanted. But if you think I'd set another woman up for a party like that, you're dead wrong."

Lorna revved her engine and reversed, shooting the big car out onto the dirt road.

Still gripped by Lorna's attack and a dark reminder that she had been set up for Leo, Maggie opened the door of her camper and stopped, keys in hand. The door was unlocked, and yet she had used the keys this morning.

The camper had been rearranged neatly. Magazines that Maggie had read and tossed into a stack were all sized, large on the bottom, smaller on top. The curtain that she had folded back and pinned for Scout to look out of the window had been released and straightened.

On the tiny table, the photographs of Beth, Celeste, and Maggie had been placed exact distances apart, and several with Scout had been stolen. The pictures of Nick and Maggie dancing at the Alessandros' anniversary party had been taken, along with those of Sissy's children in front of the old two-story house.

Also missing were two snapshots of Maggie's family. "It seems that you're lonely, Lorna, needing photographs of someone else's family and friends. I guess you can have the pictures. They're not worth accusing you of thievery."

Maggie repinned the curtain for Scout to look outside. "Hmm. I didn't know you like to clean, Lorna."

The changes in the camper were meant for sly intimidation—to let Maggie know that Lorna was set to defend her territory.

"That won't work, Lorna dear. Intimidation didn't work years ago, and it's not working now. I've dealt with powerful people before, and this time, you're not getting what you want. What's more, keep pushing and you just may lose those twenty acres you're holding over Nick's head."

Blanchefleur had become home in a short time, her friendship with Celeste and Beth rich and deep, and the first in years. Maggie wasn't leaving easily.

Ed wasn't talking. He hadn't answered Celeste's questions, but he knew something. It scurried around inside him, flashing and vicious and waiting. What was it?

She'd seen the man in the car—the one taking away her breath and bringing death to her—slipping into the alley behind Ed's tavern, and she'd asked for truth from the wrong man. Ed had denied seeing anyone, but she'd known then that he was lying—and that he was afraid.

The night and the lake called to her and Celeste knew it was her time. She slipped from her home, leaving Beth sleeping soundly.

Celeste could have ignored the silent call to her senses, but if she did, the ones she loved could suffer. And she wanted desperately to know why he had come and what he had to do with Maggie and Scout.

With a spring of lavender in her hand, she faced what would come. She walked slowly toward the lake, then along the walkway, trailing her hand over the waist-high seawall. Her dark blue caftan caught the slight wind, her long red silk paisley print scarf seemed almost alive as it fluttered, brushing her hands like a lover's caress.

A sensual woman, Celeste lifted her face to the fresh air. She'd lived her time and it had been good; she'd given Eugene that smile to carry him on through the years. It was a peaceful night, filled with lovers' sighs and sweet scents of life, the moonlight on the harbor's still water trailing toward her.

She pushed her fear aside and let her sturdy Iowa good sense wash over her—a season to live, a season to die, the goddess and her cycles.

Shadows kept the moonlight from her, the trees providing privacy. At one o'clock, the park along the water was closed and silent.

She felt him in the darkness, watching her. His hatred seared her, and a sound that could have been a breeze whispering through the leaves became the cries of women he'd hurt . . .

Like a specter, he loomed out of the shadows; only the sharp angles of his face caught the moonlight. Clawlike, his hand bit into her upper arm, holding her. His voice crawled through her fears and scratched at the night. "Hello, Celeste. I hear you've been asking questions about me."

"I knew that Ed would relay that to you. I wanted you out in the open, and now you are." Behind Celeste, the waves lapped quietly at the seawall holding them, and Celeste heard only the racing beat of her heart, the wind sighing in the trees, life saying goodbye to her. Her time had come, and this was the man she'd feared.

He leaned closer, and the smell of whiskey circled her. "Yes, Ed told me about you. He hates you with your spooky ways, and he likes money. He wants his property back and you're interfering. I've seen her at your house, and I've seen another woman. Tell me about the other woman and I'll let Beth live."

She had to know. "Why have you come?"

"For Maggie Chantel, and for my dog. She stole my dog and took away my life and now she has to pay. I saw everything from my room above Ed's. If I angle a mirror just right, I can see everything—Maggie and her friend, Nick Alessandro, right? His parents own that restaurant?"

The rubber gloves he wore had a slightly bitter scent as he artistically looped her scarf around her throat, nudging her back against the protective barrier. But the safety of concrete wasn't there, only a space used by emergency boaters from the lake to tether their lines and climb the steel ladder.

"Ask Ed." If only she could break away, warn Maggie and Beth . . .

But the red silk scarf tightened around Celeste's throat and the man smiled coldly. His other hand caught hers as she reached to grasp the metal hand bars attached to the concrete. "Let me introduce myself. I'm Brent Templeton, late of San Francisco, and a very special friend of Maggie's sister, Glenda. I met Maggie five years ago and I knew I had to have her."

Maggie's locket . . . her sister . . . the dog . . . The images swirled around Celeste and the words, "Tell me you love me." Then she saw this man slide the needle into a woman's arm, and a bright splash of copper-colored hair fell back, the hazel eyes sightless in death. He grew strong as he punished and hurt, careless of the pain to others, feeding off it. . . .

The beast within sensed her natural fear of dying and fed on it, enjoying her like a cat playing with a trapped mouse.

Celeste balanced on the edge of the safety, the water black and waiting below. He moved closer, peering into her face. "Ed says you see things, that sometimes you work for the police. What are you seeing now, mind reader? Tell me."

The shadows moved inside Celeste's mind. "You killed Maggie's sister . . . She'd become a liability. You wanted

Maggie and when you couldn't have her, you ruined the person closest to her."

The silk scarf jerked tighter as he hissed, "I suppose you should know. You're not telling anyone. Maggie ruined my life. She went door to door, stalking my friends, embarrassing them in public, calling newspaper reporters, and then she went after my wife—my rich wife. Evelyn put Maggie off, but she believed her. Without Evelyn's money, I couldn't pay my creditors, and they came after me—see how pretty I am now? Maggie gifted me with this limp. It can be fixed, but that takes money, too. Well, Maggie made me this way, and I'm going to kill her very slowly, then use that dog to get a start on a new life, breeding her and selling the pups—not much money, but it's a beginning."

If only Celeste could break free, to warn Maggie—

"You want to warn her, don't you? Well, you can't. I won't let you," he crooned as he pushed her back nearer the open space in the seawall, and the drop into the lake.

For a moment their minds ran together and then Celeste blocked his intrusion, masking her expressions until he could see nothing inside her.

Fear rose in icy ribbons, not for her own death, but for another's. "Don't kill Eugene."

"I don't know him. But if he's between Maggie and me, I might. You're not asking for your own life. Why?" he asked almost absently.

"Because I knew you were coming, and that I was the price for Maggie and Beth's safety. What do you know, inside you, I wonder? Do you know that Maggie will be your undoing? That if you have to murder me, you should leave to save your own life? Because if you stay, I will give my power to her and she'll be even stronger than before."

For a moment Brent looked puzzled, and then he muttered, "Ed said you were crazy, witch woman."

Celeste fought desperately, but he was stronger, forcing her closer to the very edge of the concrete walkway, the opening in the seawall and the drop into the water.

As he gripped her scarf and forced her over the railing, she knew—he intended to make her death look like an accident, the scarf catching on the railing, twisting in it, acting as a noose when she fell. "I'll haunt you forever, Brent Templeton. I'll be in your every nightmare, your every breath, and—"

"Time's over." Almost clinically, as if he were creating a work of art, Brent reached out in one smooth movement, gripped her hair, and slammed her head against the concrete abutment.

Someone was falling into space. Was it she?

A silvery flash tumbled past her and a man cursed bitterly.

In the heartbeat before she died, Celeste saw Iowa cornfields again and her parents, her father's big, strong, safe hands reaching out to her. Alyssa was beside him and the woman called Monique—the Frenchman's love. Celeste asked for their help to save Maggie and Beth.

Silky and strong and eternal, something sailed past her, and she willed that gift and a warning message to Maggie.

And then she saw nothing.

# THIRTEEN

Brent watched the mourners file into Alessandros Restaurant. The psychic seemed to have had the friendship of the entire town.

"Giving her power to Maggie. That's a crock. The dingbat wanted me to believe that if I stayed, I'd die. Maybe that works with the paying morons, but I'm not buying. I've hunted her for too long to be scared off by gibberish," Brent muttered, keeping behind the rags serving as curtains in Ed's upstairs storage room. The fool was frightened of Brent, and worse, he wasn't neat. He didn't understand order. The room had been a pigsty. Now it was barren, but clean and orderly.

The morning after he'd killed the psychic, Brent had been up early, waiting . . . waiting. The sound of police sirens had preceded the red lights that flashed in his upstairs window, breaking the gray dawn. On their way to the channel, people hurried to see what had happened.

Ed had given Brent a full account of how a fisherman headed out of the harbor into the lake had found the psychic's body floating in the channel, how the police had lifted her upward and placed her in a body bag to be transported to the county medical examiner. Photographs were taken, flashes of light in the gray seeping dawn. A small piece of her scarf had been retrieved from a handrail on the channel, and first guesses were that she'd stumbled somehow, probably trying to free her long scarf that had tangled on the handrails. Bending over, she'd probably bumped her head on the concrete, and had fallen. The long scarf had caught somehow, hanging her. Eventually the scarf had torn, and the dead woman had dropped into the water.

The newspaper's lengthy front-page account of her life, from Iowa farm girl to Blanchefleur's resident psychic, listed her death as accidental. The town council was already debating placing a plaque dedicated to her at the site.

Watching mourners on the street below, Brent reached to straighten the curtain and paused. Lorna Smith-Ellis, dressed in couture black, strode into the restaurant as if nothing could stop her. From Ed's description of Lorna, Brent hadn't expected her to mourn. Maybe she wasn't. Maybe she was there to make a point. And maybe he could use her; the rich had their fancies and their fantasies, and he had experience satisfying their whims, ingratiating them to him.

A covey of the town's elderly moved slowly into the restaurant and then—

There was Maggie, Nick's arm around her, his other arm around Beth—Ed had pointed her out to Brent earlier. Maggie leaned against Nick, trusting him. The big black Lab stayed close to Maggie, and she occasionally reached down to pet it.

Bitterness churned inside Brent, eating at him. "You and Alessandro are lovers. Don't lie to me, Maggie. You've been unfaithful. And you've not only wrecked my life, but you've stolen my dog. No one takes what's mine and gets away with it."

From his vantage point, Brent watched the rest of the mourners enter the restaurant. His dog obeyed another man, a man who slept with Maggie. That dog was his, and so was the woman.

He reached for his flask and cursed again. It had gone into the harbor when he'd killed the witch. His initials were on it, but only Maggie would recognize it and soon she wouldn't be saying anything.

He thought of the psychic's expression, the almost calm way she slid into death. Later a chill, a sense of being watched, had wrapped around him. Yet nothing had moved in the night, and he had been alone as her body had slid into the harbor. "It's nothing. No one is watching me. She's just gotten to me, that's all."

But then, he'd always been able to deal with anyone crossing him. Including Maggie.

Maggie ignored the heat of the afternoon sun, signing for the truck's deliveries at the back door of Journeys. It was only a day after Celeste's funeral, but on the first week of August, tourists were thick in Blanchefleur, making the most of their time before school started, and the shop needed attention. Beth didn't want to leave Celeste's house yet, holding the older woman close to her for as long as possible. But the bricks of candle wax for the shop wouldn't tolerate the heat if left to stand on the wooden platform, and Maggie carried in one heavy box to the storeroom.

She felt Celeste inside the shop, vibrant and soft and sweet. Maggie held that image in her mind, rather than the sodden corpse pulled from the harbor, the torn scarf still tight around Celeste's throat.

The night after Celeste's death, Maggie's nightmares had stalked her in vibrant horror, a blend of her father's death, Glenda's, and now Celeste's. Beth had stayed that first night at Nick's, and the sound of Maggie's screams had brought her running.

It was childish, but Maggie hadn't cared. "I want everyone in this bed now. I want to know that everyone is in one place and safe."

"I'll move," Nick had said, but Maggie had reached to grab that shaggy hair and tug him back down to the pillow beside her. "Down. Beth, on my other side. Scout is already at the foot of the bed. Now, no one move."

Maggie had lain still for a full five minutes, her hands locked with Nick on one side and Beth on the other.

It had been a long, restless night for everyone.

This morning, the telephone rang in Celeste's shop, intruding on Maggie's thoughts, and she automatically picked it up. "Journeys. We're closed for business now. Call back in two weeks."

A man's coarse breathing sounded over the lines.

"Ed, I am in no mood to play games. Beth said you'd been doing the breathing act, but she's not frightened of you anymore. You call her or me again and you're going to have real trouble."

The man didn't stop and Maggie slammed down the line. When the telephone rang again, she didn't answer.

She stepped out on the platform and found Lorna in the shadows, her red sports car parked by Maggie's truck. The brim of a large straw hat and enormous sunglasses almost hid Lorna's pale face. A tight black top cut at the midriff revealed buffed arms and a flat, muscular stomach. Her hip-slung shorts led to legs developed by exercise, and on her feet were high-top, laced athletic shoes.

"I'll miss that old woman," Lorna stated rawly. "She saw me through some rough times with dear old dad—he was afraid of her. Whatever I hated in him, I seemed to search for in my ex-husbands, and she helped me through that, too. For whatever reason, she liked you. But she's gone now, and I want Nick. Why don't you just move on down the road? If you need money, I'll pay you."

"Thanks, but no thanks. And you don't really want Nick. You don't have to prove anything to your father now."

Lorna stiffened. "I can make things rough, little girl."

Maggie ignored her and picked up another box of wax. With a hiss, Lorna hit Maggie's shoulder, spinning her around. Without her hat and sunglasses, Lorna's expression was fierce. "What do you want to bet that I can run you out of town and get Nick, too?"

"Okay, Miss Smith-Ellis. I'll bet you can't run me out of town, and if you can't, you sign over that land to Nick for its sale price."

Lorna's cold blue eyes lit as she latched on to the bet. She thrust out a hand to shove Maggie's shoulder. "I'm ready now. This could get rough. Just between you and me?"

Maggie wasn't getting pushed around for a second time in her life; she knew that Lorna wouldn't stop until she'd tested Maggie thoroughly. "Okay."

Lorna sneered. "I can handle you by myself."

"Then do." Maggie had had threats before, and Lorna didn't frighten her. She let go of the box and Lorna leaped back to keep her feet from being crushed. With a hiss, she lifted her hands in a karate position, and Maggie shook her head. "I wouldn't. But you touch me again, and I will."

She hadn't expected Lorna's fast, expert move, that sent Maggie flying in the air and landing on her back.

"Had enough? Ready to leave town now?" Lorna's disdainful sneer took Maggie back up to her feet and into action.

"Let's try that again," she invited coolly. "Nice moves, by the way."

Moments later, Maggie stood inside the softly lighted shop. The shadows and scents seemed to quiver, reminding Maggie of Celeste's distaste for violence. "Celeste, I did not hurt her. I defended myself. She was off balance in that kick, and fell from the platform. She's mad and she's bruised a little. I jumped down to see if she was okay and she knocked me over. I had to defend myself."

Maggie rubbed her back slightly. "Okay, so Lorna is good, mean and sneaky. Landing on that old stack of boards wasn't exactly like that of feathers. And I'm sure she didn't like being tossed into the dirt. So we're even . . . for now. Rest, Celeste. I'm going to be okay and so is Beth, and just maybe Lorna, too—because you seemed to care for her."

The music of the wind chimes in the front of the store slid through the closed door, and the summer sun caught the little goddess spinning within her cage of silver pipes.

The hair on Maggie's nape rose as if chilled, and she stood very still. Nothing came to her, only the waiting sense that Celeste was warning her.

"Go ahead," Beth said. "Nick is depending on you to help him at today's wine festival. I'll be fine."

In the shadows of Celeste's yard, Beth's face was too pale, a week of sleepless nights shadowing her eyes. She scanned the flowers and scented herbs running around the yard, rich with color in the first week of August. A cascade of red impatiens seemed to tumble from a whiskey barrel, a squirrel perched on top. Lavender bloomed in a bright patch, waiting to be picked and dried in bundles.

Beth held Earth close, the cat purring heavily. "They found a scrap of her scarf on the ladder's handrails. She must have hung on the channel wall for a time before dropping into the harbor. When he motored down the harbor, Maurice Livingston saw her body just floating, bumping against that concrete wall. I don't understand why Celeste had to go out that time of night, why she didn't wake me, if she wanted to walk. But then, she never did. I went all through that with the police."

"So did I. Celeste thought that someone from my past might cause her death. I went all through that, and couldn't think of anyone who would want to go to that much trouble, now that I'm away from them. I thought it better not to mention what she'd said. Maybe I was wrong. But San Francisco is a long way away in both space and time for me."

"Yeah. Some stuff is better not told. I understand."

Wind and Fire came twining around Beth's legs and she bent to pet them. "And I don't understand why she had to wear that silly scarf—her hangman's noose, Maggie. And no one was around to help her get free. I don't know why she had to be buried in Iowa. How am I going to talk with her?

But I'm going to run her shop and live in her house and take care of her damned cats, because I promised."

Maggie took Beth's hand, lacing their fingers. For the week since Celeste's death, she'd stayed close to Beth, mourning their friend. They'd cried and slept together. "You love her house and her cats, and you can talk to her whenever you like. I don't want to leave you."

"I'll be fine. I'm always fine—except for that one night at Nick's, the day Maurice found her, when we all stayed there. For the last week, you've stayed here, and that's enough. Nick has had this wine festival scheduled for months, cultivating customers to come to it, and he's going to need help. And that Jeff character, Celeste's nephew, is arriving today. He's supposed to collect her family things. I wonder how she—"

"It's only for a day. We'll be back tonight. I'll stay at Celeste's with you."

"I do not need a baby-sitter," Beth stated firmly, then added more gently. "Just call me when you get back in town, okay?"

She laughed shakily. "That was something, wasn't it? The three of us in Nick's bed, you between us. I don't think another guy would have put up with that. Maggie, you've got to do something about your nightmares—they're worse."

"I know. I can't help it. I think Celeste's death has stirred them."

Beth shook her head. "They were always bad."

"I have to go. We should be back around one or two in the morning. Nick has some pre-meetings with buyers before the festival starts at three. It's only for one day, and only three hours away if you need me."

"Scoot," Beth said with a tired smile. In the distance, a low rumble began to get louder. Then an old big Dodge pickup, road dust covering the green finish, came over the street's hill and stopped in front of Celeste's house. Between the dents, areas of dull brown said the metal had been patched.

The arm draped outside the window was big and tanned and masculine. The man who leaned his head out of the window was young and gorgeous. "Hey, ladies," he called, "is this Celeste Moonstar's place?"

"Iowa license plates," Beth noted sullenly and crossed her arms over her chest. "Probably that Jeff guy."

"Probably. Are you Jeff?" Maggie asked.

"Yes, ma'am. Jeff Ingmar. Pleased to meet you." He got out of the pickup and stood and stretched, all six feet, five inches of pure, fit, prime male, wearing only faded bib overalls and work boots. His broad, bare shoulders gleamed golden tan in the light, and muscles flexed as he lifted his ball cap and replaced it on a mop of long, curling blond hair. He began a slow amble up the walkway to the women. "Nice place. It's like her."

The goddess chime suddenly caught the breeze, tinkling within the silvery pipes, and Beth stopped drooling long enough to whisper unevenly. "That's Jeff. Celeste's *little* nephew?"

Jeff towered over them, his blue eyes warm and friendly as he took Maggie's hand. She liked the feel of his hand, safe and big and callused. He carried with him that same sense of solid friendship and warmth, of clean living and a loving, good heart, that had been Celeste's. This was the husband Celeste wanted Beth to have, and Maggie liked him already.

Beth's breath caught, and Jeff's eyes were already taking in her blouse, tied at the midriff, and her tight, cutoff shorts. His gaze strolled down her bare legs to her bare feet. "You've got nice feet. Pretty. I like those toe rings. But I'd rather you didn't ever wear long scarves, if you don't mind."

For the first time since Maggie had known her, Beth seemed to struggle for words. Then she said firmly, "You're staying here tonight."

He nodded, his expression serious as if he were accepting the vows of a lifetime. "Yes, ma'am. I'd like that."

"I loved her," Beth said in a burst of emotion that brought tears to her eyes.

With the ease of a man who soothed easily, Jeff reached out a big hand and smoothed her hair. "She's always going to be with you. Aunt Mary Lou always left a little bit of herself with those she loved. I got the feeling she wanted to leave me with you, Beth. She said you're one perfect prize. I always did like to take first place at the fair."

He bent to kiss her cheek and then her lips briefly, as if he were tasting her, and above them, the little goddess tinkled happily in the chimes. Celeste was still there, Maggie decided, watching and perhaps laughing a little.

"You just did," Beth whispered unevenly.

Jeff nodded to Maggie, who had been unable to move, spellbound by how easily the younger couple had accepted each other. Jeff was looking at Beth as if she were top grade prime. "You'll excuse us, won't you, ma'am? We've got some acquainting to do."

"Um, yes. Beth, I might not call tonight after all. We might be busy until late."

But Beth had her hands behind her back, gazing up into Jeff's eyes. She looked fresh and sweet and excited and happy.

"That worked out nicely, Celeste," Maggie said as she drove toward the winery and returned Jerry's wave and thumbs-up.

At the Alessandro Vineyards and Winery, Nick tugged her into his arms. He felt good and solid and strong. "Are you okay?" he asked against her hair.

"I'll miss her," she answered. But deep inside, she felt more than grief. She sensed the danger that had troubled her friend. "Do you really think it was an accident?"

Nick stroked her hair, his heartbeat safe and constant and strong beneath her cheek. "Celeste wandered at odd times. She did as she wanted. If the wind caught her scarf, tangled it, and she reached to free it, bumping her head, her weight enough to snap her neck—yes, I think so. Don't you?"

"She was worried about my past and danger to me. I've gone over it all. It's not likely that anyone came after me. They were all very happy when I left."

"Let it go, honey. Let her go."

"That's going to be very hard to do. I loved her—and Beth is like my sister. You should have seen her and Jeff. They didn't even miss me when I left. Nothing better happen to her."

Nick patted her bottom and kissed her lightly. His soft expression said he understood. Then his dark brown eyes filled with laughter. "Kids grow up. They leave the nest."

"Oh, you." Maggie stood on tiptoe and kissed him hard. "Let's go. I want to make a big impression on my boss."

"You already have," Nick returned, tugging her to him for a long, deep, hungry kiss.

"Getting away will be good for both of them, even if for only one day," Rosa said as she sniffed the bubbling tomato sauce in the restaurant's kitchen. Scout had come to stand at the doorway between the private family room and the restaurant's kitchen. Rosa enjoyed talking to the dog, who tilted her head and listened intently. "Anthony and I love having you here. You're so good with Tony's babies. . . . First the wine festival, then Nick has to pick up some supplies, and they'll be home late tonight. Beth left a message on Nick's machine. She's off to meet that nice boy's family and see where Celeste is resting in Iowa. Beth took the cats, too. Celeste's death was a terrible thing, so sudden, and Beth needed to put her at rest. We're all going to miss Celeste."

It was just after the coffee and pie bunch, and the lunch crowd hadn't arrived yet. During tourist season, the working regulars taking their noon break used the Alessandro private family room, and Rosa liked tending the people she considered family. As long as they cleaned after themselves, they could help themselves to the smorgasbord in the back room for minimal cost.

Rosa thought of someone who she wished would eat more—Lorna. The girl was stick-thin, and should learn how to cook. Rosa smiled; she knew the identity of Lorna's long-time rumored boyfriend, but it wasn't for her to tell. Vinnie might not like it. In these things, it was best for nature to take its course, and Lorna was starting to look at babies curiously—

Scout returned to the family room and Rosa tossed a handful of fresh herbs into the sauce. She looked at the customer just entering the door. He'd been in before, sometimes taking a shadowy corner booth usually meant for lovers, or for those waiting for their preordered takeout. He tipped an exact amount, he spoke little, and his manner was brisk, except for the times when he settled back to watch—like a snake, Rosa thought, waiting to strike.

A tall, lean man with thinning sandy hair, he moved with a slight limp. While the restaurant's lighting usually softened features, his edgy, narrow face was marked by knifelike cheekbones and shallow cheeks and a broken nose. His eyes seemed to burn within their lashless sockets. In an outdoors community, catering to the beach, sailing, and fishing crowd, his complexion was pale, not weathered and tan. He held what looked like a looped belt in his hand.

Rosa shrugged lightly; perhaps he had been ill, and tourists often brought their own problems with them. Sometimes she withheld the warmth she gave to young families and others; sometimes she sensed the darkness coursing within customers, and they were better left alone. All Rosa could do was to give him good food and a comfortable dining experience.

The man scanned the restaurant, not with the casual air of a customer wanting a place to eat, but with a hawkish, tight look of a predator. Rosa wiped her hands on her apron. If he were one of the mob, preparing to demand a cut of the profit, he was not going to be happy. The Alessandros had two generations' experience of dealing with crime lords.

This time was different. He was coming directly toward the kitchen.

"Marco . . . Dante . . ." Rosa said too quietly, and immediately, the big men dropped their smiles and conversation, rising to their feet. Scout, whom Marco had been petting, stayed in the family dining room as she had been taught.

With Marco and Dante looming behind her, Rosa pasted a professional smile on her face and picked up a menu. He had a mission, this man, she thought, gripping the menu tightly. With her husband taking a much needed nap upstairs, she did not want him disturbed. "Hello. We have a lovely bell pepper and tomato salad for our lunch special, also marinated zucchini. Chicken with prosciutto and cheese and our soup for the day, Italian bean, is delicious. May I offer you a seat?"

He glanced warily at Marco and Dante standing behind her and shoved a paper at her. The leash in his other hand unfurled at his side. "I want my dog. Here's her papers. She was stolen from me."

At the sound of his voice, Scout tore through the doorway, and with a vicious snarl, leaped on the man. The usually friendly dog's teeth lodged in the man's jeans and the next few seconds were filled with noise and motion, tables and chairs toppling, condiments spilling to the floor, as the man tried to escape. "Get her off me!"

"Dante," Rosa said quietly and her son moved forward, catching Scout's collar and dragging her back.

"Give the dog to me, now!" the man screamed. "She's mine!"

"Not today," Marco said, gracefully, quickly easing past Rosa. The butcher's massive hand gripped the back of the man's head. Marco's other hand latched onto his jeans, hefting him slightly off the floor. "Out."

Rosa hurried to open the door for Marco, who pitched the man out into the street.

"You'll pay for this," the man threatened as he stumbled and found balance, smoothing his mussed hair with a claw-like hand.

"You want more?" Marco asked quietly.

"No, Marco. Don't come back, sir," Rosa ordered firmly and tossed the leash at him.

"That's my dog! I own her!" He shook the papers at her.

She sniffed and placed her arms over her generous chest. Papers meant nothing to Rosa, only the love bond between

Maggie and Scout. "You're not getting the dog. No more talking."

While Marco stood outside the restaurant door, watching the man hurry away, Rosa stepped inside the cool interior, where Dante was straightening the tables. She bent to pet Scout, who was tense and poised to move in the doorway, as if she expected the man to come back. "He's not gettting you. I saw the cruelty in his face, the crazy look."

She looked at Dante. "When it is time, I will tell Maggie and she will settle the matter as she wishes. If the dog needs protection or if Maggie does, we will do so. She has just lost her best friend. She does not need more trouble now. Your father isn't feeling well, and I don't want him worried, either. See where the man is staying."

But when Dante stood in front of the restaurant's window, scanning the street, Rosa knew that the man had already disappeared. She prayed he would not come back, because his eyes were those of someone possessed by the devil. Rosa shrugged; she wasn't afraid to admit to herself that her grandmother's teachings lingered in her. Anthony would go crazy if he knew—but the next time Rosa saw that man, she was putting the evil eye on him.

Brent slid into Celeste's unlocked house. Furious that a butcher with a stained apron had actually touched him, that the Alessandros should only disdain, not fear his threats, Brent badly needed to make someone pay.

*And the girl, Beth, was his victim of choice—for now.*

Maggie had always been very protective, and now that her sister was gone, she had taken a new chick under her wing.

At noon, Beth would be working in Celeste's shop, and he'd be waiting for her when she returned home.

Beth had been Ed's "girl," and the bartender was furious with Celeste and Maggie. It was obvious that he feared the Alessandro brothers, but Brent had caught and locked onto the rage in Ed's eyes, playing into it. Brawny and brainless, Ed could be a very useful pawn.

But he loved Beth, and that could be a problem. Her death had to look like an accident so as not to enrage the bartender.

The hiss Brent heard was his own. Shadowy and scented, the house reminded him of the woman he had killed—intricate and crazy. He shuddered at the clutter dancing around the house—no order, no order, everything in a mess, a frightening jumble of tiny knickknacks on every ledge. The groupings didn't match—carved elephants mixed with red stone gnomes, throw pillows contrasting embroidered "Sex is for Seniors Who Know What to Do with It" and delicate English countrysides and starkly modern plaids. The room colors, blues and greens, spotted with yellows and lavenders, jabbed at Brent.

French country and modern red appliances clashed in the tiny kitchen, a huge fairy perched on top of the refrigerator with emblazoned "Bite Me." Throw rugs with lavender blooms and fringed rugs of rose designs spread haphazardly over a linoleum pattern of daisies. The makings of candles, molds and slabs of wax, ran across one counter, a shoe box filled with shavings. A row of six china cups spread across a tiny wall shelf, the saucers behind them. Brent automatically reached to adjust the third cup, turning its handle in the direction of the other five.

Every framed picture in the house—cheap prints, family photographs, and rules to live by—seemed to be tilted, and Brent began to sweat, the house closing in on him.

He wiped his hands on his handkerchief and folded it, placing it into his pocket. He wouldn't touch anything, just search the girl's room, getting a fix on her.

Then feverishly, unable to deny his compulsion, Brent whipped out his handkerchief and, using it, began straightening the pictures.

The youthful clothing in one room identified it as the girl's. It was very neat and uncluttered, a picture of Maggie and Beth on the dresser, arms around each other. He sneered at the room's cheap contents, the slightly flashy clothing, in contrast to the psychic's flowing caftans. The books beside her bed were about improving self-esteem and saying no. A three-legged feng shui frog stood on top of women's magazines, staring at him from its plastic perch of Chinese coins. A mandella of leather and feathers hung in front of the window.

Maggie had been fond of good luck charms, and more than likely she'd given it to the girl—the old witch seemed more of the crystal ball–tarot card type. Maggie's technique hadn't changed, trying to uplift her chicks' pride, to better them beyond their true slut nature.

Brent stepped into the tiny hallway and danced back from the huge rubber spider hanging from the ceiling. He eased around it and peered into another bedroom.

The jumble of color and clutter terrified him. A huge garden fairy holding layers of long flowing scarves peered back at him, unblinking eyes holding his own, chilling him.

Celeste had seemed to accept her fate, that blow to her head, the snap of her neck. There was no way the psychic could know that he would die if he didn't leave Blanchefleur. And no way was he leaving without Maggie, taking her to a place to break her . . .

Eager to be out of the smothering clutter, Brent hurried down the hallway. On his way to the back of the building, he stepped into a tiny plant-filled sunroom. The plastic pan he'd accidentally nudged spilled something onto his shoes.

His shoes were sprinkled with kitty litter. Gagging, he fumbled toward the door, opened it with shaking hands, and fled into the day's heat.

Brent stopped, caught by a sense that he was being watched, just as he had felt when disposing of the psychic. He scanned the overgrown jumble of bushes and flowers and roses and found nothing. She'd made him jumpy, talking about his death if he stayed, that was all, he decided, dismissing the idea that anyone watched.

He fought to restrain the tight, explosive pressure building in him. But eventually, everyone who came between him and Maggie would pay . . .

\* \* \*

Nick glanced at Maggie, gauging her mood. Not one of the people visiting their booth would believe that behind the warm smile, the smooth, slightly husky voice, her heart had been shattered just a week ago.

He'd held her as she mourned Celeste, and understood that Maggie was also mourning her sister, her hand often holding the locket. Her open affection and concern for Beth showed how deeply she must have loved her own sister. There were times when she saw young boys and she'd stare, but being busy with the wine shop and chatting with people had seemed to ease her.

Relaxed, friendly customers visited the different vineyards' booths, each ready to sample. Michigan tourism promoters added to the colorful mix in the shopping mall. The five-dollar entrance fee provided customers with a wineglass, and those who were swallowing were cautioned to spit and rinse after tasting. Crackers and cheese were provided, and the day moved quickly, customers buying individual bottles as well as cases of fine Alessandro wines.

Was it possible that he loved Maggie already, that he wanted to share children with her?

His instinct was to hold her close and love her.

Time, Nick cautioned himself. Give her time to mourn her friend and close away the past. If he had to, he could manage to live without the secrets she kept.

When the customer she had been speaking to moved on, Maggie turned to Nick, her smile still warming her lips and eyes.

Between them, time hesitated and slowed, and her smile gave way to a softer, intimate one that squeezed his chest tightly.

The impact sucked his breath from him and swirled in tiny warm sparks around him.

Automatically, he reached to pour wine into a waiting customer's glass. He filled it very full, to the top, just as full as his heart. "I love you," he heard himself say quietly, deeply, still holding Maggie's gaze.

*I love you . . . It was the wrong time, and the wrong way.*
Nick hadn't meant to speak of his heart, but now his words
hung in the noise, the wine-scented air.

Her smile stilled and froze, sliding away into a slight
frown. Maggie turned from him abruptly and poured wine
into a waiting glass. Her hand shook slightly, but that was the
only indication that she'd heard him speak.

A movement to one side just across the room grabbed his
attention, and hovering behind a father with a toddler
propped on his shoulders, Nick found Ed. At another wine-
maker's booth, the bartender hefted his case of wine, his hard
eyes locked just a fraction too long with Nick's. In that heartbeat, Nick sensed that Ed was controlling the temper that
bristled across the heads of the crowd to him.

Ed's eyes narrowed; his silent threat flew across the room
before he turned away. Nick decided to have a friendly chat
with Ed. If he had something planned for Maggie, it wasn't
happening . . .

Nick settled in to complete the day, taking shipping orders
and talking with customers. Maggie's glances at him were
tentative and concerned; he met them with a blandness he did
not feel. He wasn't apologizing. Period. She'd have to deal
with what she felt—he already knew his heart.

The drive back to Blanchefleur was quiet and tense.

It had been a mistake to let Maggie drive, her hand moving
sensuously, competently on the stick shift. Every move of
those strong sleek legs as she used the foot pedals sent a hard
rap of desire through him, because he knew exactly how supple and fit Maggie's body was—and how soft and warm and
tight and . . .

Nick was torn between his anger that she'd ignored his
statement, dropped it flat on the wine-splattered floor, and
sexual desire. When her index finger circled the floor stick's
smooth black knob, sex won. "Pull over. I'm driving."

Maggie started and looked at him as she negotiated a
curve. "I'm not tired. You are. You spent time with Beth and
me after Celeste. Eugene told me you got behind and you

had to work most of the night preparing for today. I don't mind—"

If her hand touched that floor shift one more time . . . "Pull over."

When Nick was in the driver's seat, Maggie settled into the passenger side. She propped her wine-stained white tennis shoes on the dashboard. With her legs folded, Maggie settled in to relax after a hard day. Those long legs—right up to the curve of her bottom beneath her frayed cutoff shorts—gleamed in the light of the dashboard, and Nick shifted a little too quickly, the truck jerking forward.

He wouldn't mention his love for her again—not to have it trampled like a used napkin.

"You're sulking. Sales were good, weren't they?"

"They were good. It's just mostly paperwork now, and we'll ship later. Thanks for helping today. It's just been a long day." He passed by the winery and slowed before approaching Maggie's camper. She'd spent the week at Celeste's with Beth, but as badly as he wanted her, Nick wouldn't ask. If she wanted to stay in that tight little metal fort of hers, that was just fine. If she didn't want to acknowledge that they had more than most people right now, then that was fine, too.

Maggie's hand smoothed his shoulder. "I didn't mean to hurt you today. I just didn't know what to say."

"You said plenty." Her silence hadn't been encouraging.

She slid close to him and nestled her head on his shoulder. The soft, feminine gesture surprised him. Maggie's reserve was always there, her past with another man separating them. "This is like a date, a little, don't you think?"

He snorted at that and despite himself, leaned his cheek against her hair, inhaling the fragrance. "No."

"Thank you for being so sweet when Celeste—"

"No need to thank me, Maggie. I loved her, too."

"You're a good guy, Nick."

"What I said today, I meant," he stated grimly. "I'm not asking for a lie in return, something you don't feel."

"I know. And I do have feelings for you. I couldn't make love with you if I didn't. . . . Are you going to put your arm around me or not?"

"No, I'm not. You'd have to shift and I'm not going through that anymore."

She looked at him blankly. "Going through what?"

He refused to answer, holding the last bit of his shredded pride intact. "Are you staying at the camper tonight?"

If she wanted to be alone tonight, either at the camper or at Celeste's, he understood, but that didn't dim his need for her.

"I'd like to sleep with you tonight, Nick. I need to be close to you. I missed you."

It wasn't a statement of love, but Nick would take it. Maggie needed him, and that was all that mattered.

Inside his house, Nick's promise to be tender and slow shattered the moment she moved into his arms.

That fierce need to possess her drove him to gather her against him. In this way, she was his, completely, fully, hungrily.

Maggie's soft mouth opened to his, the fine edge of her teeth sharp against his tongue. He dived into the scent, the softness, and the woman. She belonged to him, was a part of him.

In his mind, they were already making love, Maggie undulating against him, opening for him, tightening.

"Nick?" she whispered as his hands ran down her body, reassuring himself that she was in his arms.

"I'm not taking it back—what I said," he said roughly against her throat and then pushed himself away.

"Fine. Don't." Her voice was husky, uneven.

What had he expected? Maggie to say she loved him?

Nick rubbed his chest, where the ache for Maggie had grown tight and painful. In the shadows past midnight, Maggie's eyes were huge, her face pale, her hair tangled from his fingers. "Look, I'm sorry. I didn't mean to come after you like that. I've missed you. You've been through a lot this last week and I—"

"Shh. We're both tired." Maggie slowly lifted her shirt away, tossing it to the washer. She kicked off her shoes and opened her cutoffs, letting them slide away with her briefs. She came to him softly, easing away his shirt, kissing his chest as her hands smoothed the tension in his body, sliding over his back. Maggie's lips traveled over his skin, heating, and gently closed on his nipple, taking away his breath.

Her hands framed his face, fingers smoothing the hair at his temples as she looked up at him. "I feel so much, Nick. I'm just not certain about myself yet."

"No one is ever certain, Maggie. Most of us just have to work our way through the good times and the bad and do what we can."

She leaned her forehead against his chest, her hair silky and sweet beneath his chin. "I feel as if I've come so far. I'm working through so much. And I'm so tired. All I want to do now is to make love with you. I need you, Nick."

Maggie eased away, turned slowly toward the bathroom, and looked at him over her shoulder. "Coming?"

"I'll wait." When he'd tried to shower with her previously, she'd been terrified; he couldn't bear to see her fear now.

"I trust you, Nick. That isn't something I give lightly."

In the steamy shower, he was careful to give her as much room as possible. She moved into the streams of water like a lover, and the erotic, feminine sounds that he had heard before drew his body into a hard, tight knot.

Maggie turned slowly to him, her hair sleek against her head and shoulders, rivulets of water streaming down her body. She spoke as if discovering a precious, wonderful part of herself. "I can manage this. I can, Nick. I'm not afraid with you."

"That's good, Maggie—" But the words dried in Nick's throat as she looked down at his aroused body.

Slowly the hand that had very competently shifted the truck reached for him, gloved him briefly. Her thumb slid over the delicate tip of him, caressing, and Nick fought the rough shudder of his body, the demand to fill her running hot and rich inside him. "I think," he managed unevenly, "that I am getting out of here now. I need a shave."

"Can't it wait?" Maggie asked softly as she moved against him.

When she lay tangled against him later, Nick smoothed her still damp hair. It was enough for now, he told himself, and knew he would want more.

"I know you're here, Celeste. I can feel you."

Dressed only in Nick's shirt and still warm from his body, Maggie moved into the cool fog, making her way down the sand to the lake.

She needed this first private time to reckon with her friend's death. The lake was peaceful and black beneath the clouds, white foam from the waves seemed like lace upon the dark cold sand.

"I'm going to remember you as I saw you last, with a smile for everyone, not as you were when they found you. Beth is walking into her future even now, and she'll never forget what you gave her—the strength to become herself. Why were you there that night? What made you dress in your favorite caftan and wear that scarf? How could you have known?" Maggie asked the night, and a slight breeze came to play in her hair, swirling the ends and lifting it away from her face. Maggie closed her eyes, remembering how Celeste would touch her hair, sweeping it back to look clear and straight into her eyes—perhaps into her soul, searching for what Maggie would share with no one.

Maggie thought she caught a sweeter scent than those of earth and water, that of lavender. "He's going to want more. Maybe I've given everything I can to a marriage. Maybe I'm never going to be fully free of what happened to me. I don't think it's fair to burden Nick. And he's still tied to Alyssa— every time he sees a motorcycle, he's remembering."

The moon slid round and full between the clouds, and a perfect silver trail cut across the black water to Maggie. "Celeste, please ask Alyssa to let him go. If there is some way, please help my sister and Monique. I feel Monique stirring out on the lake, waiting. I feel Glenda's darkness now more than ever. Give her ease, Celeste, and stay with me. I need you. I'm not ready to let you go."

From a clump of grass, a drop hovered and slowly fell, chilling Maggie's hand. The fog at her feet churned as though licked by a breeze that said, "Beware."

Maggie inhaled and pulled the sensations into her, just as Celeste had said she had done. "You're telling me that something is hungry for me, waiting. But what?"

The moon vanished as quickly as it appeared, and Maggie realized that she was standing in the froth and water, the sand sucking at her feet. "I love you, Celeste. Stay with me."

A sound behind her turned Maggie. Nick stood at the top of the sandy knoll, watching her, waiting.

More than desire ran between them, and it was the *more* Maggie feared as she slowly made her way upward.

"I was talking to Celeste. I asked her to stay with me and to help Glenda, Alyssa, and Monique rest. Celeste has a way of helping troubled hearts—"

"So do you, honey. You give more than you know," Nick said as he eased her into his arms.

The warmth of his body seeped into hers as she settled against him. "This is good."

"Very good." Nick nuzzled her hair, his heart safe and true beneath her cheek. "Alyssa said that Monique called to her. She felt that if she ever died before her natural time that she would have a friend waiting for her on the other side. Celeste has given you something, Maggie, maybe something to help ease you about Glenda."

She decided not to tell Nick about Celeste's concern about a stranger from her past. When Nick's lips brushed hers, she forgot everything but the sweet tenderness, the gentleness that was Nick.

# FOURTEEN

"Stop pushing, Nick."

The big open hand at the small of Maggie's back didn't hurt, but applied enough pressure to still her. She looked over her shoulder to the man pressing her stomach down on the bed. Nick's features were primitive and harsh in the morning light, the set of his mouth grim.

His other hand traveled lightly over her shoulders and back. His hands switched places and then the examination continued down to her ankles.

"I said, I want to know where you got those bruises."

"That's a demand, not a question."

He flipped her over easily and bent to hold her wrists beside her head. "Maybe, just maybe, I've got the right to know."

"Let me go." Maggie trusted Nick to be gentle and safe, but this man, his wide shoulders taut and gleaming as he leaned over her, eyes flashing, cutting at her, was ready for revenge. "I'll handle it."

"You'll 'handle it.' Why didn't you tell me last night that

you were bruised? When I think of how I held you, how you must have hurt—"

He pushed away from her slightly and drew the sheet up to cover her nude body. She saw his self-torment, the pain in his expression. Nick was lashing out more at himself than at her.

"It's nothing," she said and knew that he wouldn't be satisfied.

He stood abruptly, naked and tall and powerful, his anger ricocheting in the room. "Yes, it is. It means you still don't trust me, no matter what runs between us."

"I trust you—"

"On one level. The other is questionable. You're holding part of yourself away from me."

"I can handle this, Nick. I didn't want you bothered."

"Dammit. Tell me. Did Ed send someone else—?"

Maggie sat up and drew her knees to her chin. "It's Lorna. We . . . have a problem."

"'A problem!' That bruise on your shoulder is three inches across, and there's another one on your butt that's no sweetheart, either. What did she do?"

Maggie didn't trust the tone of his voice, the anger in it. "If you promise to calm down, I'll tell you."

Nick's hands went to his hips. "I don't feel like bargaining, Maggie—"

"You're going to have to. If you do anything to Lorna—"

He leaned forward. "You'll what? Threats, Maggie, dear? You'll tell me now."

She patted the bed. "You'll have to lie down beside me and be a good boy."

Nick sat abruptly, his weight shaking the bed. His flat "What" wasn't a question.

"Lie down beside me."

"Great. You've been hurt and you're protecting Lorna. This isn't about some dumb promise, is it? Because I'm not promising anything." Nick eased down beside her, his arms behind his head. "Talk."

Turning onto her stomach, Maggie smoothed the wide expanse of his chest, toying with the triangle of hair there, and finger-walked down the line to his navel. When Nick captured her hand, she said, "I said that Lorna and I have a problem. It's you."

"So what else is new? She's made it clear to me that she wants you out of Blanchefleur."

Maggie tugged the hair on his chest. "And you kept that to yourself, didn't you? See? I'm not angry. Two women, one man. It equates to a little bit of trouble."

He stared at the ceiling and then slowly one of his hands came down to smooth her back. "Those bruises say it's not a little bit."

"I can't decide if the look on your face is a smirk or a snit." Maggie took her time easing over him. She traced his eyebrow with her fingertip and then his lips. Her hips nestled against his, found what she'd been seeking and allowed just that first blunt bit of enticing intrusion.

Nick nipped gently at her finger, his eyes closing for a moment as their intimacy grew and her body accepted more. "You've got my attention."

"That's what Lorna doesn't like. Celeste loved her, and that gives me reason to try to understand Lorna. I think I do. She survived a terrible childhood by being aggressive and fighting for whatever goal would please her father. It wasn't so much the goal, but the need to battle for attention. Her good points weren't reinforced as a child, and that's important. I had that—she didn't. I'd say that has a lot to do with whomever she's seeing now, with why it is such a secret. Or maybe it's got a lot to do with him, and how he feels. But she does have a good heart as Celeste said—I know it. Things just get twisted. You're just a prize, Nick. Not someone that she really wants in the long run."

"Now that hurts." The uneven rise and fall of his chest, the caress of his hand on her breasts and back, said that she had his full attention.

Maggie rose slowly, keeping him within her, her knees bent to lift and lower her body. Her hands smoothed his chest. "This is nice, don't you think?"

His hands roamed over her, cupping her bottom, skimming the backs of her thighs. "Just how did you get those bruises?"

"Lorna and I had a little discussion. It got physical. When I reached down to help her up, I wasn't expecting her to flip me. I should have known better. And she should have known better than to come after me. She's really good. Good technique."

Nick stared up at her blankly, then he cursed. "You admire her technique?"

"It takes a lot of hours and hard work to get as good as she is. We have a tiny bet and I'd appreciate you keeping your nose out of it. Will you?"

"No. I don't want you hurt. What's the bet?"

Maggie nuzzled Nick's throat, settling closely upon him. "Oh, you, and a few other things."

He lifted her slightly and began to smooth his open mouth across her breasts. "Like what?"

She closed her eyes as Nick's lips closed over her nipple, and the trembling within her began too quickly. "You talk too much . . ."

Nick paused at the winery door and inhaled the fresh air, admiring the green lines of the vineyard. If the weather continued and the frost waited, the grapes would be full and rich and sweet, holding the summer's sun and rain.

His mind swung to another harvest, the long, slow lovemaking of last night. At least Maggie had spent the night in his bed, and if Nick could manage, he'd check the inventory and return to their bed before she woke up.

Breakfast in bed should be a good way of making his point—she should move in with him.

Nick tucked his briefcase under his arm, smiling briefly at all the good contacts and orders it contained.

He unlocked the heavy winery door and pushed it open.

Because of the wine festival, Eugene had yesterday off. This morning Nick wasn't expecting to see the old man who had been trying to put the moves on Dee Dee. Apparently, Eugene mourned Celeste, but he figured she'd given him something, too. And he intended to use it.

The new orders from the wine festival needed attention before Nick returned to Maggie. He intended to get to the bottom of the bet she had with Lorna, one way or the other. Maggie had a way of distracting him . . . rather, Maggie could refocus him completely.

The too-strong smell of wine hit him. Nick flipped on the overhead lights and stopped. The entire showroom had been savaged, the display wines and cases toppled onto the floor, glass broken. "Eugene?" Nick asked cautiously.

The showroom was too still, and a sense of trouble slammed against Nick. He noted several bottles of wine missing, from the slots on the wall. "Eugene?" Nick called as he tossed his briefcase aside. Then he said softy, "Engene, I really hope you are at Dee Dee's."

He righted a display table on his way to his office. Papers had been pulled and tossed from his desk, file cabinet drawers emptied, the contents strewn everywhere. Hurrying down the stairway, Nick checked Eugene's apartment; the old man's bed was neatly made, and his coffee pot hadn't been perked this morning. His telephone messages—including Nick's—hadn't been retrieved, and Eugene was methodical about using "that silly machine," fearing it would overflow and he'd miss Dee Dee's call. Nick punched the button, and a nonstop flow of Celeste's sexy "Big Boy, you are so hot" and "stud-muffin" phone talk purred into the room; apparently Eugene had deleted all messages but those.

Nick punched in Dee Dee's number, taken from the pad beside the telephone, the sheet filled with heart-shaped doodles. Dee Dee answered briskly, and said that Eugene wasn't there. To keep her from worrying, Nick fed her a white lie that he just saw Eugene outside the window.

Nick moved quickly to the cellar doorway and turned on

the cellar lights. The yawning cool silence terrified him—
and the stronger smell of wine. "Eugene?"

A faint rattling echoed from deep inside the cool interior.
Nick picked up a two-by-four scrap board and held it as he
slowly descended the stairs. The rattling noise didn't stop as
he noted the bung holes opened on the wine barrels. The
tanks had been emptied, wine covering the floor. Nick moved
down the battered cases of wine, soaked now with their contents. Bottles had been smashed everywhere, glass glittering
in the ruined wine.

The noise became a rhythmic pounding that echoed from
the back of the cellar, and Nick rounded the toppled cases of
reserve wine to find Eugene sprawled on the damp floor.
Nick crouched beside the old man, lifting his head gently.

Blood mixed with wine on Eugene's forehead as he
sighed. He dropped the hammer he had been using on the
empty metal barrel next to him. The old man's voice was uneven and raspy. "I'm tired, Nick. Been down here awhile.
Came down here to see about the noise and got clobbered.
Didn't see who. My leg is hurting bad. I been in and out, but
Nick—Nick, I had to drink something. I crawled over to the
cases of Alyssa and found a bottle. The rest has been
smashed to smithereens. I heard the forklift run by me and
managed to roll against the wall, playing dead."

"You'll be fine, Eugene. I'll get help. Just hold still."

Eugene caught his arm. "But, Nick. All those bottles of
Alyssa—gone. That wine was special to you—"

"Eugene, stop. It's just glass and wine, not your life, and
not a woman."

The old man's eyes drifted closed. "You've moved on. I
knew Maggie would be good for you . . ."

Nick's eyes adjusted to the dimly lit interior of Ed's tavern.
With Eugene in the clinic, Nick had given the police chief,
his cousin Lorenzo, the basics, and had arranged to answer
in-depth questions later.

A crime-scene truck had been ordered with a team of experts Blanchefleur did not have, and there was enough yellow tape around Nick's winery to stretch to China. Police cars studded the parking lot, and the state of Michigan would be involved; Nick's wine had been bonded, making certain the state got its cut.

Dante and Maggie, both worried about Eugene, were at the clinic. And right now, after checking on the old man, Nick had an appointment with Ed; he wanted to get to the tavern owner before anyone else.

Seedy, old, and layered with brawls, under-the-table deals, and sex, Ed's Place served as a hangout for locals and fascinated tourists. Ed had been known to arrange private parties, such as the one for Maggie, and known prostitutes favored the bar. In the early afternoon, the tavern was closed and vibrating with country music. Stacking glasses behind the bar, the bartender had his back to Nick, his head bobbing to the beat of the music.

Shirley, a barmaid who catered to male tourists, and Ed's longtime, on-and-off girlfriend—when he wasn't busy with another woman—stood facing the door and laughing up at Ed. Beneath her hard makeup and mass of overteased hair, her eyes widened fearfully when she recognized Nick. She slid along the bar and hurried into the back room.

When Nick pulled the plug on the jukebox, Ed looked into the bar's mirror and found him. His body tensed, his expression one of surprise before he pulled on his insolent mask.

"Hello, Ed," Nick said quietly as he slid onto a bar stool. He smiled, belying the anger running inside him. He picked up a quarter lying on the bar and flipped it. It gave him something to do when he really wanted to haul Ed across the bar. "I thought I'd drop in and see how your inventory of wine is doing."

"You're not making me buy any." Ed poured himself a whiskey neat and drank it quickly. "The Alessandros are big in this town, related to everyone. But I've got some mob connections and you'd better not start anything with me."

"I'm not happy, Ed. You want to know why?"

"No, I just want you out of here. You Alessandros are nothing but trouble."

Nick flipped the coin high and caught it. "Heads, you tell me why you hurt Eugene. Tails, you tell me why you hit an old man. We'll get into the rest of it later."

Ed stared at him blankly. Then something moved in his expression, just a tiny jerk that Nick intended to pursue. Ed quickly downed another drink. "I don't know what you're talking about."

"Eugene is at the clinic with a concussion and a broken leg. I was at a wine festival yesterday. I saw you there, so you *knew* I was there. The winery was closed, and Eugene had the day off. He got back in the afternoon to a real mess. Someone broke into my winery, destroyed what they couldn't contaminate, pretty much ruined a complete inventory, and took a case or so of my best wines. But that is secondary to why anyone would hurt that old man."

"I never touched him." Ed's hand shook as he took a third drink.

With a violence that surprised himself, Nick picked up Ed's glass and hurled it against the mirror. Ed jumped back as the mirror cracked, shards of the whiskey shot glass spraying onto the bartender. "I don't know nothing!"

Nick reached across the bar to haul Ed up to his face. "I'm not feeling very gentle now, Ed. Where were you yesterday after you got back from the wine festival?"

"Came right back here. Shirley's sister was sick and she couldn't bartend. I was here, closed the place, and spent the night at JoAnn Armand's. We been doing it since Beth ran off. Just ask Shirley—she's been at me enough for playing around. She's been mad as hell at me since I took in Beth. I get tired of Shirley's griping, so I move around with women, but Beth was special, and she knew it. She's not happy about JoAnn, and you can call her if you want to," he repeated.

"I'm going to check on that, Ed."

"You do that." Ed shook loose and straightened his shirt

gingerly. He scribbled on a bar napkin. "Here's JoAnn's number. Point the law at me, I don't care. I wasn't anywhere near your place."

"Let's see." Nick leaned forward and with his other hand picked up the telephone. He cradled the receiver between his head and shoulder and punched out JoAnn's number.

JoAnn was at first glad to hear who he was and then sullen when asked about Ed.

"Tell him, JoAnn," Ed ordered roughly.

When she confirmed his alibi, Nick released Ed and studied him. The bartender was too nervous, taking another shot of whiskey. His eyes darted away from Nick's. Nick stood slowly, fighting his anger. "Everything better check out, Ed. Or I'll be back. And if you know anything about this, you'd better tell me. Think it over."

When Maggie entered the police station, Nick at her side, she took his hand. He immediately brought it to his lips. "Lorenzo is my cousin. He'll believe what you say. Calm down. You're shaking."

"I've been in police stations before. The experiences weren't pleasant. Do you think I should say something about Leo's attack?"

"It's up to you. This is just the initial interview of all people involved in the winery. The lock had been broken, and Eugene had forgotten to turn on the security system, so there will be more questions after the crime scene people do their job. Let him do his job, Maggie. He's a small tourist town police chief, but he's got a real feel for people."

Nick never left Maggie, his hand big and firm around hers, and Lorenzo briskly skimmed through the paperwork. When he was finished, he said softly, "Take it easy, Maggie. Nick tells me you're not too fond of police and that you once had a bad time proving a point to them. You're not under suspicion; this is just standard. I had to interview Eugene and got some cock-and-bull about how well he fought off his attacker, and

I pretended to take notes on that, too. This could take days, so just relax and let us do our job. Nick, there are rubber boot prints all over that place. Size ten."

Lorenzo looked at Maggie and then back at Nick. "If anyone you know has a grudge against either one of you, think about giving me that information. And Nick, the smell is so bad in there that the guys are requesting fans, so be prepared for an even bigger electricity bill."

On their way to Eugene at the clinic, Maggie said, "Your cousin suspects I'm not telling him something."

"He's leaving that up to you. You're pale and shaking. Take it easy while you visit Eugene, okay? I've got to meet Lorenzo at the winery. He's going to let me into the office for some files and paperwork I can do at home."

"Do you need me—?"

"I always need you. See you tonight at the house—you're staying with me, right?"

Maggie placed a shallow box of Rosa's food on Nick's kitchen counter. "Dee Dee has just collected Eugene from the clinic. I helped move him into her house. He'll need some of his things from his apartment. When I left, she was holding his hand and fussing over him. I couldn't tell if his smile was a leer or pain. How are you, Nick?"

She glanced at Dante, who had just passed her with one of Rosa's hot casseroles. At eleven o'clock at night, Nick's house was well lit, and he was seated at the kitchen table amid a mass of papers. The crumpled papers on the floor showed his frustration.

"I'm disgusted. I should have had a better security system, one with automatic timing, and I let an old man—a really good friend—get hurt. There's no way to fill these new orders now. Some of the equipment needs repair. We couldn't bottle, even if we had full tanks and barrels. Whoever it was wore gloves and fireman's boots. What he didn't break, he contaminated or emptied—rammed a forklift right through the cellar. It will take years to rebuild our customer base.

We've just shipped some case goods, but not enough to hold future shelf space and facing. This year's crop isn't going to stop ripening and it has to be processed. With what? The equipment is going to take a fortune to repair—I could lose the whole place."

When Maggie came to stand behind him, smoothing his shoulders, Nick leaned his head back against her and closed his eyes. He rubbed Scout's ears as the dog's head lay on his thigh. He sighed roughly. "It's been a long day. I'm glad you're here."

Dante slid into a chair. He placed three glasses on the table, and with an expert twist of the corkscrew lifted the cork out of Nick's best wine, reserved for family use. He poured it into the glasses and spoke thoughtfully. "Size ten farmer's rubber boots. Tracks everywhere. They're probably in the lake by now. He would have had wine stain all over him, so he probably wore some kind of gear. They're pretty certain it was one man by the tracks. Could have been someone on drugs . . . when they couldn't find cash in the receipt drawer, they lost control. But since you don't keep cash on hand when closed, that theory doesn't work. You do a lot of credit card and check business, not that much cash anyway."

Nick shook his head. "I don't think it was Ed. But I think he knows something—and I think he's afraid. I think he'd take a beating from me rather than talk."

"I don't think it was Ed, either. He might be a heavy breather, trying to intimidate women—"

Nick's head jerked away from her body and he stared up at her. "Has he been calling you?"

"Beth *and* me. A man like him won't just walk away—"

*"And you didn't tell me."*

"I didn't think it was important. I've had a lot worse come across telephone lines and so has Beth."

"You should have told me. But oh, no. You're used to handling your own problems, right?"

"And you're understandably upset about Eugene and the winery, so let's just stick to the problem at hand, okay?"

"If you two will stop arguing long enough, I have an idea. Lorna is pretty steamed about you and Maggie—"

Maggie shook her head. "She might have gone into my camper when I wasn't there, but I don't think she would have done anything like this. She's honest in what she wants, not sneaky."

Nick's hand grasped Maggie's wrist, and he brought her to sit on his lap. "What's this about your camper?" he demanded.

"Lorna left it very neat. She just wanted me to know that she could get to me when she wanted. It's an old game. When I got home the other day, Lorna was parked right outside the camper, waiting. I don't know why she wanted my family pictures, but I understand she's had a hard life. Maybe she wanted—"

Both men were staring at her blankly.

"Lorna? Neat? You've got to be kidding," Dante said finally. "Her housekeepers are always complaining. They usually don't stay long."

"She broke into your camper and you didn't tell me." Nick's words were spaced, accusing her.

"It's nothing to worry about. Nothing was broken. She's just pushing her weight around, that's all, nudging me."

Nick looked at Dante. "They have a bet about me. Maggie won't tell me what it is. Maggie handles everything in her life and doesn't want anyone else in her business. Things will have to change after we're married."

Maggie stared at him. "Nick—"

"I don't have anything to offer now, but a big mess. But I'll be back on my feet. I've done it before. You like puttering around a house and doing laundry. You can do that here, if you want—with my ring on your finger. What did you think? That I would let what we have go?"

When Maggie shook her head no, Nick looked back at his brother. "Don't mind her. It's going to take a while to set in. She's stubborn that way. We haven't even had a real date yet."

Maggie had tried to halt Nick's flow of words, but he wasn't about to stop. So she took the only action available to her. She lifted her glass and raised it over his head, slowly letting the wine fall, drop by drop, onto his shaggy head.

He settled in to ignore her reaction, but his arm held her tight against him. He licked the wine from his lips. "I am not in a good mood, Maggie. It's been a long day. Just sit still and let me hold you. If you want to argue, please save it for much, much later."

Nick looked so gloomy that Maggie couldn't help reaching out to dab away the wine she'd spilled on his head. She kissed him lightly. "Later, then. But don't think you're going to get away with that."

He was silent for a moment and then he said, "About Leo Knute. He wasn't exactly happy. He did a lot of threatening. Maybe he's come back to make good. But it's up to you, Maggie, if you want to tell Lorenzo. He'll get there, sooner or later, just by talking to Eugene and others and fitting the pieces together. It's a stretch for you, but this time you might trust the law."

"I have been thinking that I would."

"Leo was mad enough. But he should know what will happen if he tries anything again. But then maybe he's sent a professional." Dante swirled his wine and then sipped it. His look at Nick said his thoughts were serious. "Maybe it's time you told her. Maybe they want Scout. When she went for Leo, and it took everything I had to haul her off him."

Holding Maggie in his arms, Nick tensed. "Big mouth. She's got enough on her plate with Celeste's—"

"Tell me what?" Maggie caught Nick's hair in her fist and tugged it back, looking down at him. "What about my dog?" she demanded, and sensed that the tension in the room had shifted once again.

Nick sighed tiredly. "Someone was at the restaurant, claiming that Scout was his. It could have been anyone faking ownership papers. She's been around town enough and she's a good-looking dog. Mom ran him off. Dante can't find where he is staying. The guy is probably gone by now. They didn't want to bother Lorenzo with something so small. He's got enough problems with tourists letting off steam, and that underage bunch on drugs."

"Scout took after the man. She's become a town pet, especially with the geriatric crowd, and the children love to shake hands with her. Other than that night with Leo Knute, she's a gentle dog."

"Sometimes the threat in a person's voice will trigger a re-action like that," Nick added. "Especially if the person is holding something in his hand, like that leash. If it is Leo's doing, then we'd better keep Scout close. She's gotten into a routine of checking on the shops while you're at the gym, especially Marco's."

Maggie tore away, shivering with reaction. Flashes of Scout, muddy and unfed, with the wariness of a mistreated animal that had taken a very short time of loving to over-come, played in Maggie's mind.

Was the man Brent Templeton? Was it possible that he could have come after them?

Brent was obsessively neat. He couldn't bear to step into spilled wine, or mess up the office . . . But he was capable of using someone to do his dirty work. Brent was very good at that . . .

She wrapped her arms around herself, her fears leaping within her. A tide of memories washed over her as she clasped her locket. "What . . . what did he look like?"

The brothers studied her as Dante said, "Tall, thin, walks with a limp, thin gray sandy-colored hair, narrow face, bro-ken nose, scar along one cheek. Has a sickly look. Not a friendly guy. A loner."

The description didn't match Brent. Hours spent in a gym had honed his muscles; facials and Jamaican holidays kept him smooth and tan. He moved with a slick, winning confi-dence, and he was never alone, always surrounded by power-ful people and those who needed them. He preyed upon the latter, twisting their lives so poisonously that—

Glenda . . .

Nick rose and came to stand beside her. He took her hand between his. "You're ice-cold. Do you know this guy?"

She shook her head. She fought to dismiss her terror and yet it nagged, nipping at her. With his money and vanity, a fitness addict with resources, he wouldn't have scars or a limp. Brent would never have allowed himself to look other than perfect, and he was very smooth. His easygoing, friendly manner concealed a deadly predator who liked to play games. "No, of course not. But I think I saw that same man when I sailed with Dante. It's just been a long day. Where do you think he is now?"

"We've been hunting for him. My guess is that he left town after the incident at the restaurant. Mom has threatened to put the evil eye on him, but don't tell Dad. Nick, Maggie stayed with Eugene the whole time. She hasn't eaten, but a little that Mom urged into her," Dante said softly. "She's always taking care of other people, but she forgets about herself."

Nick drew her against him, holding her in his safe way. "Maggie, what you tell Lorenzo is up to you. But if this investigation opens up and Leo is proven to be involved, there's a question of withholding information."

Maggie didn't want Nick or Dante to be held to blame for her decision. "I'll call him in the morning—anything to help."

"Call him now. He's working on this full time to help me hurrying through this investigation and get that yellow crime-scene tape removed. I've got to get up and running before that crop comes in. Dante, I'll take care of her. Let's see about good old Leo—what he's been up to. You took down the information from his wallet, Dante. After Maggie calls Lorenzo, give it to him."

Brent had waited for the concealing cloud-covered night; he'd carefully timed the movements of the coast guard and land patrols. The small town's police and a team of investigators were working full time with investigators at the winery, and that distraction served Brent's night adventures.

Before Brent had married well, he'd worked the wealthy resort docks, and the experience had served him well. He motored a small fishing boat out onto the lake and checked the cables around Leo Knute's tarp-wrapped body. A sizable incision in Leo's midsection, plus the added weight of the sunken boat, would ensure that the body didn't resurface.

According to Brent's directions to Ed, this particular fishing boat had a large hole in the bottom, crudely repaired and already leaking. Another boat, tied to the side, would be Brent's ride back to shore. Ed knew only that Brent needed to dispose of something.

Ed—a pitiful excuse for a man—feared Brent now, feared what he knew and what he could do. The bartender was in too deep to get out now, fearing Brent and his "connections." At first, Ed had latched onto the idea of getting Scout, breeding her for the money, and his desire for revenge against Maggie still simmered. Using that, Brent had snared Ed's alliance and help.

The small-town police chief, a relative of the Alessandros, had already interviewed Ed; after that Ed, a longtime antagonist of Nick's, had been noticeably jumpy.

Brent shrugged. That was as it should be—his talent came in gauging the weak, playing them, just as he had played Maggie's sister.

But Maggie wouldn't play. She didn't understand the rules. He would have to make her understand, to make her obey his every wish—before he killed her. He kicked at the repaired hole until the water began to gush through the crack and it widened treacherously.

Leo had served his purpose, driving in that night to destroy the winery. Later, Brent had been waiting for him in a deserted garage. As they had agreed, Leo had handed Brent a thick wad of big bills for the information leading to Maggie and Nick, the bargain between just the two of them. Laughing wildly, Leo planned how he would come back and kill the entire vineyard, so that nothing would ever grow on Alessandro land. Then, high on drugs, wine, and revenge, Leo had wanted Maggie, bragging about what he would do to her . . .

Brent moved briskly to the other boat and frowned into the dark water, remembering the blank look on Leo's face as the overdose hit him, passing from pleasure into death. No one but Brent was tending to Maggie Chantel, and she would tell him that she loved him before she died, just like her sister . . .

He watched the water seem to slowly absorb Leo's boat. With care, Brent placed Leo's wine-stained farmer's boots into a plastic sack—they tied Leo to the ruined wine, and could be useful later.

Brent removed his rubber gloves and stuffed them into a plastic bag loaded with rocks. He tossed the bag into the water and began humming as he motored back to shore.

His mother had always taught him to be tidy.

# FIFTEEN

From his vantage point in the old lighthouse, Nick watched the woman on the beach. The brief call to inform his cousin Lorenzo, the local police chief, about Leo's attack had really upset her. And when Nick took the telephone, Lorenzo hadn't been too happy with him. His rapt admonishment "Nick," was followed by the hiss of a dead line and had a lot of force—Lorenzo, as police chief, should have been informed of Leo's attack.

On the beach now, Maggie had slipped from Nick's arms and his bed, just as easily as she could slip from his life. Her past was always there, locked against him, and yet touching their lives. Maggie had more to tell him, and yet she preferred to keep that distance between them.

Nick ran his hand over his bare chest and wondered what drew her to the water. Maggie had changed since Celeste's death, as if she were waiting for closure and listening to an inner voice. Even now, Maggie stretched her arms high into the brief slice of moonlight, as though she was trying to summon the answer within her.

Maybe he'd never understand. Maggie had faced her fear of sailing, and now she was dealing with Celeste's death in her own way.

Women kept their secrets, and Celeste, Beth, and Maggie definitely had a bond.

The odd thing was that Maggie had defended Lorna.

The winery's destruction and the attack on Eugene was one thing, stirring a cold anger that Nick feared releasing.

Maggie was something else: There was always that distance, as though she didn't want to fully step into their relationship. He rubbed the ache in his chest, the one that told him how much he would miss her.

And she wouldn't like what he had planned.

Nick picked up the telephone and punched in Vinnie's number. At two o'clock in the morning, the radio was playing loudly in Vinnie's garage, a sign that he was working on a very private project. When he answered the telephone, Vinnie was panting, and the sound of a welder's dying torch hissed in the background. "Yeah?"

Nick didn't want to know about Vinnie's special nighttime work. "Vinnie. I've got something I need done, and I can't do it myself."

"You got it. Heard about the winery. Bad deal. The family and I been talking about it. We figure an outsider did the deed. Not kids on a spree, but someone out to make a point, a warning."

"We're working on it. I think the wine growers association will pitch in to help me with this harvest. I've helped enough of them in the past. Vinnie, there is going to be a lot of inquiries. If you've got anything going that isn't on the up-and-up, you might call it off for a bit. Meanwhile, if you could get a few relatives together and help me out, I'd appreciate it."

"Rebuild the place?"

"Can't do that until the insurance and investigators are done, and I'm tied up with paperwork and obligations now. I can't meet those orders I just took, and I've got to work on getting equipment for this year's crop. No, this has to be done tomorrow, while Maggie is in town."

A woman's voice murmured close to Vinnie and he answered, "Sure, baby. I'll be right there. I got to go, Nick. My baby is sweaty, revved, and waiting. How can I help?"

The identity of Vinnie's girlfriends weren't for discussion. He let it be known that he liked married women, keeping his obligations in the affairs to a minimum.

Nick gave a brief description of the job and replaced the telephone. Maggie would dig in to argue, and things could get rough between them. He could lose her.

Maggie walked up the knoll to Nick's house, the sand cool and shifting beneath her feet, just as her fears stirred within her.

Lorenzo's questions had been quick and shielded, but he wanted answers: Had she given Leo any indication that she might play ball that night? Had he paid her? The questions led to Ed, and Lorenzo advised her to avoid future conversation with the bartender. Lorenzo had chuckled when she described her confrontation with Ed to protect Beth.

Maggie pushed away her uncertainty, that nagging quiet voice about Brent, and called to Celeste to help her. The description of the stranger did not fit Brent, meticulous about his physical fitness, his hair and face. A vain man, he would have repaired imperfections: If he were thinning, he would have had implants. If he had a scar, he would have had cosmetic surgery. He ran and exercised regularly, ate well, and on the outside was the picture of a healthy athlete. But his mind was sick, and the infection spread to the people whose lives he touched.

Scout moved close to her, as if understanding her unsettled emotions, and Maggie bent to hug her pet. "It isn't Brent. He's far too vain and too sly to outright come after you. He was glad to get me out of town, to shut me up. He knows I can make trouble."

Nick stood on the porch, dressed only in jeans, and standing with legs braced and arms crossed. A big man, he was a formidable sight as he watched her walk up to the house. "You're upset because I want to marry you."

"Yes, I am. I've been married. It wasn't fun. I was the good wife and I gave everything, too much."

"I got that picture."

Maggie understood Nick's pride and his vulnerability now. But she wasn't acting as a scapegoat for his frustration and letting someone else set terms for her life. She'd learned the hard way. "Now isn't the time to be discussing something like that."

"You think because my business is in the toilet that I can't handle my private life? That I don't know my own mind when it comes to the only woman in my life?" His angry thrust sailed across the shadows to her.

"You're going to work through this, Nick. You'll rebuild. That's what I'm trying to do with my life."

"Your nightmares—they're worse. Why? Did the investigation make you nervous? Lorenzo is only doing his job, honey. He's not looking at you as a suspect."

"It's not about that. I rescued Scout. The thought that anything could happen to her—it's a long story."

"I'm waiting." The demand was flat, tinged in anger that stoked her own.

"You can wait then." Maggie didn't want Nick to see the darkness she'd left behind.

He chewed on that, a muscle moving in his jaw, then demanded, "What am I to you? A temporary stop before you move on?"

Maggie fought her own anger. She'd been pushed, and hard, before in her life and now Nick's need for legal commitment nettled. "Nick, I wouldn't be here now if I didn't want to be."

"Move in with me. I want you protected. If anything happens to you—"

Maggie instantly sensed his insecurity—that he'd once let a woman he'd loved die. Instinctively, she moved into his arms, holding him tight. "Nothing is going to happen to me, Nick."

Against her cheek, his heart was racing, his arms trembling around her. "Nothing can."

When Nick picked her up to carry her to bed, Maggie held him tightly. She understood his need, and her own, to share the tenderness between them, to be one and to be comforted—because she had already started to love him.

Yet to her, love was a dangerous seduction, taking away everything—because she gave everything.

In the morning, Maggie awoke slowly to Nick's steady, even breathing. Today would be difficult for him—facing the reality of investigators, paperwork, calling customers, the legalities of dealing with a criminally ruined inventory.

She eased aside to look at him, this man who already shared part of her heart, and definitely had shared her body. The muted light from the window gentled his features. She eased back a strand of waving hair from his forehead, and he grunted, jerking away as though he didn't want to wake up. "Go back to sleep," he murmured drowsily.

Maggie studied the long sweep of his lashes, his tousled look. The arrogance was still there in the broad planes of his face, the blunt masculine nose beneath her prowling fingertip. Celeste had said that it was a stubborn, truthful nose, that men with those noses were honest and faithful—they could be trusted.

Beside the bed, the crystals in an abalone shell gleamed, the facets catching color from the early morning sunlight. Celeste had given the crystals to Nick just days before she died, her actions unexplained.

The multicolors of the abalone shell seemed to cuddle the crystals, bringing warmth and life to them as images stirred within Maggie.

She saw him as a boy, running freely with his brothers. As a grandson, helping an aged man fulfill his dream. As a son who loved his parents and family.

She saw him as her lover, intimate and honed, locking her possessively to him.

She inhaled slowly, and turned to Nick. His tall body sprawled on the bed, a sheet pushed down to his hips.

New and demanding, the need to take him, pit herself against him, rose in her. Perhaps the physical need was a release for the tension of last night, the more primitive side of tenderness, the dark possession of a predator.

Maggie nestled her bare breasts against his arm, smoothed her insole against his shin, and settled in to think about Nick.

With Nick, she simply enjoyed being a woman—at times feminine, at times playful. She enjoyed being in command of herself—and with Nick, strong and predatory, a taker. She could be what she wanted, because Nick could handle it— meeting her in equal strength.

Whatever happened between them, for the moment, she was in full possession of a man she had chosen, not one that society and surface logic had chosen for her. With Nick, she was unafraid to show her sexuality, her needs and hunger. Call it tension release, but Maggie felt alive and strong and physically ready to take on anything.

Biorhythms, Celeste had explained, were a powerful influence, and now Maggie's were dismissing everything but the pleasure of—

With Nick, she enjoyed being predatory, and now was the time to give him a sexual marathon to remember throughout a long, hard day . . .

Nick dreamed of Maggie's hand on the stick shift, the skillful movements that could make him hard. He gave himself to the luxurious sensation of those hands on him, moving him into high, erect gear.

He groaned, pulsing and hungry and—Nick opened his eyes as Maggie moved over him, kneeling to capture him fully.

With slow rhythm, she took him from one dream into throbbing reality.

Just before she went into herself, Nick caught that smile—a pleased, victorious smirk that caught him.

So she thought him easy, did she?

Taking care, Nick eased slightly away, eluding her capture of him fully.

Braced on his shoulders, her fingers dug in, her body trembling as he withstood his own release.

Everything else outside their own intimate battle, Nick caressed her hips until that first threatening orgasm eased without release.

She frowned down at him. "Nick?"

He couldn't stop his grin. "Maggie."

One hand lightly prowled his chest, and she tugged a hair gently, her expression challenging. "Don't make this difficult on yourself. Give up."

"You first." He ran his thumb over the crest of her nipple and then raised to suckle gently, edging it with his teeth before lying back down.

Watching Maggie deal with her frustration and her pride was fascinating. "You want games? I'll give you games."

She settled down atop him, her elbows braced beside his head, her hand toying with his hair. Her hips undulated slowly upon him. The tightening of her inner muscles almost sent him over the edge. She brushed her lips over his, holding his bottom lip in her teeth just that instant before releasing it. "Take that, Nick. Live and learn."

Maggie was all heat and sleek, damp, soft skin, her muscles gliding smoothly beneath his caresses.

Nick allowed the knowing feminine smirk, enjoying it, before he moved his hand down her belly, lifting her slightly.

When his fingers found the tiny intimate treasure, Maggie stiffened. "That's not fair."

This time, it was his turn to smile. "Isn't it?"

\* \* \*

Multiple orgasms with Nick had a way of making the morning absolutely beautiful, Maggie decided.

Not that she was alone in the orgasm lane, as she had thoroughly zapped Nick. Or he had zapped her.

It was a mutual experience, a most satisfying, long-lasting, draining, woozy, and filling experience. Maggie showered quickly, pleased that the man she had left that morning could only grunt and turn over after her good-morning kiss.

"I hope I haven't ruined you, dear," she'd whispered against his ear, gloating a little that she was the first to move that morning.

Her muscles ached, but then the physical release had been long and powerful—and satisfying for them both.

He'd grunted again, an apparent concession to her victory.

They had met in a balance of endurance and power, but his button move just wasn't fair.

Okay, so it was a toss-up, Maggie admitted as she dressed in an athletic bra, a tank top, and shorts. She tied her shoes briskly and noted the slight twinge in her haunches.

Maggie smiled softly. She'd left Nick belly-down, sprawled on the bed, unable to move. He'd have a hard day, but she'd accomplished her goal of giving him something to take with him.

And tonight she planned a candlelit bedroom assault. After fighting legalities and frustration all day, he'd come home to a good meal and healthy, devastating sex, which she would thoroughly enjoy.

If Nick was up to it. He'd definitely been up to it earlier, giving her only so much before starting again, lifting her even higher . . .

Maggie shuddered a little bit, remembering flashes of their match, a good healthy release of tension, a little bit of physical medicine before they both met their day.

But now she was late for her appointments, and despite the shadow of the destroyed winery, the possibility of Leo in the area, and the ongoing investigation that could take days, she was supremely happy. Anxious to meet the day, Scout was busy prancing in front of the door, whining softly.

"You are going to have to stop visiting the whole town for a while, Scout. If Leo is involved with this, I don't want to think about what he would do. Let's just stick together like we always have, okay?"

Maggie lifted her freshly shampooed hair into a ponytail, opened the back door, stepped onto the deck, and stretched.

She stopped, arms held high, and looked at the men seated in various positions around the deck. The Alessandro males—Vinnie, Dante, Tony, and others—were drinking coffee and eating cinnamon rolls. Anthony held a water hose, rinsing the siding of a big metal building . . .

Maggie blinked, and it wasn't a building at all. Her camper was parked alongside Nick's house.

"About time," Vinnie said around the toothpick on his lips. One eye was swollen and he looked as if he'd had a hard night. "Setting up a hookup is going to be a bitch. It would be easier to have one of the commercial guys come out here with a truck and empty the tanks."

Vinnie looked past Maggie. "I don't think your girl likes the arrangement, Nick. You're on your own."

Maggie turned to Nick, who stood in his boxer shorts. He yawned and rubbed his hair as if slowly coming awake. "Thanks, Vinnie. I'll handle her from now."

She stared at Nick, her tender lover of last night and the man who had survived her full athletic skills. He'd handled her all right, but there was a possessive confidence about him now—and a narrowed, determined look that matched the lock of his jaw.

Nick bent to pluck a daisy, then tucked it in her hair. His smile was tight and grim. "Good morning, honey. This arrangement is only temporary, until we know just who is behind destroying my winery. Or you could move in and make everything simple."

"Let me get this straight: I am supposed to accommodate you. You just move George's—"

With the look of an artist putting the finishing touches on a painting, Nick adjusted the daisy in her hair. "George agreed, honey. He thought it was best, too."

To the men, he smiled warmly. "She's cute when she's all worked up, don't you think? I like her freckles."

Nick had kissed enough of her freckles last night. Now he was primed for a complete takeover. Maggie batted away his finger as it traced the freckles on her cheek.

Scout was standing at attention, eyeing the cinnamon roll in Tony's hand. "Tony, if you give that to my dog, you're dead," Maggie said.

He had that little-boy guilty look. Nick didn't; he looked as if he'd dug in for a fight and he meant to have his way.

Vinnie tossed a hand unit to Nick and yawned. "We rigged an alarm system. An intercom between the camper and house. You're close enough for a good reception—and one that goes all the way to the winery, too. See you. Let me know if you need anything else. I gotta catch some shut-eye."

Anthony looked at Maggie. "My son is worried about you. We all worry about you, alone in that tin can. This is a small thing, to keep you safe. You can stay at the apartment, but you know, my Rosa, she won't like Nick . . . ah, visiting. And I remember when I was young, and maybe now, too, I wouldn't stay away from Rosa. I needed to hold her in my arms each night and know that she was safe and well. That is how he feels, I'm sure."

"I want her to marry me," Nick said with that narrowed look down at her, as if he were digging in for a war he intended to win. "It's only a short time, but I know what I want."

"Your mother wants a ring on Maggie's finger, Nick. She wants to know if we raised you wrong. I am paying a price for this, you know, boy. I was a little bit of a ladies' man in my youth, and she's blaming me for what you do. She sees you together, and she knows that it is right. Maybe you had better start talking to Tony. He could give you advice about courting a woman of today."

Maggie stared at Anthony and Nick, both men towering over her. Nick's winery should be his first concern this morning, and his family's. Instead, they were discussing why Nick and she weren't making wedding plans. "Hey. I'm in this somewhere."

"Is my son not romantic enough?" Anthony demanded as the other men started to grin.

Nick glared at them, his hands on his hips. "She's going to change her mind. She's been married before and didn't like it. She's going to like it with me."

"Oh, am I? Nick, you have important business this morning—you know, the winery? All those investigators? Your customers?"

"*This* is important business," Nick and his father stated at the same time, frowning at her.

Because actions came more easily to Maggie than words, she reached for the hose Anthony had been using. Adjusting the spray to full force, Maggie aimed the water at Nick. He stood, arms crossed, eyes closed, as the water hit his face and moved down the length of his body.

While he was standing in the pool of water, streams of it flowing over his body, and dripping from his hair and soaked boxer shorts, Maggie turned the stream on the other men, who yelped in surprise and leaped over the guardrails, standing back a distance.

Scout barked happily, running around the deck and leaping on Nick. He rough-played with her and then eyed Maggie. He blew a drop of water from his nose. "At least *she* likes me."

Maggie sprayed him again, gave the hose to Anthony, and stood on tiptoe to kiss his cheek. "Don't blame yourself. Your other two sons are sweet."

Anthony grinned widely. "I want one of those old-fashioned handlebar mustaches, a really big set that I can use wax on to curl the ends up. Rosa says no. She likes you. Maybe you could talk to her about my mustache?"

Maggie considered the older man carefully. Family was

more important to Anthony than the replacement of a business. "You get Nick to back off and I will. He's coming on like gangbusters and I like to make up my own mind. I've got a lot to settle, and he's not making it easy."

She threw up her hands. "Here we are, in the middle of a disaster, Nick's business could be ruined, investigators swarming everywhere—"

Anthony laughed loudly. " 'Gang busters.' Yes, that would be my sons. You should have seen them when they were young. Still, a woman has the right to make up her own mind—sometimes."

He lowered his voice to a serious tone. "This is dangerous, Maggie. He is only concerned about you. Forgive him his mistakes. It is a bad time for him. He held his grandfather's dream close, and he has already lost once before."

"I know, and he's emotional right now. But he can't push me around."

"That's good, to have a balance where the man and woman understand each is strong and each is willing to give."

"I understand that he is vulnerable right now, Anthony. I'm going to help him get through this and then we'll see what happens. We're each sorting out the past right now." Then Maggie turned to the other men. " 'Bye, boys. I'm running into town and taking Scout. I'm making my appointments and then I can help, Nick."

"You don't need to do that. I'm not asking." Nick's pride slapped at her through the morning light. He wasn't quite as modern a man as he thought, in his time of stress placing her neatly aside.

She'd been placed in life's boxes before and didn't like it. He needed her help and he was going to get it. "Too bad. Have fun putting my camper back."

Maggie took off at a slow pace, furious with Nick for making decisions without talking to her. Instead of running at her side, Scout doubled back. Maggie recognized the dog's affection for Nick and knew that he would care for her closely since the man's attack at the restaurant.

Brent Templeton couldn't possibly have found her—or wanted to find her, after all the attention she'd drawn to him. The description didn't fit Brent at all, and yet the image of the man standing beside the channel nagged.

She fought to dismiss the idea that Brent would be near.

Anyone could have forged papers. . . . Pedigreed dogs were stolen all the time, either for resale or for breeding. Some people didn't care about papers, they just wanted the dog for retrieving. Now, thanks to Nick's efforts, Scout retrieved perfectly; she held in place until given the "go" signal. Secure in her treatment from Nick, Scout had proved that she wasn't gun-shy or afraid of feathers.

Maggie geared up her pace into a full jog, noting in the tightness of her body that she hadn't done her full set of warmups. She'd been too eager to get away from the Alessandro men.

After the strenuous lovemaking last night, her body still felt heavy and warm and sated.

Scout barked behind her, a happy sound, and Maggie turned to see Nick in his wet boxer shorts and running shoes jogging behind her. Tony had stopped in the road; he was bent over, apparently dragging in breath, his hands braced on his knees. Dante was keeping even with Nick, and while Dante's expression said he was challenging his brother, Nick's said that nothing could keep him from running with Maggie. Vinnie's truck came alongside Dante and he leaped onto the running board, waving as he rode by her.

Maggie allowed Nick to catch up with her. Once he was beside her, she didn't glance at him. With wet, shaggy hair and unshaven face, he made quite a morning picture in his sodden boxer undershorts. "You need new shoes. Those are too worn."

He didn't answer, but grimly matched his stride to hers.

She did a double-take, noting the inside-out boxer shorts.

"I needed an athletic supporter," Nick growled. "I had to hurry."

Maggie couldn't help grinning. "You look ridiculous,

Nick. Go back to the house. I'm only going to run into town. I need to do a little business this morning and then—"

"Okay, I'll go back. But only with you." Nick suddenly turned, bent, and hefted her over his shoulder. "One way or the other."

"You're steamed, huh?" Nick said as Maggie sat beside him in his pickup.

"Being lugged around like a sack of flour—yes, I am steamed." Maggie continued staring out at the early morning, already bright and foretelling a hot, dry August day without a breath of air.

His hand slid briefly on her bare thigh, then settled on her knee. The caress was just enough to remind her of last night's sensuality—and his full, exhausting, mind-blowing possession of her. "Like I said, you're cute when you're in a snit. Your arms across your chest lift up your breasts, and the way you pout is very sexy."

She lowered her arms to her midsection. "Shouldn't you be concerned about the investigation today?"

Nick nodded, his expression serious. "I'll think better when I know where you're at and that you're protected. This is a dangerous situation, honey, and I want you safe. Is that so bad?"

"I've handled my life so far. This is a takeover. Correction: a macho takeover." She eyed him across the cab as Scout sat between them, and she looked down to the big hand on her thigh.

Nick took the hint and removed his hand from her leg and looped his arm around Scout, who was tongue-hanging-out-panting happy. "Jerry wants in on this. You wouldn't deprive him of acting as a bodyguard, would you? I'll pick you up later, or someone will bring you out to the winery. Keep Scout on that leash today."

"You're giving *me* orders?"

"Someone has to. Try to fit in with the plan and not cause trouble, okay? And if any investigators, other than Lorenzo, want to talk with you, call me first. I'll be there with you." Nick slid the pickup alongside the sidewalk in front of Journeys. Immediately, Jerry came at a run, as if he'd been waiting to seize the moment, his big chance.

Puffed up and dressed in black, the youth was dressed for duty in army camouflage T-shirt and pants. Binoculars hung from his neck, and a variety of tools hung from his belt. Jerry briskly opened the passenger door for Maggie. He slapped the loaded pockets on the side of his pants. "Got a cell phone and a walkie-talkie. Tested it with Tony and Dante. The reception is good. I'll take it from here," he announced. "She's safe with me. The checkpoints are set up. After taking care of the shop, she goes to Celeste's to water plants, then to the gym, then maybe a stopover at your folks' place. Any changes in schedule will be called in."

Maggie didn't let Nick escape her stare as he got out of the pickup and rounded it. "A little overdone, don't you think?"

A movement on the street caused her to turn. Marco stood in front of his butcher shop, a big ham bone in his fist as if it were a club. Down one block, Dante stood casually, one hand on the florist's display. He returned Nick's brief wave.

As if he were patrolling, Tony drove by slowly on the street, and Nick nodded. Then he turned to Maggie's accusing frown. "Got to go," he said almost cheerfully. "Have a nice day, honey."

When she remained silent, Nick shared a look with Jerry. "She gets that way. Take care of her, okay?"

"You got it." Jerry whipped out a walkie-talkie. "Alpha One to Dinosaur. Alpha One—"

The metallic sound of Dante's voice sizzled through the air. "You idiot. I'm not that old."

"Um. Just checking. Dinosaur Pappy, are you reading me?"

This time Tony's voice snapped. "Shut up, twerp. Don't use that thing again until there's trouble or the checkpoints have changed. Got it?"

"Someone has to be in charge of this operation." Looking

pleased with himself, Jerry shoved the unit down into his pants cargo pocket. He put his hands behind him and braced his legs in a military stance.

Maggie shook her head. "This isn't necessary. Nick . . . uh . . . Mmm. . . ."

His goodbye kiss sizzled all the way down to her toes. With the little brain she had left, she grabbed his T-shirt, ignoring his wince. "Nick, if Beth calls, you tell her to stay put in Iowa, okay? Tell her what you have to, but keep her away. I don't want her to be involved if this—"

His hands closed over hers. "I'll take care of it."

He understood her protective affection for Beth, compassion softening his dark eyes. Because he cared, Maggie stood on tiptoe to kiss him briefly. "Thanks."

After Nick left for the winery, Maggie stood very still. Celeste's goddess within the silver chimes seemed to turn slowly, too slowly, though the air was still.

As Maggie held her locket, a slight chill curled around her. The hairs on Maggie's nape lifted, as if in warning. Scout, leashed and standing beside her, also watched the slow turning of the goddess, as if she, too, had been warned.

# SIXTEEN

Just down the street, Ed noted the kid in camouflage, and saw Dante hanging around the florist shop. Dante, supposedly admiring the flowering baskets that hung from the canvas awning, had never been a fan of flowers. At this time of the morning, he was usually down at his boatyard. Yet this morning, he was hanging around town.

That damn Lorenzo Alessandro had been pushing Ed, asking questions about Leo Knute and Ed's connection with him, and when was the last time he'd heard from Leo. That cop was bad news, as much as the rest of the Alessandros. The Crazy upstairs had better stay quiet and out of sight, because if he didn't—

Nick Alessandro had just planted a big juicy one on the woman with the dog. The hotshot kid was tailing her into the old witch's shop. Ed had seen enough television to know when a surveillance had been set up. So the Alessandros were out in force to protect the woman, were they?

Shirley came to stand beside Ed. He could trust her; he knew how to work what she needed, the little compliments, the trinkets from the few heists he'd pulled in the summer people's homes. She did everything he said, believed his excuses for being with other women and his rationale for his obsession with Beth—that he never quite got over his childhood sweetheart and Beth reminded him of that sweet, good time. He had told Shirley his obsession had to run its course and then he'd come back to stay.

"What's he doing now?" Ed asked her.

"Sleeping. I mixed a dose of what you gave me in his food."

Ed snorted in disgust. Brent Templeton might have been really something once—he kept yakking about everything that he had and how he ruled the world and had women at his call. But he was really just crazy as a loon—and he believed in his power over Ed—which only gave Ed a real edge on handling him.

His time was coming, Ed decided as he took one last drag on his cigarette. He flicked the butt onto the cobblestones. There was more than one way to get rid of that spooky psychic, the woman who had taken Beth from him, and Nick Alessandro.

He'd had Shirley following The Crazy, watching everything—The Crazy killing Celeste, breaking into her house, and killing the rich idiot who tore up Alessandro's winery.

Unable to stand waiting longer, The Crazy had gone out that day to get the dog. Anyone with an ounce of sense would not have gone to the Alessandros' Restaurant like that, waving papers in broad daylight and taking on the family.

That idiot could have given everything away right then, and Ed had convinced him that the locked apartment door was for his protection—it was really to keep him under control while Ed was busy. The drugs helped control The Crazy.

Beth would be back, and nothing could keep Ed from her this time. Everything was working out fine.

He nodded, satisfied that the game was being played exactly to his liking. So he had to put up with a few problems—the idiot's demand to clean the apartment, his nitpicky obsessions. Soon Ed would be done with lugging specially prepared food up to his renter. Did Brent actually think that Ed would be satisfied with a few bills, when he could have more?

Once that witch woman was gone, nothing could stop him. When bred with a good male, that dog's pups would bring a pretty penny. Maggie had shamed him once with a sucker move, and she'd pay for that, and Nick for pushing his weight around. The Crazy would do all the work, and then . . .

Ed chuckled at how easily his superior brain could manipulate weaker minds, using their frailties against them.

He thought about Beth, how much he loved her, and how she'd come back to him. She was just a sweet kid, after all, and taking off with the farmboy would only prove that Ed was the best choice.

"Let's go in, Shirley. You're looking really good today. Is that a new shade of lipstick?" he asked and watched the compliment sink deep and strong as she preened. Shirley was a good old girl.

"You wanted to see me?" Maggie asked Lorna over the elegant house intercom. "What's this about?"

"Just a minute." Lorna opened the door and swept her hand in front of her, a grand gesture indicating Maggie should enter.

When the door closed, Maggie said, "I don't have much time. You left a message for 'Man Stealer' on Celeste's machine that you wanted to see me. You were right. I do know who you are without leaving a name. Make it fast. You said you had information about the winery and wanted a private tea party?"

A quick glance at the opulent entryway and the grand room beyond it said that Lorna's tastes were very, very expensive.

Dressed as she had been before—in a tight-fitting sports bra, short spandex pants, and high-top laced gym boots—Lorna had been working out. She unlaced her boxing gloves enough to slip them off, patted her sweaty face with the towel around her shoulders, and tossed the gloves aside on a brocade-covered bench. "Where's the dog and how did you get rid of the kid tailing you?"

Maggie ignored the question. Scout was at Tony's house and she'd sent Jerry on a "necessary errand": Jerry didn't want to go into the grocery store for feminine supplies. And she'd said she wasn't coming out of the bathroom until he got what she wanted. Once Jerry had left the house, Maggie had hurried to Lorna's. "What do you know, Lorna?"

"We're going to have to play this my way, got it? Come on back."

Maggie followed Lorna through the elegant house to a well-stocked workout room. The punching bag was still swinging. "Let's have it."

"I hear Nick's winery was pretty well smashed."

Maggie nodded; it was hard to miss the big crime-scene van parked next to the winery and all the yellow ribbon blocking off entrances to the place.

Lorna moved to a large framed mirror. At the touch of a hidden button, it swung open and a gush of cool air swept against Maggie. With an assessing look, Lorna folded her arms in front of her chest. "You'd fight for him, wouldn't you?"

"If this is—"

"You're going to have to take this package as I give it to you. I'm mixed up and know it. Therefore, I do mixed-up things. I've got two rotten marriages behind me, and Vinnie—"

"Vinnie?" The name shocked Maggie. Was it possible that Nick's own cousin—?

"It's not what you're thinking. Vinnie is a good guy. He understands me and he doesn't ask anything. He got me started on kickboxing to defend myself. I was a pampered butt once and I liked being a spoiled rich bitch. Maybe I still do. You were right. Nick was someone I couldn't have— more of a challenge than anything else. Vinnie thinks my father soured me for most men."

Lorna paused briefly and then continued as if nothing could stop her admission, "I'm Vinnie's girlfriend. I have been through everything, and he hasn't pointed any fingers at me. We work out at night, sometimes put a car together, and I like welding and machines, something Daddy wouldn't understand. I got a little worked up over this whole thing last night when we were practicing kickboxing and punched Vinnie too hard. My aim was off. I just wasn't focused. He's wearing a black eye this morning and I really feel bad about that. It was an accident."

She flicked on a switch, and light sprang from the stairway leading downward. She entered the stairway and paused to look up at Maggie. "Sixty degrees. A private cellar. And well stocked. Enough to help Nick meet some orders. It's the only thing that Vinnie ever asked of me—to help Nick. Vinnie said he understood about me holding the twenty acres of Nick's land. Just keeping something that someone else really wanted. If you think that I'm going to get you down here and do something weird, forget it."

Her voice lost that hard tone and shifted to a softer one. "Vinnie wouldn't stand for that, and I guess I love him. He's sweet, the kind of deep-down sweet that nothing is going to change. What I have or don't have, or how I act, doesn't make any difference to him. And he doesn't make fun of my cooking, either. I always wanted to learn how, and oh, no, Daddy and my ex-husbands had to hire a cook for 'the image.' "

Stunned, Maggie slowly descended the stairs after Lorna. Cases of Nick's wines were stacked everywhere. Lorna's tone turned defensive again. "I said I had problems. I was thinking at the time that if I couldn't get the man, I'd get part of something he loved."

Lorna pivoted to Maggie and shoved a fat file of papers at her. "I called in a few favors and they acted as buyers for me. Receipts, purchase dates. I'm ready to title those twenty acres back to him, too. You've got to promise you won't spread this around. Talk to Nick and get this to go down smooth—that's what you're for—he's in love with you. Any idiot can see that. The wines have aged and they're good. The thermostat daily readouts are in the file. This room has been kept at a perfect temperature—I simply enlarged after Daddy died. Nick ought to make a profit off them as a special, private stock sale. He can pay whenever. Or not. I don't care. This is for Vinnie. And maybe for me, too. But I don't want this to get out," she added fiercely. "I'd look like a stupid fool."

Amazed at Lorna's admission and her kindness, Maggie asked softly, "Lorna, why don't you want people to know how very special you are?"

For the first time, Lorna's brisk, tough attitude crumpled and tears welled in her eyes. "It started a long time ago with dear old Dad. The family image wasn't sweet and wholesome when no one else was around. You learn how to protect yourself as a kid and then it just gets deeper, the need to be special and wanted, to make that old man proud of me. Vinnie doesn't want us to go public because he says his image will hurt me. He said people will think he's after my money—what a load of macho dumb duck dung."

This woman faced her own struggle with life, just as Maggie had. Where Glenda did not have the inner strength to depend on herself, Lorna had had a lifetime of trying.

Maybe, just maybe, Maggie should have let Glenda do her own fighting. Maybe as an older sister, she'd protected Glenda too much, so that when the time came, she couldn't make the right choices.

Maggie shook herself free of the past and said, "Lorna, you are special. And I know it. I'll talk to Vinnie."

"If you hug me, the deal is off. I've got a little favor to ask though. It won't cost or hurt," she added quickly.

"Anything. Meanwhile, I've got to go see if Jerry has found my brand of tampons yet. You asked how I got rid of him. That's how. What's the favor?"

Lorna looked down and spoke quietly. "I'm rich and I've never really dealt with an everyday working woman's problems. There's a big gap of understanding about life between Vinnie and me. I want to get a job and I want to learn how to cook. I thought maybe you could help me get into both—maybe a job at Journeys, if it's okay with Beth, and maybe have Mrs. Alessandro teach me how to cook. And if you laugh, I'll clobber you and the deal is off."

"I'm not laughing, but you've got to promise not to tell Jerry that I just wanted to get rid of him, sending him to get fem supplies. He was disgusted, but at least he thought he was helping me and I was safe. It wouldn't do to let him know that I'd come here meanwhile, okay?"

"Deal."

Lorna's generosity and that knowing smile about male aversions and how to use them held a warmth that carried Maggie through the morning.

At the winery, Nick was busy with investigators amid the shambles of his business. He looked tired and drained, but drew her against him for a brief kiss. He continued to hold her tight as if nothing could happen to her.

"So this is your fiancée?" the investigator interviewing Nick asked. The man's badge read DETECTIVE RON SIMMONS.

Because Maggie didn't want to argue the point before she'd made Lorna's case, she nodded and smiled up at Nick brightly. He blinked and frowned and stared at her blankly. "What's up?"

"Nothing, honey," she managed sweetly, innocently. "If you don't need me here, I think I'll go home. I'm a little tired."

Nick's blush was fascinating, because he knew the reason for her fatigue—last night's marathon lovemaking to keep his mind from his winery. "Uh. Just so you know, I haven't had time to move the camper. Uh . . . do you mean home as in the house?"

She didn't want to start an argument now, in front of the detective, and nodded. "You silly thing. You're all upset, aren't you? Why don't you just take care of the detective here, and I'll see you later?"

Nick relaxed a bit, smiled, and shared a man-to-man look. "I was supposed to do that today. Then this came up. One of those honey-do things."

The detective, a middle-aged man wearing a wedding ring, nodded sagely and stepped in to protect one of the brotherhood. "Ma'am, take it easy on the guy. He's just lost a hell of a lot of income. Those honey-do jobs will have to wait. And he's going to have to do something about that incoming crop, and his equipment has been vandalized."

Maggie gave him her brightest a-man-knows-best smile. "Thank you, Detective. That's good advice."

Nick's puzzled frown at her deepened. He was still frowning when she kissed him goodbye.

After a session of explaining every detail of a woman's cramps to Jerry, her bodyguard settled in Nick's living room to watch a ball game, thus effectively avoiding more information and giving Maggie the privacy she needed.

Then Maggie set to work. First she called Beth in Iowa for an update.

But before Maggie could speak, Beth had her own happy update: "I think I'm pregnant. We did it on Celeste's bed with candles and everything. It's too early for a test, but Jeff has what it takes. Just within minutes of meeting him, I knew she was right. I knew he was the guy for me, and I am so in love. While we were doing it, I just got this warm snugly feeling, just like all of me was ready and revved. He said he didn't want to take a chance I might get away from him, and he was ready to plow and seed and take possession of what was born to be his. Gosh, he's romantic. And Celeste's cats love the farm's big barn. Who would know?"

Apparently recovered from the lesson on women, Jerry went out to his pickup to retrieve Celeste's plants. While he slumped by Maggie in his surly slave attitude, carrying the plants, Beth raved on about Iowa and Jeff. Maggie enjoyed every delightful word; Beth deserved every happiness.

"Beth, there's been some trouble here, and I want you to stay put. There's no reason for you to be here, and I've found someone to work at Journeys." Maggie thought it best not to mention Lorna at the moment. "I'm staying at Nick's for a little while, trying to help. This is what happened . . ."

When Maggie finished, Beth stated firmly. "I am coming back."

After a brief argument, Beth agreed to stay in Iowa, with the condition that Maggie was to call with updates.

Maggie's next call was to Vinnie. He was wary. "Yeah, sure. If you think it hurts Lorna to keep what we have going on as a secret, I sure don't want that. Maybe it is time we shook up the town. Lorna would like that."

"She loves you, Vinnie. She's terribly proud of you."

Maggie shook her head. Beth, Lorna, and Vinnie were one thing; Nick another. He wasn't going to like her proposal to let Lorna help, and Maggie intended to make it easier for him to digest.

She was just directing Jerry to arrange Celeste's plants in the living room, taking advantage of the muted light, when the telephone rang.

Maggie hurried to answer it, because if Nick needed her . . . The harsh deep breathing on the other end wasn't welcome, and Nick didn't need more trouble. "Ed, if you don't stop your little joke, I am personally going to flatten you. And if you had anything to do with the winery getting destroyed, you are going to pay in more ways than one."

The line clicked off and Maggie frowned. Now was a poor time for Ed to play games. His feet were definitely larger than tens, but that didn't eliminate him from being suspect—somehow.

The police were searching for Leo and hadn't found him; he had a few enemies, they'd discovered, and a few friends on the wrong side of the law. And, according to Lorenzo's information, Leo wore size ten shoes, the same size as the boot tracks in the wine. If Leo was around, Maggie hoped they caught him soon.

While the police worked on the investigation, Maggie had

a very different and tough job ahead of her. Right now, she had to deal with how to get Nick to accept Lorna's offer of the wine . . . and he wouldn't be happy.

The sun was round and burning, setting over the lake when Nick at last arrived home. Totally drained, he pulled his pickup into the parking space beside Maggie's small white truck. Careful not to bruise the bouquet of roses for Maggie that Dante had delivered to him at the winery, Nick checked her door locks to see that they were secure and untampered. Nick's request for the roses had been met by his brother's knowing laughter.

The camper was still against the house, the door padlocked as he had left it. He noted the goddess wind chime from Celeste's house turning in the early evening breeze, and considered it a sign that Maggie was inside.

He didn't understand her sweet-innocent act in front of Simmons. More than likely, he was in for trouble when Maggie got him alone.

She needed protection, Nick thought as his determination wavered just that bit. Sometimes Maggie just didn't know what was good for her, but in this case, he knew better.

Carrying his briefcase and the make-up roses, and feeling as if all he wanted to do was to hold Maggie, Nick stepped onto the back deck. He stopped and looked at the jumble of potted plants.

The back door opened and Jerry rushed out, scowling at Nick. "I'm outa here."

"Problems?"

"None that I want to talk about. She had me peel those apples for your pie, all the time telling me stuff I didn't want to hear. I thought this was going to be bodyguard duty, not girl's stuff. Man, women are gruesome when they want to be." Jerry blushed deeply and revved his rusted black van, leaving clouds of dust as he shot away—evidently headed for freedom.

Nick paused, his hand on the back doorknob. The delicious scents coming from inside the house were unexpected and more than welcome.

He opened the door slowly. Inside the house was cool and dimly lit. He placed the briefcase aside and carried his defense—the rose bouquet. He'd hit her with a one-two, the roses and some good, old-fashioned groveling. If that didn't work, then she'd just have to listen to good sense—until they knew if Leo was lurking nearby with revenge on his little brain.

A deep-dish apple pie sat cooling on the counter. When Nick lifted the lid to the big pot on the stove, the aroma of pot roast swirled up at him. He closed his eyes and enjoyed.

Scout's claws sounded in the hallway, running toward him. "Maggie?"

Nick scratched Scout's ears and hurried into the living room, which was empty. He brushed aside a huge stalk of bamboo plant and eased around something that looked like it could have eaten a whole jungle. Making his way down the hallway, Nick noted a flowery feminine scent. The dog acted okay, and she was protective, and if anything was wrong with Maggie, Scout wouldn't leave her . . .

Maggie was in the big bathroom, her hair piled high, mounds of bubbles in the water. Her eyes were closed, her head back. "I'm in therapy. I've missed this since the attack in my home. I couldn't bear to be in anything other than a shower. I hope you don't mind Celeste's plants. They were lonely. She always said they needed people around to make them happy."

Everything that had been troubling Nick fled into the hot summer night. Entranced by the sight of Maggie, relaxed, a feminine little smile on her lips, Nick sat on the edge of the tub. "I heard you checked on Eugene again."

"Jerry makes an excellent bodyguard and reporter, right? Eugene is absolutely wallowing in Dee Dee's full attention. I wouldn't count on him being well soon. His story about how he fought off his attacker is growing."

Nick's vantage point was good; Maggie's nipples played beneath the soapy water, bobbing like little cherries that needed tasting. Her long, sleek, curved body shimmered beneath the bubbles, her feet raised, her nails glossy and red. His hunger switched from food to woman.

Apparently she made orgasmic sounds in the bathtub, too, and every one of them lodged hard and needy in his body. She'd made those same sounds last night as she moved against him, hungry and sweet and tight and—

Her eyes opened drowsily, finding him. She shifted a little, and her breasts quivered beneath the bubbles. "Nick?"

"Hmm?" He was having trouble thinking. Images of the ruined grape crusher had been replaced by memories of last night's lovemaking marathon. They interfered with whatever his plan had been. And he was no longer exhausted.

"This is a really big bathtub."

Maggie lay on top of Nick's back, his body relaxed beneath her on the bed. She smoothed his temple with her lips, her fingertips at work massaging his shoulders. "Feeling better?"

"Umm." His back rolled beneath her breasts, a male luxuriating in the feminine softness lying over him.

"Enjoying yourself?"

"Umm." His hand reached down behind him and caressed her bottom.

"That's good." She nuzzled the side of his throat. "It's not as bad as you think—the winery and the orders, I mean. You smell like my bubble bath."

He sighed heavily as if unwilling to return to the reality of dealing with the investigation and his endangered business.

She nibbled on his ear, and Nick turned his head slightly to give her a kiss. "Thank you."

"For dinner?"

He wriggled his butt just a little beneath her and smoothed her bottom again. "That, too. I like this total body massage idea."

"I had an interesting conversation today that might interest you." If Maggie's fingers weren't smoothing his shoulders, she might have had them crossed for good luck.

"Let me guess. Dee Dee and Eugene?"

"He wanted me to sneak him some condoms."

She could feel Nick smile as her cheek rubbed against his. "Lorna invited me to her house. I sent Jerry on an errand while we were at Celeste's house, because I knew if he reported my visit to Lorna's to you, you'd be upset."

The powerful shoulders beneath her fingers tensed. "You're right; I am. And what did Lorna want?"

When Maggie briefly described Lorna's offer, Nick flipped over so suddenly that she almost went tumbling off the bed. He grabbed her and hauled her up, leaning over her. He turned on the bedside light. "*She* had buyers working for her? *Lorna has cases of my wine?*"

His quiet roar was enough to wilt Celeste's plants, but Maggie wasn't backing up. She took a deep breath and served what he didn't want. "Your best reds. They store well. She has a special cellar and temperature control printouts."

This man wasn't the lover of hours before, the weary warrior grateful for a warm loving welcome; he was a thundercloud, waiting to shoot lightning bolts. He surged out of the bed, stalking across the bedroom as if he wanted to tear something—someone apart. "Let me get this straight—she's got a private wine cellar that she's selling back to me at cost . . . when I can make payment or not . . . and she's ready to title those twenty acres back to me? There has to be a hitch. She's got something else going on."

Maggie sat lotus-style on the bed and adjusted the sheet around her nude body. "Vinnie. That's what she's got going on. Think of it as a family thing—"

"Lorna? Vinnie? Together? That way? You've got to be kidding. Why didn't I know?"

She felt sorry for Nick. He had a lot to cope with—coming to terms with a woman he didn't like *and* discovering the said woman was involved with his own cousin. She ignored his shocked look and continued, "It's complicated. I checked the cases and dates. It's your best reds. If you can make substitutes on the orders you've already taken—"

"Lorna and Vinnie. Lorna and Vinnie . . ." Nick stared at Maggie as if he didn't know her. "Who are you?"

She tilted her head. Nick was really cute with his hair standing out in clumps and that owlish, what-planet-am-I-on look.

He gestured to the bed, to the dishes of food placed on the floor as they made love once again. The owlish look slid into a grim one. "So that's what the little-woman act was about? To soften me up for one of Lorna's deals?"

"Vinnie thought he was protecting her by keeping their secret. I called and convinced him otherwise. She's not like you think."

He glared at her. "I've known her for her whole life. Believe me, Lorna never gives without getting. *You convinced my cousin to come out with whatever thing they have going on?*"

Nick's you-traitor look irritated. "Vinnie loves her and she loves him."

"That barracuda can love?"

"They'll probably get married. She'll be in the family. They want children and they'll be your cousins. She'll be at all the family gatherings."

Looking like a warrior who faced a losing battle, Nick sat down hard on the bed, staring off into space. "I'll talk to Vinnie."

"They've been together for years. Lorna is his mystery girlfriend. They kickbox and work on cars. That black eye he's wearing and the dead-dog-tired look come from being with her all night. She wants to be more housewifey and make a home for Vinnie. If I can help, I will."

His abrupt curse hit the shadows. "I don't trust her. What did Lorna want in return? Lorna always wants something in return."

"Secrecy. Only those who need to know in on it. To run Journeys and be a working girl to show Vinnie that she's just not a rich playgirl. To learn how to cook from your mother."

Nick's expression swung back to the lost-on-what-planet look. "*My mother? My family is involved in whatever she's pulling?*"

Maggie couldn't help adding a tease, "Lorna is sorry if your feelings are hurt. You were just a challenge. She offered to play-act out a scene in which she dumped you, if it would help you save face."

With a loud, frustrated groan, Nick lay down beside her, his hands folded behind his head as he stared at the ceiling. "You sure know how to lay a proposition on the table. Or in bed."

She smoothed his chest with her hand. "I enjoyed every minute, but even without Lorna's offer, I wanted to be here tonight for you."

He covered her hand with his. "You actually like her, don't you?"

"Yes, I do. And knowing more about Lorna's life, I saw more of my mistakes with Glenda. I protected her too much—my little sister—I should have let her fight more of her own battles earlier, so that when put to the test, she would have had the inner strength she needed."

Nick drew Maggie down to him, holding her close. "You've got to stop blaming yourself about your sister, Maggie. It's all about choices. She made the wrong ones. You just did the best you could."

"It wasn't enough."

She listened to Nick's heartbeat beneath her cheek and the stillness. "You're not going to let Lorna help, are you?"

"No. She's playing you. She's got an angle in there somewhere, and she's better left alone."

Maggie lifted slightly to look at him. "Nick, listen to me. Pride is one thing. Saving a business you've struggled and worked for, and that your grandfather had hoped for, is another. At least think about it."

Nick eased from her and pulled on his jeans, silently leaving the house.

Aching for him, Maggie climbed the steps to the lighthouse. Nick needed time alone, balancing Lorna's offer against his pride. The wind played in Maggie's hair and the sheet over her body. She listened to the peaceful tinkling of Celeste's chimes and prayed that Nick would consider Lorna's offer and that his business would survive the blow.

Maggie also prayed that his anger at her would ease. Nick's silence hadn't been encouraging.

The lake spread black in the night, a trail of silver cutting through the waves. Scout whined softly and leaned against Maggie. With her hand in Scout's thick coat Maggie wondered about Monique who had died on the lake, about Celeste who always seemed near, and about Nick's Alyssa, always hovering close to him.

When Maggie turned toward land, Nick stood amid the grapes that would be ready for September harvest. They wouldn't wait.

Once he'd sold land to pay for Alyssa's medical expenses. Now, to save what he had built, he would have to bend his pride once more.

Enveloped by shadows, Brent held the earpiece of the bugging device to his ear. Planted on an overhead light fixture, the device had proven invaluable when he was blackmailing for his deals, and he was never without it. Ed wouldn't suspect that he'd been followed, that Brent could easily leave his room by simply picking the lock. Through the window, he watched the man inside the salvage yard garage—it always paid to know what the underlings around him were doing.

Ed was talking to himself. "Waste not, want not, my ma always used to say."

Brent frowned; Ed had somehow known where Leo's car had been stashed, in that old garage. The bartender had collected the car and would likely sell off the parts.

And whatever Ed's mother used to say was familiar; their

mothers were of the same bottom-grade ilk. But Brent had raised himself above the low-class start he had in life. He sneered at Ed, who still showed his shack-town roots.

Ed guzzled beer from a bottle. He ripped off the tarp covering the new sports car, the one Leo had rented in Louisville, Kentucky, and set to work. "Good old Leo. By coming in from Louisville the same as The Crazy, and driving up here he took care of any clues that might put him in this area. Have to give The Crazy credit for suggesting it to good old Leo. There are always buyers for these babies. I'll repaint and sell to a customer wanting a high-class model at a low price."

Disturbed from its nest, a huge spider crawled on top of the shiny hood.

Ed's fear rose and swelled and screamed, echoing in the cluttered garage. Picking up a bat, Ed pounded the hood of the car, the spider skittering across it to disappear within.

Panting fiercely and winded, Ed stood back. He wiped the sweat from his forehead and blinked at the car. The red shiny surface was battered; the spider reappeared and then returned inside the car. Ed grabbed a can of insect spray and began fogging the car. "If the witch woman is haunting me, I'm finishing her off for good."

Overcome by the fumes, he coughed and staggered back. "Another time, Celeste," he said as he flung the tarp back over the car and left the garage.

With a keen distaste for the garage's junk and smell, Brent eased inside moments later. He held a handkerchief over his nose as he lifted the tarp and viewed Leo's rented car.

The battered hood pinpointed Ed's desperate fears. "Always interesting to know what they fear," Brent crooned softly. "Well, this is coming along nicely, Maggie. He's doing all the work and will take the blame for what happens to you. Too bad he won't be around to enjoy it."

# SEVENTEEN

"*I don't want you doing what you did for him.*" Nick slapped the file of Lorna's receipts onto the kitchen table, and the plant Maggie had been tending there quivered in the fragrance of morning coffee as he continued, "I should be taking care of *you,* not the other way around. And there are plants everywhere. This place looks like a jungle."

He lifted the damp cloth over her unbaked and rising cinnamon rolls. "You don't need to get up early and start cooking. I don't need—"

Nick's bristling, laying-down-the-law male role grated on Maggie's nerves, so she said, "The cinnamon rolls are for Eugene. Not you."

"Oh . . . well, okay." He sounded disappointed.

But Maggie knew that the cinnamon rolls or the plants weren't Nick's real problem. Maggie almost felt sorry for him—a big, powerful male locked in a battle with necessity and fighting his macho instincts.

He studied her coolly. His inspection of the overlarge cotton shirt and sweat pants she had borrowed was so long and thorough that Maggie shifted uncomfortably. "My other clothes are in the camper. It's locked, you know—a great big padlock."

Nick ignored her reminder that he had moved and locked the camper. He leaned back against the kitchen counter and crossed his arms. "This is what you do, isn't it? You are a facilitator, smoothing out other people's lives. Like Vinnie and Lorna. You just had to step in that, didn't you? What happened to Miss Mind Your Own Business?"

Maggie removed the last of the plant's dried leaves. From the challenging look of the man who had loved her well last night, she needed to smooth out her own life. "I've learned that it doesn't pay. I can't make life choices for other people. I don't want to hear any more of your groaning about Vinnie and Lorna. They are in love, Nick, whether you like it or not. I wasn't going to get involved with Blanchefleur, but now I am."

"You are *involved with me*. We're lovers, Maggie. I want to marry you, and I won't be placed into the same category as your ex-husband. I won't have you making-do for me or cowing down to Lorna to help me."

"Leave Ryan out of this. I am not arguing with you. You have a simple choice, Nick, to let her help you or not. I think Lorna would have made the offer whether or not I was involved—because of Vinnie and because she's basically sweet." Maggie didn't want to think about how she'd given her life to a man who, in the end, cared only for himself.

Her distrust of giving herself totally to her new relationship to Nick had definite ties to her past, and they both knew it.

Nick walked out of the kitchen into the early dawn. He stood with his hands on his hips surveying the vineyard.

She understood his dilemma, pride battling survival; she'd faced enough of that herself. So he was angry that she'd been the messenger of an offer he didn't want to accept.

On the other hand, she wasn't happy with his high-handed macho-man protect-the-little-lady attitude, either. It was *her* camper padlocked and perched against his home. If he needed thinking room; he'd have it.

She went out onto the deck and held her palm upright. "I want the key to that padlock."

He turned to glower at her. "Why?"

"Because that's my home, that's why. I want to be in my house."

"You're being ridiculous. It's locked for your own protection. The police are trying to locate Leo. He *does* wear size tens, the same size as the footprints in the wine. He could be anywhere, and that camper is like a sardine can. He could break in—"

This time, Maggie's hands were on her hips, her legs braced apart. "Stop deciding my life for me, Nick."

The sweet morning air quivered between them, and Scout whined softly, looking from one human to the other.

Neither one looked at Dante, who had just pulled up in his pickup. He walked to the deck and studied them. "Problems?"

"Not a one," Nick said curtly.

"He's shoving me around and I don't like it," Maggie said.

"She's being stubborn. They still haven't located Leo, and I don't want to take the chance that he might be after her." Nick glanced at Vinnie's black van, which had just pulled beside the other vehicles. Lorna was in the passenger seat. His short flat curse said he could have done without the visit. "What are they doing here?"

"I invited them. You are going to be nice."

"This should be interesting," Dante commented, then raised his eyebrows at Maggie's silent warning.

"Dante, would you please go in the kitchen and put my cinnamon rolls in the oven? Just follow the directions in the cookbook next to the stove. Make some icing while you're at it, please. As soon as you can, bring out some coffee and juice for Nick's guests. You can serve the rolls when they're done."

Dante looked blank for a moment, then he said firmly, as if reaffirming himself, "I can do this. I can do this . . . About Leo. Here's Lorenzo's update: Three days ago, Leo flew into Louisville and rented a sports car. It's likely that he did that as a diversion in case anyone was checking on his whereabouts. From there, it's an easy shot up to Michigan and Blanchefleur. They've alerted the state patrols. His friends said he was pretty ticked over what happened when he was here and that he was out for payback. He's a size ten lead, anyway. And they can't locate that car."

Nick reached to scoop Maggie protectively against him. Unused to anyone's help, Maggie floundered between comforting him and the decision at hand. Nick's scowl at Vinnie and Lorna wasn't friendly. Maggie decided that Nick was on his own, and moved away from him.

"Hey, man," Vinnie said as he held Lorna's hand. On the deck now, Nick's cousin had an air of a man squiring a lady and proud of it. In a white ruffled peasant blouse and a long cotton floral skirt and sandals, Lorna looked feminine and wary; her hair was now a soft brown.

While Nick stood immobile, his scowl locked in place, his arms crossed over his bare chest, and his jeaned legs braced apart, Maggie smiled brightly. "Hi. We're just about to have breakfast. Dante is in fixing it now. Have a seat."

She noted Lorna's nervous glance at Nick and decided that powerful chest would upset any woman. Maggie hurried inside, took one of his shirts from the dryer, shook it briefly to remove the wrinkles, and found Dante looking at her. "What's up?"

"Lorna can help Nick and he's not being friendly."

Maggie briefly described Lorna's offer, and Dante whistled. "Good luck. He won't buy it though."

"Just don't ruin the cinnamon rolls, will you? There's a serving tray in the closet. Be sure to bring napkins. Put the rolls on a plate, the juice in a pitcher, and don't forget the forks. If the situation gets difficult, get lost. Do laundry or something in here."

Dante had that disgusted look, the same one as when Sissy asked him to change his nephew's diapers. Clearly Alessandro men had definite ideas about man-woman roles.

Outside, Nick wasn't budging. Maggie pinched his butt lightly, and when he scowled down at her, she held up the shirt. He put it on, but left the buttoning to Maggie. She added a little warning jerk and a look when adjusting his collar. Nick's dark eyes locked with hers, then shifted over her head to Lorna.

"What's the deal?" he asked abruptly.

Vinnie moved closer, protectively, to his girlfriend, just as Nick had done with Maggie earlier. "It's a woman thing, man. They do weird stuff, but that's what makes them what they are. You gotta appreciate the little differences in their thinking. She could make a bundle off that aged wine, but instead she's following her heart."

"Sit down, please?" Maggie offered as she nudged Nick to a big wooden lawn chair and pushed him. He eased down into the chair as if he would make up his own mind about doing anything, however everyday common.

To ensure Nick wouldn't move, Maggie sat on his lap. Vinnie's arm went around Lorna's shoulders as they sat on a plastic love seat. "Now this is real nice," Vinnie said in the obviously tense silence.

"I like the plants," Lorna said quietly.

"They're Celeste's. We put some here in the house and on the front porch. The wind chime was hers, too. I like to think of her as always being with me. Would you like a start from them? That would give you a little piece of what she loved."

"I'd love that. Thank you."

Another long silence, then Nick asked Lorna, "What's the catch?"

Obviously nervous, Lorna shot back. "You've got the offer. Are you interested, or not? Hey, bud, I can always sell that inventory to someone else—"

"Now, hon—" Vinnie began.

"Pretty day, isn't it?" Maggie said, hoping to lighten the

moment as she placed her arm around Nick's tense shoulders. "Nick?"

"You'd really do that, wouldn't you, Lorna? Sell my wine to someone else, so you can make a profit?"

"Hey, bud. It's *my* wine. I bought it."

"You'll never be the cook my mother is."

"You just try me. I'm already planning a family do at Vinnie's, and I won't have it catered, either."

" 'A family do?' " Nick repeated harshly. "If you think that I'm coming to anything you—"

"Well, this is going well, don't you think?" Maggie asked in her best cheerful tone.

Vinnie shook his head. "I know them both. It's just something they have to go through before making the deal. Both stiff-necked as hell. But Lorna's neck is a whole lot prettier and sweeter and—"

He leaned to nuzzle Lorna whose frown gave way to a girlish squeal of delight.

This time, it was Nick's turn to shake his head. "Sure. Why not," he said in a doomed voice. "It's a deal. I'll try an extenuating circumstance plea with the state board to iron out legalities of transfer and resale."

The kitchen door opened and Dante warily studied the people on the deck. "Can I come out now? Look what I baked—"

Maggie waded through the tension on the deck to play hostess. From this point on, everyone had to make his own choices.

"I'd like this recipe," Lorna said, as Vinnie sucked the frosting off her fingertips.

Nick groaned painfully and his stare accused Maggie. "I suppose before I do any finger licking, I will have to—"

She held out her hand. "You're right. You will have to kiss it. But right now, give me that key."

After a day of Nick's frowning and gloomy silence, and visiting Lorna's extensive cellar with him to keep peace, Maggie decided she needed a little space from brooding males, and her camper was like a cool, quiet oasis.

Maggie ignored the big man on the deck. He paced, using his cordless telephone to make business calls and substitution offers—while he watched her unlock the camper.

The hum of her tiny air conditioner was comforting, almost a melody as she settled down with a stack of women's magazines. She smiled as she thought of Beth's baby news and set forth to wallow in sloth with a cinnamon roll, chocolate milkshake, and salty munchie orgy. She totally deserved every calorie.

The knock on her door was ominous. "Yes?"

Scout whined softly, and her pleading look said her buddy Nick was at the door.

"Are you coming out?"

"I don't have any plans at the moment."

"Make plans."

She waited, letting him think over the pushy male routine. "What was that again?"

The long silence said Nick was thinking very hard. "Thanks for helping," he said finally.

"You're welcome."

"Would you open this door?"

"It's locked, like you told me to." With a sigh, Maggie rose from her luxurious peace and potato chip sloth, and opened the door to Nick.

He looked tired and wary as he thrust a bouquet of roses at her. "Celeste's plants miss you. So do I. How long are you going to stay in here?"

Nick looked closely at her. "Whatever you're eating is all over your face."

"Chips, cinnamon rolls, a chocolate milkshake."

"Is that what you do when you get upset?" He looked so worried and confused that Maggie's desire for ultimate peace slid into a warm puddle.

"You're not exactly a stress-free-maintenance item." She

tentatively lifted a finger laden with frosting and potato chip crumbs.

Nick's mouth was hot and warm and the look in his eyes sent definite hungry messages to her body.

"When was the last time you spent the night in a camper?" she asked, fisting his shirt and tugging slightly.

"Is that an invitation?" But he was already moving toward her with that look that said he intended to be very thorough.

Like an artist, Brent studied Ed's slumped body, and the suicide note next to the whiskey and pills. Experienced with drug effects, Brent checked Ed's pulse and lifted his eyelid. In an hour or less, Ed would no longer have any problems. The bar had been closed for two hours; Shirley was due in the morning and would probably let herself in when Ed didn't answer.

Investigators had been snooping around Blanchefleur all day, and Lorenzo Alessandro was busy digging for information too. According to Ed, his notable, ongoing conflict with the Alessandros had made him a perfect suspect. The police were only gathering evidence now, but they would soon pressure Ed in hard interrogation, taking off the gloves. It was only a matter of time before he revealed the identity of his upstairs guest. The incident with the spider in the garage said Ed was unstable and would likely break under intense interrogation.

And Ed had made the mistake of arguing with Brent, of telling him what to do.

"My ultimate conclusion, Ed, old boy, was that you had to go. Thanks for the hospitality and the tranquilizer dart gun for the dog."

By the time Shirley found Ed, Brent would be like any other tourist, sleeping in his anonymously rented hotel room. He ran through his checklist: The telephone records would show that calls from Ed's phones had been placed to Leo just prior to Leo flying into Louisville and renting a car. That car was in Ed's salvage garage, complete with Leo's wine-stained boots. The stolen bottles of Nick's best wine were easily seen on the tavern's bar.

Brent walked to turn one bottle until the labels were exactly straight and even. He wiped a spot off the otherwise gleaming bar and took one last look to see if all the pictures in the bar were straight.

His new instant tan, his wig and glasses and padded waistline, were perfect disguises. Rented with a fake ID, his car wouldn't be questioned—not with all the tourists in town.

He hummed as he bent to read the note Ed had written at the point of a gun—and a threat to Beth.

*The poor dumb jerk really seemed to love that slut, probably enough to die for her.* Whether Brent kept his promise not to harm her depended on if Beth was in his way or not.

"I can't live with myself any longer," Ed's note read. "I'd had all I could stand of Nick Alessandro and I called Leo Knute because I knew he'd had a run-in with Nick. Leo took care of Nick's winery, and when Leo started shooting his mouth off about my girl, I saw red and we started a ruckus. He's out in the lake somewhere, but his boots are in my garage. It's easier this way. The law won't have trouble matching us up. I'm not serving time again. I did once. Ed."

"Thank you, Ed. That was nicely said," Brent said as he picked up his bag. In it was the tranquilizer gun that Ed had provided for the dog.

Brent let himself out into the alley. "It's neat enough to let everyone go back to their business, relax a bit, and then I can attend to Maggie."

Out of habit, he reached inside his light jacket for his silver flask and cursed when he found it gone. It was all he had left of his power and money—Maggie had taken everything else away.

With the ten thousand cash and a box of heisted jewelry from Ed's private cubbyhole in the floor and Leo's ten thousand traveling-money, Brent would have enough to get back on his feet again.

Breeding the dog constantly, selling her pups for a healthy price, was just payback for obeying another man.

Maggie's payback would be slower, and she'd beg him. Brent looked forward to the begging part, when he felt all powerful. When they told him they loved him. Maggie's sister had done it very well.

Brent heard a tinkling of wind chimes, the sound eerie, echoing off the bricks of the alley. The sound made the hair on his nape lift and goose bumps ride his skin, though the August night was hot and still.

He mocked himself with a grin. "Ed's fear of the witch woman must be contagious. Well, now they're together."

Yet the tinkling found him in his dreams—in the nightmare of the giant spider wrapping its silk around him. Then Brent awoke to his own scream.

Dante nudged Nick as they stood in front of Ole's gym, looking through the window. Maggie was doing push-ups inside, a reminder of their lovemaking on the single bed in the camper. Nick swallowed tightly, his body responding to all that long, sweet, very fit feminine softness on the mat inside.

Dante spoke quietly. "Lorenzo and the investigators have their hands full now with Ed's suicide. His note was backed up by the evidence—your missing case of wine, Leo's car in Ed's shop, the phone records proving Ed contacted Leo."

When Nick didn't answer, Dante continued, "Just a guess, but I'd say whoever came after Scout was probably hired by Leo. I never thought Ed would be a neat freak, but according to Lorenzo, that upstairs apartment was almost sanitized. They say he must have been on a cleaning binge before he died. Every bottle in the place was systematically arranged."

Nick had just decided that Maggie had the cutest behind and shook himself back into the bright daylight. "Huh? Oh. Uh-huh. There will be enough stock to hold our shelf space and take care of our orders. The customers were happy with the replacement. We'll be able to limp along until next year.

The winery has been released and we can sanitize it and try to salvage whatever."

He watched Scout trotting down to Marco's shop. His cousin held a big fat knuckle bone out to the dog, who took it and the rough ear rubbing before trotting across the street. Scout disappeared into the alley that led to the Alessandros' backyard, there to gnaw in pleasure.

If Nick could give Maggie back her sister and her friend, he would. But Maggie hadn't said she loved him; she hadn't agreed to marriage, and they seemed a long way from the future he wanted . . .

From the old lighthouse that night, he watched Maggie with Scout on the beach. She needed thinking space, and he needed her.

The most difficult task in Nick's life was waiting for Maggie to trust him, to turn to him fully—there was always that distance.

She stepped into the waves, surprising him. Working with her fears, Maggie had kept him away.

Nick heard the windowsill creak beneath the grip of his hands. There was always that tenuous distance, the feeling that at any time she would leave, and he could only wait.

# EIGHTEEN

The waves washed over Maggie's feet, sucking the sand beneath them. She walked slowly, thoughtfully, as she cradled Glenda's locket in her hand. Out on the lake, tourist sailboats skimmed the water, making use of the wind that came to play in Maggie's hair.

In the last three days, everything had become so clear—as if a black cloud had been wiped away.

The medical examiner had confirmed that Ed had committed suicide. Though the investigators were clearing up paperwork, his note and the evidence had eased questions about the vandalism at the winery and Leo's death.

Scout was safe now, free once more to roam on her visits to town. In Nick's vineyard, his grapes were growing, and he was hard at work, salvaging his business. Profits would be almost nonexistent, but the all-precious customers' goodwill, shelf space, and facing had only been slightly damaged. The wine growers' association had already sent offers of help.

Nick was still nettled that Lorna had come to his rescue, and his pride said he didn't want Maggie working beside him in the winery. His instinct was to protect her, and he wasn't shy about pointing out her mistakes. She loved him, of course, but she'd had enough of male pride and men setting rules for her.

And within her lived the past, the ridicule of another man, the angry pain that she had given everything, just as her mother had taught her to do. Who was she really?

Who was the woman she needed to know fully before giving herself to Nick? And why hadn't the nightmares eased? Why was she uneasy? There was always the sense of an unfinished place in her life, but then Glenda's death left no room for closure, did it?

Maggie watched two boys fly a kite over the waves, and she instantly ached for Glenda's sons, Seth and Cody. The boy with sandy hair was wearing a backpack, and he waved to her. "Where's Scout? I've got a Frisbee."

"Hi, J.C. She's at Tony's, playing in the kiddie pool."

"She'd have more fun with us than a bunch of babies," J.C. stated with a ten-year-old male's arrogance. "Hey, do you want to see what I've got?"

Leaving the kite flying to his friend, he ran toward her. J.C. sank into the sand, digging at his bag while Maggie came to stand beside him.

He pulled out a net bag of prize shells, a piece of driftwood that looked like a deer horn, bluish gray and reddish stones perfectly smoothed by water, a baseball cap that had seen better days, and—

Grinning proudly, J.C. held up his prize to her. "Mom washed it real good. It smelled like whiskey. Fancy, huh?"

Maggie slowly took the silver flask, and the bright sunlight on the metal blinded her for a moment. She smiled, turning the prize slowly in her hand. "That's beautiful, J.C."

"It has initials—see? Mom said I'd have to give it back if anyone asked around for it, and I had to leave a note at the city lost and found. Irma said I could keep it meanwhile, if I took really good care of it. See those initials? Mrs. Friends writes that old-fashioned way—"

The initials B and T, ornately engraved, curled on the silver flask, and Maggie's world stopped turning, her blood running cold.

*It was the same flask that Brent Templeton had taken out of his pocket the day she pushed her way into his men's club, accusing him of ruining Glenda. While his powerful friends watched, he'd handed it to her, wanting her to have a drink and calm down. She'd thrown it back at him—*

"You like that? It had some pretty thread on it. Let me show you." J.C. dug into his bag and came up with a scrap of red silk.

*Slender and gleaming in the sun, that tiny scrap matched Celeste's favorite paisley scarf.* "Can I have this, J.C.?"

"Sure, I guess."

She thought of how many times Glenda had described drinking with Brent, his special little flask "just for us." Maggie couldn't bear to touch the flask, but the tiny part of Celeste she'd keep. The channel's current must have wound the scrap around the bottle, keeping them together—or was it Celeste?

"Listen very carefully, J.C. I want you to take very good care of that flask, because it's important. Don't ask me why, but someday someone might need it."

Her heart pounding with fear, Maggie set out at a run, her fist clutching the scrap—the physical proof tying Celeste and Brent at the same place. No one had believed her about his involvement with Glenda, but this proof couldn't be denied. If Brent were near, he was capable of anything—and that included hurting the Alessandros and Maggie's friends . . .

In her panic, she could think of only one thing—that she couldn't stay in Blanchefleur, endangering the Alessandros or anyone else. Brent wouldn't stop. He would use other people to do his dirty work; his tentacles ran insidiously, spreading into other lives, twisting them. Lorenzo and his men couldn't stop Brent; his friends were powerful, attorneys . . . The nightmare engulfed Maggie.

She had to leave—to lead Brent away, and she couldn't let him find Scout . . .

"Nick? Has Maggie called you? Has she turned up at the winery? She can't find Scout and is frantic. She's calling everyone and asking them to hold Scout for her. She said she had an errand to do and she'd be right back. I've never seen her so upset."

Over the telephone, Sissy's voice was worried. From his office at the vineyard, Nick noted Maggie's pickup racing down the dirt road to his house, clouds of dust in its wake.

"I just saw her go by. She's okay. Let us know if Scout turns up. I'll be with Maggie."

"Please tell her I'm sorry, Nick. Scout took off like she does when she knows you're nearby, and I didn't think anything of it. She's run off to the winery a couple of times and I know Maggie doesn't like that, but I didn't want to worry her."

Logically Maggie should have called. She hadn't. Scout had made independent visits in town and though scolded, she continued her regular visits when off the leash. Eugene, Marco, and the restaurant were regular stops.

Taking care not to alarm his parents or the others, Nick placed a few brief calls. Sissy had already reached them, asking them to hold the dog.

And yet Maggie hadn't called Nick, the man who loved her and wanted to marry her. Scout was missing, and though Maggie knew Scout might make an independent trip out to the winery, she hadn't called Nick.

Nick punched out Dante's number at the boatyard. In late afternoon, Dante would be winding up his day, getting ready to baby-sit at Tony's. "See if you can find Scout, will you? She might have heard some kids on the beach and gone to play. She knows better, but check it out anyway, okay?"

Nick closed the winery and drove slowly down the road, balancing his concern for Maggie against his anger that she hadn't called him when in distress. If she left his house, she'd have to pass him, and would have a hard time doing so. He wasn't above throwing a blockade in front of the woman he loved.

When he saw her packing her pickup, anger took over. In front of the camper now, Nick reached inside the pickup, collected the keys, and slid them into his jeans pocket. He crossed his arms as he leaned back against the driver's door and waited, his hurt and anger building. He'd be logical and listen; he'd understand whatever Maggie chose to do.

*The hell he would. He loved her and in everything but words, she had told him that she loved him. People who loved didn't run out on each other. Not in his book.*

Hurrying out of the camper, Maggie stopped when she saw him. Sissy was right; Maggie was badly frightened and apparently in flight. His anger slipped a notch. "Let's have it. The note you left for me. I deserve that much."

"Have you seen Scout? Is she in the house? I don't hear her barking—"

Nick reached out a hand to grip her upper arm, stopping her from running into the house. "She's not here. If she were, she would be running circles around us now. What's up?"

Maggie's eyes pleaded with him in her pale face. Her hand shook as she shoved a strand of reddish brown hair behind her ear. When she spoke, her voice trembled. "Nick, I wasn't planning to stay in Blanchefleur. You know that."

His anger hitched back up, his gut churning with pain and passion that he exposed to few. "I thought things had changed. You know—my marriage offer, telling you I loved you, those sweet little nothings in bed that make a guy feel like he's the only one in your life. Or do you just go around the country collecting guys like me and leaving them? Is that how you get your kicks?"

As her lover, the man who loved and was fascinated by Maggie, he recognized every move of her body. Now it read that she wanted to hurry away from him, that she was frightened—

Nick locked onto that incredulous thought. He pushed away from the pickup. "Maggie, are you frightened of me?"

She bit her lip and hefted her canvas bag into the pickup bed. "I have to go, Nick. It's time."

Torn between frustration and confusion and anger, Nick grabbed her wrist, holding her still. "Maggie, I deserve some answers."

Tears brimmed in those brownish-green eyes as she tried to tug away. Nick looked at the tear that had just fallen onto his hand. Gleaming and warm, it sent an emotional punch into his gut. "Maggie, please. What did I do wrong?"

"It isn't you—" She flung herself into his arms, pressed tightly against him. When Nick's arms locked around her, she pushed back and stood free. "It's me. I'm no good for you. I'm no good in a relationship. You'll find someone—"

There in the late afternoon sun, Nick's emotions swung back to confusion and anger and hurt. "What the hell are you talking about?"

She seemed to brace herself, swallowing and dashing away the tears clinging to her lashes. "I've just got to go. It's better this way."

"That you would take my life and my heart from me? That you would take every dream and breath with you? How is it better? Explain that."

"I'll call you later. We'll talk."

"Dammit. Talk now. I'm bleeding to death right in front of you."

With that, Maggie seemed to crumple, to fold into herself as if holding inner pain that could escape her control. With her arms around herself, she rocked silently.

Unable to stand more, Nick drew her into his arms, holding her tightly. He felt the trembling of her body as if her heart were trying to leap free. Against her damp cheek, he whispered rawly, "Maggie, don't do this to us. Tell me why you're afraid. Let me help. We'll work through this together."

She began to cry, really cry, deep draining sobs that seemed to be drawn painfully from her soul. Nick stroked her hair and rocked her, waiting for the worst to come.

When suddenly her arms pushed free and wrapped around him as if she would never let go, Nick began to hope. "You love me."

"With all my heart."

Her firm answer gave him more hope. Whatever had been between them was close and opening and raveling. "Then, Maggie, help me understand why you want to leave."

Maggie shoved free again and her eyes were haunted as she looked up at him. She took a deep breath and said unevenly, "Nick, I'm bad luck. I've always been. For my family and for my friends, and I don't want anything happening to you—or your family. I love them all."

"I don't follow. What makes you think so?"

She laughed shakily, but her gaze scanned the vineyards and the marsh. "I've had a lifetime of it. Do you think Scout could have been bitten by a snake out there?"

"Maggie. Think. Scout doesn't go into the cattails unless she's headed to my house. If she was bitten, she could still make it there. Now what is this about?"

Maggie shuddered slightly, and when Nick smoothed back her hair and wiped away her tears, she whispered, "Celeste died because of me. I know she did. The winery break-in, your business almost being destroyed, and Ed's suicide. Oh, Nick, none of that was an accident. Ed didn't commit suicide. He's here . . . Brent Templeton is here and he's . . . he's after anyone dear to me. He's going to destroy everything dear to me, just like before. He's after Scout. He'll hurt her, Nick."

When Nick frowned, Maggie stood back from him. "You don't believe me, do you? You don't believe—"

"Maggie. I'm just trying to place the name with a face. I don't know him."

"I do. He's evil and corrupt and insidiously destroys everything that comes in contact with him. You don't believe that one person can do that, do you? Well, he can. He destroyed Glenda, and—"

Nick couldn't breathe as he waited for her story. He felt as if everything in their future hung on what she told him. "What, Maggie?"

"And he destroyed my life. I met him five years ago. When he failed to seduce me, he went for Glenda. He insinuated that she was second best, playing on her insecurities. He virtually pitted my own sister against me, and I became her enemy—at least in her mind. She rebelled against everything and played right into his hands. He's very good at what he does—controlling people, hurting them. He's smart, insidious, and obsessive. Toss cruel into the mix."

Maggie shivered in the warm air and continued as she seemed to step into the past. "He got Ryan under his thumb and Ryan didn't believe me, and then the first thing I know, Brent is a full partner in our business. Poor-quality workout machines that would hurt someone were arriving at the gym, and there were harmful power energy boosters and body building drugs that Brent wanted us to market on the sly, and he got to Ryan. He got to Ryan so badly that Ryan was convinced that I had flirted with Brent, encouraging him. Ryan believed Brent. *My own husband didn't believe me.* He wouldn't support me to protect Glenda. Brent told me that he destroyed my sister because he couldn't have me."

She wrapped her arms around herself again, as if holding in her fears. "You're frowning. You don't understand. I've seen that look before—on Ryan . . . when he thought I was making everything up—"

Anger spiked again and Nick inhaled slowly. "I . . . am . . . not Ryan."

"You don't understand. If I leave now—with Scout— you'll all be safe. I don't know how Brent found us, but he has and he will destroy anything—anyone—close to me. He used to call, breathing like that, nothing more. It wasn't Ed, as we had thought, it was Brent, letting me know he was around and waiting—he likes those games—and I was so certain that was all behind me that I didn't think—"

Maggie paused for breath and shook her head. "But maybe I did. I never truly felt as if it were finished, the battle between Brent and myself. I had no closure to that, and now I know why—he's not a man to stop destroying and he isn't finished with me. I want you safe . . . your family safe, Nick. And Beth—Beth is expecting a baby. He'll stop at nothing, even that. He made Glenda have abortions. He twines himself into everyone's lives and then he twists and ruins. You don't believe me, do you?"

"I believe you. Just tell me how you know he's here. You've been fighting this, haven't you? But now you have proof?"

She seemed stunned. "You . . . you believe me?" she asked incredulously.

"Of course. Now go on." Now wasn't the time to tell Maggie how badly she had hurt him, that she hadn't trusted and believed in him and their love.

She blinked and shook, her eyes wide upon him. Her expression, the silent movement of her lips said she struggled to find logic and words. "I . . . J.C. found Brent's whiskey flask on the beach. I recognized it. He was never without it. There was a scrap of fabric with it that matched Celeste's scarf. He killed her, Nick. From where Celeste died, the current from the river coming into the harbor from the land side would have taken that flask from the channel out to the lake . . . and then it would have washed back to the beach where J.C. found it."

Maggie's voice shook now. "Brent killed Celeste. I know it, just as I know he somehow used Leo to do his dirty work at the winery, and then Brent must have—Brent must have killed Ed—Ed knew what he was. He killed them both! He's the man from my past that Celeste warned me about!"

Nick had to comfort her; the panic rising in her with every heartbeat, her shoulders tense beneath his open hands. *Oh, Maggie, trust me . . .* "Maggie, we'll work through this. There are plenty of tourists in town. Scout could be playing in a hotel pool with kids—you know how she loves that. We'll find Scout and—"

"I should have watched her better. I'd had her on the leash for so long while we were traveling that I'd been letting her run more, and everyone has watched her so well. I should have—"

Nick shook her gently, trying to ground the panic flying through her. "That's right. Blame yourself. That's what you love to do—tear yourself apart. Everyone in town loves her. They watch her, and so do I. Someone will call and she'll be fine. Meanwhile, we'll call Lorenzo."

Maggie's eyes were rounded, as if another realization had just struck her. She reached to grip his arm. "The man who came after Scout in the restaurant could have been Brent. I didn't think it was him. I just couldn't see him not keeping up his looks, or coming after us. He's a powerful man, a rich man, who takes care of how he looks. But he was tall and had sandy hair. He's vain and he's compulsive-obsessive. That's why Ed's upstairs room was so neat—Brent has been staying there, watching everything. That's why the bottles on Ed's bar were turned so exactly—that wasn't Ed's work or his employees—that was Brent. He has to have everything in a line, in order, pictures straight on the wall—Nick, I know it is him. I'm not imagining this. He stole those pictures of my family as a threat, as a memento."

Nick smoothed her shining reddish hair, warm with sun and a vivid contrast to her pale face, the freckles dancing upon her skin. How many times had she fought alone, struggling for a justice that never came? "I never said you were. The thing is to keep you safe—and Scout. We'll find her, Maggie."

She stared at him as if she didn't know him. "Nick, you didn't ask to see that scrap of Celeste's scarf. You just believed me. Why?"

"Because I love you. It's that simple. I don't need proof to know that you are scared stiff, and while we're at it, it's a little bit irritating to know that you don't trust me."

When she shook her head, Maggie's bright hair caught the wind, the ends almost fiery in the sunlight. "I'm sorry, Nick."

This wasn't the time to weigh Maggie with his frustration. Nick gathered that silky hair into his hand and shook her head gently. "Take it easy. We'll find Scout and—"

"Nick? There's one more thing. I took Scout from him. Brent was furious when she didn't perform in front of his buddies. She was untrained and young and it wasn't her fault—it was his. He hates failure and they laughed at him. I can't let her go back to him. He'll kill her eventually, just because I love her—and worst of all, from his viewpoint above the tavern, he would have seen her obey your hand commands—he could never get her to respond to him. Nick, while I stay here, you and your family are in danger. He can't tolerate other men succeeding when he fails."

"He's not getting her. Take it easy, Maggie. You need to be calm to tell Lorenzo everything." As Nick drove Maggie into Blanchefleur, he pushed aside the pain that she hadn't trusted him and concentrated on her safety. He tucked the unread note she'd written into his shirt pocket. After she and Scout were safe, Maggie would make her own decision.

Worst of all, Maggie hadn't trusted him to believe her.


"Nick said you were to stay here while he checked on Scout. Lorenzo agreed it was safest to keep you here."

Dante settled into the restaurant's upstairs apartment with Maggie to play cards and to bodyguard. "You're not going anywhere. Downstairs is too busy and we're going to sit this one out up here until Nick or Lorenzo calls. The police are going door to door now, asking questions about suspicious characters and giving out that man's description."

Maggie lifted the curtain aside to scan the street. In front of Journeys, the goddess chime was catching the dim light, flashing silver as she turned. Maggie wrapped her arms around herself, her body chilled at the ominous sign. If that was Celeste's warning, it was effective. Brent was capable of anything, and Maggie had led him here to kill her friend—and maybe Nick.

From the window over the tavern, Brent would have seen everything. He would have seen her love for Nick and that would snap any sanity he had left, because Brent could not tolerate women outside his maneuvering—like herself. "It's getting dark outside. Nick hasn't checked in for the last hour."

"He will."

"I did not want to go to the police with this. I've been through all that before and no one believed me."

"Lorenzo did, and he's seen a lot. And Nick believes you. Did you think he wouldn't?"

"I . . . I didn't know what he would think. I just panicked. I still am." Maggie shivered as she remembered Nick's dark anger, the chilly, brisk stashing of her in Dante's care. She'd hurt Nick terribly.

Dante sat at the table, laid out a solitaire game pattern, and began slapping down cards. "He believes you enough to have the whole family alerted. Pop is really enjoying this. Jerry is at the back door, playing guard with his cute little walkie-talkie, and Marco is frisking people at the front door—now that would be an experience. Lorna and Vinnie are downstairs, dressed in black leather, and I don't want to know what they are packing beneath their jackets. Lorna is all revved to show off her hand-to-hand technique. If Vinnie gets any more worked up, just watching her, we're going to have to put them in the backyard and turn a cold hose on them. . . . Don't spoil the cavalry's fun by making them worry about you being safe. Nick will find Scout and he'll call. Meanwhile, we're sitting tight."

Maggie studied Dante, who was evidently enjoying his role. "You know, there's a certain arrogance about you Alessandro males that makes me want to take you down. I should be out there, hunting my dog."

Dante flashed a superior-male wolfish grin. "Try getting by me, half pint."

"I could hurt you, Dante," she warned darkly, but didn't intend to carry through her threat.

His grin widened. "Now I'm real worried. Settle down, will you?"

Maggie turned to Dante. "You see things down at the boatyard and in town. Did you ever see that man again?"

Dante inhaled slowly as if he were preparing his answer. "I did. But I lost him. And now I know why. Ed must have gone to a lot of work to get that upstairs storage room clean enough."

Maggie leaned her head against the cool glass and studied the goddess slowly turning within the wind chime. "What are you trying to tell me, Celeste?" she whispered.

"What did you say?" Dante asked.

"Not a thing." But every sense in Maggie was alert and still and warning her that Nick was in danger. She couldn't be kept safe, while he—Maggie didn't want to think about what Brent might do to Nick, the man whom Scout obeyed, the man she loved.

Brent would destroy everything Nick loved—the vineyards, the winery, his home. The Journeys wind chime began turning quickly, almost frantically as the wind began to sweep down Blanchefleur's main street, tossing leaves against the apartment window.

In that instant, Maggie knew she had to find Nick and Scout; she couldn't wait. Every instinct she had said they needed her.

If Brent had Nick and saw anyone but her coming, he'd kill Nick without a second thought.

But he just might take Maggie as a substitute. If she found Brent, he might just leave Blanchefleur with her, and the Alessandros would be safe—

"Dante, I can't relax. I'm taking a long soak in the tub. Let me know if Nick calls, okay?"

Minutes later, Maggie turned off the tub's faucets, made some splashing and relaxing noises, and then opened the window. A similar escape diversion had worked with Nick's cousin; she could only hope it would work with Dante. She heard him call down for a food delivery. He'd be eating alone.

With little effort, Maggie hefted herself upward and out of the window. The rain-scented wind lifted her hair, chilling her nape, as she stepped out onto the roof and edged her way around a corner. Her fingers gripped the damp bricks, jutting out a bit from the rest to make a design; her shoes found the edges and she inched her way to another angled roof.

The rusted iron fire escape was old and unused, but strong enough to hold her weight until she dropped to the ground. She scanned the street, cars parked on either side; she had to get to Nick's house. A missing vehicle would draw attention, and if Brent were pushed too soon, Nick could be killed.

Lorenzo's deputies cruised slowly by the restaurant, and Maggie slid deeper into the shadows. *If she could just find Nick . . .*

The health-conscious Martins, local residents, often walked to the restaurant, their children following on bicycles and skateboards, which were deposited in the alley while the family ate inside. Maggie quietly worked Oliver's fast racer from the metal tangle and pulled back into the alley when a group of elderly women on their weekly night out passed by. Mrs. Friends turned to look at Maggie, and at Maggie's silent shush signal, she nodded and continued chatting. "If Eugene wants to spend time with Dee Dee, he's perfectly welcome."

Taking care to stay away from the streetlights, Maggie eased out of town and sailed toward Nick's winery. The wind pushed her clothing against her, fierce and angry, as the damp moonless night enclosed her.

Celeste had said to focus on her senses, and everything in Maggie told her that she had to find Nick and Scout. If Nick was hurt . . .

Maggie's lungs hurt as she sucked air into them and dropped the bike, running up the old footpath that led to the winery.

Then through the soft rain she saw the light in the Frenchman's old lighthouse, and she knew . . .

"Down, Scout. Down. Sit," Nick ordered firmly as Scout's claws dug at the kitchen's slick linoleum, stretching the chain around her neck tightly.

Brent studied the dog critically as she snarled at him. "It's truly amazing how those spikes dig into a dog's throat when they don't obey. She'd better get used to it. She's got a life-time—what's left of it—waiting for her."

"Easy, girl." Behind him, Nick's wrists were slick with blood; his fight against the plastic ties were futile. His arm hurt where the tranquilizer dart had hit, but in his fear for Maggie, the blows from Brent's tantrum did not hurt.

Somehow Brent knew that Maggie would come to him. Meanwhile, he seemed content to batter Nick. "How did you get her to come to you?"

"Simple. She remembers the sound of my voice. I parked in the woods and talked to myself—planning how I was going to watch you die—and she came snarling after me, just as she did in the restaurant. The dart hit her perfectly. I got in the car and waited until the tranquilizer worked."

"And now you want Maggie." Nick recognized Maggie's description of Brent, how he enjoyed hurting—his obsession to be powerful and rule others.

"You took her away from me. You shouldn't have done that. And she shouldn't have ruined my life and stolen my dog. Look what she's done to me: This—" Brent tapped his nose with the gun. "This and the scar were because I couldn't pay my creditors. She studied my friends' haunts and habits and she tracked them down, embarrassed them in front of their business associates and friends. She harassed and turned my friends against me and my wife . . . my rich wife with enough attorneys to make that prenup stick. Maggie provided the limp. My wife wouldn't pay to have it fixed, or the therapy I needed later. But I'll have it all fixed, once I've finished here."

Nick's mistake—calling Scout and looking for her rather than the man who wanted to harm Maggie—could be fatal for her. He'd been so worried about Scout that he barely felt the burn of the dart. Somehow Brent had managed to get Nick's limp body into a kitchen chair, securing his hands and feet with plastic cord restraints. And then his rage set in, beating Nick before he was fully conscious.

Winded, Brent had stopped to gather his strength and apparently to savor the moment as he waited for Maggie.

Nick had surfaced with a prayer that somehow he could free himself. "How much will it take to leave now, without Maggie? I can get cash—"

"You don't understand, do you? I have cash. Now it's time for payback. While you were having your little nap after our last session, I went up to that tower. Using those binoculars, I saw Maggie. She's coming. It was only a shadow of a bicycle racer powering down that dirt road, but I knew who it was. Only Maggie would be riding a bicycle in the wind and rain. I've always admired her fitness and that elegance, that class few women have. When she's aroused, fighting mad, she's like a tigress, but I will tame her. She gives everything—and I intend to make her beg for me. Just like her sister and the others did."

Footsteps sounded on the wooden deck, and Maggie slowly opened the kitchen door.

Brent aimed the automatic at her. "Hello, Brent," she said, as if she had expected him to be just there, waiting for her.

"Maggie—" Nick struggled against his restraints and was surprised to see her smile glitter coldly, brilliantly at Brent.

She moved to pick up a napkin and blot the wound on Nick's forehead, the bloody cut on his lip. "Hi, Nick. I told you that I was his. Now see what a mess you've made. Brent doesn't like messes. Do you, Brent? You washed your hands after you did this, didn't you? Or did you wear gloves?"

"You know me so well," Brent almost crooned, his eyes burning at her. "I wore gloves, of course."

"That's good. I wouldn't want you to become infected by his blood."

Brent's horrified expression was quickly replaced by a sly smile. "You're so considerate, my dear. She fences well, Nick, trying to undermine me, throw me off balance, and that only makes winning more enjoyable."

Maggie smelled of wind and rain, her face pale beneath the spray of summer freckles. Nick noted the way she breathed, straining not to show her exertion, belied by the rapid pulse in her throat. Those earth green eyes glittered at him just once, a flash of fear as her smile held in place.

She reached to pet Scout, and Nick noted that she stealthily loosened the choke collar. Then Maggie walked slowly to the kitchen sink and filled a glass of water. On the opposite side of the room, she drew Brent's attention from Nick as she chatted almost conversationally. Only a man who loved her would know how badly Maggie was frightened, how her hand trembled as it pushed back those thick, reddish brown strands. "You're not looking so good these days, Brent. What happened?"

His face contorted with rage. "Because of you, I lost everything—that's what happened. You pushed and shoved and harassed, and none of them wanted to be my friends after you got done smearing my name all over. Just after you disappeared, Evelyn divorced me, cut me off. *You ruined me.*"

Nick noticed the quick flaring of Maggie's nostrils, the almost imperceptible softness of satisfaction held deep inside. But her lips curved slowly. "I shouldn't have done that. I'm sorry."

"I'll make you sorry," he snarled. "You ruined my life," he repeated violently.

His thin body tensed threateningly, and Nick knew that Maggie was baiting Brent, that she was balancing her fitness and agility against his gun. "I'm good at what I do, working with individual health problems. You look like you need a personal trainer. I'm available. I can have you back in shape in no time."

She ignored Nick, shifting her body seductively to show the curves beneath her damp T-shirt and shorts, the length of her legs. Brent's indrawn hiss said he hadn't missed her open sensuality. "She's magnificent, isn't she? Strong, feline, smart . . . opportunistic. She's circling me now. Quite the prize. I've missed you, Maggie. The little challenges you offer. We've been waiting for you. You're almost too late for the party. Tardiness doesn't pay. Now, the first thing you must do is call and make everyone feel that you and Nick are safe. If you don't call them off, he's done right now. Do it."

Maggie shrugged lightly. "Suit yourself. I was planning to move on anyway. He doesn't matter."

Brent's cold eyes flared, his tone bitter. "I saw you laughing at him, playing with him. It looked like you cared. You were all over him."

In a flirtatious gesture, she flipped her hair and studied him coolly. "Get smart, Brent. I used him. I needed a good contact—the Alessandros know everyone. I thought I could go back to playing the little woman, but that's not me. I know who I am now and fairy tales just don't exist. I've changed. You taught me that."

Brent considered her statement and then began a crooked, knowing smile.

Despite the bruises and pain of Brent's rough treatment, a worse pain twisted around his heart. *Maggie didn't love him . . . It was all a lie . . .*

His stomach churned, and he felt as if his heart had stopped forever.

She moved seductively again, drawing Brent's attention, and then Nick understood. Maggie had said that Brent would destroy anyone dear to her, those she loved—

*She was protecting him.*

*She loved him . . . "With all my heart," she'd said.*

Oh, he had plans for her later, Nick thought grimly. "You are going to get what you deserve, sweetheart."

Brent gripped Maggie's hair and tugged, placing his skeletal face next to hers in a pose as they faced Nick. "Her hair is the same rich penny color as her sister's. I used to like Glenda's on my skin. If I had time, I'd let you watch. Sort of a parting gift from me to you. I think I'm going to keep her for a time. Maggie, *call off the Alessandros now*."

Her body arched at an odd angle as Brent held her hair, but she reached for the telephone. She hesitated for just that second and then she dialed the restaurant. "Hi. Dante? Sorry about the slip. Yes, I know Lorenzo is fuming. I am definitely champ of the window escapes, but I couldn't just sit there. I'm with Nick and we've got Scout . . . Yes, everything is fine. Hmm? Scout found a friend, a little Yorkie, and they've been doing the beach thing. We're going to try to find who owns the Yorkie—cute little thing. Yes, everything is fine. I just didn't like that Alessandro man-thing you and Nick pulled about protecting the little helpless woman. We're sorting things out here, so don't bother us. I'll apologize to Lorenzo later. See you in the morning."

"Very nicely done, Maggie," Brent said when she hung up the telephone. He released her hair and walked to Nick. "She was always independent. In some ways that is good for a woman, but they really need to know who is boss—and that takes me back to this fellow here."

Brent's fist crashed against Nick's face. When Nick surfaced again, he saw Maggie's pale face, her fingers gripping the counter. He heard Brent say, "You know you belong to me, Maggie. You're going to work like Glenda worked and get what I need."

"You're high," Maggie observed quietly.

"Just to kill the pain of my knee while we take care of business. I knew you would come tonight because we are locked together, perfect mates, except of course, I am much superior. I knew I would be your master from the time I met you. Cut the ties on Nick's legs. We're going for a boat ride. We'll use Nick's fishing boat to get out to mine, a little cabin cruiser that I borrowed. It's just perfect for our reunion, Maggie."

"I look forward to it. But first, would you like something to eat? You need me to take care of you, Brent. To do as you say."

Brent took the suggestion with a nod. "Something to eat would be lovely. One of those delicious instant things you used to do when I came home to dinner with Ryan."

He turned to Nick. "Ryan didn't deserve her. He wasn't man enough. I knew that and so did he. Maggie used to be a perfect wife, a perfect hostess, working so hard to help their business grow. Yes, make me something delicious and just for me. Nothing that takes too much time, because we have work to do. And nothing with a knife, please. I wouldn't want you to hurt yourself."

"An omelet then. Not that tasty without chopping mushrooms and onions, but I'll throw in some dry herbs. We'll put you on a vitamin and nutrition program right away, Brent," Maggie said as she began breaking eggs. Nick recognized Maggie's stubborn look—that she intended to have answers. If only he could distract Brent long enough for Maggie to escape . . .

The omelet sizzled into the hot pan and Maggie seemed to concentrate on it. "So here we are. You and I. You killed Celeste, didn't you? And my sister?"

Brent's smile was wolfish, sly, predatory, seeking her weaknesses. "The witch woman was dogging me, following me. She was asking Ed questions. Her house is a nightmare. She should have died for that alone."

She carefully turned the omelet, her voice distracted. "You mean that it wasn't orderly. I can understand that. And my sister? She was too weak, wasn't she? And you were done with her? Glenda must have been a real liability. She was to me, too."

Maggie's expression changed for just a half of a heartbeat into grief and anger. If she moved against Brent now, he'd fire . . . Nick shifted on the chair, enough to make a scraping sound, warning her.

But Maggie hadn't moved, her silence demanding, heavy and ominous in the kitchen. The wind picked up slightly and the wind chime began its music. Maggie seemed to go too still, her head tilted, as if she were listening to the sound.

Brent shrugged and smiled slyly. "Sure. It was easy. She was already gone, really. I just helped a bit and gave her what she wanted, that last shot. She begged me for it. Your name and her kids' names were the last words she spoke. After she told me she loved me."

"Okay. I just like to have everything straight between us. I think I always knew you would come for me," Maggie said slowly, casually, as she served Brent the omelet. "You're not done yet, are you? You're coming back for Nick's family and for Beth?"

"Of course. Ed might have told the girl something that might have implicated me, and the Alessandros need pay-back for running me off that day. I thought I'd burn their restaurant down, maybe with them in it." He indicated with a gesture of the gun that she was to sit at the table. While he stood and ate ravenously, Brent watched Nick and Maggie closely.

Maggie seemed at ease, but Nick knew the pain inside her—and the fury. It seemed to radiate from her in hot waves. *Don't, Maggie. Not now . . .*

When he finished, Brent said, "Now. Come get the knife and cut the ties on his legs. Then put the knife back slowly."

"He's too big for us to move. If you want to get him into a boat, he's going to have to be conscious. Don't hit him again." When Maggie bent to cut the ties, she gave Nick a grim warning look that said not to talk or resist—not to infuriate Brent. That brief glance terrified Nick. He understood perfectly. She was playing for time, for opportunity. She'd fought for Glenda, and she would fight for him.

*And she could be killed.*

"Why don't you just let Brent and me sort this out, Maggie? You could tie her up and leave her here, and come back when you're finished with me," he suggested as he stood unsteadily, suddenly dizzy.

"Didn't you know? He needs me to see everything—how strong and smart he is—don't you, Brent?" Maggie answered as she shoved him lightly.

Nick faked a stumble, because Maggie's thrust wasn't enough to unbalance him. She was taking chances to save his pain and his life. On the path down to the lake, she picked up a stick and prodded Nick's back. If she managed to look like she was hurting him, Brent would enjoy the spectacle. In her other hand, she held the chain that led to Scout's choke collar.

Nick understood the scene she was creating—the strong fit woman maneuvering a big man with a stick, prodding his back, and controlling a dog with her other hand. In his need to show that he was all powerful, Brent would become even more obsessive about having her—and perhaps distracted from killing Nick . . .

"Sweetheart, you are really going to pay for this," Nick murmured as he stepped into the small aluminum boat with Brent.

She walked into the water, pushing the boat out into the waves that were growing stronger with each moment. She hefted her body up into the boat and at the indication of Brent's gun, took her position at the motor.

Maggie hadn't showed Brent her fear of water, but Nick saw it in her tense expression before she closed it away.

Brent preyed on fears, and Maggie wasn't giving him that edge—she was playing for time—because she planned to protect Nick and the others with her own life.

She intended to finish with Brent tonight, one way or the other.

# NINETEEN

While Maggie fought Lake Michigan's massive swells, steering the small fishing boat toward the cruiser, she focused on chipping at Brent's weakness—his ego. "I think I always knew that we were meant to be together. I knew you would come after me, Brent. Somehow, I knew. You found me through Leo, didn't you? And you talked him into coming here and destroying the winery."

"I worked the health spas, because I knew that would lead me to you. You don't really know how to do anything but play the good wife and be a trainer. Leo recognized your picture right away. He wanted to help and I merely let him. I lost everything because of you. And you're going to repay me—one way or another. It's just a matter of time before I'm back on my feet, and you're going to work for me every minute."

Maggie fought the fear squeezing her; *she had to save Nick's life and Scout's.*

She'd almost cried out and ran to Nick when she first saw him tied to that chair. For the first time in her life, her rage was so great, she wanted to kill Brent. Now, Nick's face was bruised and swollen, one eye almost closed, a cut along his cheek. From his painful movements, his side was injured. But then, Brent needed to bring others down to his level.

The anger flashing in Nick's eyes terrified Maggie. If he decided to move too soon . . . *Don't, Nick, please don't . . .*

The waves battered Nick's small boat against the cabin cruiser. "Cut his hands loose. He's going into the water. I want him too busy to cause trouble while we board. One wrong move and I shoot—you, the woman, and the dog. Even if you somehow manage to live, I figure it will take you a while, if you can make the swim back to shore, and by that time, I'll have paid your parents a visit—and maybe your brother's kids."

He tossed a pocket knife at Maggie. "Catch. I want that back, and he'll get it right now, if he tries anything. If he dies now, that's okay. I'd prefer to take my time, though."

At Nick's warning look, Maggie stopped her fearful protest. His hands free, Nick slid over the side of the small boat, the waves washing over him. Brent balanced with one hand and smashed his foot against Nick's clinging fingers. "Hands off."

Brent's gun flashed at Maggie. "Up. He can bring the dog. It will keep his hands busy. If he can't make it, I'll finish them both off right now."

Maggie swung onto the ladder, trying not to look back at Nick in the deadly waves. If Brent sensed how deeply she cared, Nick would die. Waiting for the right moment, she obeyed Brent. If she tried to overpower him now, she might lose, and Nick and Scout would die.

Brent swung onto the deck after her and held the gun to her ribs as they watched Nick struggle out of the cold water and into the small boat. "Keep that chain on her and untie the boat," Brent yelled against the wind.

"Not a move," he ordered as Nick managed to place Scout onto the deck. "Go back down and capsize the boat. Make one wrong move and I shoot her."

"So it's going to be a drowning, is it?" Nick asked grimly and with a nod set about Brent's task.

Maggie tried to mask her fear for Nick, but her stomach was in knots.

Brent glanced at her and smiled evilly. He would use any weakness. "Still afraid of water, Maggie? Remember how your father died?"

She pushed away her fear and smiled, because Nick needed her. *Oh, please, let me find a way to distract Brent.* "You're behind. I told you I'd changed. I swim now."

When Nick stood on deck again, dripping and shivering with the lake's cold water, Brent was ready. "Tie his hands again, Maggie . . . tight. I'm checking them. Then we're going farther out. With the lake this rough, you'll die before you reach shore. Drowning is awful, they tell me. I'll watch you, of course, Nick. It will look as if you drowned while out on the lake with Maggie and Scout. You fell, got battered by the boat a bit, and finally gave up. They won't be found, just some of Maggie's clothing and Scout's collar artfully tied to a life jacket. Because they'll be with me."

Maggie instantly swung in to pick at Brent's plan, upping the pressure on him, because he hated his mistakes served back to him. "Nick's wrists are scraped and bloody. They'll know he's been tied. Maybe—"

Brent blinked as though surprised at a flaw in his plan. Then his anger fired again. "That can't be helped. They'll think he got tangled in the rope and tried to fight free. Tie them."

With a look, Nick warned Maggie not to challenge Brent.

Her look said she wasn't finished with Brent, even though revenge now could cost her life. "Some things are better let go, Maggie," he cautioned quietly.

"I heard that," Brent yelled. "She can't let go. She's tied to me, the same as I am tied to her."

Maggie's eyes held Nick's, willing him to understand. "He's right, Nick. I'm just sorry that you're in this, too. I think I always knew it would come to this. That we'd meet someday in different circumstances."

His anger slashed at her. "Just you and him, right? I'm not in the picture? You take care of things yourself, cutting me out?"

"I'm so sorry you're involved." When Maggie was finished, her fingers gripped Nick's briefly. His frustration and anger throbbed in the stormy air, nipping at her. When Brent checked her work, her eyes locked with Nick's, telling him of her fear, her sorrow, her love for him. Then her stare turned, purposely directing his to a sliver of broken glass, caught in a crevice at the back of a seat.

When Brent straightened, Maggie shoved Nick's chest, seating him near the glass, and he went to work. "Quiet," he ordered Scout, who was growling at Brent.

*If Nick could just get his hands free . . .*

Only a few feet from Nick and Scout, Maggie prayed that he could work free, and tried to ignore Brent's hand squeezing her bottom—an obvious show of ownership. Repulsed by his touch, she followed Brent's orders, expertly steering the cruiser into the waves. Not even a strong swimmer could make the distance to shore now, even in calm, warmer water.

*Nick could drown, just as her father had . . .*

Working to distract and upset Brent, Maggie chipped away at him. "You shouldn't have killed Ed. You should have kept him, made it look like he did this. You could have used that gun. Then we'd be away free."

"Shut up." The rage in Brent's expression said that he'd lost his temper with Ed and acted sooner than he had planned.

Maggie glanced back and saw that Scout's choke collar was gone. That she was obeying Nick's quiet command to stay still. *That meant Nick's hands were free and he was just waiting for the right moment . . . He could be killed if she failed to distract Brent . . .* "Oh, I see. The original plan didn't work when Ed started—"

"He was a liability. If he got pushed hard enough, he'd tell everything, and they were certain to do a thorough interrogation. I couldn't have him ruining my plans. He was frantic and he thought I might hurt his little girlfriend, Beth. When he started playing hero, I knew he had to die."

"That was smart." She pulled Brent back by the compliment, playing to his confidence, then served him another flaw. "What was the plan the day you went into the Alessandros Restaurant for Scout? Didn't that expose you too soon? But then, you probably—"

"I said, shut up."

But Maggie had successfully placed the nudge—the reminder that Brent's furious temper had erupted and escaped his control.

Then she pushed again, tilting that same confidence. "Celeste knew you were coming. She's here . . . on the lake. Can you feel her?"

Brent shivered and looked fearfully into the windy night, the clouds sweeping across the moon. In the distance, Blanchefleur's lighthouse sent a rhythmic dull beam into the night; it seemed almost like a living pulse, a slight hope to grasp.

Maggie decided to push once more, preying on Brent's exposed fear, fueling it. "Celeste felt she had bonded with Monique, the Frenchman's lost fiancée—she went down on a ship, just off that tiny island in the far distance. Oh, you can't see it now, but they say Monique walks beneath the water, waiting to show a drowning person her home. Do you think that can be true? Or that he waits for her?"

"Shut up. I don't believe in ghosts." But she had scored a hit; Brent nervously searched the lake as the wind whistled eerily around them.

Maggie played to the violence of the storm, the sound of the wind. "You can't see them. You can only feel them. Or hear them."

"Maggie," Nick cautioned behind her, the sound soft and dangerous, carried by the wind.

With her hands on the controls, she braced herself; when Brent turned once more, she would pit her weight against him—taking them both over the side.

When Brent looked back at Nick, Maggie feared he planned to kill Nick right then. If she shoved now, the gun could go off, wounding Nick. She played for time, attempting to draw Brent's attention back to her. "Then believe this. You can't breed Scout. She's been spayed. She isn't going to be your private puppy mill—and that's what you had planned, wasn't it? To get back what you'd lost? Get back into your buddies' good favor? Gee, another plan gone wrong."

For a moment, Brent's expression went blank; then with a wild scream, his fist lashed out, catching her jaw. "I need those pups for my friends!"

Maggie staggered backward with the blow, just as she heard Scout's warning growl. In the night and the rain, Scout leaped toward Brent, his gun flashed, and the dog yelped.

Then Nick was on Brent and Maggie pushed herself to her feet, instantly killing the motor. She plunged at the two struggling men, and Nick's open hand found her face and thrust her back gently. "Could you trust me, just this once? Get out of the way!"

Balancing against the toss of the waves, Maggie fought leaping back into the battle to protect the man she loved. "I love you! You can't expect me to not help you!"

"Give me a break, will you?" Nick's grip on Brent was that of a fit workman against a much frailer man. He tossed the gun into the water and reached for a coil of rope, quickly binding Brent, who was muttering wildly.

Muscling Brent past Maggie, Nick pushed him down on the deck and, placing a knee on Brent, jerked up a cushioned seat. He prowled through the tools and came up with duct tape. In minutes, Brent's arms and legs were secured and when he didn't stop raving, Nick applied a strip across his mouth.

He turned to look at Maggie who was leaning over the

side, her flashlight searching for Scout. "Scout? Scout? Nick, she must have gone overboard!"

Terrified for her dog, Maggie called until her throat was hoarse, but the flashlight showed nothing in the water. The wind rose, lightning fingered down from the clouds and rolling thunder followed. After a half hour of searching, Nick said quietly, "Maggie, it's getting rougher. We have to leave."

"Just a bit more—"

"Maggie . . ."

She recognized the warning in Nick's tone, and defeated by odds she could not control, sat as he steered the cruiser toward shore. Nick eased it onto the sandy beach and cut the tape on Brent's ankles. "Jump in."

The force of the waves took Brent under, but Nick jerked him up. "One wrong move and I let you drown. Freezing, isn't it?"

He turned to Maggie, saw that she was managing and pushed Brent to shore. When Maggie stood on shore, scanning the lake one more time, Nick said, "We'll hunt for her in the morning. Come on, Maggie. We've got to take care of this garbage."

Cold, wet, and exhausted, they worked their way up the sandy knoll. Maggie's mind was on Scout, grieving for her, and she moved automatically. "You took the key to the cruiser."

"I wanted to make certain you didn't go back out without me. It's too dangerous."

"Nick—" She started to cry, unable to control herself any longer.

Nick couldn't bear to see her grieve, seeming to fold within herself, coming apart before him. There was no way Scout could have been wounded and survived out in the lake. Her body would probably wash up onshore.

Maggie had lived through a real nightmare with her father's death, and her sister's, a good friend, and now a pet that she loved dearly. Her pale, tear streaked face turned to him, but Nick couldn't give her the answer she wanted.

"You'll get through this. We'll look for her tomorrow. Come on," he said gently, and pushed Brent ahead of them. "Get up on the porch."

Brent shook his head, the tape over his mouth muffling a terrified, high-pitched protest, and pushed back against Nick's hand. Nick hauled the slighter man up by the collar and shoved him up the steps to the porch. "Maggie, come on."

Nick watched her move slowly, painfully up the steps. Brent was twisting now, trying to get away, his eyes wide with fear. Busy holding him and watching Maggie, Nick barely noticed the hooded slight figure moving out from behind the huge, tropical plants that had been Celeste's.

Maggie grabbed Nick's arm in warning, and lightning lit the hard face of Shirley within her plastic raincoat. In her hand was an automatic.

"Hello, Shirley," Nick said quietly and frowned when he noted Maggie edging in front of him.

"You want me, Shirley. I'm the reason Ed got tangled up with this man. Let Nick go."

"I've had enough of your sacrificing-hero stuff for tonight, sweetheart." Nick reached his free hand out to capture Maggie's arm, dragging her back.

Brent was fighting furiously now, making terrified noises, and Nick struggled to control him. Terror had given Brent strength and agility.

Nick's blood stilled as Shirley aimed the gun at Maggie, who now stood a few feet from him.

"Yes, you brought him here. He followed you," Shirley said slowly. "He killed my Ed. I never told the law, because I wanted to settle his hash myself. I knew he'd be coming out here and I saw you sneak out of the alley."

She pointed the gun back to Brent. "I knew when I saw how neat everything was—I used to deliberately tilt the picture frames to irritate him. But when Ed died, all the frames and the bottle labels were arranged—just after I had left them deliberately messed up. Ed wouldn't have killed himself. That note didn't even sound like him. He loved me. He just played around to make me jealous. But he always came back. I knew everything about Mr. Brent Templeton. Ed had me following you. Who do you think cooked all that fancy food you had to have, Mr. Glove Man? Did you know I spit in every dish you got? I saw you go into that witch woman's house, and kill her and that fat slob who tore up the winery. Not much goes by old Shirley. We laughed over how crazy you are, up there pacing and raving about Maggie."

At that, Brent stopped squirming. He straightened and looked haughtily down at her.

"You heard me, Mr. High and Mighty. I spat in your food every time Ed took it up to you. You didn't think poor old Ed was doing all the cooking, did you? He couldn't fry an egg. I've been waiting. I saw Nick's boat go out and I knew. I knew that one or the other of you would come back, and I didn't care who I finished off. Take off the tape on his mouth. I want to hear what he has to say, before all of you die—The Crazy because he killed Ed, Maggie because she brought The Crazy here, and Nick . . . well, he has to die because he'll be a witness. I can't let him live," Shirley said.

Nick didn't waste time with a slow, gentle removal and ripped away the tape. Brent grimaced with pain and then smiled slowly. Previously, that smile might have charmed, but now it was a crooked grimace. "I didn't kill Ed, Shirley. It was Maggie. She tried to get Ed and when he wouldn't have her, she worked Nick, getting him to help her. Nick is in on it with her."

Shirley's gun moved slightly, aimed at Maggie. Then Nick reached to put her behind him.

"So it's like that," Shirley murmured. "You'd die for her."

"I would. But you don't want to do this, Shirley. You've lost Ed, isn't that enough?"

"Get out of my way, Nick," Maggie said beneath her breath.

Brent leaned forward, eager to sway Shirley. "They planned it."

The gun swung back to Brent. "Ed never should have got mixed up with you. I told him that you were trouble, a real crazy. But he thought he could handle you."

Brent hissed, "I am not crazy. Ed died raving about how much he loved the girl, you old hag—"

The blast was deafening, the flash of light from Shirley's gun brilliant in the night—just before Brent toppled forward.

Nick and Maggie swung into action; Nick grabbed Shirley, controlling her. When she was secure, Maggie crouched to listen to Brent. The fallen man was fatally injured, his raspy whisper punctuated by a deathly rattle.

She nodded, and in a soothing gesture stroked his forehead. "You can go now, Brent. You're tired of fighting, aren't you? Just let go; there's nothing more for you to do here."

With a last rattle, Brent's head fell limply aside and he lay still.

Maggie looked at him for a long time. "He's dead."

"What did he say?" Nick asked when Maggie stood. On the porch was the man who had ruined so many lives, twining inside them, insidiously tearing them apart.

Her hand found her sister's locket once more. "He said that Celeste said he would die if he didn't leave after killing her. She was right. He said that Celeste gave her power to me."

Maggie was too stunned to do anything but stand and look at the dead man, the man of her nightmares, who had finally found her.

Nick hovered near her, lifting Shirley's arms high behind her back. In his expression was torment mixed with love. "Maggie, come inside. I've got to call Lorenzo."

"No, go ahead. I just want to stand here and know that he will never hurt anyone again. That it's done, finally done now. I . . . always felt somehow, someplace inside me that it wasn't finished, and now it is."

In the eerie aftermath of the violence, the sound of the chimes curled through the fresh, rain-washed air.

"She's out there, needing me, Nick. I can feel it." Maggie looked out of the old lighthouse windows, the panes slashed by rain. A streak of summer lightning split, forking across the night, outlining her taut body and gleaming on her tearstained cheeks.

Nick sat on the arm of the wooden chair. Hours after Shirley had been collected and jailed, Maggie's fear for her dog hadn't eased. Nick had immediately pushed her chilled body into the shower, chafing and holding her as the warmth set in. He'd dried and dressed her. She should have been exhausted; she wasn't, and Nick ached for her grief.

"We had to come back, Maggie. The squall was getting worse. We did everything we could."

"She was wounded. I should have—"

"Maggie, stop it. You were ready to shove Brent overboard and you with him to save us. We'll go out again in the morning. Meanwhile, let's get some sleep. You're running on nerves."

She turned to him suddenly. "You see what I mean, Nick? That I'm bad luck?"

"If you are, then why are we both alive?" Nick rose to his feet, waiting for her to decide she needed him. His own emotions were unsteady, the aftermath of seeing his love, his heart in danger, of understanding what she must have gone through years ago.

She swayed and looked at him helplessly. "I love her so, Nick. She's a part of me. Just like Glenda. And Celeste, and you—I couldn't bear the thought of him killing you, Nick— I love you so."

So he was human, Nick decided. He needed that much from her. "Maggie, come here. Let me hold you."

She came into his arms, holding him tightly, while the storm tore into the night, lightning streaked like crooked spears, and thunder rattled the windows. "If anything would have happened to you . . ."

"Nothing did. You were protecting me."

Maggie was silent for a moment, and then she said, "And you didn't like it one bit."

He nuzzled her damp hair, inhaling the fragrance, and reveled in Maggie, safe in his arms. "Men like to play heroes, you know."

She shook her head. "Brent was mad. I should have done more years ago. I should have stopped him."

This time, Nick shook her lightly. "You tried. Why does everything have to be your fault?"

Maggie was still for a moment, then she eased away, looking small and vulnerable in his T-shirt. "Nick, you have to let Alyssa go."

"Where did that come from?" Nick rammed his hand through his damp hair and down his unshaven jaw. One minute he was comforting her, and in the next, Maggie had turned to his guilt about Alyssa. "Now, that one was my fault. She should have been wearing a helmet. I should have made her put it on."

"Think of it this way—you saved me tonight. That evens the score, doesn't it?" Maggie came to look up at him, her hands smoothing his jaw. "You look awful."

"I wanted to protect you tonight—and I couldn't. I walked right into a trap that endangered you."

She eased his head down to lightly kiss his bruised face, his swollen eyelid, the bruises on his forehead and jaw. "But you did. You're my hero. You were wonderful."

A little of his ego slithered back, and Nick angled his jaw for her kiss. "You missed a place."

Maggie held him tightly, her face warm against his throat. "Just hold me."

Nick sipped coffee from his thermos as he steered the boat out onto the lake, searching for Scout's body. Leaves and branches rolled on the waves, evidence of the storm's violence. The ghostly gray, the predawn spread out onto the peaceful lake.

He'd left Maggie sleeping deeply to climb up to the old lighthouse.

Maybe she was sleeping. Or maybe she just couldn't take any more pain until she was ready. He'd opened the windows to the damp, chilly air, needing the clean freshness to sweep through him. There was the sound of the waves, the gentle wind twining through Celeste's chimes, the steady drip of last night's rain from the branches. He had to give Maggie peace, even if it was Scout's body, and suddenly he'd been in motion.

Taking care not to make noise, Nick had descended the stairs and dressed quickly in the kitchen. He had scooped up the keys to the cabin cruiser, and automatically reached for the thermos of coffee left by a sheriff's deputy.

On second thought, he didn't want Maggie to hope or to worry about him. He'd reached for a pad and pencil and said, "Be back soon. Wanted to check on damage at the vineyard. Wait for me."

The stolen cruiser was still aground on the sand, just as they had left it last night. Straining with all his strength, Nick had managed to free it from the sand.

In the approximate location where the cruiser had been last night, Nick cut the motor and held very still, surveying the huge black swells for a sign—anything to take back to Maggie.

He saw something in the water, lying low and flat, and started the motor, steering toward it. Close now, Nick identified it as a log, and once more cut the motor, scanning the swells.

The wind rose slightly and Nick tilted his head, listening to the faint sound. It could have been Mac Donovan's collie down the road. Or a tourist's dog on a leash.

*Or it just could be Scout.*

He tossed the remainder of the coffee into the lake and powered the motor, traveling toward the sound and then stopping once more.

In the predawn and the fog, Monique's tiny island was an impossible distance for a wounded dog to swim—especially in a storm.

Yet the sound came again, a dog's excited bark, and Nick shoved the controls into full forward, heading for the island.

"He should have waited for me."

Maggie stalked the beach, watching the cruiser moving swiftly over the water toward her. She'd already made a fast run up and down the shore. She'd searched for Scout's body and *Nick had gone searching on the lake without her*.

She braced her hands on her hips and decided that he could just take her out again.

"Look at that," she muttered to herself as the cruiser came closer. "He's grinning, proud of himself. He's been out conquering the world, doing the dirty work to save little old delicate me from—"

Then Scout's black head popped up beside Nick, and Maggie held her breath—and prayed that she wasn't dreaming.

"Scout!" She waded into the water just as her dog leaped from the boat, swimming toward her.

Scout met her in a final lunge that took her under water. Only knee-deep, she struggled against the sucking waves, and suddenly she was being hauled up by her sweatshirt.

When she sputtered and shook the water from her face, she found Nick frowning at her. While Scout barked and bounded around them, he mopped the water from her face and shook her slightly. "Are you okay?"

Maggie blinked at him. She moved her feet, struggled to find her balance while Nick peered at her, and her left canvas shoe came off. Scout happily snatched it and ran to shore, ready to play fetch. "Am I dreaming?"

"If you are, it's a good one." Nick grinned and chuckled

and hefted her up to his shoulder. "Come on, Scout. She's fine, just a little flesh wound. I don't know how she managed to make it to a small island. We'll take her to the vet as soon as you change clothes—"

"No, now—"

"Maggie, sometimes you are just better off not arguing with me."

She braced her hands on Nick's backside. "You can put me down now."

"Not a chance. Scout is too excited to obey and she'll take you down again. I saw you in danger enough last night."

"You love this he-man stuff, don't you?"

Nick didn't answer, but his pat on her bottom confirmed her accusation.

Maggie smoothed his taut butt, letting her hand wander between his legs. Nick stopped walking up the hill. His body tensed and that little hip-wiggle thing said he wasn't averse to her prowling hand, which wandered around to firmer fare. "What."

"All this macho stuff is turning me on."

This time Nick's pat turned into a caress, gliding over her backside. "You're going to have to wait. . . . I can feel your heat through our clothes. Maggie, you are not starting something we can't both finish now."

"My hero. You deserve a nice warm reward. One of those flavor-ripening, peak-temperature, full-fruit-bursting kind of things."

Nick's coarse, choked sound said he understood perfectly. But then he served her a simmering invitation of his own. "Harvesting at the perfect time means waiting for that plump, skintight fruit, juicy on the inside, to give a full-bodied taste. It's going to start at the top of your head and work down to the bottom of your feet. And there are a few interesting areas between, the supple, fruity kind."

Nick eased her down from his shoulder. He reached for her face, cupping it as his lips and tongue devoured ruthlessly.

"That will have to do, love. Because eventually you'd fret about Scout, and once we start, it could be a very, very long session. I want to know and feel that you are alive and with me and I don't want any interruptions."

She nestled close against him, her breasts already peaked and aching and ready for harvest, just like the rest of her. But there was more, so much more, and it ran tender and sweet between them now. "Then it could be a long session. I need to know the same."

"You're shivering. You're getting in the shower before we go anywhere." He eased her damp hair back from her face. "You didn't panic under water. You were already surfacing when I hauled you up."

Maggie hugged him tighter, laying her head on his chest, where his heart beat strong and safe. The sound of Celeste's chimes seemed happy, and the clumps of grass remained damp from the fog that was slipping away to a beautiful day. "I knew you would fish me out, and Scout was alive. I don't think I'm afraid of water anymore."

This time when he lifted her face, his kiss was brief and tender, matching the softness in his dark eyes. "Good. I'm glad."

When they were in his pickup, driving to Blanchefleur, Maggie held her sister's locket. It was time to let Glenda rest. "Nick, I want to go to that island."

"Why?" Nick smiled briefly. "To escape the lecture Lorenzo is set to give you?"

"Oh, I know that is coming for sure, and I appreciate him putting it off this long. I should have called him when I sensed you were in danger. I know now that he would have listened to me, when others hadn't. And he's already told me that I'm going to work that mistake out by baby-sitting . . . There's something I have to do. After Scout sees the vet and we're finished with whatever statements we have to make, please take me to that island where you found her."

*　*　*

Nick sat on his haunches and built the campfire. Through the smoke and ash, he watched Maggie walk along the island's tiny shoreline, Scout at her side. The late August night was cool, foretelling of fall and Nick's ripening harvest.

In the exhausting sessions of interviews and statements and working at his winery, Maggie had been withdrawn, speaking little, but curling into his arms every night as if Nick were her safe harbor. They moved through the necessities of day-to-day living, and Nick realized that she was working through the past, trying to heal.

Camping on the island for a couple of days was a good idea—getting away from telephone calls and business, and making sense of all that had happened. Maggie needed this time, nothing else mattered. At times she walked to him and simply slid into his arms, her head on his chest. Lovemaking was long and sweet and reassuringly tender without words.

He understood the tears that Maggie silently shed as he held her, the dampness warm upon his skin.

Nick stood as Maggie went down on her knees. He silently walked closer, because if she needed him—

Maggie turned, and the moonlight caught her face, pale and haunted. "Come here, Nick. I know you're there."

As if she were inviting Nick closer, Scout trotted to him, heeling perfectly as he walked slowly to Maggie.

The necklace was a stream of silver in the moonlight, flowing from Maggie's hands as she cradled the locket. Nick went down on his knees beside her, his arm around her. "I've never seen you open that."

"I couldn't, but it is time now." Slowly, she opened the locket and there was her sister. Maggie's finger traced the smiling image so like her own. "Her sons look like Glenda. She needs peace. Celeste said she did."

With a deep breath, Maggie reached inside her light jacket's pocket and held the scrap of Celeste's scarf. Silently, she dug a hole in the sand. She carefully placed a lacy hand-kerchief inside it.

"That was our mother's," she explained softly as she placed the locket and the red scrap in the handkerchief and folded the edges over them. "Goodbye, Glenda. Goodbye, Celeste. Sleep tight. I'll always love you."

# EPILOGUE

By mid-September, Nick was exhausted. By working from before dawn until late at night, he was slowly getting the winery in shape for the crop that would be full and luscious in another week.

Nick had had to make some personal attitude adjustments: Lorna was obviously the best fix-it "man" around when it came to anything mechanical, and Nick had been forced to admit that to her. The sight of Lorna swaggering around in greasy coveralls with a tool belt strapped around her hips was too much.

Another full-blown argument with Maggie had made him feel like a jerk. After a hard work day, he settled in to brood over a glass of Pinot Noir at the family dining room table. Closed for the night, the restaurant was quiet as his family came to sit at the table.

Echoes of his last argument with Maggie circled him:

"You need me, Nick. You're short on help, with too much to do. I know the inventory. Don't be so bullheaded."

"I will not have you working for me without pay. In fact, I don't want you to work for me at all."

"It's your pride. You don't want to be compared with Ryan, who basically used me. Nick, this is different, you know it is. I love you and I want to help."

"You've done enough. Just do whatever you have to do, but you're not working for me. A man likes to think that he can provide—"

At that point, Maggie had picked up the dinner rolls she'd just finished baking and started throwing them at him. Nick had caught a few and then simply let the rest of them bounce off his body. "Now that's a waste."

"If you think that you're anything like Ryan, forget it. You've got this man role–woman role thing going on. I can't just sit on my hands while you're working yourself to death. I want to help you."

"That's what we are, Maggie. A man and a woman."

"All this comes down to me not telling you everything—"

"We were lovers. I had a right to know about your life and your nightmares. I had a right to your trust. I love you, Maggie."

"Those nightmares are gone, Nick. Those grapes are coming in and you need help."

"Not you."

With just two weeks to go before the harvest at the end of September, Nick had dug in firmly—he refused to let Maggie help him put the winery back on its feet. Or to lend him the money that Celeste had left to her. Or cash the bonds her mother had left her for absolute down-and-out "bottom money."

Just after Brent's death, Maggie had been locked in a struggle with the past, and Nick had ached for her every minute. She'd taken long walks, watched Lake Michigan, and cleaned his yard—and his house. Gradually, she'd eased away from all but the necessary gym classes, keeping those clients with definite health problems.

Nick understood that she was distancing herself from a life and a profession that she didn't really feel were hers.

Every foot of his house had been scrubbed and polished, the furniture rearranged. Since this seemed to be therapeutic for Maggie, Nick hadn't complained. And then she'd regrouped, and all hell broke loose—a mix of arguments, sulking, determined lovemaking, and stalking him.

Not that he minded Maggie stalking him, or her persuasive methods—such as that night she appeared in the vineyards carrying a blanket and a basket of food. She hadn't been wearing anything beneath that peasant blouse and full skirt.

Nick swirled the wine in his glass, watching the liquid catch the light. Maggie had licked the wine she'd dropped onto his body and in the moonlight had moved over him . . .

"I love you," she'd whispered, nuzzling his stomach and working her way up to his nipples.

That soft, sweet lovemaking was the perfect end to a day he never wanted to repeat.

While Nick brooded over Maggie and his current standoff with her, his father asked, "Where are the girls tonight?"

"Lorna, Sissy, Beth, and Maggie are at Celeste's house, settling details. Vinnie wants to buy the house for Lorna, and Beth is going to move to Iowa, but be a partner in Journeys."

"Your mother is with them. I don't like it—"

As if on cue, Rosa and Maggie entered through the back door. Dante was with them. He looked half terrified and half hopeful. His hand shook as he poured a glass of wine and quickly downed it.

Maggie came to look down at Nick, her expression tender as she smoothed his hair. "Hi, Big Guy. You look tired."

She came easily when he tugged her into his lap, kissing her. Nick leaned his head against hers. Everything he'd wanted in the world was in his arms, giving him peace—unless she brought up working at the winery. "Hi."

Rosa tied on her apron with a firmness that said she had made up her mind. "We're going after my grandson tomorrow. Anthony, you and Tony move Dante's things in with

Tony. Sissy will baby-sit during the day—or I will. We're a family—we'll do this together and Dante and his son will be together. Maggie said it's time, and I think so, too. A little boy will feel better with his grandmother and a future auntie coming to get him with his father. Dante, you go call that woman who calls herself a mother. Make the arrangements. As Maggie says, 'We're settling in as a family.' We have things to do, all of us. And Nicholas, you must realize that a woman wants to help her man. Just as I help your father— because it is my place to do so. You cannot stop Maggie from—"

Maggie lifted her face to study Nick's expression. She toyed with his hair. "He's cute when he sulks, isn't he, Rosa?"

Rosa beamed at both of them. "Very cute."

"My son is terrified of me," Dante said unevenly. "I don't think—"

"Oh, shush," both women said at once.

At Nick's house, Maggie took her shower, and the erotic sounds she made soon had Nick joining her.

Their hunger shot into heat immediately, and Nick had hurriedly carried Maggie to his bed—where she belonged.

They'd made love gently, thoroughly, many times, but this time was fierce and demanding, rising to the peak and then easing, only to rise again.

Panting delicately, Maggie held back her orgasm, one that Nick demanded from her.

Because he was fighting her demands as Maggie pitted herself against him, biting lightly, suckling, undulating beneath him.

Nick had pinned her hands at her side, their fingers locked, rising over her, pressing deep within the cradle of her thighs. "You like this, don't you? Testing me?"

"It has its pleasures. I like the other sweet times, too. You're just a big, fantastic playground. I'm an athlete, dear heart. I enjoy our bodies, and you're so easy." She panted, fighting the release he demanded of her, because his own was threatening to escape his control.

"You're going to marry me."

"Yes, I am. Because I love you. Every stubborn part of you. I think I showed you that a minute ago before you started rushing me. It's time, Nick. Now," she whispered breathlessly.

"When are you going to marry me?" He plunged in to taste her breasts, not sparing her, seeking that rich, luxurious clenching of her body, the ripe fruit that was his to claim.

Maggie pushed back, her hair damp against her face, her lips swollen with those deep kisses that drove them both—"No more waiting until the flavors blend just right. You're full and ripe now, Nick. Just ready for harvesting. One crush, just one squeeze and you'll—"

With all his strength, Nick controlled his release, easing slightly away. "When? When are we getting married?"

"When I come to you. There are things I have to do—"

Nick shuddered, fighting the warm, enticing clench of her body. "After Dante's boy—like what?"

"Like this—" With a high, keening sound, Maggie went into herself the way he loved, holding him tightly, her pulses became his, and Nick gave himself to her.

When he could breathe again, Nick nuzzled Maggie's damp throat as she stroked his scarred thigh, soothing him. "Like what? What do you have to do before we get married?"

Maggie gripped the gearshift of the moving van and eased the heavily loaded vehicle onto the dirt road leading toward Alessandros Winery and Vineyard. In the first week of October, she was hot and tired and dirty, pushing across country from San Francisco to Michigan—but she'd never felt so good, so clean and new and excited. Professional movers could have helped—but this was her journey, one she had to make by herself, coming from the past into her future with Nick.

At the winery, cars were parked in the visitors' lot. In the vineyard, the Alessandro family appeared to be just finishing tidying up. Dante stood near his parents, a small boy sitting on his shoulders. The boy's black hair shone in the sun, his grin matching Dante's.

Nick was still arguing with Maggie before she flew to San Francisco to collect her family's things and see her nephews. "I'll come with you. Just wait until harvest is done and—"

"You're not letting me help you, and I've got things to do. I want to clear my life, the past, and then I'll be back. Stop pushing me."

"I like pushing you. You like pushing me, so what else is new?"

"Everything," she'd said. "Everything is new and wonderful—with you."

Nick hadn't liked Maggie going alone, fearing for her. But she knew that he loved her and understood—as much as he could.

Through the dirty windshield, Maggie saw Nick—shirt open, jeans dusty, hair even longer and blacker than she remembered, a red bandana around his forehead.

Her heart did that little roll-over thing that said she loved him, and she eased the rented moving van to a stop. The man watching her didn't smile, but across the distance, she felt the impact of that hard body, the tenseness riding him.

She tilted her head a little, admiring Nick's walk toward her—that unhurried masculine swagger as he took off his gloves.

Tough? Definitely. A man to last and to love? Most certainly. A good family man whose love ran deep.

Those black eyes pinned her as he came close to stand beside the truck. He stuck out his thumb in a hitchhiker's gesture, and she nodded.

Nick opened the door and Scout leaped inside, controlled by the man who followed her into the cab. "Hi, lady."

Maggie hugged Scout, scratching her ears, but her eyes never left Nick's.

"Hi." She loved him. Whatever happened between them, however they would argue, there would always be love.

She shifted the gears, and the van lumbered into movement. Nick handed her a small, folded, worn piece of paper. She recognized the note that she'd left for him when she'd discovered Brent was near.

When her look questioned Nick, he shook his head. He'd never opened it.

Maggie slowly tore the paper into pieces and tossed them out the open window. The Maggie who wrote that note, terrified by the past, was completely gone. She'd come through a lifetime just for Nick.

"So is Lorenzo still steamed at me?"

Nick shrugged, and his lips pushed down a smile. "Sure. Expect a few more lectures on how you should trust police. Bake him some cinnamon rolls. Better yet, promise to supply them on a regular basis for him and for any bake sales for the police uniforms or retirement fund."

"Sounds fair enough."

Nick's arm stretched across the back of the seat, behind Scout. He removed Maggie's ball cap and smoothed her hair, his eyes warm with tenderness and understanding. "So what's new?"

He spoke easily, waiting for her to come all the way to him. She'd made a difficult journey, but she needed to come to him on her terms, new and ready for the future.

"My nephews are coming to visit. They've grown. If you don't mind, their father and his new wife are coming, too. I like her . . . I thought we'd go for the big Italian wedding, if that's okay with you? Invite the winegrowers who gave you so much help?"

Nick seemed to stop breathing, and he said quietly, "I'd like that. I make mistakes, Maggie. You shouldn't be anything, do anything, but what you want—just for you. If you want to work with me, you should. I mean, you can. Your call."

"Oh, I'll be helping you. And I intend to get paid, very well. Maybe not with money."

His grin shot across the cab's shadows—because he understood perfectly. And because he knew her, Nick asked, "And what else?"

"I'll have plenty to do, and everything that I really want to do. Lorna wants babies, and that means she'll need help at the shop. Then I want to start an herb garden, maybe a really big one, and there are the tulip bulbs to plant, of course. Oh, I have a lot to do. And I think I'll start with a shower—"

She loved Nick's blank expression, and his delight. "Gotcha," she teased.

"Not yet. If you don't stop handling that stick shift, it may be sooner than later."

The van lumbered toward his house, and Nick and Maggie crossed through sunshine and shadow, just the same as when they first saw each other—and just as they would spend the rest of their lives.

A week after their mid-October wedding, Maggie stood in the Frenchman's old lighthouse, Nick's arms around her as they looked out at the moonlit lake.

The slight wind brought the sound of falling leaves and Celeste's wind chimes through the open window.

On the small table, there were two framed wedding pictures. The brides were in lace and white—Alyssa with a young Nick, and Maggie with a solemn older Nick.

"Beth, in Iowa, feeding chickens and loving it," Nick mused. "Now that's a picture."

"It's a beautiful picture."

"I know how the Frenchman felt, waiting for the woman he loved, watching for her," Nick said quietly. "I could have waited for you forever."

Maggie leaned back against this strong, good man who always did his best. "I feel their peace, all of them. I'm glad Alyssa gave you to me. I felt that she did, that she wanted you to be happy."

"It's good," Nick stated simply as he held Maggie closer.

"Very good."

A romance from Avon Books is always a welcome addition at the
🎴      beach, the park, the barbecue ...      🎴

Look for these enchanting love stories in August.

### TO LOVE A SCOTTISH LORD by Karen Ranney
*An Avon Romantic Treasure*

The proud and brooding Hamish MacRae has returned to his
beloved Scotland wanting nothing more than to be left alone.
But Mary Gilly has invaded his lonely castle, and while it's true
that this pretty healer is beyond compare, it will take more than
her miraculous potions to awaken his heart.

### TALK OF THE TOWN by Suzanne Macpherson
*An Avon Contemporary Romance*

Nothing puts a damper on a wedding day quite like discovering your Mr. Right is *Mr. Totally Beyond Wrong*, which is why
Kelly Atwood knocks him flat and boards a bus to tiny
Paradise, Washington. One look at the gorgeous outsider and
attorney Sam Grayson gets hot around his too-tight collar,
because this runaway bride is definitely disturbing his peace.

### ONCE A SCOUNDREL by Candice Hern
*An Avon Romance*

It was bad enough when Anthony Morehouse thought he had
won a piece of furniture in a card game, but when he discovers
that *The Ladies' Fashionable Cabinet* is actually a women's
magazine, he can't wait to get rid of it. Then he sees beautiful
Edwina Parrish behind the editor's desk, and Tony is about to
make the biggest gamble of all.

### ALL MEN ARE ROGUES, by Sari Robins
*An Avon Romance*

When Evelyn Amherst agrees to her father's dying request, she
can scarcely imagine the world of danger she is about to enter —
or that it will bring her tantalizingly close to Lord Justin
Barclay. Here is a man to turn a young lady's head, but Evelyn
refuses to be diverted from her mission, especially not by this
passionate yearning for Justin's embrace.

REL 0703

# Discover Contemporary Romances at Their Sizzling Hot Best from Avon Books

WHEN NIGHT FALLS                 by Cait London
0-06-000180-1/$5.99 US/$7.99 Can

BREAKING ALL THE RULES        by Sue Civil-Brown
0-06-050231-2/$5.99 US/$7.99 Can

GETTING HER MAN              by Michele Albert
0-380-82053-6/$5.99 US/$7.99 Can

I'VE GOT YOU, BABE             by Karen Kendall
0-06-050232-0/$5.99 US/$7.99 Can

RISKY BUSINESS        by Suzanne Macpherson
0-380-82103-6/$5.99 US/$7.99 Can

THEN COMES MARRIAGE      by Christie Ridgway
0-380-81896-5/$5.99 US/$7.99 Can

STUCK ON YOU                 by Patti Berg
0-380-82005-6/$5.99 US/$7.99 Can

THE WAY YOU LOOK TONIGHT   by MacKenzie Taylor
0-380-81938-4/$5.99 US/$7.99 Can

INTO DANGER               by Gennita Low
0-06-052338-7/$5.99 US/$7.99 Can

IF THE SLIPPER FITS          by Elaine Fox
0-06-051721-2/$5.99 US/$7.99 Can

........................................................................................................................

Available wherever books are sold or please call 1-800-331-3761 to order.        CRO 0203

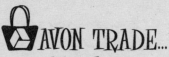

# AVON TRADE...
## because every great bag deserves a great book!

## Avon Romantic Treasures

*Unforgettable, enthralling love stories,
sparkling with passion and adventure
from Romance's bestselling authors*